THE PRESIDENTIAL ARCHIVE

THE PRESIDENTIAL ARCHIVE

John Griffiths

CARROLL & GRAF PUBLISHERS, INC.
New York

First edition 1996

Carroll & Graf Publishers, Inc.
260 Fifth Avenue
New York, NY 10001

ISBN 0-7867-0316-4

Library of Congress Cataloging-in-Publication Data is available.

Manufactured in the United States of America.

THE PRESIDENTIAL ARCHIVE

Prologue

April 1996

IN THE WAR ROOM it was just short of midnight and the players were watching TV. Just the four of them now in that dim and sound-proofed chamber, Porcher and his principal assistants, gathered around three sides of the conference table, chairs slewed to face the flickering screen. The men had at some point removed their jackets, rolled up their shirtsleeves, loosened their ties. Intended to indicate commitment to business, this informality had accomplished the reverse. Shirts were rumpled, sweat-stained around the armpits; in places buttons had incontinently popped. They looked, these men, demoralized and scruffy, a point not lost on the woman of the group; her own crispness of manner and appearance, thanks to regular visits to the rest room, had scarcely wilted in the hours they'd been there. The oak-veneered table at which they were sitting was strewn with the visible results of their labors: chewed ballpoints and stubs of number two pencils, memo pads covered with rococo doodles, drafts abandoned after one or two phrases. The trashcans were filled with crumpled sheets of paper, each the fetus of some stillborn bright idea. On the wall behind the TV, above a patchwork of demographic charts and a map of the Texas electoral districts, was a two-by-ten banner of computer paper. On it was printed in large black letters:

THIS TIME IT ISN'T THE ECONOMY, STUPID

Porcher, in whom for the past two hours the desire for a smoke and two fingers of bourbon straight up had threatened to become an obsession, allowed his eyes to stray from the screen. Porcher, some said, had the sharpest mind in politics today; others said it was not the sharpest, just the most devious, which was different. He himself

1

would not, at this moment, have wanted to claim either title. His eyes rested briefly on the banner and its message before moving on to survey his lieutenants. They were, if not the ablest team in the campaign, close to it. So how come, he wondered, that in more than four hours of collective brain-beating the best that anyone had been able to come up with was the monument to the obvious tacked above the TV?

It would take a whole lot more than that.

It would take, he thought gloomily, returning his gaze to the TV, nothing short of a fucking miracle.

On-screen Richard Telfer, senior senator for Iowa, emerging from a thicket of tangled syntax and sweating from the heat of the camera lights, was introducing, to an audience of the faithful, the cause of the War Room's current anxieties.

"Fellow Republicans, fellow Americans—fellow victims, for the past three years, of executive incompetence and legislative gridlock—I give you the landslide winner of these caucuses and of every Republican primary so far. I give you"—he paused to gather breath for his peroration—"THE NEXT PRESIDENT OF THESE UNITED STATES."

Pandemonium among the faithful. The TV cameras, panning the packed auditorium, registered scenes of borderline hysteria. People screeching, jumping up and down, clenched fists punching the sky in triumph. Total strangers hugging each other. The banners and flags, dementedly waving, resembled a cornfield hit by a tornado. Streamers flicked through the air like comets. There, in that Iowa high school auditorium, the din was a serious threat to the eardrums. Here, in this padded and soundproofed chamber, the decibel level was still uncomfortable. Reaching for the remote control, Porcher cut it a click.

The action released a volley of comment from the players:

"Next president, my *ass*. First catch your bear, dickhead, *then* skin him."

"Dickhead is wearing the wrong color shirt. And as usual sweating like a pig. Someone should introduce him to Number Seven Pancake."

"Someone should introduce him to his father."

"Someone should have strangled him at birth."

Wearily Porcher gestured them to silence. He had no tolerance for this kind of chat.

"Shut up and listen, why don't we," he growled. "We might just learn something. God knows we need to."

On-screen the new Republican messiah stepped forward. Tall and patrician-looking, with cropped black hair and piercing blue eyes, Hal Reynolds wore his gray business suit like a uniform, carried himself like the soldier he'd once been. In spite of the heat from the camera lights he was not, it was instantly noticeable, sweating.

He held up his hand for silence. Didn't get it. (And didn't, Porcher thought, expect or want to get it, since the frenzy that greeted him obeyed its own momentum and in any case was music to his ears.) So he stood there while a minute extended into two, acceding gracefully to the will of the people and smiling the boyish, self-deprecating smile that was worth, Porcher thought, God alone knew how many points in the polls. And he was right to smile, no call for self-deprecation, for his nomination was all but in the bag. His election, too, if the polls could be relied on.

On-screen the frenzy abruptly redoubled. A passage opened in the throng of campaign workers on the platform, and through it, in a wheelchair expertly maneuvered by a nurse, the candidate's wife now made her entrance. She'd been beautiful once and was handsome still, though showing the ravages of multiple sclerosis from which she'd suffered for the past fifteen years. Her expression was grave, her features sunken and cadaverous, but her large gray eyes were alert and mobile, surveying the scenes of fervor below with an interest in which—or so it seemed to Porcher—there were traces of irony, hidden amusement. When his wife had taken her place beside him, the candidate bent down and kissed her on the cheek. Then taking one of her hands in his, he attempted once more to stem the applause.

"Jesus . . . it's the total fucking package." Porcher gave an exasperated snort. "Handsome war hero. Crippled, gallant wife. Only thing missing is the loyal family mutt. Labrador, maybe. Golden fucking retriever."

On-screen the candidate, at last granted silence, began to speak. He did so gracefully and with humor, also briefly. He gave thanks to all the appropriate people, credited them, not himself, with the victories so far. He offered a vision of a future so rosy its actual features remained indistinct, and avoided in the process offending anyone, even, Porcher noted, the lunatic right. Which was not to say that the candi-

3

date had no message—indeed he did, and even a platform; it was moderate, centrist, full of common sense, and therefore perhaps just a tiny bit dull—but rather that the message was not in the words. The message, Porcher knew, was the candidate himself. Hal Reynolds *looked* like a president. He looked like a man Americans could trust. More important, since in the matter of trust American hearts were so calloused by betrayal that at this point they consisted of little but scar tissue, he looked like a man by whom they would never be embarrassed, a man they could (without cringing) imagine rubbing shoulders with distinguished foreign statesmen or even, stern test, taking tea with the Queen. He looked, Porcher thought, the incarnation of those family values Americans expected in spades from their leaders— the more so since they failed so signally to practice them themselves.

"The sumbitch is good," Adam Steiner commented. Steiner, *summa cum laude* from Princeton, was Porcher's media relations wizard. "You've got to give him that. He not only looks good, he *is* good."

"The sumbitch is more than good." This from Bill Raeburn, Ph.D. (Wharton), pollster. "Sumbitch is perfect, that's what he is. War hero. Family man. Distinguished public servant. Fucker makes our guy look like Gollum . . . Gollum." Raeburn brightened, diverted by the thought. "That's exactly who our guy is. Subaquean. Slimy. Giving off that faintly fishy glow." He turned to the others, smiling sardonically. "I think that expresses our problem in a nutshell. What we are doing, sitting around this table, is figuring out how to reelect Gollum."

"That would be some achievement." Maggie Howard, fund-raiser, smiled tartly. "*If* we could find a way to pull it off."

"Rhetorical question," Steiner again. "If character is destiny, what is *lack* of character?"

Rhetorical bullshit, Porcher thought. Demoralized bullshit at that. High time to cut it off.

"Fine. So we're all agreed. Reynolds is perfect. Let's cut the whining. Where does that leave *us?*"

"Facing a landslide loss." Raeburn shrugged. "A wipeout in the Electoral College."

If anything, this was an understatement. According to the poll in Porcher's briefcase, were the election held today with Reynolds the Republican candidate, the president would lose in the popular vote by a 35 percent margin. What this would translate to in terms of elec-

4

toral votes Porcher hadn't bothered to compute. Perhaps—the thought flitted wanly through his head—to the first recorded shutout.

"Tell me something I *don't* know." He frowned. "Offer me words of encouragement and hope. Show me a way we can win this thing."

"A way?" Steiner shrugged. "I can offer you several: The voters are afflicted by collective amnesia. Gollum's fish stink turns magically into charisma. Reynolds suffers a heart attack, retroactively steps on a land mine."

Defeatist talk from Adam Steiner. Porcher hadn't heard it before, didn't want to hear it again. Time, he thought, to rally the troops.

"Let's cool it with the gallows humor, shall we? Anyone here thinks we can't win should leave. Ditto for anyone thinks we *won't*."

He paused, his look challenging each of them in turn but lingering an extra moment on Steiner. Adam was the youngest, but also the smartest. Adam had the fiercest will to win. If he couldn't sell Adam, he couldn't sell the others. It would help quite considerably, Porcher thought, if at this point he could even sell himself.

Steiner looked back at him, eyes expressionless.

"I mean it, Adam." Porcher didn't blink. "You can leave now, and my blessing with you."

Steiner said nothing. But he didn't get up from the table.

Relieved but not showing it, Porcher turned to the others.

"Look, people, we're at crunch time and the message is very simple: Winning, losing, it happens in the head. When you're thirty-five points behind in the polls, you just can't afford the luxury of doubt. I won't have anyone on this team who isn't totally committed to winning."

Henry V before Agincourt it wasn't. But eloquence had never been his forte. This crew, in any case, had spent half their lives around politicians; eloquence, to them, was always suspect. He surveyed them once more, his gaze unwavering.

"Another thing I need to make clear: Our candidate is the president of the United States of America. We will not—repeat, *not*—refer to him as Gollum."

He paused.

"Okay. Now back to the business. What, right now, do we have going for us?"

No prizes for the answer. Maggie Howard supplied it.

"What we have going for us is this: The election isn't being held right now."

"Correct." Porcher nodded. "This is April. We have until November. And in politics, as everyone knows, six months is a lifetime. *We still have time to turn things around.*"

"More to the point, Reynolds has time to screw up—and he *will* have to screw up," Steiner said. "He will have to screw up *bad.*"

"Don't count on it." Raeburn looked doubtful. "So far he hasn't made one false step."

"Or rather," Maggie Howard corrected, "not that we know of." She thought for a moment, then continued, "But he has to have sometime, it's only human. No one's as perfect as he seems."

"Amen to that," Porcher agreed. "We've all got our skeletons in the closet."

"Except the president." Steiner smiled faintly. "Most of his skeletons are out of the closet—which accounts, perhaps, for the thirty-five percent margin."

He paused.

"But the polls offer this consolation, at least: If this election were fought purely on the issues, we could win. Our problem is character. That's where he's killing us. So the bottom line is simply this: Either Prince Hal has a skeleton in his closet—and it better be nasty and stink like a skunk—or *we* are competing for second place."

"He has one." On this point Porcher's conviction was total; he'd lived around politics for twenty years. "What we have to do is find it."

"It's not as if we haven't been looking," Raeburn said.

"Then we haven't looked hard enough," Porcher snapped. "As of now I'm making this top priority. I want people on it around the clock. Go back through his records. Check tax returns, investments, business associates, the lot. And let's not forget the sex angle, either. That wife of his has been crippled the last fifteen years. Don't kid yourself he's been sleeping alone."

He got to his feet. This meeting had depressed him long enough.

"We need to find that skeleton and quick. And, people"—he fixed them with his steeliest glare—"let's not misunderstand each other here. I'm not saying *try,* I'm saying *find* it."

PART I

Moscow, April 1996

Chapter One

WHAT YOU DIDN'T LIKE was the waiting.

Which wasn't really surprising, he thought, because waiting gave you the leisure to think. And thinking, the mind being what it was, led sooner or later to worry. And worry, which was simply the investment of emotion in the knowledge that not everything was under your control, was pointless almost by definition. Fact was what mattered, not contingency. If Volodya didn't show, he didn't show; you went home and made other arrangements.

But Volodya would show. After twenty years' acquaintance you could read him like a book. Volodya would show because *he* had set up this meeting. And given his instinct for circumspection, he would show some thirty minutes early. And when he did, he would come up here, to this place inexplicably open to visitors in this season of the year when there were no visitors. To gain the high ground, he'd explain, indulging a fondness for military analogy, to check out the lay of the land, to give himself a feel for the position. Not that in this case, he'd hasten to add, he'd imagined any need for such precautions. But forewarned was forearmed. Better safe than sorry. Old habits died hard . . . Volodya was the creature of his training.

It was puzzling, in view of this, the religious adherence to precept and maxim, that he seemed to have failed utterly to grasp their essence. The essence, surely, was to have no habits.

Habits were what got you killed.

It looked as if spring might come early this year. To the east, in a sky the color of brass, a compound of sulfur particulates and fog, the sun, now making its first appearance in weeks, hung dim and cold like a tin medallion. And today again, to judge by a dripping from the eaves, the temperature had edged above zero. In the courtyard below, from the asphalt pathway along which Volodya would presently approach, the last snow had been shoveled into heaps that a week's alternation of thaw and frost had compacted into miniature alps and the city air had veiled with soot and grime. The smog in Moscow got worse every year. This ought to have been surprising, but wasn't. Industrial production was down. Industrial pollution was up.

Accomplishments of the new regime.

This wasn't the meeting place he'd have chosen. Too isolated, for one thing; too quiet, for another. The sort of meeting place that advertised itself for what it was. But Volodya had always picked places like this. Even in the days when they'd ruled the old schoolyard in Zagorsk with a rigor worthy of Stalin—Volodya always the velvet glove, he the iron fist inside it—even then, before their special talents had commended them to those whose business was to notice special talents, Volodya had liked to be somewhere high up, surrounded by wide-open spaces. He liked—it was another of his maxims—to spot trouble before it spotted him.

Such thinking had a flaw, of course: It relied overmuch on assumption. If trouble happened to spot him first, a vantage point could become a death trap.

But this bell tower, it had to be admitted, gave wonderful all-around views. To the northeast, the Kremlin. To the south, Lenin Stadium and the university, whose gigantic fortress and spire reminded you always of a concrete wedding cake. To the west, the Savvinskaya Embankment and the river. To the east and spread out directly below, the Cathedral of the Smolensk Icon, arrangement of delicate slender towers, five emerald domes encircling one of gold; and adjoining, gateway from this world to the next, the graveyard.

Khrushchev was buried there, he seemed to recall, somewhere among those leafless, dripping trees. Also others of his ilk. Chekhov and Gogol, Scriabin and Prokofiev, writers and artists, scientists and statesmen. Clever people now lost to sight.

Clever temporary people.

His mother had liked to visit this place, former retreat of the noble and reclusive. It spoke to something in her spirit, she'd maintained, reminded her of where she had come from. *How* it had done so remained a mystery. His mother had been neither noble nor reclusive.

10

Stuck fast in the lower echelons of the *nomenklatura*, she'd been a notorious troublemaker and in the worst, bureaucratic, sense of the word, a snob. Life with her—five people crammed into three small rooms—had been turbulence without intermission, an unrelenting struggle for *Lebensraum*, psychic and otherwise. He might easily have ended up killing her, he thought, had cancer not saved him the trouble.

Not much traffic on the roads today. Returning his mother, Khrushchev, and company to their shared and merited oblivion, he crossed to the east side of the tower, scanned as much as he could of Bolshaya Porogovskaya. In the distance he could make out a small white car nosing its way down the street toward him.

Volodya's VW? It was too far off to tell. Presently, when it got nearer, it would either continue in the direction of Smolensk or turn in here at the gateway. Not everything in life was under your control. No point getting excited.

He was conscious, nonetheless, when the white car, making the turn, drew up outside the gateway, revealing itself as a VW Rabbit and disgorging its driver, that his pulse rate was up, his breathing shallower and faster. This was normal, of course; in these encounters there was always danger. In his own case, granted, the cause was not just the danger. But this, as the training school shrink had insisted (he'd been one of the people whose business it was to notice special talent), was nothing to be embarrassed about. One didn't get to choose one's likes and dislikes; indeed, it was the other way around. And *his* likes, furthermore, were the state's quite considerable good fortune. There was certain work—vital, necessary work—that could only be done by people who liked it. These efforts at tact had been laughably misplaced. Embarrassment, at least in *that* mealymouthed sense of the word, had never been part of his makeup. He liked what he liked. It was as simple as that.

Volodya, he observed, was entering through the gateway.

He couldn't make out the features yet, but he could tell it was Volodya by the gait and, especially, the coat. The gait reminded him always of a fox, the steps short and mincing, the feet set down gingerly—provisionally, almost—as if their owner were poised for flight, or in this case (as was reasonable, given the condition of the path), worried about slipping. The coat was a piece of foolish ostentation, one of Volodya's several vanities, the cloth a heavy lamb's-wool-cash-mere mix, the collar beaver, the lining marten, a label on the lining of the inside breast pocket bearing the name of a noted London tailor. Volodya had bought the coat, with the proceeds of some timely specu-lations in the foreign currency market—you could never get hurt, these days, betting *against* the ruble—from a former ambassador, now a cabdriver. Since the coat was full length and the former owner at least six inches taller than the current, the skirt, on Volodya, hung down almost to the ground. Volodya, however, resisted alteration; he maintained it would destroy the classic lines. His vanity made him look like a clown, which was his problem. But it also got him noticed and remembered, which was sometimes a problem for those who had dealings with him. It was wiser, professionally speaking, to confine one's dealings to people more obscure. Volodya was known, to the world on whose fringes he lived, as "the little pimp with the coat and the computer."

Today, however, he was without the computer.

Maybe he had left it in the car. Normally you didn't leave *anything* in cars—in Moscow, a current witticism had it, when parking on the street it was best to remove the radio, the seats, and, if at all possible, the engine—but since this place was to all appearances deserted, per-haps he'd decided to take a chance. This would be slightly out of character, but then this whole enterprise was out of character, a de-parture from a lifetime's avoidance of unnecessary risk, an abandon-ment so remarkable you could almost admire him for it.

Almost but not quite.

You could never admire the abandonment of friends.

All of which left unresolved, of course, the question of the com-puter. But with knowledge so imminent, speculation was redundant. Volodya would be here in half a minute. And however grossly he had lately betrayed the larger commitments of his life, he was clearly still faithful to the small ones. For skirting the cathedral and the graveyard, he was heading straight for the bell tower.

Spotting trouble before it spotted him.

In fact, his arrival took more than half a minute. There were five long flights of steps, and Volodya, who was badly out of shape, paused before each to catch his breath. His footsteps, echoing up the spiral stairway, would stop, recommence, the gritty scrape of leather on stone counterpointed by the rasp and wheeze of his breathing. At the top the entrance to the stairwell was enclosed by an ornamental doorway, creating on either side a shallow setback. Volodya was several steps into the chamber before he checked himself, turned.

Saw who was waiting for him.

*   *   *

THE CHESS PLAYER FISCHER, you recalled reading somewhere, explained the satisfaction he derived from his profession in a single terse sentence: *I like to see them squirm.* Fischer, of course, derived his satisfaction from a game, but his explanation, if coarsely phrased, applied more or less to your own situation; it was far more apt, at least, than the tactful inanities of the training school shrink. Like Fischer, you delivered understanding, final lucidity packaged as ultimate defeat, and what you liked—it was an intellectual pleasure—was the moment when that understanding dawned.

You could say this for Volodya: He was not slow. There was no silly standing there, mouth agape. His reaction time, indeed, would have done credit to his laptop computer. A microsecond was all he needed to receive the message transmitted by the eyes, combine it with inputs retrieved from memory, leap to the appropriate conclusion.

What you liked was the moment when understanding dawned, when your eyes locked on to the eyes of the other and you saw, in that horror-struck, enlightened gaze, time reduce to this fugitive instant, past and future rushing through a hole in the present.

Chapter Two

On the metro, Cass felt she was being watched.

She'd felt it since she left the bank. It was different from being noticed. Noticed was okay, more or less. Noticed meant looks, smiles, whistles, invitations ('Excuse please, miss . . . you want I explain you Moscow?), and remarks in varying shades of bad taste made about her as she passed and pitched just the wrong side of inaudibility. The remarks she could do without, but the rest she had learned to live with. It was inevitable, really. She was blond, obviously foreign, well (or at least expensively) dressed, and she stood in her bare feet five feet eleven and three-quarters inches, which by Russian standards was tall for a woman. (Russian standards *baloney*, she thought, by *anyone's* standards it was tall for a woman.) But tall, blond, and obviously foreign didn't explain what was going on today. It didn't account for the sense she had that her every move was followed, and noted, by watchful eyes.

She checked again in her right-hand coat pocket. It was still there. Just as it had been the last time she checked and the twenty or thirty times before that. The wad of bills in the envelope had that reassuring thickness and texture. Real money. Dollars. Not the Monopoly money even the Russians didn't want. It was dumb to have put it there—she knew she should have put it in an inside pocket—but moving it now, in plain view, would be orders of magnitude dumber. People got mugged here all the time. In this city where the spirit of free enterprise was king, you could get yourself mugged for the price of a bottle of vodka.

For a thousand dollars you could get yourself murdered.

But that was ridiculous, wasn't it? No one could know about the money. No one but the Citibank teller, an American. And Comrade Dolokhov, of course. But *he* must be on the other side of the city, traveling by a different route entirely. Her own route, she told herself, that detour through Red Square to Arbat, involving a change at Borovickaya and adding fifteen minutes to the journey, had hardly been predictable. And these women on either side of her, both seemingly absorbed in their knitting, had been on the train when she boarded. So had the man directly across, the one shooting her covert glances and pretending to read *Notes from Underground.* (He was either pretending, she thought, or else he was a *very* slow reader.) So either she accepted the ridiculous premise that they, along with the Citibank teller and half a dozen surveillance men (all keeping in contact by telepathy, no doubt) were part of a complex, labor-intensive plot to separate her from her lousy thousand dollars, or she kept *some* slender hold on reality and conceded this feeling that people were watching her was most likely paranoia.

Or guilt.

Or, to be more accurate, fear. Her moral sense owed no particular allegiance to the laws of the Russian Federation; she just didn't want to end up in jail. Though she didn't know for certain that what she was doing was illegal, common sense told her it must be. Otherwise this Dolokhov—or whatever his name was—wouldn't have insisted on surrounding the transaction with this web of elaborate precautions. He hadn't actually admitted that the document was stolen, and she hadn't, yet, agreed to buy. But these were technicalities, she thought; they wouldn't do her a whole lot of good if she found herself explaining her part in the deal to an officer of the State Militia. (Especially since the document in question belonged to the state and was no doubt classified to boot.) She didn't know much about the jails in the new democratic Russia; in the old one they hadn't had a good reputation.

She shouldn't be doing this, she thought. She should have given him the brush-off. Or at least referred him to Professor Kuryagin. Had she done so, of course, he might have crawled back into the woodwork, taking his interesting document with him. In all probability he *would* have, she thought, and that might have been a considerable loss to her branch of Soviet Studies. But at least she wouldn't be sitting here now, with a thousand dollars in her pocket, feeling like a guppy in a tank full of sharks, and morally uncomfortable as well. And the moral discomfort was merited, wasn't it? For surely the reason she *hadn't* brushed him off had little to do with historical truth or even professional advancement. "You could ask your uncle"—his leer as he'd switched off the player and pocketed the tape had haunted her then and haunted her still—"Better yet, ask your father."

Ask her *uncle* about something Gorbachev had said?

Her *father?*

*   *   *

WITH A HISS of brakes and a lurch of deceleration, the train began its approach to Park Kultury. The woman to Cass's left stood up. So, a moment or two later, did the man in the seat opposite. The relief Cass felt was short-lived, however. The woman was getting off. The man was moving to the vacant seat beside her.

"Excuse please, miss: Are you being American tourist?"

If the English was shaky, the tone was confident. But the feelings with which she greeted the approach were closer to relief than annoyance. A surveillance man would hardly proposition his subject. And propositions she could generally handle. Move number one—it was normally enough—was to feign complete ignorance of the language.

Any language.

"American tourist?" he persisted. "You want I explain you Moscow? Is not for money. Is"—he searched his memory for the phrase he wanted, found and offered it, beaming self-congratulation—"for my pleasure."

Spoken like a man, Cass thought. She flattered herself she'd perfected the look she returned him. Perplexity mixed with a hint of regret. No suggestion of outrage or rebuff. Hostility was counterproductive, the male ego, wounded, unwilling to retreat.

This one showed no intention of retreating.

"*Parlez Français?*"

It didn't sound as though *he* did, she thought. She returned him the same blank smile, the same perfect incomprehension.

"German? Norwegian? . . . Swedish? . . . What language *do* you speak?" He fell back, frustrated, on Russian.

Continuing to smile, she shrugged and spread her hands. She'd be

16

very happy to talk, she conveyed, but alas was utterly without the means.

But conversation, apparently, was not among his requirements. Words exhausted, he resorted to gesture. Pointing first to himself, then her, and walking his fingers down the armrest between them, he contrived to convey that his escort services were at her disposal.

Velcro-man. *Fuck* . . . and a member of that charmless fraternity, it seemed, for whom the enjoyment was the chase, obstacles merely a turn-on. Not an easy type to shake.

In her pocket, next to the money, was a tourist map of the metro, the station names given in Cyrillic, transliterations in brackets underneath. Pulling it out, she showed it to him, pointing to Borovickaya, then tracing with her finger a route to Leninsky Gory. He grinned, pointing at himself and nodding. By the strangest of coincidences, she gathered, Leninsky Gory was his stop, too.

The prospect of her company in the future seemed to satisfy him for the present. Apart from catching her eye when he could and grinning like an ape when he did, he made no more attempts to communicate. She was thankful for this; his overtures, or rather the attention they'd attracted from the other passengers—she'd noticed a duo of babushkas opposite clucking disapproval like a pair of mother hens—embarrassed her considerably. She was angry with herself for this, the lack of logic so often displayed by her feelings. The embarrassment shouldn't be hers, but his.

Presently, she intended, it would be.

When the train's loudspeaker announced Fruzenskaya, he caught her eye and shook his head. She nodded, seeming to understand. At the station she sat, not looking at him, waiting for the doors to clear. When they did, she stood up abruptly.

"Not this one." He laid a hand on her arm, a subscriber, clearly, to the widespread local belief that Russian, spoken slowly and loudly enough, commanded universal comprehension. "This is not our stop. Our stop is next."

Very deliberately she removed the hand from her arm.

"Thank you. But I think you are mistaken." She spoke a little louder than she needed, enunciating clearly, taking care with the accents. The loudspeaker was warning people to stand clear. She figured she

17

had maybe five seconds. "This is my stop, Fruzenskaya. *Your* stop, Leninsky Gory, is next."

Her Russian, though not perfect, was light-years ahead of his English. And what she enjoyed most, when the subway doors had rattled shut and she was able to face him through the window, was the laughter on the faces of his fellow passengers and the look, absurdly plastered on his, of dumbstruck amazement and outrage. The look of a predator foiled by its prey. Of a shark, she thought, that had gotten itself bitten by a guppy.

The satisfaction she felt at this maneuver sustained her through the station and onto the street. But on the street anxiety returned. As she made for the convent she found herself glancing behind. Looking for what, she wasn't sure, but it struck her that Velcro-man *could* have been a decoy. But if so, if people *were* following her, how could she hope to spot them? Presumably surveillance people went to some lengths not to look the part. She remembered her father telling her once that even merely competent surveillance was next to impossible to spot. Here, of course, it would be better than competent. In Moscow, for much of its recorded history, a significant percentage of the population had received a monthly paycheck from the government to keep a weather eye on the rest, and this tradition had achieved its finest flowering under the auspices of the KGB. When it came to surveillance, her father had told her, the Russians were simply the best.

If she had any sense, she'd turn around and go home.

But she couldn't let herself do that, could she? Not just because going home would be prudent, and prudent was for her just a fancy name for scared. Something mysterious was going on here. Something mysterious and possibly sinister. And somehow it involved members of her family: her uncle, who was running for president, and her father, who until not long ago had been someone very eminent in the CIA. She *couldn't* just turn her back and walk away. And even if she did, it wouldn't solve anything. Dolokhov might crawl back into the woodwork, but sooner or later he'd resurface. She might as well deal with him now.

The hell with all those ex-secret policemen.

Like fear, resolution nourishes itself. By the time she reached the gatehouse, she'd talked herself out of her misgivings. The ex-secret policemen were evidently otherwise engaged. No one was tailing her. No one was even around. No one but the janitor, or maybe he was the curator, and *his* indifference could hardly have been more pronounced. As she passed, he barely glanced up from his magazine—some local version of *Playboy*—then, with that laconic eloquence of gesture Slavs seemed to share with the Latins, he half rolled his eyes and almost shrugged, thereby contriving to suggest that her choosing to visit at this season was crazy, but anyhow it was not his problem.

Crossing the courtyard, what she noticed was the quiet. It was something she hadn't gotten used to yet, the way the city all winter long was blanketed by this white silence, this stillness that movement and even sound—the occasional muffled slither and thud of snow breaking loose from the branches of trees—served only to cast into starker relief, seemed only to intensify and deepen. Winter, she thought, was the natural condition of this city. Though she'd made its acquaintance in the summer and come to know it better in the fall, parks rioting then in colors that were brilliant, even shocking, she'd always felt these seasons were aberrations, that only in winter was Moscow truly itself.

At the foot of the first flight of steps she paused. Her watch informed her she was seven minutes late. There'd been no cars in the parking lot; if he was here already, he must have traveled, like her, by metro and on foot. Probably he *was* here, she thought. He'd struck her as the kind of man who'd be careful about things such as time and money. Probably he was watching from up there, making sure she wasn't being followed. The thought—being watched by a dealer in stolen documents with whom she was about to do business—made her stomach give a small premonitory lurch. It occurred to her that this was her very last chance to draw back, and she had, suddenly, an image of the future as laid out for her inspection like those branch diagrams they'd used in school to explain evolution or whatever. Each choice excluded, but some much more than others; the wrong one could send you on a shortcut to nowhere.

Melodramatic nonsense. What her father called the chicken-shit reflex. She despised herself for entertaining it. The choice was made, wasn't it? She'd made it when she listened to the tape, heard Comrade Dolokhov's disquieting innuendo. This wasn't something she *could* leave alone. If the tape was real, it was a bombshell, a bombshell

19

with shocking implications. She didn't know their full extent, but that could wait for the moment. She needed to take this a step at a time. Endeavor to authenticate the tape. Ask her father about it.

She needed to take this a step at a time. And the first was in front of her.

Right here. Right now.

* * *

HE WAS WAITING, as she'd expected, at the top of the bell tower. As she mounted the last of the five flights of steps she saw him, in the overcoat that was much too long, hunched over an embrasure that looked out to the embankment and the river. He was leaning out over the broad stone parapet. Leaning way out, she saw, almost lying, his head down, his back to the entrance of the stairway. Something must have caught, riveted, his attention, for though he must have heard her footsteps, must have known who it was approaching, he didn't greet her or turn, even when she entered the chamber.

He didn't move.

He didn't move either when she called out his name. But by then she'd been struck by something awkward in his posture, something absolute in the quality of his stillness. He was not looking down, she realized; he was not looking anywhere. So she was almost prepared for the moment when he did turn. *Almost*, she thought later, but not quite; if it happened every day you could never be really prepared. And what chilled her then when her greeting, her hesitant tap on his shoulder, went unanswered and she tugged, hard, on the shoulder of the overcoat and he rolled over and showed her his face, what chilled her was not the sightless, astonished gaze, nor the small, bluish hole in the center of his forehead. What chilled her was the thought that someone had put him on the parapet; someone, having killed him, had taken the time and trouble to prepare what amounted to a gruesome practical joke.

Had someone known who would find him?

Chapter Three

Ivo Sokolnikov, lieutenant, State Militia, placing his hands behind his head and leaning back comfortably in the janitor's chair, gazed at the suspect with satisfaction. At last, he thought, a case that wouldn't depress him.

He'd been depressed, professionally speaking, for most of his eight-year career. When he'd joined the Militia from the Training Academy (graduating first in unarmed combat, third overall in a class of nearly two hundred), he'd been under the illusion he was going to fight crime. Crime, that was, with a capital C. Mobsters and gang lords, black marketeers, a competent and energetic evil. The selection process and the training had conspired to foster that illusion. The batteries of tests going in, or so he'd been repeatedly assured, had eliminated all but the finest. And the training—two years of systematic torture, cramming the mind to the overload point with courses in law and forensic techniques, languages and criminal psychology, driving the body to ever higher peaks of fitness and endurance—had instilled in him, as in all who survived it, a belief that he was special. What stuck particularly in Sokolnikov's mind was his weekly engagement with the obstacle course, a grueling, mile-long gauntlet of ditches (most too wide to jump, and filled, he'd suspected, with sewage), rope climbs, jumps that stretched nerves and muscles to the limit, crawls through claustrophobic, bug-infested tunnels, teetering dashes across swaying logs or along the tops of fifteen-foot walls, the whole thing (naturally) taken at the double and punctuated, usually at moments of maximum exhaustion, with interludes of panic in which hidden assailants came at you suddenly with clubs or knives. You couldn't conquer the obstacle course—and he had conquered it, finally, in

21

ninety seconds less than the required twelve minutes—without seeing yourself as part of an elite, a sort of commando for Order and Justice, vanguard of Russia's fight against the wicked. It had come as something of a letdown to discover that, for most of the crime he had to deal with, the c was decidedly lower case, the obstacle course not remotely relevant. What he found he was fighting most of the time were drunkenness, drugs, domestic violence. Not so much evil as despair.

That last murder case he'd handled, for instance. A woman had figured in that case, too. She and her lover had murdered the husband, stabbed him to death as he lay in a drunken coma on the very bed they'd deceived him in. It had taken Sokolnikov about three minutes to deduce what must have happened, another ten to break her down. Her ID said she was only forty, but she'd looked, with her frizzy orange hair, her wrinkled skin and rotten teeth, her dumpy, potato-thickened figure, at the very least fifteen years older. (It had bordered on the grotesque, he recalled, to imagine her having a lover.) She had sat there, in that cramped and filthy kitchen, staring at but not seeing him across the cheap deal table, and intoned like a mantra: "I killed him. I killed him. I killed him." She had sat there like a parody of grief, clutching herself as if she were cold and swaying back and forth to the rhythm of her words, the tears cutting furrows in her mask of rouge and powder, and it had come to him that what she was doing was not so much confessing as releasing. The killing had purposed, been pointed toward, this confession; together they enacted a surrender, submission to a world in which every day dawned without promise. Evil, Sokolnikov thought, had perhaps been present at that scene, but if so, it was an evil abject and flabby. An evil imponderable, vast, and ancient. As huge and hopeless as Russia itself.

But this case promised to be different entirely. The evil that was operating here was brisk and purposeful, intelligent, sardonic. An evil with imagination and even a sense of humor: A man in an overcoat four sizes too large had been ambushed in the bell tower of Novodevichy Convent. He'd been shot in the exact dead center of the forehead with a small-caliber pistol, presumably silenced (since no one seemed to have heard the report), and by someone who had subsequently rifled his pockets, removed the contents (and, of course, every trace of identification), and then leaned the body (facing outward)

22

over the parapet of an embrasure so whoever found it would be dealt a nasty shock. All this had been done by someone, moreover, who had entered the convent unnoticed by the janitor, left it, or apparently left it—the jury was still out on that one, Sokolnikov thought—and had apparently driven off, again unnoticed, in the victim's own vehicle, a white VW Rabbit.

Here was an evil worthy of the obstacle course.

Sokolnikov continued to gaze at the suspect, giving silence time to do its work. He was proud of his interrogation technique and especially this gaze he'd developed. He had encountered it first on the face of a legal psychologist and had made it his own by practice in front of a mirror. Impersonal but friendly, curious but not very, it seemed to promise willingness to listen, no interest whatever in judging. Since in fact he was rather quick to judge, perfecting this aspect had cost him some trouble, but he felt results had justified the effort. His look—the record supported his opinion—had a quality that almost compelled confession. It had certainly worked wonders on the woman with orange hair.

But this Cassandra Wolfe was a different proposition entirely. Nothing abject or flabby about her. Twenty-six, good-looking, clearly intelligent—you could sense the intelligence, Sokolnikov thought, without being told she was from Georgetown University and here to do research in the Kremlin archives—she stood two centimeters taller than he and held herself straight as a rifle. Moreover, she was obviously rich. By Russian standards, of course, most foreigners living here were rich, but she looked rich by *American* standards. At current rates of exchange, he guessed, her cashmere turtleneck, sable hat, knee-length boots in soft Italian leather, beautifully tailored, fur-collared coat would have set the average Russian back about half his annual wages. What it all added up to was confidence, an armor of self-possession that hadn't been noticeably dented by her finding herself involved in a murder, or indeed by being treated as a suspect. She'd submitted without batting an eyelid to a search of her handbag and pockets, had declined the services of an official interpreter, and had raised no objection to having her statements recorded on tape.

Good looks and self-possession: a formidable combination, one to which Sokolnikov was far from indifferent. He found himself wanting to ruffle that calm surface, to churn up the depths he was sure it concealed. But it was hard to be certain what prompted this wish, his being a man or his being a policeman. She was, this elegant American, the kind of woman he sometimes dreamed of. The kind he always wanted, never seemed to get. She was also—he needed to remember this—a woman mixed up in a killing.

It had to be admitted, however, that she wasn't, or not directly, a suspect. He could see her being capable of murder. He could see her being cool enough to go through the dead man's pockets, strong enough to have hoisted the body, some sixty or sixty five kilos of dead weight, onto the parapet of that embrasure. What he *couldn't* see her being was dumb enough to hide the murder weapon (and presumably the contents of the victim's pockets) in the convent grounds, where they'd certainly be found in short order. But if she'd killed him, that had to have been what she'd done, since no weapon had been found in her possession and, at least according to the janitor's report, no more than five minutes had gone by from the time she'd entered the convent grounds to the time she'd reported the murder. Events could still prove him wrong, but he'd bet a year's wages they wouldn't. The search of the convent and grounds would find nothing, because both the weapon and the contents of the victim's pockets had departed with the killer in the victim's white VW. They'd departed, further-more, some time before this Miss Wolfe had arrived. You couldn't, reasonably, suspect her of doing this murder.

What you could suspect her of was lying.

* * *

SHE HAD STARTED LYING—started evading, at least—almost as soon as the preliminaries were over.

"Describe for me, please, how you found the dead man."

"Do you mean how I *happened* to find him, or how he was when I did?"

An important distinction. But not, Sokolnikov had thought, one you'd expect to occur to someone who'd just stumbled onto a murder. Your normal witness just blurted things out, left it to you to make distinctions. She wasn't a normal witness, of course; hers was a careful, discriminating mind. But the care she'd seemed most to be exercising here was to answer only those questions she was asked.

Which suggested there were those she would rather avoid.

24

"Actually," he'd said, "I meant both. Start, please, with how you came to find him."

"I came to find him because I arranged to meet him."

Again a somewhat stilted response. And not, he'd thought, because of problems with the language. Her Russian was admirable: fluent, idiomatic. Far better than his English.

"You arranged to meet him? Then at least you can tell us who he was."

"I can tell you his name: Dolokhov. Vladimir Dolokhov. Beyond that I know nothing about him."

"Not even where he lived? What he did for a living?"

She'd shaken her head. "As I said, I didn't know him. I met him just once, at a party."

"When?"

"Three days ago."

"Where?"

"At the home of a friend."

It could get tiresome, this studied economy of response. Sokolnikov had let his voice take on an edge.

"The name of this friend, please."

"Dmitri Kuznetsov."

Dima Kuznetsov . . . she moved in fast company, this one. Dmitri Kuznetsov was known to the State Militia. He was known to them on the basis, admittedly, of suspicion rather than fact; known for nothing more criminal, in fact, than belonging to the pack of instant millionaires who, since the collapse of the Soviet state, had descended like wolves on the Russian economy. At a time when 99 percent of their countrymen were fighting tooth and nail just to stave off ruin, Kuznetsov and his ilk were prospering and prospering obscenely. They produced no goods, they supplied no necessary service, they contributed nothing, they simply traded. And though the commodities traded in varied—foreign currency one week, certificates of ownership the next—they all had this attribute in common: Whether the price was rising or falling, the traders made staggering profits. And if that wasn't a crime, Sokolnikov thought, it should be. To him Kuznetsov was simply a criminal against whom nothing had so far been proved.

What had this Cassandra wanted with a man she'd met through Dima Kuznetsov?

25

Sokolnikov had thought he could hazard a guess.

"You met him at a party and arranged to meet him here, in the bell tower of Novodevichy Convent? Why?"

"He had something he wanted to sell. Something he thought I might want to buy. I agreed to meet him to see if I did."

She'd hesitated then, seemed about to elaborate. Sokolnikov had waited. His next question was predictable, inevitable. Surely she'd save him the trouble of asking.

She hadn't. She'd just sat there, regarding him calmly. If he wanted answers, her manner had implied, he'd have to ask the questions.

At that point he'd switched off the tape recorder.

"Listen very carefully," he'd said. "I'm investigating a murder here. I need to know why this man was killed. I've no wish to poke into private matters." He'd paused then, caught her gaze, and held it. "Allow me to make my meaning clearer. In the Russian Federation it isn't a crime to form the intention to purchase drugs."

"Drugs?" She'd looked startled, then indignant. "You think I wanted to buy drugs?"

"If not, what did you want?"

"I don't do drugs."

Her tone suggested this truth was self-evident. On reflection he'd found himself almost persuaded. In his experience Americans and drugs went together like love and disappointment, but she looked too healthy to be a user. Too healthy and too indignant.

"Statement noted." He'd shrugged. "But my basic point is the same. Whatever it was you were planning to buy, planning is different from buying."

"And contemplating is different yet."

"If you say so."

"I do say so."

He'd shrugged again, reactivated the tape recorder.

"You've stated you met the dead man because he had something he wanted to sell you. What?"

He hadn't known what to expect. Something on the black market, probably. An icon would be in the right range. The low end, at any rate. Genuine antiques, export prohibited, usually went for more than a thousand dollars. Possibly the dead man had been hoping to palm her off with a fake.

Her answer had brought him up short.

"He wanted to sell me a tape recording."

"A tape recording? A *thousand dollars* for a tape recording? That seems out of the normal price range."

She'd eyed him coolly.

"This was not a normal tape."

"Evidently not. What was so extraordinary about it?"

"He claimed it was an important historical document." She'd paused. "The actual verbatim record of a meeting of the Soviet Politburo."

He'd paused to consider. If this was a lie, its sheer unexpectedness lent it credibility. Except, it had struck him, for one very cogent objection:

"Why would you pay a thousand dollars for a document to which you, as a historian, can have access for nothing? The Kremlin archives, as I understand it, have been open to scholars for years."

"Most of the archives have," she'd agreed. "But not Politburo records. They're part of the so-called presidential archive. It hasn't been declassified as yet. Probably won't be for years."

In the silence that followed this announcement, her gaze had taken on an aspect of defiance. She knew what she'd just admitted, he'd thought, knew that he knew it, too.

"In other words, what you were planning to purchase was a secret document belonging to Russian Federation?"

If he'd hoped this would shake her, it hadn't.

"An allegedly secret document." She'd corrected him calmly. "And, as you earlier informed me, contemplating is different from doing."

"An allegedly secret document." He'd accepted the amendment. "And for this allegedly classified document you were willing to pay a thousand dollars? Sight unseen?"

"I'm not stupid," she'd said. "Not that stupid. What I agreed was to hear the tape. The money was in case I decided to buy."

"You didn't suspect him of setting you up?"

"To be mugged? . . . It occurred to me." She'd shrugged. "He didn't look the violent type. I was more worried about being conned."

"But in any case you agreed? You agreed to meet this man you'd met just once before, at a party. You agreed to meet him in the bell tower of Novodevichy Convent to *contemplate* the purchase, for one thousand dollars, of an alleged tape recording of an unspecified Polit-buro meeting." He'd paused. "Does that accurately summarize your story?"

She'd considered the question for a moment.

"I might object to your use of the word 'story,' but otherwise, yes, in most respects, that's a reasonably accurate summary."

"In what respects is it not accurate?"

"It wasn't an unspecified Politburo meeting. It was held on the twelfth of March 1990."

"The date struck you as especially significant?"

"That date struck me as profoundly significant. Those were the final months of the regime. Each decision made then affected . . ." She'd broken off then, given him a quick, embarrassed smile. It was the first smile he had from her, the first time she'd addressed herself to *him*, acknowledged his existence as a person, and he'd caught, suddenly, a glimpse of a wholly different woman—not the disdainful amazon armored in wealth and self-possession, but someone more sensitive, less sure of herself, more vulnerable altogether.

He would need to be on guard against that smile.

"I'm sorry," she'd said, "that was presumptuous, a foreigner lectur-ing *you* on your history, a history you lived through at first hand. I should have said that the date was significant because Lithuania had declared independence the day before. Dolokhov claimed the Polit-buro meeting that day was devoted to deciding how to respond, whether or not to send in troops."

She'd paused.

"You can see why this would interest me. If what Dolokhov said was true, his tape was the original, authentic record of that meeting. Apart from its enormous inherent interest, it could also serve as a check on eventual releases from the archive."

"As a check?" He'd been a little slow to follow her. "What kind of a check?"

"For changes or deletions, of course." She'd looked at him as if he were a halfwit. "Why do you think the archive is still classified? Quite a number of people, I imagine, would pay big money to edit those Politburo records."

"Edit" was good, Sokolnikov had thought. Good and very Russian. The Soviet state had been apt to edit. No state had ever edited,

28

indeed, with such barefaced effrontery and on quite such a scale. The emphasis, of course, had always been on erasure. Opposition, mistakes, confusion, defeats, betrayals had vanished forever at the stroke of some bureaucrat's pen. Uncounted millions of lives had in this way and others been "edited" out of the record. It was far from inconceivable, then, that someone had said something at this meeting in March 1990 and now wished to make it disappear. It was far from inconceivable, also, that some farsighted businessman, apprised of the fact, had seen in it the chance to turn a profit.

Some farsighted businessman now dead.

A scenario was starting to outline itself here, but it seemed to raise more questions than it answered. Price was the main one. If earlier it had sounded too much, a thousand dollars now seemed absurdly little to ask for a document someone was willing to kill for. And wasn't the identity of the chosen purchaser almost as hard to explain? Why would this Dolokhov offer his tape to a foreigner, a woman? And why to this Cassandra? And was her account of her behavior plausible? Would anyone as smart as she obviously was risk a thousand dollars on a strange-sounding story from a man she'd met once at a party thrown by Kuznetsov? And why, if her story was true, had the killer been so concerned—for what else explained the rifling of the pockets?—to conceal the identity of his victim?

Answer these questions, Sokolnikov had thought, and *then* you would have a workable scenario.

You might even have a suspect.

"And this is everything you know about this tape?"

"Yes. That's correct. That was all he told me about it."

She'd nodded as she said it, met his gaze without blinking. But her own gaze, he noted, had been oddly opaque. Truth, in any case, seldom showed in the eyes. As a cop he'd been lied to much of the time, probably more often than not, and mostly by people who'd met his gaze without blinking. But lying tended to make people tense, a fact exploited by polygraph machines, and the tension had to express itself somewhere. In lying, what separated the novice from the expert was not the eyes but rather the mouth. He'd noticed, when she'd finished speaking—using, moreover, too many words, making her denial three separate times—an involuntary compression of the lips.

Evading, he'd thought, had just toppled over into lying.

* * *

FOR THE SECOND TIME in about five minutes, Cass noticed, this lieutenant had switched off the tape recorder. It could get very confusing, this off-the-record/on-the-record routine.

"Cassandra Wolfe, I think you are in trouble."

Extremely welcome end of uncomfortably protracted pause. But he'd blinked, Cass thought, so she'd won that round. Now he was evidently planning to scare her. This mightn't have been such a bad move, she thought, except for the inconvenient fact that she could hardly be more scared than she was already.

"I imagine you'll get around to telling me why, eventually."

Her voice seemed to issue from somewhere above her. It, and the hostile, snotty tone, seemed to belong to someone else. It also seemed to be the only tone she could manage at the moment. Was that how one dealt with fear? Erected a facade, a fearless adult persona, for the terrified child to hide behind? If so, she thought, it made her sound like a bitch, and in a way she was sorry for that. In other circumstances she could have liked this lieutenant. Beneath his small, harmless vanities, the facade of shrewdness bordering on omniscience (borrowed, quite clearly, from the cop in *Crime and Punishment*), there lived an intelligent and decent man. It showed in how he referred to Dolokhov. It was always *myortvii chelovek*, dead man; never simply *trup*, cadaver.

"I think you're not telling me everything."

Well, of *course*, she thought. You can think that till you're blue in the face. The question is: Can you prove it?

"What is it, exactly, that you think I'm not telling you?"

"If I knew"—he shrugged—"we wouldn't be talking about it. I will, however, tell you what I think."

He paused.

"I think it is true that the dead man offered you this tape. I think he was killed because he offered it to you. I think that the killer and whoever hired him—assuming he wasn't working for himself—used to belong to the KGB. And this, of course, is why I think you are in trouble. . . . They may decide to kill you next."

No surprises there, she thought. The same line of reasoning had occurred to her, in fact, as she'd stood over Dolokhov's body, learned

30

he no longer had the tape. (She still couldn't believe she'd actually done it, had forced herself to look in those lifeless eyes and more or less calmly rifled through his pockets.) But her logic was different from this lieutenant's. Indeed, it went in the other direction: If they'd wanted to kill her, they could have already. That they hadn't suggested that they didn't see the need. This must mean, in turn, that they didn't know she'd listened to the tape. And this, of course, was one very compelling reason for *not* confiding in this lieutenant.

There were others, of course, but this would do. In Russia, she knew, the distinction between cops and robbers was often entirely a matter of uniform.

"You think they may want to kill me next. . . . Are you going to offer me police protection?"

He shook his head. "In Moscow, Miss Wolfe, there are not enough policemen, too many people who break, or *contemplate* breaking, the law. A more helpful witness we might want to protect, but you . . . ?" He shrugged. His eyes never left her face. "You, Miss Wolfe, must protect yourself."

"How am I going to do that, exactly?"

"By helping me put these people in jail. By telling me everything you know."

"I have told you everything."

She didn't know why she bothered to say it. His look conveyed he didn't either.

He shrugged again, took a notebook from his pocket, wrote something in it, and tore off the page.

"It's possible you will change your mind. You can call me anytime at this number."

She knew she should shut up now, but she couldn't.

"You can't change your mind about what you don't know."

Giving her another of his skeptical looks, he once more switched on the tape recorder.

"Miss Cassandra Wolfe, I have this to say for the record: You are a material witness in a murder investigation. Until this case is resolved or unless you are otherwise notified by the State Militia, you may not leave Russia or travel beyond fifty miles from Moscow. Should you attempt to do either, you will be treated as a fugitive from justice. This would not, I assure you, be a comfortable experience."

31

* * *

AND THAT, Sokolnikov told himself afterward, had been the note to end on. It had not been one of his more successful interviews; the advantage had definitely rested with her. But his parting shot had obviously given her pause. It was still, moreover, early in the game. She would soon find out, this American princess, that Ivo Sokolnikov of the State Militia was someone *not* to be lied to. He was tired of her calmness, her armor of self-confidence. He intended, in due course, to dent that armor. He intended to pierce it through and through.

If someone didn't kill her first.

Chapter Four

CASS SAT IN THE EMPTY OFFICE, staring out over the street, where a thin mist was threatening to turn into drizzle and the passersby were hunched against the damp. She wondered where the hell Reddaway had gotten to. He'd promised to be back "in no time at all," but had now been gone for fifteen minutes. Add that to the forty it had taken her to get here, the twenty she'd spent waiting to see him in the first place, and the further twenty explaining what she wanted—fruitlessly explaining, she suspected, since he hadn't seemed to grasp why she was there—and what she was left with was a wasted afternoon. When she'd registered with the U.S. consulate she'd been led to believe that its primary function was to render assistance to American citizens, especially those who ran into problems with the Russian authorities. Coming here, she'd had some notion of confronting Sokolnikov's restrictions on her movements with the majesty and menace of the United States of America: a strongly worded protest, at least, from the ambassador to the Foreign Ministry. This notion, it seemed, was sadly misplaced. Reddaway's rank was several steps lower than ambassador—he was actually third secretary—and his idea of rendering assistance was to make her repeat, three times, her account of the morning's events and to urge her "very earnestly" to cooperate with the Militia. That in other circumstances this might have been sound advice did little to mollify her feelings. She'd several times assured him that she *had* cooperated, and he'd no way of knowing that she hadn't. His urgings struck her as uncalled for, and his departure "to consult with a colleague" as a confession of incompetence. People were always talking about getting rid of waste in government. If they wanted to do more than talk, they might profitably start with the U.S. Foreign Service.

33

The feeling persisted ten minutes later when Reddaway, returning, introduced his colleague, then excused himself, pleading another appointment. His colleague, Arthur Quine, looked competent, and whatever else, he clearly wasn't consular. A tall, gangling, pipe-smoking man with wispy red hair, he seemed to belong to that class of diplomats her father referred to as "gentleman amateurs" and sometimes, more scathingly, as "amateur gentlemen." The rumpled condition of his three-piece tweed suit served only to emphasize the elegance of its cut, and his oxblood wingtips had been made for him, she guessed, by one of those places on Jermyn Street, probably in about the year she'd been born. His bow tie informed you he'd attended Yale. His smile was boyish and designed to charm, his eyes bright blue, intelligent, appraising. His age, she judged, was late forties or early fifties.

"You know," he began, "I used to know your father."

Not exactly a recommendation, but good manners extorted a response.

"Really?"

"Your uncle, too. That was some time ago, of course. Before he became national security adviser. In those days he was special envoy to SALT."

She wondered how he had known who she was, and whether this casual establishing of links was his way of acknowledging her importance or a subtle method of conveying his.

"You must have been posted in Brussels then."

"I was. Were you ever there yourself?"

"Once. Fourteen years ago. For my mother's funeral."

This put a stopper on the social niceties. He murmured something about being sorry, then:

"Do I gather you're in some kind of trouble?"

"I don't know that I'd call it trouble. This morning in Novodevichy Convent I discovered that someone I'd arranged to meet there had been murdered. I reported the fact at once to the police, explaining how I came to be there and the circumstances in which I found him. They seem to feel that I didn't tell them everything I knew. They've forbidden me to leave the country or travel farther than fifty miles from Moscow." She paused. "Since I planned to stay through the summer, this isn't a serious inconvenience. But it's an awkward posi-

34

tion to be in. I thought I should notify the embassy, get some idea of my legal position."

"Very sensible." He nodded. "Perhaps you could give me the details."

"I've already given them, I thought rather thoroughly, to Mr. Reddaway."

"Of course." He gave her the boyish smile, high beam. "And he conveyed the gist to me. Things sometimes get garbled in transmission, however. I'd appreciate hearing your own account."

It struck her even at the time as odd that in telling him exactly what she'd earlier told Reddaway she was never once tempted to tell him more. It wasn't that she felt he wasn't to be trusted, but rather that some instinct seemed to warn her that his interests and hers were different, possibly opposed.

She would give him this: He was a good listener. He didn't cut in or ask her to repeat things. He just sat there quietly absorbing what she told him, waiting until she'd reached an obvious stopping point before interposing with a question.

"This murdered man, this Dolokhov . . . how did he happen to approach you?"

"It was at a party. Given by Dima Kuznetsov. I imagine you know him, or know of him?"

He nodded but registered no particular reaction.

She continued, "Well, somehow I got into this argument—about history. One of those abstract, theoretical debates the Russians seem so fond of. About objectivity, whether it's possible, how much of it history can achieve. I took what you could call the pragmatic approach: 'Let's start by assembling the data, worry about interpretation later.' This begs all sorts of questions, I know, but at least it gives you something to get on with. Especially when you're dealing with the Soviet Union, where there's still so much assembling left to be done." She paused, feeling suddenly awkward. His interest in historiography probably was somewhere between slight and nonexistent. "I've probably told you more than you wanted to know, but it helps explain how he came to approach me."

But it really didn't. The argument had been just a pretext. He'd been lying in wait for her all evening. Not for anyone else, for her.

"I asked." Quine flashed the smile again. "Tell me anything that

35

strikes you as relevant. If it strikes you as that, the odds are it is." He paused. "This Dolokhov was involved in the discussion?"

"No. That was what was strange. He wasn't. Not directly. He must have been listening, though I didn't notice him. It was only later, just as I was leaving, that I first became aware of his existence. . . ."

* * *

THE PARTY ITSELF had been something of a blur. At all Moscow parties, whether in Tatyana's two-bedroom apartment or Dima's palace on the top floor of the House on the Embankment, two things flowed in torrents: talk and drink. Sometimes music was also provided, but usually only as background. At Dima's there'd been some kind of Gypsy ensemble sawing away doggedly all evening, but its chief effect on the assembled throng had been to make them raise their voices. And the talk had been fueled, *turbocharged,* by the drink. At Dima's it had been real champagne, served by mess-jacketed waiters. Dima, like some modern Trimalchio, kept urging his guests to greater consumption. "Not nearly enough dead soldiers!" he'd shouted, gesturing at the lengthening rows of empties beneath the long table that was serving as a bar. "Tonight we will take no prisoners, please. I'm expecting a bloodbath, a real massacre of the innocents." But if there had been any massacre that night, it had not involved many innocents. Dima's acquaintances were colorful and eclectic, drawn from almost every walk of life: mafiosi and ministers of state, politicians and diplomats, street merchants, cabdrivers, and pimps. She had listened, guzzling Dom Perignon, to gangsters arguing fiercely about poetry, to hookers holding forth on the nature of love, to former *apparatchiks* welcoming democracy, to all and sundry on the merits of free enterprise. By midnight her senses had been pleasurably swimming, and ignoring Dima's boisterous reproaches ("Cassandra, please, I *forbid* you to be a lightweight"), she had sought relief in fresh air and silence. It was then, in the hallway, when Dima had given up and she was getting her coat from a servant girl dressed bizzarely in a Ukrainian costume, that Dolokhov materialized beside her.

"*Izvinite, pozhalsta.* . . ."

A short, slight man in an astrakhan hat, rubber galoshes, and a fur-collared overcoat several sizes too large, he held himself stiffly, as if for her inspection, regarding her with mournful spaniel's eyes.

"You are Cassandra Wolfe. . . ." He said it with an air of discovery, like Stanley greeting Livingstone in Africa.

"I am." She'd sounded, deliberately, not much pleased to be greeted.

He held out his hand.

"Dolokhov, Vladimir Ivanovich. . . . My friends call me Volodya."

His friends could call him what they liked, she'd thought; she intended to keep things formal.

"Mr. Dolokhov, it's a pleasure to meet you. What a pity it didn't happen earlier. Now, alas, I'm about to go home. . . ."

He brushed this aside.

"I was listening to your discussion. About history and truth, the problems of establishing fact. I happen to have in my possession something that will interest you greatly, something, I think, that would establish certain facts."

She subjected him to a quick appraisal. If this was a pickup, at least it was original. Why not let him run with it awhile?

"Something that would establish certain facts? . . . Why didn't you join the conversation? It didn't strike me as the kind of party where you had to wait to be introduced." She paused for a moment, considering. "What facts?"

He didn't answer. Clearly whatever he wanted to tell her wasn't for the servant girl's ears. His look, it now struck her, was not so much mournful as anxious. Not embarrassed or awkward, anxious. This was not, she was convinced, a pickup. But in that case, what on earth *was* it?

"Perhaps," he suggested, "we might walk a little together?"

So they'd taken the elevator down, started along the embankment. Presently he'd stopped, looked back at the apartment block they'd left.

"If buildings could speak," he'd said, "consider what that one could tell us. There must be more truth concealed in it than in all your archives put together."

He was probably right, she thought. What was recorded in archives was only the fraction of things said and done that someone had thought proper or safe to write down. And this was no doubt particularly true of the archives *she* worked with, the official records of the Soviet bureaucracy, many of whose most powerful figures had lived in the House on the Embankment. They had always been riven by faction, those people, those Central Committee and Politburo members. What they said in open debate had been only what they allowed themselves to say, only what was politic and safe. This accounted for the sense you got, reading their recorded discussions, of things not said, or said but not meant, of cracks in the fabric of government smoothed over by the plaster of consensus. But *there*, she thought, in that stronghold of privilege from whose top-floor windows the strains of Dima's revels could still faintly be heard, whispering mayhem to the Moscow night, there, if anywhere, they'd been able to murmur their secrets in the ears of trusted cronies—except, of course, that they probably hadn't, because even the cronies had never been trusted, and in any case the whole place had probably been bugged.

"This thing you have that will interest me," she said, "what is it exactly?"

He regarded her for a moment without speaking.

"I presume you have heard of the presidential archive?"

"Of course—it's the Politburo records. But it hasn't been opened to historians."

"Why do you suppose it hasn't yet been opened?"

"I think it's obvious." She shrugged. "Most of those people are still around. A lot of them are still influential. Before they release the Politburo record, they want a chance to edit it, cover up their nasty little secrets."

"Exactly." He nodded. "And you historians will eventually get an incomplete, distorted version of events. From this you will then write your articles and books, for which you will claim the authority of 'fact.' "

"I doubt we'll claim anything of the sort." She shrugged. "We all know objectivity is relative. We just hope our books and articles will be closer to 'fact' than anything previously written. Closer than *The Short Course*, for instance."

He smiled, acknowledging the hit. "Since *The Short Course* was written by Stalin, *Grimm's Fairy Tales* would be closer."

He paused then, suddenly serious.

"What would you give for access? The presidential archive, I mean. What would you give for uncensored versions of the Politburo minutes?"

38

"What would I give?" She stared. "The presidential archive is the single most important set of documents from the period. Most scholars would sell their souls for access."

"I'm not speaking of most scholars, I'm speaking of you, Miss Wolfe. What would *you* be willing to give for access? We're speaking of dollars," he added dryly. "In Moscow the market for souls, even yours, is at present regrettably sluggish."

"How much would I be willing to pay?" This time she really stared. "Are you claiming you can *get* me access?"

He nodded. "Not to the entire archive, but to the minutes of certain Politburo meetings. Originally the meetings were taped, you see. The minutes were transcribed from these tapes, and no doubt received their first editing then. Afterward the tapes were destroyed." He paused. "*Most* of them were destroyed. A few, as it turns out, were not."

"And those few are now in your possession?"

"Six of them are." He nodded. "Six *very* interesting tapes, all dating from 1990, when the Soviet Union was starting to break up. For instance, the tape of the meeting held on March twelfth."

"March twelfth?" She consulted her memory. "That would have been around the time Lithuania declared independence?"

"Correct. The Lithuanian declaration was made on March eleventh! The next day's Politburo discussion, not unnaturally, dealt with the problem of how to react. Specifically, whether or not to use force. A lot of the discussion focused on the probable U.S. response to an invasion. I'm sure *you'd* find it fascinating, Miss Wolfe. Especially the exchanges between Gorbachev and Kryuchkov." He paused then, looked at her sideways, slyly. "Kryuchkov, as of course you recall, was at that time head of the KGB."

Why me particularly? she'd wondered, noting the emphasis, the sly, sidelong look. Why me more than other historians?

"It's easy to guess what you're thinking," he continued. " 'How can I buy tapes from a classified archive? If I buy them, how can I use them? How can I even be sure they're authentic?' I think there are solutions to these problems. But before we come to them, we need to settle what one might call the sixty-four-thousand-dollar question: Are you interested, Miss Wolfe?"

Pause.

"Let's put it this way," Cass said. "I'm curious—and one of the things I'm curious about is what makes you think I have money."

He smiled indulgently. "Intelligent sellers look for qualified buyers. Your family connections are not a secret. I know you have money or access to money."

"What makes you think I'd want to spend it on something like this?"

"On something like this?" He shrugged. "I think when you know what 'this' is really like, you'll be more than willing to spend your money."

"And how am I ever going to know?"

He stopped then, looked around, reached in his pocket, and handed her a slip of paper. Scrawled on it in pencil was a number, a telephone number.

"I'm going to give you a sample," he said. "If you want to hear what was actually said at that meeting of April twenty-ninth, you can call me at three o'clock tomorrow afternoon. Not five minutes before or five after." He fixed her with his mournful gaze. "Three o'clock, precisely."

* * *

Her account was received without discernible reaction. Quine was a *very* good listener, it struck her. Good, no doubt, because practiced. And practiced, probably, at detecting lies, more practiced at detecting than she was at telling. She would have to be careful here, more careful than she'd been with Sokolnikov. Don't invent, she told herself, don't elaborate.

Omit.

"So of course you called him." He was stating, not asking. "As I would have done in your shoes. . . . You called him. What did he tell you?"

She had it by heart now, this part of what she had come to think of as her "story," her edited account of what had happened with the tape. She told it tersely, in summary, exactly as she had to the lieutenant. Again Quine made no comment.

"So he offered to meet you at the convent in order to play you this tape. . . . Did it occur to you to ask how he got it?"

"Of course it did." Did he think she was an idiot? She could have

40

taken offense but dismissed the temptation. Irritation could make you careless. "He promised to explain in due course, if and when we agreed upon a deal. He said he was already at considerable risk; he didn't want to add to it unnecessarily."

"He believed he was at risk." Quine raised an eyebrow. "What happened would seem to prove him right. Yet he offered to sell you this tape for peanuts, a thousand dollars. Didn't that strike you as odd?"

"Not sell." She shook her head. "Loan. The thousand was simply an advance—a good-faith payment, so to speak. If I wanted the tape, I'd pay him the thousand, he'd loan me a copy for authentication. Once it checked out, he said, *then* we could start talking price."

"If it checked out? How were you going to do that?"

"Voiceprint analysis, he suggested. Voiceprints were like finger-prints, he said. Everyone's were different, unique."

Quine seemed about to comment on this. Instead he asked another question.

"So you never did get to listen to the tape?"

She shook her head. "By the time I found him he was dead and it was gone. Or at least," she amended, "the police claim not to have found it."

"Claim?" he inquired. "Meaning you tend to doubt them?"

She shook her head. "Meaning I have no way of knowing."

"You didn't look yourself, then?"

This was uttered casually enough, but his gaze was suddenly prob-ing.

Pause.

"Mr. Quine"—she let chill into her tone—"I don't know how many murders *you've* discovered. I found the experience terrifying. The last thing I'd have thought to do was rummage through his pockets. I wanted to get out of there."

"Understandable." He smiled, then paused for a moment, consider-ing. "Then you really have no idea what was on this mysterious tape? What Gorbachev might have said to Kryuchkov or vice versa?"

She thought about this. Important not to act too dumb. Too dumb or too incurious.

"I wouldn't say no idea. I could make a guess, but that's all it would be, more or less informed speculation."

41

"So guess," he encouraged. "The worst you can be is wrong."

It occurred to her to point out that they'd strayed a long way from the original purpose of this discussion. She decided not to. Better not to seem reluctant or evasive.

"Okay." She shrugged. "According to Dolokhov, the discussion that day dealt generally with whether or not to invade Lithuania. We know from other sources that at that point Gorbachev was opposed by a coalition of hard-liners. Dolokhov said that much of the discussion dealt with the probable U.S. reaction. This was the context in which he mentioned exchanges between Gorbachev and Victor Kryuchkov." She paused. "It's possible what they discussed was the KGB's assessment of the likely U.S. response and how this assessment was arrived at."

Quine weighed this for a moment.

"So you think the exchange concerned sources, KGB sources?"

He was quick, she thought, remarkably quick.

"It may have." She shrugged. "If there was an exchange. Or even a tape, for that matter. But assuming there was and it was why Dolokhov was murdered, you have to wonder what could make it so important. Protecting sources springs to mind. But remember, this is only a guess, more likely to be wrong than not."

She paused. Continuing, she let impatience into her tone.

"So . . . now you know everything I know and then some. Now I have a question for you, Mr. Quine. Can you get the State Militia off my back? Or have I wasted my afternoon entirely?"

"Oh, no." He smiled. "I wouldn't say wasted. I'm sure we can get them off your back. A word in the appropriate ear should do it."

He stood up. It seemed that the interview was over, his curiosity exhausted. So his final question, asked while he was seeing her to the door, seemed to come as an afterthought.

"By the way, that number he gave you to call, you don't still happen to have it, do you?"

"As a matter of fact, I do." She fished for it in her purse, found it, handed it to him. "I don't think it will help you much. I'd say it's almost certainly a phone booth."

"A phone booth?"

She nodded. "Isn't that what you guys use when you think your own lines aren't secure?"

" 'You guys'?" He looked puzzled. "Who do you mean by 'you guys'?"

"You and Dolokhov." She shrugged. "Whoever else is involved in all this. What I mean, Mr. Quine-Who-Used-to-Know-My-Father, are that curious subspecies of so-called diplomats who gather around mystery like flies around garbage. I refer, of course"—she smiled at him sweetly—"to spooks."

* * *

AND THAT, her insistence on letting him know she knew what he was, had been smart-ass, she thought later, but not all that smart. What he was had been fairly obvious; he hadn't, in fact, made much effort to conceal it. His interest in Dolokhov's tape, moreover, had been neither casual nor accidental. His swift homing in on Gorbachev and Kryuchkov had shown that: *So you think the exchange concerned sources, KGB sources?* He had shown remarkable intuition; intuition so remarkable that she wondered if it *was* intuition. Perhaps Mr. Quine had known about the tape, perhaps he was already familiar with the contents. Perhaps, in that case, his purpose in talking to her had been to find out how familiar *she* was.

Cassandra Wolfe, I think you are in trouble. . . . They may decide to kill you next. She'd brushed off Sokolnikov's warning then, but now it demanded to be taken seriously. "They," it seemed, were a multiple threat, a monster more various than she'd imagined. "They," she thought, might well want to kill her.

They would if they learned she'd listened to the tape.

Had heard about the agent code-named Oracle.

Chapter Five

Lieutenant Sokolnikov was curious. Curious and apprehensive. He wondered why the general wanted to see him. General Rev, chief of the Criminal Investigations Division, was an eminence majestic and remote. Normally one's contact with him was limited to a rigid salute as the general swept by in his chauffeur-driven Chaika. Facing him now across the vast mahogany desk in an office that, subdivided, would have yielded living space for half a dozen families, Sokolnikov, studying the general's coffin-shaped face, the general's unsmiling features, wondered what he'd done wrong.

"Lieutenant, I'm informed that you're handling the inquiry into yesterday's murder in Novodevichy Convent. Please acquaint me with the details of the case."

Sokolnikov had been expecting this. It confirmed his instinct that the case was highly unusual. It didn't, however, enlighten him much. The last time he had looked at the statistics, murders in Greater Moscow were occurring at an average rate of 8.5 per day, and the vast majority never excited a flicker of interest from the general. This killing was admittedly out of the ordinary, both in regard to the method employed and in its involving a foreigner as a witness. These aspects, plus the curious substance of the foreign witness's very much suspect testimony, justified at least some higher-level interest. Had his captain inquired into the case, or even the chief of his section, Sokolnikov would have regarded it as normal. When the general inquired, it was abnormal. More than abnormal.

Ominous.

Sokolnikov allowed none of his misgivings to show on his face or color his account of the case. He gave a succinct but detailed statement of the facts and a summary of the steps he had taken. Since the steps had led nowhere, this didn't take him very long.

"What you seem to be telling me"—the general's voice was even—"is that you haven't yet established the identity of the victim. You haven't found the murder weapon nor the victim's car, and you have neither motive nor suspect." He fixed Sokolnikov with an expressionless gaze. "Would that be a fair statement?"

Fair, Sokolnikov thought, but hardly reasonable. The case was scarcely thirty hours old; the last time he had looked at the statistics, 55 percent of murders reported in Greater Moscow were still unsolved after thirty days. He wasn't about to point this out, however. The general was known to despise excuses.

"It's an accurate statement, General."

He placed no particular emphasis on "accurate"—the general was known also to despise impertinence—but the shift in sense wasn't lost on his superior.

"Accurate but *not* fair, you're suggesting?" The general gave a sudden, surprisingly charming grin. "Not fair in failing to acknowledge, perhaps, the intelligence and effort so far expended by Lieutenant Sokolnikov and his subordinates toward a solution of this baffling case?"

"I wouldn't presume to put it that way, General." Sokolnikov allowed himself an answering smile. "What your summary failed to acknowledge, perhaps, was progress that's been made in a negative way."

"Progress in a negative way." The general turned the phrase over in his mind. "To me that sounds like going backward. What progress?"

"The murder weapon, for instance. Ballistics confirms that it was, indeed, a silenced twenty-two automatic, fired at a range of greater than ten feet. I believe we've established that it wasn't abandoned or hidden in the grounds of the convent. I would guess that at this point it's somewhere in the mud at the bottom of the Moscow River."

"You would guess . . ." The general seemed less than impressed. "We're making progress in a negative way by *guessing?* What else would you guess?"

"The killer was a professional," Sokolnikov said. "This is suggested not only by the choice of weapon, but also by the choice of shot. The man was shot in middle of the forehead, at a range of *greater than ten feet*. By someone confronting him, that is. Someone he could see, whose intention must have been plain." He paused. "He would have attempted evasive action. And the twenty-two has no stopping power whatever. Only an extremely competent and confident marksman would have attempted that particular shot."

"I see." Sokolnikov was gratified to see the general looking a shade less skeptical. "What else?"

"The rifling of the victim's pockets," Sokolnikov said. "Not only this alleged tape, but everything, every piece of personal ID was removed."

The general shrugged. "Obviously the killer didn't want the victim identified." He paused, then added sourly, "I'd have to say he's been successful in that."

"Successful so far," Sokolnikov qualified. "We'll identify him sooner or later. We have photographs to show around. Fingerprints and dental records to check. Clothing. Presently his car will show up, or someone will come forward to report a missing person—"

"What's your point?" the general interrupted testily. "I, too, attended the Training Academy. It was back in the last century, admittedly, but even then we had procedures. Please spare me the obvious and make your point, Lieutenant."

"The killer wanted identification deferred," Sokolnikov said. "Not prevented—he must have known that wasn't possible—but delayed."

"Buying time?" The general reflected a moment. "It makes sense, I suppose. . . . Buying time for what?"

"I don't know," Sokolnikov admitted. "It suggests to me that the killing, the hypothetical recovery of this hypothetical tape, isn't the end of the story. Something remained to be accomplished. A search, perhaps, for copies of the tape."

"You believe in this hypothetical tape, then?" The general eyed him shrewdly.

"I believe there was a tape, yes. I believe it may have been the motive for the killing. . . . That American woman who discovered the body, she was remarkably cool about it. But I doubt she was cool enough to invent the whole thing." Sokolnikov paused. "Again this is only my impression, General, but the details rang true to me. The details she consented to give me, that is."

"The details she consented to give you. . . . You think there were details she withheld?"

Sokolnikov nodded. "I believe so, yes."

The general considered for a moment.

"What were you thinking of doing about that?"

"Scaring her." Sokolnikov's answer was prompt. "Letting her stew for a bit. Hauling her in later and leaning on her a little. Maybe, if she continues to be uncooperative, locking her up for a few days."

This was received without comment or visible reaction.

"What do you know about her, this Cassandra Wolfe?"

"She's here on an extended visa." Sokolnikov paused. Alarms were going off in his head. So far as he could recall, and his memory was excellent, he hadn't mentioned the name of the witness. "She arrived last July. Home address: Washington, D.C. Doctoral candidate in Soviet history, sponsored by Georgetown and Moscow University to conduct research in the Soviet archives. In Moscow she lives with a fellow historian, one Tatyana Rostova, professor of history at Moscow University, also a researcher in the archives. She—Cassandra Wolfe, that is—is six feet tall, blond, blue-eyed, twenty-six years old . . . unmarried." He paused. These last particulars, obtained from the visa application, were irrelevant for professional purposes. Unsure why he'd mentioned them, he added, "She's also apparently an acquaintance of the millionaire businessman Dmitri Kuznetsov."

Still no reaction from the general.

"What steps have you taken to establish her history and background?"

"I've cabled our embassy in Washington to find out what they can. But you know the Diplomatic Service. They're unlikely to give it a high priority. I imagine we can expect to hear back from them in a month or two. By summer, possibly." Sokolnikov shrugged. "I thought of asking the U.S. embassy here, but why would they put themselves out to help us?"

"An interesting question." The general's voice was dry. "And not so rhetorical as you might think. The U.S. embassy has been at some pains to be helpful—if that's the correct word to decribe their attitude."

"You mean somebody's already asked them about her?" Something in the general's eyes caused Sokolnikov another stab of misgiving.

"Not at all." The general's voice was bland. "They volunteered the information. The U.S. ambassador himself called the Ministry of Justice this morning, ostensibly to inquire about restrictions you've apparently placed on the movements of this woman, but he also happened to let fall in passing some details concerning her background, which details the minister passed on to me." The general paused. "It seems that this Cassandra Wolfe is the daughter of one Nicholas Wolfe, a journalist who writes regularly for *The New York Times* and occasionally *The New Yorker*. Mr. Wolfe, I should add, is scheduled to arrive here on Tuesday." The general paused. "Should this information not make you reconsider your plan to 'lean on her a little,' perhaps you should know about the uncle: Miss Wolfe's uncle is Henry Reynolds. *Senator* Henry Reynolds. Perhaps you have heard of him? He was national security adviser to the last Republican administration and is currently a candidate for president. I don't know exactly how conversant you are with domestic U.S. politics, Lieutenant, but according to the latest polls, Senator Reynolds has the Republican nomination more or less locked up. Indeed, were the election to be held today, he'd be favored, overwhelmingly, to win."

The general paused again, this time for about fifteen seconds, his eyes gleaming with what Sokolnikov was stunned to identify as amusement.

"In other words, Lieutenant, the woman you were planning to 'lean on' is the niece of a man who in all probability will be the next president of the United States."

* * *

IT HAD BEEN, Sokolnikov thought later, a day of surprises, not the least of them the general's follow-up: Sokolnikov was to contact Miss Wolfe. He was to apologize for the restrictions erroneously placed on her movements, to notify her that these restrictions were now lifted, and to thank her for her cooperation. All of which was only to be expected. What was not to be expected was the "but"—Sokolnikov was to apologize, certainly, *but* he was by no means to relax his efforts to arrive at a solution of the case; indeed, he was to give it his undivided attention. The general was receptive to the view that the former KGB was involved in the case. Sokolnikov was to investigate this theory, and any others that commended themselves to him, with unre-lenting vigor. He was also to report his findings—and this was perhaps the biggest of the surprises—not to his captain or the chief of his section, but to the general himself, personally.

Chapter Six

"But of course you'll meet him at the airport?"

"I hadn't thought of it." Cass shrugged. "He'll be on expenses; he always is. The paper pays for everything: hotels, transportation, the lot. It won't hurt him to take a taxi."

"But Cass, my God: He's your father. You must."

The bewilderment and horror on her roommate's face told Cass she'd just struck a cultural nerve. Tatyana's idea of the family bond was Russian and thoroughly sentimental. The truth of this was evidenced by the state of her apartment. Cass surveyed the ambient clutter. Parents and grandparents framed in silver on the mantel, lesser relatives crowding every wall: drawings, silhouettes, snapshots, daguerreotypes. Photograph albums and packets of letters littering every available surface. Boxes of memorabilia stacked, three deep, along one wall. Family was everything with Tatyana. And, of course, she'd worshiped her own father.

That, Cass thought, always helped.

"It's not as if we're close," she said. "The last time I heard from him was Christmas. And that was just a greetings telegram, probably sent by someone in his office. This is the first letter in something like a year."

Perhaps it was because of their history, she thought, because these days their meetings were so few, that she found it easiest to read his letters as if she'd run across them in an archive; as if, like the records of a long dead past, they were best subjected to dispassionate analysis, scrutinized carefully for subtext. This one, however, had struck her as mostly surface.

Dear Sass,

It seems I'm to be sent to Siberia for a while. Or if not Siberia, Moscow. My editor, whose nostalgia for the Cold War reveals itself occasionally in twinges of Russophobia, wants a survey of the current political situation, with emphasis on the lunatic right and what he terms the "Zhirinovsky Menace". I suggested he had writers more qualified for this assignment, but he maintained that what Moscow needed was me. I arrive Tuesday the 24th, local time 1640, on American Flight 317 and will be staying, initially, at the Metropol.

While I'm there, may I hope to see something of you? A lingering parental instinct is joined in this query by the wish to make use of your expert local knowledge. My Russian, never fluent, is these days hesitant to the point of paralysis and my circle of acquaintances in Moscow deplorably limited. I think you'll agree that State Department stuffed shirts and agency hacks are not the most promising of sources for the "fresh and offbeat perspective" my editor expects me to provide.

I hope your stay to date has been enjoyable and your researches productive.

Love,
Nick

Almost *entirely* surface, in fact. In spite of that disingenuous "May I hope to see something of you?," he clearly—why else include the flight information?—expected her to meet him at the airport. (And she would, she supposed, if only to get Tatyana off her back, or else because not to would seem childishly discourteous.) As for the rest, it probably meant *less* than it said. What he wanted, obviously, were contacts and help with the language. The only instance of subtext she could see was in his use of her childhood pet name. This was reverse psychology, of course—pure, unmistakable Nick: the tip of an iceberg with nothing underneath. If his pet name for her had been deserved on occasion, it was also not for nothing that hers for him had been "Slick."

The letter had arrived three days ago, the day before she'd met Dolokhov at Dima's party. In retrospect, its arrival, right on cue, seemed ominous. *You could ask your father,* Dolokhov had said. And lo and behold, here he was to be asked. What, she asked herself, could her father know about a 1990 meeting of the Soviet Politburo and a KGB agent code-named Oracle?

51

She also wondered, not for the first time, if someone had been reading her mail.

"Just because he doesn't write"—once Tatyana got her teeth in a subject, it wasn't always easy to get her to let go—"doesn't mean he doesn't care about you. Some men aren't comfortable writing."

"Tatyana"—Cass entered a mild remonstrance—"he's a journalist. If *he's* not comfortable writing, who is?"

"I meant letters, of course." Tatyana tossed her head. "Some men aren't comfortable putting their feelings on paper. It doesn't mean they don't have them. I'm sure he loves you. He's your father, isn't he?"

Tatyana was right about one thing, Cass thought. Nick had always been undemonstrative—"not much," as he put it, "for wearing my heart on my sleeve." But its absence from his sleeve was no proof of its existence elsewhere. Actions spoke louder than words, and his, since her mother's death and before, had never been hard to interpret.

"I know I must strike you as odd," she said, "and probably unnatural. But your family and mine are worlds apart. It's not just culture," she added. "There's a history. The past exacts reparations. You can't just forget it. You of all people should know that."

"I know it very well." Tatyana nodded, a little primly. Like Cass, she did research in the Soviet archives; unlike Cass, she was a full professor, part of the team appointed by Yeltsin to write a history of the KGB. "But not forgetting it is not enough. To move beyond it we need to understand it." She paused. "What is there in this past that you can't forget or at least forgive?"

What is there? . . . There was so much, Cass thought. There were years and years. It was hard to know where to begin. She didn't, moreover, have much inclination. But she knew a refusal would be taken as a snub. Tatyana was not only her roommate, she was also a generous mentor and friend. And while most Americans might find her curiosity intrusive, Cass knew it was merely warmhearted and—though Tatyana was only just out of her thirties—motherly; a concern that was natural and expected in Russia, where teachers were surrogate parents to their students, and the care and correction of the young was almost exclusively the province of women.

"*All* of it. For instance . . ." Cass hesitated. Her instinct was not to confide. What was there to be gained by it? But she'd started now,

52

she might as well go on. "I told you—didn't I?—that twelve years ago my mother killed herself."

"You did." Tatyana was sitting on the floor beside Cass's chair. She reached up and, taking Cass's hand, held it in both of her own. "You think your father was to blame for that?"

"I don't know. At the time I thought it was his fault . . . when I wasn't thinking it was mine, of course." Cass considered. "I guess I still think it was his fault, at least indirectly. She was fine till he cheated on her, left. I don't believe she ever got over it. . . . But that wasn't what I was talking about." She paused. "She killed herself in Brussels. I was fourteen when it happened, at a boarding school in Concord I hadn't wanted to go to. I got this phone call from my uncle—my uncle, you'll note, not my father. I was devastated, absolutely shattered. . . . I must have needed to punish someone—my father, myself, both of us, I didn't care—so I told him I wasn't going to live with him, I wanted to live with my aunt and uncle. I imagine part of me must have meant it, but part of me was hoping he'd protest. I kept waiting for him to tell me not to be silly . . . hug me . . . look sad . . . *something*." She paused again. "You know what he actually did? He just looked at me. He gave me that look he used to give my mother, the one that tells you you're being emotional and tiresome, and he said: 'Whatever you want, Cass. Just tell me what you want, and I'll make the appropriate arrangements.' I felt as if he'd kicked me in the stomach."

"Poor Cass." Tatyana gave her hand a sympathetic squeeze. "Poor Cass. It's easy to imagine how you felt. But think for a moment how he must have felt. He must have been blaming himself, too. He, too, must have wanted to punish himself. Or maybe he just wasn't able to show his feelings. Men often can't, you know."

"Or maybe"—Cass wasn't buying—"he just wasn't feeling very much."

"No. . . ." Tatyana shook her head. "Excuse me, my dear, but that's stupid. I'm sure he cares about you—if he didn't, he wouldn't have written—but you're still angry so you won't accept it." She paused. "You say the past exacts reparations. That's true in the case of history, perhaps, but between people it seems to me the attitude of an accountant. If we're always adding up who owes what, where is there any room for love?"

"I don't know." Cass sighed. "Maybe you're right. Maybe the problem isn't him, it's me. Maybe I'm the one who doesn't feel. Maybe I've been trying not to for so long I've lost the knack of it." She paused. "You know what I think, Tatyana? I think Oscar Wilde was right."

"Oscar Wilde?" Tatyana stared. "Right about what, exactly?"

"About parents and children."

"Did he even have children?"

"Oh, yes," Cass said. "Two sons, I believe. And this is what he said: 'Children first love their parents, then they judge them, but they rarely, if ever, forgive them.' "

Tatyana frowned. "I think that's terrible."

"Oh, yes," Cass nodded. "So do I. But would that stop it being true?"

Chapter Seven

At the airport, Cass found herself recalling Wickenburg.

It wasn't strange that she should think about her father—she was here to meet his plane, after all—but it surprised her that of all the possibilities, this scene, Wickenburg, was the one she had chosen to replay. She hadn't chosen it consciously, she thought, but she must have chosen, it, some part of her must. And why? she wondered. Why this one now? Why not the scene in the library of the house in Santa Barbara when he told her that he and her mother were divorcing? Or the one a few years later in Brussels, in the limousine returning from her mother's funeral? Why, she wondered, with so much psychodrama to choose from, did she so often opt for the simple thriller, the western?

* * *

She knows they are bound for Santa Barbara, but she can't remember any longer how come they are driving through Wickenburg. She recalls Nick saying that, for the hundred-mile stretch between Wickenburg and the California border, Route 60 was quicker than the interstate, but what they are doing in western Arizona, where exactly they are coming *from*, are details that escape her now. The ones that stick are that they're traveling at dawn—he says to avoid the worst of the heat, but she thinks it has more to do with the absence of highway patrolmen. The Porsche's top is down, the speedometer needle hovering around a hundred and ten, the slipstream threatening to scalp her, and sleeping towns with names like Wenden and Vega are flicking by almost as fast as the mileposts.

Then, up ahead, maybe a quarter of a mile, barely discernible in the luminous gray-purple of the dawn, a figure can be made out on the blacktop. Nick cuts the speed back to eighty, and as they get closer they see it's a man and he is flagging them down. Not thumbing, flagging. Waving his arms and hopping up and down in a dance, almost comic, of distress. The Porsche fishtails to a halt some thirty yards past where he's been standing, and already he's hurrying toward them, treading gingerly, as if hobbled.

They notice he has nothing on his feet.

"What happened?" Nick grins. "Someone steal your boots?"

"Them, my damned truck and all my damned gear." He's about twenty, faded Levi's and T-shirt, bareheaded. His suntan ends halfway up his forehead. He's agitated, trying not to show it. "I give this feller a ride. Picked him up outside Phoenix. Seems like a nice enough feller. Presently he offers to take over driving for a bit. I'm set to doze off when he stops, pulls a gun, and orders me out of the truck. Didn't even give me time to grab my boots and hat." He pauses. "Son of a bitch."

"How long ago?" Nick asks.

"Not long . . . five minutes, ten at the most."

"Get in." Nick reaches over, unlocks Cass's door. "Sass, hop in the back, will you? You're smaller."

"Eddie Cox." The young man holds out a hand. "I appreciate you stoppin', mister. . . . Thing is, he don't have much gas. He'll have to stop in Blythe. Maybe sooner. There's nothing before Quartzsite. We should be up to him by then."

In fact, they are up to him inside ten minutes. The state highway, though only two-lane, is well maintained, straight as a needle. Nick takes the Porsche up past one-thirty, and in no time at all—too soon, indeed, for Cass, who at ten years old enjoys the speed but doesn't like the sound of that gun—the truck, an aging Ford pickup, comes into view up ahead. It slows as they come up on it, inviting them to pass, but Nick tucks the Porsche in behind it, keeping some eight or ten car lengths back.

"What are you going to do?" Cass whispers.

"Stay on his tail." Nick shrugs. "Await developments. He knows we're here. It's his move now."

"But Dad . . ." It occurs to Cass in retrospect, though it can't have at the time, that she almost never calls him Dad. "Eddie says he's got a gun."

"I heard." Nick nods. "And right about now, I imagine, he's starting to wonder what good it's going to do him."

"Look, mister"—something of Cass's nervousness has infected Eddie Cox—"it's just an old truck and some gear. I wouldn't want anyone to get killed for it."

"Me neither." Nick gives him a grin.

"Then why not just drive to the Highway Patrol in Quartzsite?"

Nick grins again but doesn't reply.

At this point the truck pulls over.

Nick passes. Cass expects him to drive on, but instead he pulls over, twenty yards ahead. He takes the Porsche out of gear but leaves the motor running. As he gets out, he tells Cox to take the wheel. He tells him if anything goes wrong to take off, drive like hell for the Highway Patrol in Quartzsite. He tells Cass to keep her head down. She is scared by this, but reassured, for the moment, by how calm he is. And how big. Six-feet-four, two-forty, the broad neck and heavy shoulders a legacy of the oarsman who once rowed for Yale. He reminds her of a buffalo or maybe an elephant: quiet, unpredictable, dangerous to mess with. But this reassurance doesn't last. The man who emerges from the truck is young, seventeen or eighteen at the most. Too young, Cass thinks, to be having a gun, much less threatening her father with it. But that is exactly what he is doing. And the rest of him—what he looks like, what he's wearing—gets lost in the dread that surrounds this perception. Even later, this—how young he is— will be all she remembers of him. And the gun, of course, which she knows is the real thing, a snub-nosed revolver with the bluing worn around the muzzle.

"What the fuck do you want?" The voice is strained, high-pitched, belligerent.

"Eddie here would like his truck back," Nick says. "Also his boots and the rest of his gear."

He takes a casual step forward.

"Hold it . . . right there." The young man gestures with the gun, his voice rising higher, skirting hysteria. "I'll use this if I have to. . . . I don't want to, but I will."

"Of course you don't want to." Nick stops. His voice is relaxed,

57

conversational, even friendly. He could be talking about the weather. "Right now you're not in that much trouble. You're facing car theft." Pause. "*Attempted* car theft. Three months in jail. Six at the most. If this is a first offense, maybe even a suspended sentence. . . . Kill me, on the other hand, it's first-degree murder. That's life imprisonment . . . or worse." Another pause. "I'd say the choice is worth thinking about."

The young man appears to do that, briefly.

"Why don't I just pop the three of you and take off?"

Nick shrugs. "You'd get picked up inside a day . . . assuming, of course, that you managed to pop us. It's hard to shoot someone when he's driving away. Especially"—pause—"when you don't really want to."

"Who says I don't really want to?"

"You," Nick says. "You just did. Remember?"

Silence.

"Then maybe I should just take your car. Shoot out the tires on the truck and leave you here, thumbing."

"It's an idea." Nick ponders it, shakes his head. "You might make it as far as L.A., but I doubt it." He pauses. "What's your name?"

"My name?" The young man looks utterly startled. "What the fuck d'you want with my name?"

Nick shrugs. "I'd like to know who's threatening to shoot me. . . . I know what you look like. Why not your name?"

Another silence; then, very reluctantly, "Wayne."

"Well, Wayne," Nick tells him, "you have to decide how much trouble is enough. You can give me the gun, or you can kill me. . . . If you're going to kill me, now would seem to be the time. Because sooner or later someone's going to drive by, and then the whole thing will be out of your hands."

He pauses, allowing the thought to sink in.

"What I think you *should* do is give me the gun."

At some point in the long, tense silence that follows, he puts his hand out, takes a slow, deliberate step toward Wayne. Nothing happens. He takes another . . . Eddie puts the Porsche into gear. Cass is aware of a tightness in her chest, a knot of grief and terror in her throat that stops her breathing, threatens to choke her. The whole scene has an unreal quality. Like a nightmare, she thinks, except that in a nightmare something always tells her she is dreaming and here she is certain she is not. And though in part of her mind time has slowed and fragmented, so each instant is an image, separate from the next, an individual frame in a movie, she is nonetheless conscious that the camera is rolling, that in five frames or ten the uneasy truce between impulses warring in Wayne will be broken one way or the other, and that when it is, her father may be dead.

And she hears herself say, "Don't shoot. . . . Please, Wayne, don't shoot my dad."

"Shit . . ." The disgusted monosyllable seems forced from Wayne against his will. Very slowly he lowers the gun, offers it, butt first, to Nick.

Nick takes it from him, breaks it open, ejects the bullets onto the soft shoulder, nudges them with the side of his foot one by one into the ditch. Eddie takes the Porsche out of gear, expels his breath in a long, drawn-out sigh. And Cass, who let hers out when Wayne lowered the gun, discovers suddenly that she is crying.

* * *

WHEN HER MOTHER HEARS, there's an elemental row, the first real row Cass has witnessed between her parents. Patsy Wolfe is overcome with fury that her husband would take such a chance. Not with his own life, she's at pains to make clear—he's welcome to do what he likes with *that*—but with Cass's. When she learns he didn't turn Wayne in to the police, just left him standing there out in the desert, because, as he explains, they'd already lost time and turning him in would have wasted the rest of the morning, outrage is added to her anger.

"Then the whole thing was just some stupid game." Her voice is cold, venomous. Cass has never seen her so angry. "You didn't give a damn about catching a thief. Nor about getting that man his truck back. You just had to prove to some teenage boy that your dick was longer than his. You're a jerk, Nick Wolfe, and an idiot to boot. A contemptible, self-centered ass."

Nick receives this tirade unblinking. "There wasn't any risk. I knew he wouldn't shoot."

"You knew. And how, may I ask, did you know?"

"He was talking too much. And the odds were overwhelmingly

against it. Not many people can kill in cold blood. Fewer than one in a thousand, I'd guess." Nick shrugs. "I just knew he wasn't the one."

"You just *knew*." The look Patsy gives him is withering. "You just took one look and you knew."

Nick nods. "One does sometimes."

"Does one?" Patsy says nastily. "Well, speaking for myself, I think I'd have shot you. I really think I might have, if only for the huge satisfaction of seeing the surprise on your face. . . . Mr. Brassballs, the hotshot poker player, who gambles even with his daughter's life, calls one wrong for a change." She pauses. Her anger has either subsided now or undergone some kind of chemical change. In its place is something Cass hasn't seen before, or perhaps, though the notion occurs to her only much later, something she hasn't allowed herself to see. It's dislike—the discovery dismays her—an antipathy cold and abiding, bordering on hate. "I actually believe that if I had been he, I *would* have shot you, just to deny you the pleasure of winning."

"Would you?" Nick's voice now is drained of all expression. Cass knows the tone; he uses it for scenes that have gone on too long, stories that are losing his attention. "In that case maybe *you* are the one."

"The one?" For a moment Patsy is lost.

"The *one*." Nick shrugs. "The one in a thousand."

* * *

WHEN CASS CAUGHT SIGHT OF HIM, in the line at Immigration, half a head taller than anyone else and standing there with the seasoned traveler's air of rumpled patience, his carry-on in hand and a suit bag slung over his shoulder, her heart gave a small, involuntary leap. She reverted to being, for a moment, the child she had been that morning outside Wickenburg. It was almost as if the events of the years in between hadn't happened. And, indeed, she noted, time hadn't marked him very much. At fifty-two there was a thickness at the waist there hadn't been sixteen years earlier, and the reading glasses hanging from a cord around his neck bore witness to the impact of years on his eyesight. But otherwise he didn't seem different. His hair was still thick and unruly, the black hardly dusted with gray. And he carried himself as straight as always, still moved with the ease and lightness of an athlete. He was almost the same as he had been then. She was the one who had changed.

He caught sight of her, put down the carry-on, waved.

She waved back. Impossible not to.

"That's him?" Tatyana asked. "That's your father?"

"That's him."

"My God, he's big." Tatyana paused, appraising. "Handsome."

"He breaks hearts." Cass nodded. "You could call it his hobby."

Tatyana looked reproachful. "Cass, please . . . try not to be bitter today. After all, he is your father."

"That," Cass said, "is mostly the problem."

"Well, forget your problem, at least for today. . . . We go out to dinner. We have a good time. Tomorrow, if you must, you can quarrel." Tatyana looked over at Nick again and waved. "I think your father looks nice."

*　*　*

AND THAT WAS A PROBLEM, too, Cass thought. (He was through Immigration now and standing before them.) Nick did look nice. Legions of women had thought exactly that, had been suckered by that intriguing facade—the gleam in those greenish-blue eyes, the habitual air of amused detachment—into wanting to explore what lay behind it, wanting to possess, more often than not, a spirit that resisted possession. At Yale, her Aunt Josie had told her, he had cut a swathe through the debutantes of her season, leaving behind him, in various hotel rooms, a litter of broken hearts.

"Hello, Sass."

"Hello, Nick."

They stood there a moment, uncertain. Then, setting down the carry-on, he leaned forward, brushed her cheek with his lips.

"It's good of you to meet me. . . . I wasn't expecting it."

"Weren't you?" Cass shrugged. "You told me the flight number and the ETA, and Tatyana here volunteered to drive me." Aware that this was less than gracious, she hastened to make introductions. "I'd like you to meet Tatyana Rostova. She's working in the archive, too. She's my friend and mentor. Also my roommate. Tatyana, this is my father."

"Mr. Wolfe . . ." Tatyana, extending her hand (and, Cass noted, a brilliant smile), greeted Nick in her pleasantly accented English. "It is great pleasure to meet you. Your daughter has told me many things about you."

If this should have given him pause, it didn't seem to.

"Ms. Rostova." He took her hand, holding it a shade longer, it struck Cass, than courtesy strictly demanded.

"Tatyana . . . please call me Tatyana." Another brilliant smile. "The father of my friend is also my friend. No?"

"I hope so." His own smile had always been charm incarnate. "And, of course, you must call me Nick."

"But Nick is familiar form for Nicholas, yes? To be correct I must use Nicholas. But I will call you Nick, I think. Because really, Nick, Cassandra is like a daughter to me." Tatyana paused. Reflecting perhaps on the possible implications of her previous statement, she qualified. "Not daughter, perhaps . . . sister is better, I think."

"Well, I certainly hope you won't call me Nicholas. Only my mother called me that, and only when she was angry with me."

"Then I will call you Nicholas only if I am angry with you."

"In that case, I must do my best never to give you cause."

"I was right." Tatyana turned to Cass. "He is very nice, your father. Very charming. I think it will be difficult to be angry with him."

"Difficult perhaps." Cass, conscious of his gaze upon her, turned and met it, expressionless. "But not impossible, you'll find."

And again she was conscious of putting herself in the wrong, of sounding like a bitch. But though it was unreasonable to blame him for Tatyana's insistence on flirting, it made her uneasy, or irritated, and part of her did blame him—if only for being, as always, so willing to be flirted with. It was almost with relief that she heard someone say her name and turned to find herself confronting the uniformed figure and unsmiling features of Lieutenant Sokolnikov.

* * *

"Lieutenant . . . I guess I should feel flattered. Now I have my own personal police escort, making sure I don't leave the country. But don't worry. I'm here to meet a plane, not catch one."

Before he could reply she turned and introduced him to Tatyana and Nick. He extended a hand to each in turn, bowing slightly and

clicking his heels. But he did it woodenly, without smiling, and there-
after ignored them completely.

"I, too, am here on personal business," he told her. "Meeting you
was a matter of chance. I do, however, have something to tell you. I
intended phoning you tomorrow, but I hope you'll permit me to take
this opportunity instead."

She saw he was angry about something. And perhaps for this reason
he was having trouble keeping icily dignified from toppling over into
pompous. Hard to resist baiting him a little.

"You have my permission, Lieutenant."

He hesitated, shot her a suspicious look; then, meeting nothing in
her gaze but innocence, he continued: "I'm instructed to inform you
that restrictions on your movements have been lifted."

Interesting, she thought. Obviously Arthur Quine's doing. He'd
been remarkably prompt. She'd have to remember to call and thank
him.

"I'm relieved to hear that. And thank you for telling me in person.
Does this mean I'm no longer a material witness?"

"It means that, subject to the normal restrictions applying to all
foreigners in Russia, you are free to come and go as you please."

Silence. She was conscious of her companions' curiosity as an almost physical pressure. For the time being she ignored it, however.

"I notice you say 'instructed.' Do I gather these instructions don't
meet with your approval?"

"They're instructions. I carry them out. Whether they meet with
my approval is not important."

"It is to me." She met his gaze and held it. "I'd prefer not to have
your bad opinion."

He looked at her steadily.

"As to your character I have no opinion. But as to your candor I
continue to have doubts. I should add that I've expressed these
doubts to my superiors." He shrugged. "They seem not to carry much
weight. Less than the fact that your uncle is a candidate—as I understand it, the *leading* candidate—in the U.S. presidential race."

He paused and again bowed slightly. "No doubt we will speak again.
. . . Now, if you'll forgive me, I, too, have someone to meet."

* * *

"WHAT WAS ALL THAT? . . . That guy was State Militia, wasn't he? A cop." Nick eyed Cass with quizzical amusement. "My daughter, the scholar from Georgetown . . . in Dutch with the police?"

"But Cass, my *God* . . ." Tatyana's reaction, predictably, was stronger. "Restrictions on your movements have been lifted? . . . What restrictions? Who is this person from the State Militia? . . . Why didn't you tell me about him? I have friends in Ministry of Justice. They could help you, maybe."

"Tatyana, relax." Cass laughed. "You heard him say the restrictions have been lifted. I contacted someone in our embassy here, who must have friends in the ministry himself." She turned to her father. "It's someone who claims to know you, actually—a colleague, I think, from your previous incarnation. His name's Arthur Quine. He said he knew you in Brussels."

Silence.

His expression, she saw, was neutral, even wary. But whether at her mention of Quine or Brussels was unclear. Probably both, she thought. If his memories of his former occupation were unlikely to be uniformly pleasant, his memories of Brussels would have to be worse. Brussels had witnessed the end of his CIA career, the loss of his friendship with Hal.

Brussels was where her mother had killed herself.

"Arthur Quine," he said. "Yes, I know Arthur Quine. How did you happen to contact *him?*"

"Actually, I didn't. I contacted someone at the embassy. It was he who insisted on my meeting Quine."

Interesting, she thought, that her father's curiosity should focus on Quine rather than on why she had contacted him, what kind of trouble she had gotten herself into. Arthur Quine was clearly a spook, and equally clearly no friend of her father, who had been a spook himself. And once a spook, always a spook. *You could ask your father.* The Agency had always been much more than a profession; it was more a religion, like being a Catholic. You could do your best to forget the church, but the church would not forget you. Ever.

"But Cass, what did you speak to these people *about?*" Tatyana's frustration had caused her to lapse into Russian. "Why does that policeman consider you unhelpful?"

"He seems to think I know more than I'm telling." For her father's benefit, Cass gave her answer in English. She'd been planning to leave this for later, but it might as well be now. "You see, I happened to discover a murder."

Chapter Eight

"CASS," NICK SAID, "it's late. I've been up a long time. Suppose you tell me what this is all about."

Cass looked around. Perhaps this *could* have waited. There was only a handful of diners left, and their waiter had greeted their arrival, received their order for two beers, no food, with ill-concealed resentment. It was almost midnight. Tatyana had long since gone home to bed. But Cass, having checked Nick into his hotel and in spite of his reasonable protest that it was late and cold and they could just as well drink in his room, had insisted on going out for a nightcap. They could drink in his room, but not talk. Not properly. Not about what she had in mind. She wasn't sure what went on now, but in Cold War days, rumor had it, every hotel room in Moscow had been bugged.

"It has to do with what we talked about at dinner, the murder I told you I'd discovered."

He considered this. It occurred to him perhaps to demand why this required a fifteen-minute cab ride. Instead he took a swallow of his beer.

"What about it?"

She hesitated. Now that they were down to it, she felt a strange reluctance, a temptation to just pass on by, pretend that nothing had happened. But it *had* happened. A tape had been stolen. A man had been murdered. And the things that man had told her couldn't be ignored or forgotten. *You could ask your father. Better yet, you could ask your uncle.* She had to ask. Not in spite of, but precisely because of, her instinct that in this case the past was much better left unexplored, that in digging it up she'd be disturbing a grave, raising ghosts that were better let lie.

"There's more to the story than I let on, stuff I didn't want to share with Tatyana."

He received this without visible reaction.

"You want to tell me about it?"

She nodded. "But first I want to ask you a question."

"Then ask. If I can, I'll answer."

Hit him with it straight off was best. Catch him off guard. Don't give him time to think. Not that lying was really his style. Evasion was, however.

"Oracle." She hit him with it. "What can you tell me, Nick, about a KGB agent code-named Oracle?"

Silence.

She *had* caught him off guard. At her mention of the name a shadow, surprise or dismay, had flicked across his features. Now they'd turned into a mask.

"Oracle? . . . How did you happen to hear about Oracle?"

"I heard it on that tape," she said, "the one Dolokhov tried to sell me. When I asked who it was, he referred me to you. 'You could ask your father,' he said. So I'm asking: Who was he, Nick? Why should I ask *you* about him?"

More silence.

"Then you did get to listen to this tape?"

She nodded. "The day after I met him at the party. I called and he set up a meeting. A contact, he called it. Very spooky."

* * *

BUT NOT SCARY. It had not yet been scary. What it mostly had been was irritating. On the phone he'd insisted on 4:00 P.M. sharp, but at twenty past she was still waiting, perched on a couch in the lobby of the Hotel Tsentralnaya—all threadbare velvet and imitation French Empire—pretending to read a copy of *Newsweek* and wondering if she looked as conspicuous and flustered as she felt. She'd not been the only woman waiting in that lobby: There were others, two others, whose miniskirts, six-inch heels, and bras designed to emphasize their cleavage had left little doubt what *they* were waiting for. It was plain that they saw her as unfair competition. She had almost decided to beat a retreat when a bellhop appeared and handed her a note. "Take the elevator to the fourth floor," it instructed. "Wait there three minutes. If you're sure no one's watching, take the stairs to the basement, leave through the service entrance. If at any time you think you're being followed, leave by the front entrance and go home."

Melodrama, she'd thought. An attempt to hype the value of the tape. No one had followed her into the elevator. No one was around when she'd reached the fourth floor. No one in the whole place, indeed, had betrayed the least interest in her presence, except, of course, the women in the lobby.

The service entrance led out into an alley. There, at the wheel of a white VW, was Dolokhov. She'd given him grief at first about his elaborate precautions, the embarrassment of having to wait in a lobbyful of hookers. His apology had lacked conviction. Given the nature of their dealings, he'd explained, one couldn't be too careful. At the time she'd dismissed this as more sales talk.

Now it was clear he hadn't been careful enough.

* * *

"YOU DIDN'T TELL any of this to the police?"

"I haven't told anyone but you." Some need to justify made her add: "I didn't want to make myself a target."

Nick seemed tempted to comment, didn't. He was still, she noted, wearing his poker face.

"And this tape was made in *1990?*"

"March twelfth, to be precise." She frowned. "I seem to recall *I* was asking the questions."

He made a gesture of impatience.

"I'll tell you what I know when I *know* what I know. If that sounds Irish"—he smiled faintly—"bear with me. What was said about Oracle on the tape? What was said *exactly?* I mean. I imagine you can remember."

* * *

SHE DID. She could recall the words, just as she had heard them in Dolokhov's car. Not just because of her gift of accurate recall, which she sometimes thought was her sole intellectual distinction, but also because he had played her that part twice. He'd stopped the tape, rewound it, played it over. To make sure she hadn't missed it, presumably. And unnecessarily, since even an idiot, nodding off, could hardly have failed to grasp its significance. She could still hear inner echoes of those voices: Gorbachev's patient, deliberate, schoolmasterly; Kryuchkov's quicker, high-pitched, abrasive. The exchange had come halfway through the meeting. Ustinov, the defense minister, proposing an immediate invasion, had asked Kryuchkov to predict the U.S. response.

> KRYUCHKOV: The American response is easily predicted. . . . They will yell murder but sit on their hands.
> GORBACHEV: This prediction of yours, esteemed Yevgenyi Petrovich, is it speculation, or based on something?
> KRYUCHKOV: It is based on something, respected Mikhail Sergeievich. Specifically on information obtained from a highly reliable source.
> GORBACHEV: Are we speaking of an *authoritative* source, or just the usual State Department flunky?
> KRYUCHKOV: Completely authoritative, Mikhail Sergeievich. A source with access at the very highest level.
> GORBACHEV: At the very highest level? . . . You mean Oracle? [Here there was a protracted pause.]
> KRYUCHKOV: Respected Mikhail Sergeievich, I must once again implore you not to specify sources. Not even by their code names, and not even in these confidential surroundings.

When she'd finished, Nick said nothing. He sat there, blank-faced, staring off into space, as if what he'd heard had turned him to stone. . . . Dolokhov had been right about one thing, she thought.

Nick knew.

"Well?" she demanded.

"That was all?"

"That was all—the only time Oracle was mentioned. But the meaning is obvious, don't you think? . . . 'A source with access *at the very highest level.*' It would have to be someone in the cabinet, wouldn't it? Someone, at least, with the ear of the president. In 1990, that tape is suggesting, the KGB had a source in the White House."

She paused, awaiting a reaction. It seemed he had nothing to say.

"Dolokhov said *you* would know who he was."

He ignored the prompt. "That bothered you?"

"Puzzled more than bothered." This wasn't true. It had bothered her considerably at the time; it bothered her now even more. "I know you used to be some CIA muck-a-muck, but not in 1990. I recall you were in London then, correspondent for the *Post*. . . . I noticed I'm still answering your questions, however. Isn't it time you answered mine? Do you know who Oracle was?"

He gazed at her a moment, sighed.

"I used to think so."

"And now you're not *sure?*" She didn't try to hide her disbelief. "Okay, then, who did you think he was?"

He hesitated.

"Technically that's classified information, Cass. Why is it so important that you know?"

"It's a little late to start acting dumb." She was getting tired of these evasions. "My interest isn't academic. Dolokhov was killed for this tape. A day after offering it to *me*. I want to know why he offered it to me. I want to know why someone killed him. If he can get killed, then so can I." She paused, anger welling up in her now. "If you want to talk important, let's talk about *that*. . . . Which is more important to you, Nick, your daughter's life or some fucking Agency secret?"

She saw he had that look on his face. The one he'd always worn when her mother made a scene. It signaled an emotional withdrawal, shutters coming down behind the eyes.

"No need to comment," she added. "I know the answer already."

"At least," he said evenly, "you *think* you do."

"Think . . . know. Whatever. Let's skip it and move on. Who did you think Oracle was?"

"Okay." He shrugged. "I used to think he was a man named Marcus Werner. He was fairly senior in the State Department. When your uncle was special envoy to SALT, Werner was a member of his staff."

She stared.

"When Hal was special envoy? . . . That was '84 or '85. We're talking 1990. At which time, so far as I recall, there was no Marcus Werner in the U.S. cabinet."

"Correct," Nick nodded. "There wasn't."

"He couldn't have been some high-level staffer?"

Nick shook his head. "In 1990 he was nowhere near the cabinet. Nowhere near Washington, even. He was in Sacramento, pumping gas."

"Pumping gas?"

"I guess he couldn't get a better job. He'd been fired from the

Foreign Service, on suspicion of selling secrets to the Russians. An inquiry revoked his security clearance. He was fired without pension rights, benefits, anything."

"On *suspicion* of selling secrets? You mean he was never convicted?"

"He wasn't even tried." Nick shrugged. "Most of the spies we catch never are. You know how it is when you bring an indictment . . . CIA secrets all over the front page. Lawyers fishing in Agency files. Shitloads of negative publicity. Convictions always cost us more than they were worth." He paused. "Werner could have sued *us* for wrongful dismissal, but he didn't. He swore he was innocent, but he never sued us. That was the clincher for me—that and the fact that the leaks dried up. I was satisfied I'd nailed the right man."

Again Cass stared. "*You* nailed him? Personally?"

"You could call it my swan song." Nick's smile was sour. "In late '84, at your uncle's request, I found myself on TDY to the SALT team in Brussels. Military secrets had been leaking to the Russians, evidently from someone on the team. My job was to identify and nail him. . . ."

Nick paused again. He was sounding tired.

"At the time it seemed open and shut. The evidence—most of it—pointed to Werner. We had pictures of him talking to a KGB officer. He had money in the bank he couldn't account for. That kind of thing. When confronted, of course, he claimed the KGB had framed him. To divert our suspicions from the culprit." Nick paused. "I'm afraid I didn't find that persuasive. Nor, I might add, did the inquiry."

"But now you think he may have been telling the truth."

"It crosses my mind." Nick's voice was dry. "If Oracle was active in 1990 it would seem to entail that he *couldn't* have been Werner."

"Only if there was just the one Oracle," she objected. "Could the Russians have had two sources with that code name, one in Brussels in 1984, another in Washington six years later?"

"Reusing code names invites confusion. So far as I know, the Russians never did." Nick shook his head. He looked bleak, she thought, stoic. "If your tape is real, I nailed the wrong man."

"*If* it's real? . . . Why wouldn't it be real?"

He shrugged, didn't answer.

"Why?" she insisted. "What motive could there be for faking that tape? To mislead visiting American historians?"

"Them among others." His voice was like chalk. "I'll say this: I hope it's not real."

"Because if it is, you nailed the wrong man?"

He shook his head. "Because I *didn't* nail the right one."

She frowned. "I'm not sure I share your priorities. I'd worry more about convicting the innocent."

She noticed he was looking at her oddly.

"Oh," she said. "That wasn't what you meant. You meant that if Werner wasn't your man, you know who was?"

He nodded, seemed about to speak, then stopped and shot her a warning glance. Their waiter was hovering with the check. All the other customers had left. Nick paid in rubles, adding five dollars as a tip. Shrugging, the waiter went back to his station.

"We should leave," Nick said. "Let the poor guy get his sleep."

"You haven't answered my question."

"Who was my man, if Werner wasn't?"

She nodded.

"I'm surprised you haven't figured it out. By elimination, if nothing else. Who do you know was in Brussels in 1984 and the U.S. cabinet in 1990?"

She felt as if she'd been sandbagged.

There was only man she knew who had been in Brussels in 1984 and the U.S. cabinet in 1990.

Her uncle, Hal Reynolds.

Candidate for president of the United States of America.

* * *

LATER SHE COULD CONSIDER THINGS more calmly. Logic was a method, not a guarantee. The art, as some wise man once said, of going wrong with confidence. At the time, however, she'd been shaken, therefore angry.

"I don't believe I'm hearing this. I don't see how you can calmly sit there and tell me my uncle was a spy."

"I'm not telling you that." He met her gaze steadily. "I told you, since you asked, what I knew about Oracle. The inference is purely conditional."

"So *hypothetically* my uncle is a spy?"

"Either that"—he'd nodded—"or your tape is a fake."

72

"And you see these alternatives as equally possible?"

"I didn't say that. I said they were alternatives."

"Then you don't believe Hal Reynolds was a traitor?"

He looked unhappy. "I for damn sure don't want to believe it."

"I wish I could believe that," she retorted. "I'd find it easier if I didn't know you were enemies."

"That's horseshit, Cass." He said it calmly. "I was best friends with Hal for half my life. Still would be, had it been left up to me."

"Then you ought to know what to believe," she flung back. "You knew him so well for so long. You guys were in school, in college, together. Don't you just know he couldn't be a spy?"

She waited. Apparently he didn't.

"Have you forgotten *everything* about him? While you were pushing paper in Langley or somewhere, he volunteered, twice, for Vietnam. He was wounded three times, got captured and escaped. He was a war hero, for Christ's sake. He won the Congressional Medal of Honor. In the Senate and as national security adviser he was always a foreign policy hard-liner. He supported Star Wars, boosting the military budget. . . . Does that strike you as the profile of a typical KGB agent? Or are you going to tell me that his whole career was cover?"

He shook his head. "I'm not going to tell you anything. As I said before, I don't know."

"But *why?*" she insisted. "Why don't you know? If the tape suggests Hal spied for the Russians, then the tape is bullshit. I don't know who would fake it or why. I just know someone did." She paused. "Can you give me a single reason, apart from the tape, for thinking Hal is a traitor?"

For a moment Nick said nothing. Finally he nodded.

"I'm sorry, Cass, but I can."

Chapter Nine

"Okay," Cass said. "Let's hear why Hal is a traitor."

Nick sighed. He had not looked forward to renewing this discussion. He'd had little sleep, and that had been restless, troubled by memories of Brussels. This dredging up the past had not been what he'd had in mind when he'd wangled this assignment to Moscow. His recent relations with his daughter seemed to have been governed by the very worst of luck. Or rather, since honesty compelled him to admit his share of the blame for the way things stood between them, there seemed to be sins for which heaven, or fate, would accept no reparation. He didn't believe in heaven—or fate—so perhaps he shouldn't have believed in sin. He did believe in it, however, and this morning he found himself tempted to believe, if not in a deity bent on revenge, at least in some agency other than chance in whose arrangement of recent events a sense of irony had played a major part.

If not, how come his attempt to reconcile with Cass had met with an immediate reverse? And why should the issue that threatened to divide them still further originate precisely in the period of his life he had zero inclination to revisit?

Was it sin coming home to roost?

He wished now they'd been able to finish this last night. But they'd both been tired, the restaurant had thrown them out, and there'd been nowhere else for them to go. Nowhere comfortable, private, and willing to stay open to all hours. The alternative, tramping the freezing streets till dawn, had not recommended itself. But leaving the business unfinished was like sleeping on a quarrel. (Not *like*, he thought; it *was* sleeping on a quarrel.) It had given her anger time to grow cold, her attitudes to harden. She'd greeted him, just now, like the enemy.

"I don't," he began, "have much enthusiasm for this."

"I would hope not."

"I'm not arguing a case, you understand. I meant it when I said I didn't know. I'll set out the facts as objectively as I can. You can make up your own mind about them."

"As objectively as you can?" She eyed him coldly. "I don't imagine you'll have any problem. Objectivity was always your strong suit."

"I hope you'll still think so when you've heard what I have to say." He paused. "To understand, you need the background—how we heard about Oracle, how suspicion came to focus on Werner."

He paused again, assailed by a sudden reluctance. What was to be gained from looking once more under this flat stone? For him, he thought, there was nothing.

"This started in May of 1984. I was in charge of debriefing a KGB defector. His name was Krasov. Viktor Krasov."

* * *

DEBRIEFING WAS WHAT THEY CALLED IT, the awkward business of looking a gift horse in the mouth. A misleading word, he'd always thought, for a process more like trial by exhaustion. In Krasov's case it had taken three months . . . *three months* of eight hours a day, six days a week, sometimes seven. Requiring the services of fifteen officers: relays of debriefers to ask the questions, researchers to think them up, analysts to scrutinize the answers. If you'd joined together the reels of magnetic tape on which those questions and answers were recorded, the result would have stretched, some humorist claimed to have figured, from Moscow to Langley and back. They had taken the better part of a month to convince themselves that Krasov was what he claimed: a Line S KGB officer attached to the residency in Vienna, with previous postings in Bonn and Geneva, who had managed to Minox a bunch of files and, slipping his leash one afternoon, had shown up on the doorstep of the U.S. embassy, asking for the duty officer.

Debriefing was what they called it. It was, Nick thought, about the most slippery enterprise, intellectually and morally, he'd ever taken part in, an queasy mix of research, detective work, and poker. The purpose was to pick apart a story. You placed your subject in isolation, deprived him of normal human contact, then you drove him almost to

75

the brink of insanity by bombarding him with literally thousands of questions—questions designed to test the statements he made against the statements he'd *previously* made and facts you had in your possession. And you understood, even as you labored to pick it apart, that if the story he was telling was fiction, its authors had labored to anticipate your questions, had built it to withstand these questions, had spent more time building it, probably, than you would trying to explode it, had already subjected your defector to a full-dress rehearsal of this very process, the details accurate down to the last fly button on the army fatigues you would give him to wear, to the Solzhenitsyn novels and copies of *Playboy* you would place on the bedside table of the windowless cell you would house him in. You understood, too, that stories can never be proved, just exploded, that however long the process dragged on, doubt could never entirely be extinguished, that in the last analysis what you'd be left with were questions and still more questions. . . .

"*What did cigarettes cost when you were in Bonn?*"

"*What is the principal German-language newspaper in Geneva?*"

"*Who was the resident when you were there?*"

"*His given name and patronymic?*"

"*Approximate height and weight?*"

"*The color of his secretary's hair?*"

"*What was the weather like that summer?*"

Like poker, it became in the end a matter of statistics and psychology. Not so much a matter of wrong answers—there were normally not many of those—as of not enough or too many "don't knows" and "don't remembers," not enough or too much consistency. Above all it was a matter of patience. You asked a question, got an answer, asked the same question three weeks or six weeks later, checked to see if the answer was the same. And you kept this up, week upon week, until somebody's patience—you hoped it was his—was exhausted.

When Krasov convinced them he was who he said, they'd turned their attention to the files. In particular to those—there'd been half a dozen—in which a KGB agent was mentioned. This KGB agent, the files suggested, was a member of the U.S. SALT team and was supplying the Soviets with military secrets.

The agent's code name was Oracle.

76

These files were what the whole thing was about. As Krasov candidly admitted, these files were his passport to the promised land—a new identity (agency-devised) and a new future (agency-funded). The question was whether the passport was phony. These pieces of paper Krasov had Minoxed, furtively over several months and, he claimed, at risk to his life, were they real or were they not? In the two months they'd spent circling this question, his debriefers kept returning to a single crucial point: Why *these*? Why had Krasov selected, from all the files he might have Minoxed, the ones he actually had? To which Krasov's answer was consistent and disarming: Since the files *were* his passport, he'd naturally chosen those most likely to be of interest.

The Oracle files *were* of interest, weren't they?

This, which left matters no farther forward, was where Hal Reynolds had come in.

As soon as he learned of the Oracle files, Nick had alerted Reynolds, in an "Eyes Only" telex, to the possible presence of a spy on his staff. Though Krasov's story could be a fabrication, mission security should be tightened and anything suspicious reported. For six weeks, apart from an acknowledgment, he'd heard nothing. In mid-June, however, just as the debriefing appeared to be at a standstill, opinion as to the subject's credibility being about equally divided, Reynolds had flown in from Brussels and asked Nick to meet him for lunch.

The invitation was nothing unusual. Nick and Reynolds had known each other for years. Contemporaries at Exeter, they'd become, when they moved on to Yale, bosom buddies. Reynolds had rowed bow and Nick six in the boat that beat Harvard their junior year and had gone on to win the Grand Challenge at Henley. When Nick went to Oxford on a Rhodes scholarship, Reynolds had opted for a year at the Sorbonne and had spent more time in England than in France. No one had been much surprised that the women they married were sisters, daughters of a New England manufacturer of fine-quality paper. Their friendship subsequently had not been shaken either by a divergence in careers (Nick into relative obscurity in the CIA, Reynolds into the circus of national politics) or by Nick's divorce, after twelve years of stormy marriage, from his wife, Patsy. When Reynolds flew in from Brussels, Nick was usually the first person he looked up. What was different this time had emerged only after they'd had lunch. Reynolds insisted, in spite of the heat and humidity, on taking a postprandial stroll. In the course of it he'd revealed to Nick that not only did he now believe Oracle was real, but also that he knew who he was.

* * *

"IT HAD TO DO WITH SALT," Nick said. "The way the negotiations were going. We were playing a kind of poker with the Russians. Some hands you won, some you lost. . . . Hal got to feeling the Russians were winning too often. From a little before Krasov defected, Hal said he'd had the uneasy feeling that every time they came to the table they knew exactly what cards he was holding."

"You could have pushed him into that," Cass said. "Maybe your telex colored his perceptions. Maybe he thought he detected a pattern only because you'd prompted him to look." She paused, considering. "I don't quite see where you're going with this. . . . If Hal confirmed your suspicions about Oracle, that's surely evidence *exonerating* him."

"Of course." Nick nodded. "But he didn't just confirm our suspicions, he also directed them at Werner. And his purpose could well have been preemptive. After Krasov's defection someone was bound to be suspected. Hal could have been trying to make sure it wasn't him. That, at least, was Werner's story. Guilt, he said, is quick to point the finger."

"Which is flimsy reasoning, if I ever heard it, and applies about equally to Werner himself."

"It does," Nick agreed. "Though Hal pointed first."

"But presumably with reason," Cass objected. "He can't just have picked Werner at random."

Nick nodded. "He had reasons. Actually, two. Sometime after my telex, Hal said, he went to talk to his deputy chief of mission. He found Werner, alone, in the deputy's office. On the desk were some Pentagon reports for which Werner didn't have clearance. Hal said he couldn't be absolutely sure, but he thought that as he entered he saw Werner put something down. When Hal asked him what he was doing there, he said waiting for the deputy, who was taking a leak." Nick paused. "Technically this was a security breach and mostly on the deputy's part. What Hal should have done was reprimand both and note the fact in their personnel files. But by now, he said, he was pretty much convinced someone in the mission was a spy; if Werner was that someone, zapping him would put him on his guard. This made sense, but perhaps it was unfortunate Hal *didn't* play this one by the book, or at least report the incident to me. Instead he decided to set a trap."

"Unfortunate?" Cass queried. "Unfortunate why?"

"That way we would have had proof that the incident actually happened. As it was, the deputy didn't remember. Werner, of course, simply denied it. He claimed Hal had made the whole thing up. It came down to a question of word against word. The same was true of Hal's other piece of evidence, his trap."

"It was word against word?" Cass frowned. "I don't see any problem there. I don't think I would have had much trouble deciding whose word to take."

"I didn't," Nick said. "Neither then nor at Werner's inquiry. I believed the man I'd known for twenty years. But this, the fact of my friendship with Hal, became the cornerstone of Werner's defense. He was able to point out that suspicion of him rested, initially, on Hal's unsupported word. He was facing an inquiry, he claimed, because I had known Hal twenty years."

"What was he suggesting? Prejudice or collusion?"

"Either or both." Nick shrugged. "Prejudice more than collusion probably. Werner claimed that, because of our friendship, I excluded Hal from the list of suspects and swallowed—hook, line, and sinker—all the 'evidence' provided by him."

"But there must have been more," Cass objected. "You surely didn't investigate Werner just because of that one incident."

"We didn't." Nick paused, considered. "It's hard to tell this without running ahead. Everything connected. Everything was open to interpretation, usually conflicting interpretation. . . . Was Krasov a defector or a KGB plant? Was Werner a traitor or an innocent framed to deflect suspicion from Hal? Was Hal a distinguished public servant, a hard-nosed negotiator bent on outsmarting the Russians? Or was he a traitor, using his position to sell out his country and conspiring with his masters to cast suspicion on a hapless subordinate, Werner?" He paused again. "The spy business was always like that, of course. But in this case, because of my friendship with Hal, it seemed worse. I ended up distrusting everyone, including myself. As for the truth"—he shrugged—"by the time I'd heard all the conflicting accounts, even the concept seemed provisional."

"History's that way." Cass shrugged. "Journalism, too, I imagine. We can never draw final conclusions, but surely we have to draw *some*. Provisional truth is better than none. You can't just leave things in a fog of 'perhaps' and 'don't know.' Sometimes you have to trust your instincts."

"Easy to say when it's not your call. But what about the consequences, Cass? . . . Historians, if they change their mind, can always write another book. Since we held that inquiry, on the other hand, Werner has been pumping gas. If I screwed up, it cost him his career. What reparation can I make? I can't give him back the twelve years."

He seemed genuinely troubled. Clearly he wanted not to have been wrong, and this only gave his doubts more weight. For the first time Cass felt a stab of misgiving. Nick, God knew, had faults in battalions, but dishonesty had never been among them.

"Tell me," she said, "about the trap."

* * *

THE TRAP, Nick thought, had been the beginning. The onset of doubt. Or paranoia. Either way, the first hairline crack in the trust that existed between him and Hal. Hal had set a trap, sure enough, but what kind of a trap and for whom?

The trap for Werner had been something right out of James Bond. Nick could recall still the scene where Hal told him about it. They'd been sitting on the steps of the Lincoln Memorial looking over the ornamental lake toward the Washington Monument. Middle-aged men in business suits, ties loosened, jackets slung over their shoulders. Hal, as he embarked on the story, had given him the classic Reynolds grin. Self-deprecating, almost goofy, it reminded Nick why he'd liked Hal so much. Because Hal, in the course of a twenty-year friendship, hadn't really changed very much; beneath the air of *gravitas* he put on for public life, he was still the irreverent fifteen-year-old who, arriving first in the dorm room they were slated to share, had greeted Nick with a smart-ass remark: "I felt sure, since I hear you're such a jock, that you wouldn't mind sleeping in the draft."

* * *

"THIS MAY SEEM SOPHOMORIC," Hal says, "but I thought that if Werner made a habit of snooping in offices, I should give him a chance to snoop in mine."

"Don't tell me . . ." Nick rolls his eyes. "You invited him up on some pretext or other, then pretended you needed to pee. You left him in your office with classified documents arranged in a pattern on your desk, and when you came back they'd been moved."

"Not very original or clever, I admit." Hal gives him the grin again. "I'm sure you guys would have managed something *far* more sophisticated. The point is, it worked. I was gone for maybe five minutes. When I came back Werner was where I had left him, but the documents weren't, not exactly."

Nick thinks about this. "You didn't tell anyone? Before you did it, I mean."

"Didn't tell a soul. Not before, not after." Hal pauses. "As per your sage advice, you'll remember. It was you who warned me—wasn't it?—to keep my mouth shut about this. Which made perfect sense and still does, since until we've identified our spy, everyone, technically, is suspect." A thought seems to strike him, for he pauses again, adds casually, "Which group must include me, I suppose."

"Which group does *not*." Nick shakes his head. "I wish you'd alerted me, though, when that first Werner incident happened. That way, when you set your trap, we could have had corroboration."

Hal stares. "Corroboration?"

Nick shrugs. "Well, he's going to deny it, isn't he? He's going to say you're lying or mistaken. Another witness would have taken this thing from the sphere of your word against his."

Silence.

"I had hoped"—Hal's tone is, perhaps, theatrically starchy—"that my word carried weight with my friends."

"Hal, don't be silly," Nick tells him. "Your word is golden with me, always has been. It's just that when we confront him, two words are better than one."

"Who's talking about confronting?" Hal stares. "That strikes me as distinctly premature. I mean, granted he was nosing through my desk, but that doesn't prove he was spying for the Russians. What it does, I think, is give cause for alarm. That's why I'm here, why I'm talking to you first. I'm going to insist on an inquiry, Nick—round-the-clock surveillance and complete background checks: politics, finances, sex life, the works." Hal pauses. "I'm going to ask for you to be in charge."

"Me?" It's Nick's turn to stare. "Why me?"

"Because I can trust you." Hal says. "Because I know I can rely on your discretion. Because I know you'll do this fairly and cleanly, without letting things get out of hand. You won't go chasing down every wild hare."

"Wild hares?" Later the remark will come back to haunt Nick. "Are there likely to be many of those?"

Hal shrugs. "About the number you'd expect, I'd imagine. Diplomats are people. They commit indiscretions. They get plastered sometimes, fuck the wrong wives. What I'm trying to say is, this is serious work we're doing. I'd like to keep distractions to a minimum. I want this Oracle nailed and soon, but I don't want a squad of heavy-footed goons turning my office upside down and getting everyone all stirred up. And that," Hal concludes, "is why I want you."

"I see. . . ." Nick pauses, struck by a thought. "Speaking of getting people all stirred up, I wonder how this will sit with my ex-wife? I gather she's staying with you."

"She's there for Josie." A cloud seems to cross Hal's face. "There's a ton of entertaining connected to this job, and Josie can't do it anymore. Patsy's pinch-hitting, acting as hostess. . . . We've persuaded her to stop hating you. Or at least"—he grins—"to stop hating you as much. Anyway, she won't know I asked for you. You'll be there under some kind of cover. Routine security inspection or some such bullshit. You won't have to see her a whole lot. If she doesn't like it, she can do the other thing."

He pauses, suddenly serious again.

"They'd assign you if I requested you, I think, but not if you don't want the job. So I'm asking you, Nick, do this for me. I'd consider it an act of friendship."

* * *

AN ACT OF FRIENDSHIP . . . In retrospect the phrase seemed to drip with irony. The act had ended the friendship. Had there been less friendship, Nick thought, he might have been more alert, might have picked up the discordant notes, those tiny alarm bells with which, in echo, that whole conversation seemed to ring: *Diplomats are people.*

They commit indiscretions. They get plastered sometimes, fuck the wrong wives. . . . I'd like to keep distractions to a minimum. . . . It wasn't so much that he hadn't noted the subtext, but rather that he hadn't focused enough on the question of who that subtext might refer to.

At the time, of course, he hadn't met Natasha.

Chapter Ten

"So," Cass said, "you went to Brussels."

A whited sepulcher—that, she recalled, was what Conrad had called it, the city where his narrator, Marlow, had gone to be briefed for his trip to the heart of darkness. Her own view was perhaps less harsh—that the place had attracted such abnormal concentrations of diplomats and government officials didn't make it, necessarily, a sinkhole of corruption—but she thought she knew how Marlow felt. Twelve years later she still couldn't hear it mentioned without a sinking of the heart. For her it would always be a place of loss. One of the very low points of her life.

"I went to Brussels." Nick nodded. "In Washington around that time Hal was very much the blue-eyed boy. What Hal wanted, Hal tended to get. Once he'd gotten my agreement, everyone else fell into line. Within a week I was ensconced, officially making an inspection of the CIA station, unofficially heading up what came to be known as the 'Oracle Inquiry.' Only it really wasn't that. It was actually the 'Werner Inquiry.' No other candidate was seriously considered."

"What are you trying to say?" Cass stared. "Hal biased the investigation? Lied about Werner in order to focus your attention on him?"

"I'm not saying that"—Nick shook his head—"though Werner certainly did. I'm pointing out that what Hal told me, whether or not it was true, did make us center our attention on Werner."

"Whether or not it was true? Had you reason to believe it wasn't? Had you ever, in fact, known Hal to lie?"

"Not at that point."

"At that point. . . . You mean you did later?"

"Yes," Nick said. "I regret to say I did."

"Knew him to lie?" Her tone was incredulous. "About what?"

"Well, for one thing about knowing Natasha. Or about not knowing her. But, of course, you don't know who Natasha was." Nick paused. "I'm getting ahead of myself again. I need to stick to the time line here. Otherwise it's going to get confusing."

"It's confusing already." Cass frowned. "You said 'was' . . . I didn't know who Natasha *was*. Does that mean she's dead?"

He nodded.

"How did she die?"

"Apparently . . ." Nick hesitated. He hadn't expected to get here so quickly. "She seems to have killed herself."

"In Brussels? In 1984?"

"Yes."

"Like my mother." Cass's voice was expressionless. "*Two* women connected with you killed themselves while you were there?"

"Nice of you not to remark on the coincidence." Nick's voice was dry. He paused, added gently, "I could bite my tongue for mentioning her now. I should have known it would remind you."

Cass shrugged. "Presumably you'd have had to, sooner or later."

"True." He nodded. "But sufficient to the day is the evil thereof. . . . Natasha will enter the story soon enough. In the meantime I can tell you this: Natasha wasn't connected with me, and her death had nothing to do with your mother's."

* * *

SHE'D OPPOSED THE IDEA of Brussels from the start, Cass remembered. From the moment, on that August afternoon when her mother and Josie, in a two-pronged attack that must have been prearranged, ambushed her in the summer house on Martha's Vineyard, she'd resisted. She'd objected, first, to Patsy's even going; then, when it was obvious *that* battle was lost, to the further plan of leaving her behind and, in the interests of her education—she did want to get into Yale, didn't she?—enrolling her in boarding school in Concord. . . . There had to be schools in Brussels, she'd argued. A city with so many resident expatriates probably had an American school. Besides, European education was better; it would give her a chance to perfect her French. And at least if it meant her going to boarding school, she didn't give a damn about Yale.

"But there wouldn't be anything for you to do." By that point Patsy's patience had been fraying. "It'll just be boring social events, receptions, and dinner parties. And as I've said, I'll have work to do. I won't have time to give you the proper attention. It's not as if you won't ever see us. You'll be spending much of the vacations in Brussels." She'd paused, added darkly, "Most of them, if I know your father."

"Oh, I *see. . . .*" Cass had affected enlightenment. Patsy, it seemed, would never learn. As a parent, she aspired to personify sweet reason, but in arguments she was easy to trip up and usually ended by losing her temper. "In the term time, when I'm mostly at school, I won't have anything to do with my time and you won't be able to give me the proper attention, but in the vacation, when I'm home all day long . . . no problem."

"God, grant me strength." Patsy had rolled her eyes. Sensing, no doubt, the weakness of her present position, she attempted a retreat to defensible ground. "Look, darling, try to understand . . . I've got to do this. It's important to Hal, don't you see? He needs me."

Important to Hal?

"I thought it was Josie who needed you, not Hal."

At this the two women had exchanged glances. Not the kind of glances, Cass noted, that seemed to be in any way revealing. Not glances of alarm or warning. Just a brief interlocking of eyes.

"Hal . . . Josie." Her mother shrugged. "What's the difference? Hal needs someone to help him entertain. Josie can't do it any longer. I can. It's as simple as that."

As simple as that. . . . But it wasn't, Cass had thought. The thing about sweet reason was it had to make sense. There was something here that didn't. Was there something they weren't telling her?

"It's for the family," Patsy pursued. "Sometimes you have to put others first. It won't be bad and it won't be forever." She paused. "We need you to be a team player."

"A team player," Cass echoed bitterly. "Help the team by *staying home?* In other words, I'd be in the way. . . . Thanks a lot for the compliment, Mother. It makes me feel all warm inside."

"I didn't mean that—"

"What else did you mean? What else could you have meant?"

"Look, darling . . ." Patsy had started to wheedle, then in one of the sudden mood swings she'd been subject to of late, she got angry. "Christ, Cassandra, I don't have patience for this. I'd hoped you might have the maturity to understand, but if you don't, you'll just have to accept . . . I'm going to Brussels to help Josie and Hal. You're going to boarding school in Concord."

As she'd stormed out, she'd turned to Josie. "See if you can make her see sense. I'm not in the mood for teenage temperament."

"*Teenage* temperament?" Cass had been stunned. "See if you can make *me* see sense?" She'd turned in appeal to Josie, tears starting in her eyes. "What the hell is there to understand? Why can't she have the honesty to admit she just doesn't want me?"

"It isn't that, darling." Beckoning Cass over to the sofa, Josie had put an arm around her, rested Cass's head on her shoulder. "Really it isn't."

But it was. That was exactly what it was. Cass wasn't so much hurt at the thought as indignant; she didn't feel unloved but rather excluded. If they didn't want her, there had to be a reason. Why wouldn't they tell her what it was?

"If it isn't that, what is it, then? Why did she flare up like that? I'm entitled to a viewpoint, aren't I?"

"Of course you are," Josie comforted. "But you have to make allowances. I think the divorce hurt her more than she's admitted. She still hasn't really gotten her life back together."

"And *I* get in the way of that?"

"Of course not. But I think"—Josie hesitated—"I do think a change of scene would do her good. A new life, new people, work she can lose herself in. She wasn't exaggerating about that, you know. She'll have her hands more than full organizing Hal's social life."

Organizing Hal's social life—it didn't sound like such a monumental task. What was involved in it, after all? Making sure the help toed the line, issuing instructions to the cook. Patsy could do that without getting out of bed. She'd been doing it most of her life.

"Okay. Then, when she's got her hands full, you and I can look after each other." The idea had struck Cass as logical, brilliant. "Mother takes your role; you take hers."

Silence.

It had seemed for just a moment as if Josie were considering it. She was considering something, at least, for her face clouded momentarily

87

in thought. Then she'd shaken her head. "I'm sorry, darling. It's not going to work. Your mother has made up her mind about this, you're not going to budge her." She'd paused then. Removing Cass's head from her shoulder, she'd fixed her with huge, sympathetic eyes. "Patsy needs this, you know, and I need it, too. I want you to trust us about this, Cass. It's all going to work out all right."

Trust *us?* . . . She trusted Josie, Cass had thought. She could trust Josie for anything. Patsy, however, was less dependable. What Patsy could mostly be trusted to do was whatever she thought was in her own interests.

"You know what I wish?" She'd struggled to hold back her tears. "I wish you and Hal had been my parents."

And then, when Josie said nothing, she'd burst out: "Why did Nick have to walk out on us? Why did he have to be such a jerk?"

* * *

HER DEATH had nothing to do with your mother's. Nick had made the statement with rather more assurance than he felt. Now, watching his daughter digest it, he wondered why he had made it at all. Had it been to reassure himself? Patsy, too, had lied about Natasha. He'd always assumed she was protecting Josie, sparing her knowledge of Hal's infidelity, but he'd never been really sure. Of the many things obscure to him about Brussels, this—Patsy's death—was as obscure as any.

"Getting back to Werner," he told Cass. "The first thing I did when I got to Brussels was put him under surveillance."

"Under surveillance" . . . It was another deceptively simple phrase, reducing to fewer than half a dozen syllables a process that had taken days, and miracles of organization, to achieve. . . . Rooms to be rented in the houses, front and back, overlooking Werner's. Bugs to be placed on Werner's phones. (The office had been a piece of cake, but the other had been a bitch. Werner's housekeeper—they referred to her as the Death Watch Beetle—was a harridan in her sixties, funereal in dress and manner, who spent her time spying on the neighbors and seemed never to stir out of doors.) Belgian visas to be obtained at short notice, a ton of electronic gear to be imported through special NATO channels. Cars to be rented in relays of six. (Since license plates are easy to remember, they'd had to change vehicles every other day.) And all this before the watchers arrived. In Werner's case, the surveillance being strict, the number of watchers required was sixteen: one and a standby in each of the houses; mobile units, both employing six, alternating eight-hour shifts. (Several of the watchers had been women, which complicated the living arrangements.) The cost to the taxpayer had been staggering—close to fifty thousand dollars—and for more than a week it had been money thrown away. They'd turned up nothing of interest whatever: no unusual contacts, no mysterious phone calls, no suspicious or eccentric behavior. Werner's private life, it seemed, was a perfect bland model of diplomatic decorum.

And then, the second weekend, he had flown to Geneva.

They'd almost lost him. Of the mobile team that followed his car to the airport only two watchers, both women, had happened to be carrying passports, and only one managed to make Werner's flight. That she hadn't lost him was the purest of luck: At Geneva, close behind him in the line for taxis, she'd heard him ask for the Baur au Lac. It was luck, too, that he waited till the next day (by which time others on the team had straggled in) before contacting the man they would come to refer to as "The Stamp Collector."

Later, protesting the innocence of that transaction, Werner would produce a letter from the dealer. Postmarked Brussels and dated four days before that sudden dash to Geneva, it begged leave to introduce to "cher Marcus" a Herr Manfred Branconi of Geneva, who was interested in items from his stamp collection, notably the Madagascar misprints. It was true that Jules Le Gallet was a dealer in rare stamps and of some repute among collectors. It was also true that he had sent the letter. What other occupations "Mon cher Jules" might have had was a question later extensively researched but never satisfactorily resolved. What was resolved and quickly—the CIA station in Geneva had no problem making the ID—was that the "Manfred Branconi" with whom photographs showed Werner exchanging fat envelopes in the outdoor restaurant of a yacht club on the outskirts of Geneva was in fact one Vladimir Ivanovich Panev, officially attached to one of the U.N. agencies but actually an officer of the KGB.

* * *

"WERNER CLAIMED someone had set him up?" Cass had seen where this was headed.

"Of course." Nick nodded. "He swore black and blue that, prior to their meeting, he'd never set eyes on Branconi. He claimed that some weeks before the meeting he'd appointed Le Gallet to help him dispose of items from his stamp collection, in particular the Madagascar misprints. Le Gallet had received an inquiry for the misprints and put buyer and seller together by letter, relying on *'cher* Marcus' to pay him the appropriate commission."

"And Le Gallet confirmed this?"

"Every particular."

"How did Werner know how to contact Branconi in Geneva?"

"It told him in the letter. He was to phone Branconi between three and three-thirty on the afternoon in question."

"Did you check out Branconi's number?"

"Teaching your grandma to suck eggs?" Nick cocked an eyebrow. "The number belonged to a downtown bar."

"A bar?" Cass stared. "That didn't strike Werner as suspicious? Surely if he'd been a real collector, this Branconi—or whatever— would have given his home or office number. He wouldn't have done business in a bar."

"You'd think not," Nick agreed. "But Werner claimed not to have known where he was calling. He said he called the number he'd been given. Branconi answered, and they set up the meeting." Nick paused. "On the surface, the story had a certain plausibility. Werner did own a valuable collection of stamps. He had been selling it off, and mostly through Jules Le Gallet. What could be simpler, he demanded, than to have some KGB man pose as a collector and, by purchasing one of the items for sale, make an innocent transaction look guilty?"

"But that would have to mean that the KGB already knew Werner was under surveillance," Cass objected. "How else could they know the transaction would be photographed? But how could they have known that . . ." She broke off, the question dying on her lips as an answer suggested itself. "Oh, you mean Werner claimed Hal had told them."

"Exactly." Nick nodded. "Like everything else in the case, the stamp sale was perfectly ambiguous. Either it was cover for a contact, or Werner was framed by someone who knew we were watching.

Which someone, Werner claimed, was Hal." Nick paused. "And that, in turn, was perfectly consistent with the rest of what Werner was claiming. Hal, he pointed out, was his original accuser. Our suspicions were based on Hal's unsupported word. The surveillance, too, was Hal's suggestion, and made, Werner claimed, so the Russians could set up the stamp sale. Werner swore what he'd sold had been rare postage stamps, not secrets. If someone had sold secrets, that someone had been Hal."

Cass considered this.

"So again it came down to a question of word against word. Whose to believe, Hal's or Werner's?"

"Mostly," Nick agreed. "Though Werner's story did raise some interesting questions: Why did Le Gallet write to him, for example, when they lived only blocks apart and saw each other on a weekly basis? Werner claimed the letter was to document the fact that Le Gallet had made the introduction, in case he, Werner, tried to gyp him out of his commission. But why would Le Gallet bother to document *that* when he was willing to trust his 'very good friend' about such vital matters as price and whether a sale had actually been made? You could also wonder, if Werner was framed, how the KGB knew he was selling the stamps. Presumably from Jules Le Gallet, which would argue that *he* was in their employ, which in turn might strike you as stretching coincidence a little. But all of this was essentially speculation. What it boiled down to was word against word." He paused. "That was why the polygraph was troublesome."

"The polygraph?" Cass stared. "Hal submitted to a polygraph test?"

"Not Hal, Werner. And he didn't submit, he volunteered. Actually, he insisted. Since we obviously doubted him, he said, we owed him the chance to clear his name."

"And he came up clean?"

"As a whistle." Nick nodded. "Which wasn't conclusive. People have fooled the polygraph before. But if it didn't clear Werner's name, it certainly muddied the waters. And it did so at an awkward time. Because just when the polygraph seemed to exonerate Werner, the lovely Natasha appeared on the scene."

* * *

THE *LOVELY* NATASHA. . . . Somehow, Nick thought, when she came to mind it was always with adjective attached. And naturally so, he supposed, since the beauty was what had stayed with him. Or perhaps what had stayed was his own response to the beauty. He'd seen her just once, only briefly, so the picture he had was blurred by time. He could summon, with effort, an image of brilliant eyes, so blue they shaded into violet, of prominent Slav cheekbones, a complexion that seemed almost translucent, a child's face on the body of a woman, but this recall was essentially verbal, a catalog description of a painting long lost. What came back undimmed was the force of the sexual attraction. She'd appealed directly to the hormones, aroused in him, that night in the office, a surge of lust whose force surprised even him, in whom surges of lust were everyday happenings, familiar as tremors in a region of volcanoes. It was not that she'd worked to invite this response; she was just surrounded by an aura of sex. And the fact that she'd seemed oblivious of it—or else was one hell of an actress—only increased the effect. That he'd not been alone in his reaction was clear from the phone call he'd gotten from Reception. Reception that night had been a marine corporal, a youthful sophisticate with whom he sometimes played poker. . . . "Mr. Wolfe? There's a lady here asking for Mr. Reynolds. I told her he's gone home, but she says it's urgent. She seems upset about something. I think you ought to see her, sir." The corporal's tone had become confiding. "I think you really ought to see her."

* * *

"MY NAME," she announces, "is Natasha Oblonski."

"I'm Nicholas Wolfe." Nick hopes he isn't staring. "Is there some way I can help you?"

"I am needing to speak with Mr. Hal Reynolds. Is where he is working, is it not?"

The speech is liquid, characteristically Russian. It reveals the normal Russian confusion regarding the workings of the English present tense. The focus is completely on Reynolds, no interest to spare for late-working spy catchers or marine corporals. "Upset," furthermore, is marine understatement. "Distressed" is the word Nick would have used.

"He works here, but I'm afraid he's gone home. Technically we're closed." Nick glances at his watch. It is close to seven-thirty. "Is there any way *I* can help you?"

"No." Very sharp. Lips set in a stubborn line, then relenting. "You are very polite, Mister. . . ." Pause, while she fails to remember his name. "I am wishing also to be very polite, but no. Is Mr. Reynolds who must help me."

Must, Nick notes, though the verb's significance is unclear; it could be taken to imply obligation but might also mean that only Hal *can* help her. If the former, Nick thinks he can guess the nature of Hal's obligation. This should bother him—later it will—but for now his reaction to the Russian is all but lost in his response to the woman.

"Does he know you?"

She nods emphatically. "He knows me."

Of course he does, Nick thinks. Lucky old Hal.

"I'm afraid you'll have to try again tomorrow. We open at ten, close at five. Better call first, though, and make an appointment. Mr. Reynolds is extremely busy."

Apparently this doesn't satisfy.

"I must speak with him tonight. Is matter of great importance." She pauses, considering options. "Will you explain me, please, where Mr. Hal Reynolds is living?"

He shakes his head. "I'm not able to do that, I'm afraid."

"Then will you tell to me, please, a number for his phone?"

"I'm sorry. I can't do that either."

"Please"—the blue eyes begin to fill with tears—"is very important."

Beauty in Distress . . . Nick, aware of the corporal's disapproving gaze, not to mention a strong urge to offer consolation, hesitates. This has all the makings of a scene. Hal is here on a diplomatic mission, and Nick, though a diplomat only in name, is familiar with the profession's First Commandment. Whatever Hal's connection with this siren, the last thing he needs is a scene.

"What I could do," Nick offers, "is call him at home. Tell him you want to talk to him."

"Please . . ." Her smile is like sunshine through rain; then it clouds. Her gaze travels to the desk, where the corporal is openly gawking. "But is not convenient to speak to him here. I must speak to him in private."

"Then we'll find you an office. I'll put the call through there—if he's able to talk to you, that is."

*   *   *

But when he called Hal, he got Patsy instead.

Chapter Eleven

ABSOLUTE JUDGMENTS invariably fail. Nick remembered reading this, in a biography of Mozart, at about the time of the Werner investigation. He had noted it with wry approval. It seemed so apt to his current researches, not least in its undermining of itself. It had struck him, both then and since, that biography and his CIA work had more than a little in common. Both aspired, from the incomplete record of events, to reconstruct the truth about a life. And the judgments of both must always be provisional, since the record was always fragmentary, the truth about lives invariably hidden, even, or especially, from their owners. But absolute judgments were the prerogative of youth. (The truth of *this* had shown in Cass's face as soon as he'd mentioned her mother.) And judgments formed early, left undisturbed, tended to harden into articles of faith. An instance—it was more than an article, it was almost a whole theology—was Cass's view of her parents' marriage. She believed that Patsy, devoted to him, had been devastated by his infidelities. His own recollection was different. What had happened between him and Patsy was the standard mismatch of expectations, the usual slow erosion of commitment, the union held together mostly by inertia, and collapsing, when it did, not from one dramatic betrayal—his fling with the actress had been more like the straw that broke the camel's back—but from fifteen years' accretion of small ones.

As Hal had predicted, his presence in Brussels had not much bothered Patsy. He'd seen her as little as he decently could, and when they had met, at diplomatic functions, there had not been much awkwardness between them. She had treated him mostly with chilly indifference, the chill more palpable because the indifference was real. What had bothered her, the night Natasha had shown up, was not the fact that he had called her. What had bothered her was what he'd had to say.

* * *

"*Who* wants to speak with Hal?"

Tone chilly, he notes.

"She's Russian. At least I think she's Russian. The name sounds Russian: Natasha Oblonski."

A pause here.

"What does she want to speak to him about?"

"Won't say. She claims it's important but refuses to specify."

Another pause.

"And you say you're calling from the office?"

"Yes."

"And she's there? Now?"

"Yes to both questions." Nick is getting impatient. "Patsy, let's skip the catechism, can we? Just let me talk to Hal."

"He's in a meeting with the German ambassador. I can tell you right now he won't want to come to the phone."

"Are you speaking as his sister-in-law, or his personal assistant?" Nick lets his irritation show in his voice. "If I didn't think he might want to know, I wouldn't have called. Why don't you tell him and let *him* decide?

Silence.

"I take it this is some spook thing or other." Contemptuous emphasis is laid on "spook." Patsy has never approved of his career.

"Patsy, I don't know what it is. She says it's important, she seems upset. I asked her if it couldn't wait for the morning; she said no. Beyond that she didn't confide."

Another silence. Then, in the tone of one humoring a child, "All right . . . I'll see what he wants you to do."

Certain things, later, will strike Nick about this exchange. In his experience women are curious about people, particularly other women. Patsy tends to be more curious than most. But in this case her interest in what the caller wants is coupled with indifference to the caller herself. There is also the matter of the name. Patsy has never been good at names. She's apt to claim that when introduced she fixes

96

on the person, not the name. But she seems to have no trouble re-membering Natasha's, though Nick is sure he has mentioned it only once. But these are things that will strike him only on reflection. At the time their significance more or less escapes him, obscured by the disquiet induced by Hal's message, which is relayed, in a tone of some triumph, by Patsy:

"Hal doesn't know a Natasha—Oblonski or otherwise. He's in an important meeting and is not about to leave it for some pretty young thing he has no recollection of meeting, who probably only knows him from his picture in the paper."

"Hal said that?"

A moment's pause. Intake of breath by Patsy. When it comes, the reply is icy. "Are you suggesting I'm making it up?"

"He used those words?"

"More or less."

"He wants me to get rid of her, then?"

"Correct." Patsy's tone is withering. "It shouldn't present any prob-lem. It's what you're best at—isn't it?—getting rid of women."

In this case, however, it does present a problem. On hearing Hal's message, albeit diplomatically worded, Natasha bursts into tears. Nick hovers ineffectually with Kleenex while the corporal phones for a taxi. This, of course, takes an age to arrive, all attempts at consolation meanwhile meeting with indifferent success. Natasha has developed a remarkable ability to cry attractively as long as she wants. When Nick and the corporal shepherd her into the taxi, under the driver's indig-nant stare, she's been sobbing on and off for fifteen minutes and still presents a picture of Beauty in Distress.

* * *

"So"—CASS'S EXPRESSION HAD NOT BEEN SOFTENED by this narrative—"you *assumed*, since she was so very attractive and so devastated by Hal's refusal to see her, that something must have been going on between them, and therefore that Hal lied about not knowing her. . . . Could it be you were judging him by yourself?"

The dislike in her voice, the contempt in her look, were as painful as slaps in the face. A special power to hurt, he thought, connected parents and children. It was hard to see her as a child, of course; she was twenty-six, in command of herself, and she used her power precisely, like a whip. But the instinct to hurt had been prompted by hurt received, and hurt received in the defenselessness of childhood. It was pointless to plead absence of intent. He'd never meant to hurt her, but he had. In the eyes of childhood, he knew, the unforgivable sins were usually those of omission.

"Actually," he said mildly, "you have it backward. I suspected Hal of lying, not because Natasha was a stunner, but because of what he *said*. Once I suspected him of lying, of course, an obvious motive suggested itself. The point is"—he paused—"I never told Patsy a thing about Natasha, apart from her name and her being upset. But Patsy, quoting Hal, referred to her as 'some pretty young thing.' Now, if Hal had no idea who she was, how the hell did he know she was young? Or pretty?"

"Maybe he assumed it." Cass frowned. "He was always being pestered by groupies. Maybe he assumed she was one."

"That was how Patsy explained it." Nick nodded. "At least it was *one* of the ways she explained it. She also said that she didn't remember what she'd said, that maybe she'd hadn't been quoting Hal directly, that maybe it was she who'd assumed it."

He paused, shrugged.

"Patsy never was much of a liar."

It was strange, he thought, that though in recent years he'd almost never thought about Patsy, he could call her to mind now without effort, instantly, as if her impatient ghost, standing just the far side of memory's threshold, had all the while been waiting for his summons. Or perhaps, since their marriage had forged this bond at least, that each possessed to a unique degree the capacity to disturb the other, it had actually been she who had summoned him. That conversation in Brussels, in the library of Hal's rented house in the opulent suburb of Schaerbeek, was as vivid in Nick's memory still as if twelve years ago had been yesterday. It had been their first encounter in a couple of weeks—their first, indeed, since she'd taken his call to Hal about Natasha. It was also the last time he saw her alive. What was said had been disturbing to them both.

It was almost as disturbing now, with Cass's eyes distrustfully upon him. A few days after that conversation Patsy had gone to bed with a bottle of sleeping pills and never woken up. Cass held him responsible for that. And though he could absolve himself—whatever the cause of

Patsy's despair, it had not been his departure from her life—he'd always suspected that last conversation had played some part in her death. Patsy had been involved in all this. She'd known something about it at least.

If not, why had she lied?

* * *

"HAL'S AT THE OFFICE." Patsy, entering, doesn't bother to greet him. "Shouldn't you be there, too? Making the world safe for democracy? Unmasking the agents of the Evil Empire?"

"That's what I'm doing," he says. "At least in a manner of speaking."

She receives this in silence.

She looks unwell, he observes, as if she hasn't been sleeping. The classic features look pinched and sharp, the skin everywhere stretched very tight, as if bone is pushing to break through. She's dressed with less than her normal care. It's not that she looks untidy, or unkempt, but as though—it would be a first for her—she's indifferent to her appearance.

"Are you sick?" he asks. "You don't look well."

"I've been better." She shrugs. "Don't tell me you're here to ask about my health."

"I'm here," he says, "to ask you a couple of questions."

"A couple of questions . . . you sound like a policeman. A couple of questions about what?"

"You recall that phone conversation we had? About the woman who came to the office demanding to talk to Hal?"

"Vaguely." She seems wary. "What about her?"

"I was curious about something you said. Actually, something you said Hal said. . . . You said Hal claimed he didn't know her. You said he referred to her as 'some pretty young thing he has no recollection of meeting, who probably only knows him from his picture in the paper.' "

"And?" She's definitely wary now. And trying not to show it.

"Did you say that?"

"I may have." She shrugs. "I don't recall it as well as you seem to. In any case, what does it matter?"

He ignores her question.

"Did Hal say that?"

"If I said he said it, I imagine he did." She pauses. "This is getting tiresome. I presume there's a point?"

"I think so."

"Which is?"

He hesitates an instant, brings it out abruptly.

"I was wondering. If they'd never met, how he—or you—could have known she was young. Or pretty."

"I see." She studies him for a moment, considering. When she resumes, there's an edge to her tone. "At least I think I see. And what I think I see I don't much like. . . . You're suggesting one or the other of us lied."

"I'd rather put it this way." He attempts, unsuccessfully, to lighten things up with a smile. "There's a seeming anomaly here, for which I've no doubt there's a perfectly straightforward explanation. I'm anxious to hear it, is all."

"Anxious." She turns the word over in her mind. "Do I gather, then, that you haven't asked Hal?"

He shakes his head. "Not yet."

"Then maybe you should. He's the one who said it."

"That's actually what I'm asking you." He pauses, reiterates gently. "Did he in fact say it?"

Her eyes narrow. "Didn't you ask me that before?"

"I did. . . . I'm not sure you answered."

Pause.

"Oh, *I* understand." Now she sounds bitter. "If anyone lied, it would have to be me. Not your old school pal, Mr. Straight Arrow. You know what?" she adds. "I've often thought this: It was you two should have gotten married."

"You may have a point." He tries once more to lighten the mood. "The problem was, we both like girls."

At this she is, quite suddenly, furious.

"Oh, don't I know it. Men! What an abject species you are. So fucking dishonest, especially with yourselves, so pompous about what you get up to. . . . Saving the World for Democracy, Foiling the Communist Menace. High-minded, hypocritical crap like that. . . . You never admit that, when it comes right down to it, all you really care about are your dicks." She seems to realize this outburst is misplaced, for she pauses then and, collecting herself, continues more calmly. "What an ugly place your mind must be, Nick. No room for innocence in it. Everything just has to be sinister. . . . Maybe I just *assumed* she was young, this Natasha Oblonski or whatever her name is. Or maybe Hal assumed it. Maybe you said something that made me assume it. . . . I expect, if I thought for half a moment, I could offer other 'perfectly straightforward' explanations. But the thing is"—she pauses again—"I really can't be bothered."

He could pursue things, but he doesn't see the point. The contradictions in what she's said must be as obvious to her as they are to him. As he lets himself out, closing the door on that conversation, the last they will ever have, he hears behind him the sound of her weeping.

*   *   *

"THIS IS BULLSHIT," Cass burst out. "A shoddy apology for logic. Patsy's confused, and that makes Hal a liar? Natasha was pretty, that means they were having an affair? . . . Don't let's forget she was also Russian. In your book, no doubt, that would make him a spy."

"Cass, knock it off." He met her anger calmly. "At the time, as you very well know, Hal was my oldest and closest friend. I wasn't falling over myself to suspect him. If anything, it was exactly the reverse. . . . If Hal had been seeing Natasha, what bothered me wasn't the fact that she was Russian. What bothered me was who else she'd been seeing."

"Who else?" Cass stared. "Don't tell me you started spying on *her*."

He shook his head. "This was something I learned by chance, and only after she was dead. You must understand that in those days everyone on our side—we, the Brits, the Germans, even the French—swapped certain kinds of intelligence. We all had our tight little kingdoms, our closely guarded treasure chests of secrets, but one thing it made sense to all of us to share was information about opposition players. . . . It happened that about the time we were investigating Werner, the Brits were running a surveillance in Geneva. They believed they'd identified a KGB case officer, and to prove it they offered a cartload of pics of him with his various contacts. In due course these made their way to me." Nick smiled, a little wryly. "If I seemed, earlier, to be stressing unduly what an absolute stunner Natasha was, it wasn't just salacious reminiscence. The point was, you didn't forget her. Nor mistake her for anyone else. If there wasn't much doubt in the minds of the Brits that the man they'd had under surveillance for weeks was a KGB case officer, there was none whatever in mine that the woman with whom he'd been photographed leaving a Geneva hotel—this was five days prior to my encounter with her—was Natasha."

"There *wasn't much doubt* he was KGB?" Cass wasn't buying this. "In other words, you don't know that he was. And if he was, you don't know that Natasha knew. And if she did, you don't know that Hal knew her. And if he did, you don't know they were having an affair." She paused. "The chain of your logic, it seems to me, consists almost entirely of weak links."

"Almost," he agreed, "but not quite. . . . The careful Swiss were sufficiently impressed by the evidence gathered by the Brits to expel the alleged KGB man. And I'm sure that Patsy was lying to me, and if she lied, so did Hal. He paused. "We weren't able to get Natasha's version of events, but her behavior seemed eloquent. After we put her in the taxi that night, she went home and stuck her head in the oven. The autopsy established, among other things, that at her death she was two months pregnant."

He paused again, inviting a response. Receiving none, he continued.

"You're right, of course, about weak links in my logic. At the time, of course, I wasn't building a case. What you have to remember is the timing. That, and my awkward friendship with Hal."

"Awkward?" Cass stared. "Your 'oldest and closest friendship' *awkward?*"

He nodded. "In context it was. At the time, we'd just gotten through polygraphing Werner. The polygraph said he was telling the truth. And Werner was proclaiming, to anyone who'd listen, that someone, Hal, was out to frame him and that I, being biased, was protecting Hal. And then, lo and behold, up pops Natasha. Native-born Russian, two months pregnant, KGB contact (witting or no), and at least conceivably linked to Hal Reynolds."

Nick stopped here, caught Cass's gaze.

"You accused me earlier of being too objective. I hope you can be objective enough to see I was trapped between conflicting imperatives: I had to be loyal to Hal, but I also had to be fair to Werner. At the very least I had to check into Natasha."

"I see that," Cass conceded. "Though in your place I think I'd have started by asking Hal."

"That's exactly what I did." Nick nodded bleakly. "I asked Hal. It ended our friendship."

Chapter Twelve

CASS WAS REMEMBERING pictures from Patsy's collage.

It was odd how selective memory was—or perhaps, since theory had it that one didn't really forget anything, just suppressed it, how random the process of retrieval was. For a time after leaving Sarah Lawrence her mother had enrolled in an art school in London. It was not that she'd been planning a career in the arts, she'd gone over to keep tabs on Nicholas Wolfe, who was enjoying life at Oxford and, since he wasn't enjoying it with her, conceivably enjoying it too much. But until such time as he could be persuaded to marry her, the pretense of studying had had to be maintained, so Patsy had dabbled in design. Her most successful effort still hung in the gazebo she'd converted to a studio in the family's summer home on Martha's Vineyard. Titled *Remembrance of a Misspent Youth*, it memorialized that year she'd spent abroad, the same year she and Nick had gotten engaged. She'd assembled it from bits and pieces, scraps from the paper trail left by a life that, as far as Cass could see—not that she disapproved at all—had that year been devoted exclusively to pleasure: engraved invitations to parties and dances, tickets to Glyndebourne and Covent Garden, labels from bottles of Krug and Veuve Cliquot, a program from the Folies Bergères, all these, together with newspaper clippings and cutouts from snapshots taken at the time, arranged as if in a careless scatter, yet functioning superbly as a piece of design.

The snapshots had always fascinated Cass, and they were what returned to her now: Nick and Hal in white tie and tails, lounging side by side in a punt, brandishing bottles of something or other and wearing delighted if slightly sozzled grins; Nick dripping wet in rowing shorts and team shirt, posing on the deck of his college barge, he and his crew, which earlier had bumped Trinity, having just submitted to a dunking in the Isis; Hal, in a gray morning coat and top hat, all gussied up for the races at Ascot; Hal, Nick, and Patsy in some Paris nightclub or other, heads together, giggling drunkenly, all three mugging for the camera like gargoyles. As a child Cass had never tired of hearing about them. "Tell me about that one," she'd demand, and whichever participant happened to be with her at the time would be bullied into reconstructing the event. In the end it became a game of tall stories. The adults, bored by too much repetition, started by simply embellishing the truth but wound up inventing alternative scenarios, each more improbable than the last. Hal attired for the races at Ascot became Hal dressed up to be knighted at Buckingham Palace (for services unspecified, but undoubtedly heroic, performed on behalf of a beleaguered queen). Nick the Victorious became Nick the Unfortunate, bumped and captured by the pirates of Balliol, forced in consequence to walk the plank, and rescued in the nick (ha-ha) of time by the gallant and devoted Patsy. The plots of these stories varied with the teller, but their spirit was always that of the collage: youth at play in the fields of an Eden where the serpent of discord never raised his head. So perhaps, Cass reflected, it wasn't so odd that these should be the images summoned by Nick's story, since for her they were icons of a paradise lost, of the family group destroyed by his defection, of the fellowship, now broken, between him and Hal.

Later, after that falling out, Hal had wanted to banish the collage. But Josie had refused to hear of it. Patsy had given it to her, she said; it spoke to memories she personally cherished. Indeed, she still spoke kindly of Nick, and not, Cass sensed, from the wish to be tactful, but because she liked and admired him. "Your father," she had once remarked, "is at heart an old-fashioned aristocrat, with the virtues of that vanishing breed. These include honesty, loyalty, and courage. Sexual fidelity, alas, is not among them. . . . But Patsy knew what she was getting into. She knew and chose to ignore it. . . . He should have had me," she'd added surprisingly. "I'd have known better how to handle him. But Hal met me first, and Nick respected that. They never competed over women" . . . An odd way to talk, Cass had thought at the time (as if the sisters had been prizes at a fair). It seemed to her it was Josie who was choosing to ignore, specifically Nick's many failings. Since the day she'd been diagnosed with multiple sclerosis, Hal's devotion to her had been unfailing. Nick, Cass thought, if faced with the same demands of duty, would pretty soon have abandoned ship. She'd expressed this view to Josie at the time, but her aunt had simply shaken her head. "My dear child, if that's what you think, I'm afraid you don't begin to know him." . . . But she did know him, didn't she? As well as she wanted to, at least. He'd betrayed Patsy, deserted *her* (seemingly without a backward glance), and had offered in justification the flippancy that "one shouldn't get married to one's mistakes." All of which made her more furious now at this implausible, self-serving tale of Hal's assumed involvement with this woman. It was Nick, not Hal, who welched on commitments, Nick who had extramarital affairs, Nick whose careless saunter through life was marked by a trail of broken hearts.

How dare he question Hal's fidelity.

"This," she said, "is the flimsiest thing I ever heard. Your whole case rests on a piece of hearsay—how Patsy reported Hal's answer to your message. It could have been pure misunderstanding."

"It wasn't, Cass." Nick met her anger calmly. "Natasha told me Hal knew her. Her tone suggested he knew her well. Hal, on the other hand, told me he'd never met her. Now, one or the other had to be lying, and Patsy's slip suggested it was Hal. I never told Patsy Natasha was a pretty young thing, and I gave her no reason whatever to assume it."

"How can you be so sure of that?" Cass demanded. "Are you certain that in talking to Patsy you never once, for instance, referred to Natasha as a 'girl'?"

He nodded. "I'm certain."

"How can you be?"

"I'm certain because I was very careful not to."

"*Careful?*" She stared. "Why did you think you had to be careful?"

"Patsy was Josie's sister . . ." He hesitated, had at least the grace, she saw, to look awkward. "I thought she might be anxious . . . on Josie's behalf. I didn't want her jumping to conclusions."

"Especially conclusions you'd already jumped to." Cass's tone was dry as chalk. "Conclusions that got worse as time went on. You mentioned earlier that Natasha was pregnant. I hate to think what conclusions you jumped to from that."

He shrugged but said nothing, continued to look awkward.

"Let me guess," she pursued. "You thought Hal was the father. You believed your oldest and closest friend had gotten this woman pregnant and then dumped her. And then, because of your need to be 'fair,' you confronted him with these suspicions. . . . I can't say I'm surprised it pissed him off."

Again he didn't respond for a moment. As if he hadn't heard her, she thought, as if he were someplace else altogether. Brussels, no doubt, in 1984.

"Were you surprised?" She brought him back to the present. "Did you think for a moment he wouldn't resent your suspicions?"

"Surprised?" Nick appeared to consider. "Yes, I was. It seemed to me he overreacted. Had I handled it the way you suggest, had I put it to him that baldly, it wouldn't have surprised me in the least. But I didn't. I didn't go in there like some prosecuting counsel, flinging accusations around. I put it to him, as a friend, that Natasha's demanding to see him that night raised questions that, had I not been a friend, might very well have struck me as awkward."

"Oh, *very* diplomatic," she mocked. "Too bad he chose to ignore the soft words and focus instead on the hard truth behind them. That you felt the need to 'put it' to him at all must have seemed to him like a betrayal."

He looked at her sadly.

"You don't understand, Cass. You're not even trying. Before, you said I should have asked him. Now you're saying I shouldn't. Whatever I'd done, you'd call me disloyal."

"Well, weren't you?" she demanded. "Wasn't it disloyalty, precisely, that Hal was accusing you of?"

"He seemed to see it that way." Nick nodded. "And he might have had a point had I shared my concerns with anyone else, but I didn't. I asked him, I accepted his answers. I didn't believe them, but I trusted him."

"You didn't believe them, but you *trusted* him? . . . You thought he lied about Natasha, you mean, but you didn't think this meant he was a spy? You went out on a limb for him by not telling the inquiry?"

"I did go out on a limb for him." Nick nodded. "I went way out. Boy, did I ever . . . so perhaps you can grasp why this tape is so disturbing. . . . The inquiry never heard about Natasha. Nor did Werner. I told that corporal to clam up, and he did. You could say I

107

withheld evidence, and technically I did. But by the time the inquiry was held I was certain that Werner was Oracle and therefore that Natasha was irrelevant. I persuaded myself that bringing her up would just be confusing the issue, handing Werner a bucket of mud and inviting him to dump it over Hal." Nick paused. "And that was the rationalization I used in dealing with the Belgian police."

"The police?" Cass stared. "How did they come into it? If you kept quiet and the corporal kept quiet, how did they come to be talking to you?"

"The cabdriver sicced them onto us. Natasha's death was reported in the papers. The driver apparently read about it and went to the police. He remembered her because, apart from anything else, she was crying her eyes out when we put her in the taxi. . . . It happened about a week later, I think. The corporal who'd been on the desk that night happened to be on duty again. He called up and told me the police had come by. They wondered if I could shed any light."

* * *

THEY WONDERED *if I could shed any light.* . . . In fact, Nick recalled, there'd been just the one policeman. He'd been chosen, clearly, for his diplomatic skills. Dry, deferential, extremely soft-spoken, Inspecteur Lem had behaved throughout as if it were he who was in a foreign country, as technically perhaps he was, since the immunity Hal enjoyed as special envoy extended to his office, his house, and whichever of his staff he chose to claim it for. Not that in this case there'd been any need to claim it. Lem had made no accusations. Nick gained the distinct impression that his purpose was more to convey information than obtain it. The deceased, Lem said—once the preliminaries were over her referred to Natasha only by that term—had been native-born Russian, twenty-five, single. At the time of her death she'd been approximately two months pregnant. Fluent in French, German, and Russian, passable in English, she'd maintained herself as a freelance translator. In 1979 she and her father, an orchestral musician now dead, had defected during a concert tour and applied for Belgian citizenship. This had been granted in 1982. In 1981, however, with her citizenship still pending, she'd applied for a post as a translator with NATO. Her application had been turned down, apparently for security reasons. NATO security had found her being allowed to accompany her father abroad "unusual enough to be suspicious." Some days before her death, according to a passport found in her apartment, she had spent two days in Geneva. On the night of her encounter with Nick, she'd apparently gone home, shut herself in her kitchen, closed the windows, turned on the oven (plus all the burners), but omitted to light the gas. This scenario, at any rate, was one Lem was "more or less inclined" to accept, though perhaps it was unusual that she'd left behind no note. Suicide, being "essentially a statement of despair," was normally accompanied by "clarification." It was in the hope of obtaining this that he'd ventured to seek Nick's assistance. He gathered Nick had seen her that night. He therefore hoped Nick might be able to shed light, in particular on two very interesting questions: Why had she come to the special envoy's office? Why had she left it in tears?

*   *   *

"SO NATURALLY, you sicced him onto Hal, this very diplomatic policeman."

"I didn't sic him on anyone." Nick frowned. "I told him only what I knew. That she'd asked for Hal and no one else, and that Hal, who didn't think he knew her, had been busy and unable to see her. I didn't see the need to share my own suspicions, especially since at that point I hadn't yet shared them with Hal."

"You hadn't shared them with Hal." Cass stared. "You mean you hadn't talked with him about her at all?"

"Oh, sure. I mentioned her in passing the day after her visit. Hal said it was weird, a total stranger coming in and asking for him like that. He wondered what the hell she wanted. . . . I let it go. At the time the whole thing didn't seem important. I didn't know then that Natasha had killed herself. I didn't know about her background. I particularly didn't know that she'd recently visited Geneva and had been photographed leaving a hotel with an officer of the KGB."

"A suspected officer, you mean."

"If you insist." Nick rolled his eyes. "He was 'suspected,' let's say, in the same sense the moon is suspected of orbiting the earth."

She ignored this.

"Did Hal say anything then about her being young or a groupie?" Nick shook his head. "He said he'd gone to the office later that night, around ten, to look for some piece of paper or other, and the corporal on duty had told him about her. He said that to judge from the corporal's description he rather wished he *had* seen her. He said he sincerely hoped she'd be back."

"And you let that slide? You thought it was a lie, but you let it slide?"

"I did. I thought . . ." Nick broke off. "You already know what I thought."

"I do indeed." She nodded grimly. "How did Lem react to what you told him?"

"He asked to speak with Hal."

"And did he?"

"Oh, yes. Hal was very gracious. He told Lem exactly what he'd previously told me. Even the part about wishing he had seen her."

"That struck you as significant?"

"Perhaps just because I already didn't believe him. Something I learned debriefing defectors was distrust of stories told always the same way."

She thought about this.

"Perhaps," she suggested, "what you learned debriefing defectors was distrust."

"Perhaps."

"Did Lem seem to have problems with what Hal told him?"

"Not that I could see. But before he left, he said something interesting. He said the obvious was often not the truth, but since in this case it was all he had, he guessed he'd have to be satisfied."

"Did you ask him what he meant by that?"

"Of course. He told us that in the autopsy a discordant fact had emerged. Natasha had died from inhaling gas, but she'd evidently, and just shortly before, received a blow to the head. There was bruising at the base of her skull, the kind of bruising that could have been made by her falling and hitting her head, or conceivably by a blow from the traditional blunt instrument. Falling seemed more likely, Lem said, since a blow would have had to be delivered upward, but that alternative couldn't be ruled out."

Nick paused.

"We asked Lem what he made of that. Nothing necessarily, he said. But the gas hadn't turned itself on. If she hadn't done it, then someone else had. A murder scenario, on the other hand, had only the bruise working for it. Working *against* it, together with the virtual absence of supporting evidence and any suggestion as to motive, was the implausibility of the means. If someone had killed Natasha and disguised the murder as a suicide, it argued a high degree of premeditation. Lem found it hard to believe that anyone planning to kill her would choose a method so haphazard and risky. It might seem a simple thing, he said, to knock her out with a blow to the head, stick her in the kitchen and turn on the gas, but a moment's reflection would alert you to the fact that she might wake up before the gas took effect. You could always tie her up, of course, but that would mean hanging around at the scene, waiting for the gas to take effect. And then, of course, you'd have to go in and untie her. To be capable of that, you'd have to be completely without nerves, not so much calculating as ghoulish. Besides, there was no evidence she had been tied up—no marks, for instance, around her wrists and ankles. It was only her background that prompted him even to consider murder. NATO security had evidently suspected her of KGB involvement. If they were right, all bets were off. In his experience, if you wanted ghoulish, the KGB was where to look."

"He thought the KGB might have killed her?"

"He thought it was conceivable." Nick nodded. "But if they had, it would probably never be known, much less proved. And speaking for himself, Lem said, if he couldn't prove it he'd rather not know."

"And that was the end of it?"

"The last we heard from Lem." Nick nodded. "What struck me most about his visit was he told us a lot more than he needed. About Natasha's background, for instance. I had the impression he was trailing a coat, floating things past to watch our reaction. 'Look, guys,' he seemed to be saying, 'I know that the spooks, yours or the Russians', have been up to something or other here, and I want you to know that I know.'"

"Why would he want you to know that?"

"To remind us perhaps whose turf we were on. A gentle hint: Forbearance has its limits."

"So how did you react?" Cass asked. "More to the point, how did Hal react?"

"About as you'd expect. With roughly the degree of interest Lem's

111

story seemed to merit. Hal asked all the expected questions, answered those he was asked. Gave Lem all the time he wished. Never even glanced at his watch."

"And afterward?" Cass queried. "What did he say afterward, when you told him you thought he was lying?"

Nick looked startled.

"I didn't," he said. "Not then, at least. It bothered me, of course, to hear that NATO security had its doubts about Natasha. But it wasn't until later, when we learned who she'd been seen with in Geneva, that I felt any need for confronting Hal."

Chapter Thirteen

CONFRONTING HAL: It was easy to say, but to this day, Nick thought, it was the most unpleasant thing he'd ever done. What Cass had said was essentially right: However diplomatically expressed, what he'd had to confront Hal with was blunt and ugly. It made no difference that he could claim, with honesty, to be acting with reluctance and only in the interest of justice. There were questions in which judgments were implied, doubts that once uttered couldn't be retracted.

Hal had grasped this as quickly as Patsy.

* * *

"WHAT YOU'RE SAYING is you think I've been lying." His stare is as bleak as the Antarctic. "To you and to the police."

"You're overreacting." Nick attempts evasion. "What I'm doing here is playing devil's advocate. Asking the questions Werner would ask if he knew enough to ask them. . . . I told you, didn't I, that he passed the flutter test?"

"You did, and I'm not impressed. I still think he sold us down the river."

"You're probably right. The problem is, he's saying the same about you. He's also saying that I won't listen because you and I are old friends."

"Are we?" Hal's stare hasn't thawed a degree. "You sure as hell could've fooled me. . . . What are you doing here now, one might ask, if not *listening* to the son of a bitch?"

"I think you could say I'm going through necessary motions."

"Horseshit." Hal isn't tempted to buy this. "You wouldn't be wasting my time and yours if he hadn't gotten through to you to some extent. You wouldn't keep asking me, or Patsy, how we knew this Natasha was young and so forth, unless in some corner of your shithole of a mind it occurred to you to wonder if he might not be right."

Me or Patsy, Nick notes. Patsy must have said something then. Odd, in that case, that Hal hasn't mentioned it before. Why has he waited for *you* to bring it up?

"That isn't it, Hal. Actually, that isn't it at all."

"Okay, so tell me. If it isn't that, what is it?"

"I'm trying to give Werner a fair hearing. He's entitled to that, don't you think?"

"Depends what you mean by fair." Hal shrugs. "You've known me more than twenty years. How long have you known Marcus Werner?"

"I don't think that's really the point. I think being fair means not having preconceptions. It means, for the purposes of this investigation, setting aside our friendship, checking his claims as carefully as yours, subjecting *all* the evidence, no matter what the source, to the same impartial scrutiny." He pauses. "I have to do that—don't you see?—especially in view of the polygraph. I can't give him the chance of muddying the waters, have him claiming he's been railroaded."

"No danger of that." Hal sneers. "When it comes to setting friendship aside, I'd say you're doing an exemplary job."

"Well, try to quit getting all bent out of shape and put yourself in my place for a moment." Nick's temper, too, is starting to fray. "Especially since it was *you* who insisted on putting me there. You think I'm enjoying this conversation? . . . Werner is claiming somebody framed him. Actually, he's claiming the somebody is you. Now, apart from your testimony, which he claims is false, the only hard evidence against him right now is his contact with that Russian in Geneva. His explanation for that is possible, if not plausible, and it's corroborated by the stamp dealer and apparently by Werner's own polygraph test." Nick pauses. "Now enters this Natasha Oblonski. Soviet defector, gorgeous, recently turned down for a translator's job with NATO for quote/unquote security reasons. Shows up at the office demanding to see you, insisting that she knows you. She could be lying, but if so she's a hell of an actress. And your response, as transmitted by Patsy, is amazement expressed in rather too much detail. Patsy, I might add, is not one hell of an actress—"

Hal cuts in. "Now, hold it right there."

"No, *you* hold it. I'm not finished. I speculate at the time, not knowing jack about Natasha, that maybe Hal has been screwing around and is naturally reluctant to have the fact known. It's not a totally unheard-of situation and in any case none of my business, so I keep my speculations to myself. But then, unfortunately, the Brits send me these." Nick points to the photographs he's placed on Hal's desk—photographs, he notes, that Hal has barely glanced at. "Eight-by-ten glossies of this very same Natasha leaving a Geneva hotel with a Russian. And not just your garden variety Russian, but a KGB officer previously photographed buying stamps, or whatever, from Werner." Nick pauses. "Now, you tell me, Hal. What am I supposed to do now? Not even ask you about it? . . . Did you bring me here to investigate, or to rubber-stamp your indictment of Werner?"

"I brought you to investigate." Hal's face is set and furious. "I asked for you because I trusted you to do it without turning the whole place upside down. Because I thought you had a brain in your head and could be relied on to use it."

"Meaning what exactly?"

"Meaning that I hoped, at least, that you could work through the logic of your own suspicions."

"I told you, I don't have suspicions. What I have are questions."

"Oh, bull. Don't patronize me, Nick. Your questions amount to suspicions, and if you won't articulate them, I will. Maybe it's Hal who's spying for the Russians. Maybe this Natasha is a cutout, reporting to that KGB guy in Geneva. Maybe, to deflect suspicion from himself, Hal trumped up those charges against Werner, then conspired with the KGB to fabricate an incident further incriminating him." He pauses. "That *is* it, isn't it? If not exactly, at least in the ballpark?"

"Suit yourself," Nick tells him. "This is your fantasy."

"Not yours? How very reassuring. That makes me feel all warm inside." Hal pauses. "But since we have it out on the table, let's take a moment to examine it more closely. For consistency, logic—details like that."

"Go ahead."

"Then let's start with this: The whole ridiculous theory presumes a

115

link between me and this Natasha. But the only evidence for it was furnished by the woman herself. If she hadn't come to the office that night, we wouldn't be discussing her now. Correct?"

"Correct."

"But according to the theory, Natasha is a KGB cutout, isn't she?"

"According to *your* theory, yes."

"But if she's working for the KGB any evidence furnished by her is automatically suspect, isn't it?"

"Agreed," Nick says. "But—"

"I listened to you." Hal cuts him off. "This time I haven't finished. Your theory suffers from an even more serious problem. Not only is it inconsistent, it's also inherently implausible. Even if Natasha was telling the truth, she can hardly have been working for the KGB. If she was, why would she have come to my office? To draw attention to herself? To arouse your suspicions? I mean, tell me, Nick, from your vast experience of the KGB, does it normally advertise its intentions?"

* * *

AND THAT, Nick recalled, had been pretty much that. Hal's defense, he'd been forced to admit, was compelling. And compelling, one could hardly fail to notice, without Hal's even answering the question of his knowing or not knowing Natasha. He should have left then, Nick thought, but he'd been angry, so he'd pushed it. Because Hal was taking such a damn snotty tone, insisting on trust he felt he was owed but clearly unwilling to extend it, staking out claims to high moral ground to which he was far from entitled. So he'd *made* Hal answer the question directly, indulge himself in the dubious satisfaction of forcing his friend to lie to his face.

"Then you've had no contact with Natasha Oblonski?"

The look Hal gave him then was one he had never forgotten. As if a door had been slammed in his face, as if by asking he'd become a stranger, unwelcome in a house he'd hitherto treated as his own. A line had been crossed, a trust irreparably broken. . . . Hal said, not bothering to meet Nick's eyes, not pretending to care whether Nick believed him or not:

"I have had no contact with Natasha Oblonski."

116

He'd shrugged. "Well, I had to ask, didn't I?"

"No, Nick. I think you really didn't." Hal had met his gaze for a moment, then turned his attention to the papers on his desk. "Now if you'll excuse me, I have work to attend to."

Chapter Fourteen

IT WAS SOMETIMES next to impossible, Cass thought, to enter the heads of men like her father and her uncle. Listening to Nick's account of his falling out with Hal, she found herself reminded of a story Josie had told her. About when Nick was a senior at Exeter, an incident Josie had heard about from Hal. . . . He and Nick had been rowing a race against St. Paul's. At the very start, the first or second stroke, with both crews straining every muscle for the lead, Nick had pulled with such ferocity that his sliding seat had come off its track, leaving him sitting on the rails. The race, Hal said, should have ended right there. Indeed, there'd been some seconds of confusion, a faltering of tempo in which St. Paul's grabbed a lead of maybe as much as a boat length. But Nick never stopped rowing, Hal said, and the Exeter boat recovered its rhythm. There'd been no way they could win, of course—you could hardly hope to under that kind of handicap—but they'd managed to stay in contention. The course had been more than a mile in length. Every stroke must have been agony for Nick, but he'd never eased up for a moment. He'd rowed sliding up and down on those rails, the sharp brass edges cutting grooves in his ass, his shorts by the end soaked through with blood, and once across the finish line he'd fainted. It was hard, Cass thought, to fathom an action like that. The motive might be easy enough to articulate, but it utterly eluded your efforts to imagine it. The courage made you want to weep, the pointlessness made you want to smack him. Was there anything, she asked herself, was there any sacrifice her father and Hal were *not* prepared to lay upon the altar of the will? Certainly they hadn't spared their friendship. All through Nick's account of his interview with Hal she'd found herself hearing what they *hadn't* said, silences screaming with words they should have spoken. With just a little give, she thought, a mutual willingness to step back from positions staked out, or even to shut up for a moment and listen, everything might have been different. But instead of talking, they'd jousted. They'd turned the thing into a competition, their words increasing the distance between them, encasing their feelings like armor, suits of tin with deaf men inside.

"So tell me," she said, "how *did* you come to snag Werner in the end? Presumably you found other evidence."

Nick nodded. "Actually, we found two things: The stamp dealer, Le Gallet, turned out to have KGB connections. That wasn't conclusive. Werner could easily claim, and did, that Le Gallet had been part of the plot to frame him. But then we found something he couldn't convincingly explain: a Swiss bank account with a ton of money in it."

"A numbered account? How did you get the records? I thought that by law those accounts were confidential."

"They used to be"—Nick nodded—"but there's been some erosion. The Swiss are above all practical people, especially when they're dealing with the U.S. government and the matter relates, as we hinted it did, to drug deals and laundered money. There was three hundred thousand in that account, deposited in chunks of twenty or thirty thousand over a period that neatly coincided with the time Oracle was thought to have been active."

"What did Werner have to say about that?"

Nick shrugged. "He stuck with the tried and true, what by then we'd come to know as 'The Philately Defense.' He'd gotten the money from his various stamp deals. But unfortunately for him, he couldn't remember the details nor produce any documentation."

"And on that basis you convicted him?"

"The inquiry did." Nick nodded. "I decided there was evidence enough to hold one. The inquiry, having heard that evidence, voted to pull Werner's security clearance. As I told you, he was never indicted, but he lost his job, plus benefits and pension."

"But at least he had the three hundred thousand. And presumably some marketable skills." Cass considered for a second. "Why did he end up pumping gas?"

"Who knows?" Nick shrugged. "Maybe he was trying to dramatize his injuries. Lying down, yelling 'foul,' refusing to get up. He claimed at the time he was shafted." Nick paused. "I gather he still does."

119

"And *now* you think maybe he was?"

For perhaps ten seconds he didn't answer. His eyes rested on her briefly, then wandered off around the restaurant. The waiters had started laying the tables for lunch, but their own table, Cass noted, hadn't even been cleared of the breakfast dishes. In the past two hours she hadn't set eyes on their waiter. Nick must have asked him to leave them in peace.

"*Do* you think maybe he was?"

Nick met the question indirectly.

"You know the awkward thing about security? It doesn't use legal standards of proof. There's no such thing as the presumption of innocence, and can't be. Grounds for suspicion are enough. In Werner's case we just couldn't take the risk. I still think we were right, that we did the only thing we could, but it wasn't the same as finding him guilty. I'm not at all sure a jury would have. Even at the time, I think, there was room for reasonable doubt." He paused. "Did I tell you I ran into him after the inquiry? That meeting always bothered me a bit. He behaved with a kind of bitter dignity, like a man who knew he'd been wronged."

"I don't think that means a thing," Cass objected. "If he could fool the polygraph, he'd hardly have had trouble fooling you."

"I know it." Nick nodded. "But even so, I was relieved to learn that after he was fired, the leaks dried up. Or seemed to."

"Seemed to? Meaning you don't think they did?"

"Meaning I don't really know. Hal said they did. At the time, I was happy to believe him." Nick paused, added neutrally, "Your tape, on the other hand, seems to say they didn't."

Cass didn't need to think long about *this*.

"Then the tape," she said flatly, "is bullshit."

He noted the defiance in her voice, the stubborn belligerence of her look. This, he thought, is where it gets nasty.

"It may well be," he said. "What bothers me is that none of this seems to make much sense. It doesn't make sense that Hal spied for the Russians, and it doesn't make sense that Dolokhov's tape is a fake."

She looked at him as if he were weak in the head.

"It makes perfect sense to me. Hal is running for president, right? Barring accidents, he's going to win. One way to stop him would be with a smear, float a rumor he sold out his country to the Russians. It's obvious to me that somebody faked the tape, then murdered Dolokhov to make it look authentic. You suggested the latter idea yourself, if you remember."

He considered this.

"If I did"—he shook his head—"it doesn't bear up under scrutiny."

"Why not?"

"Well, for one thing, the tape originated *here*. I can't think who in Russia would benefit from Hal's not winning. If anything, it's the reverse. He's the most pro-Russian of the candidates. . . . I suppose you could argue that your Russians are working for one of the others, but that raises problems, too."

"Such as?"

"Well, in order to smear you have to publish, correct? You have to get your smear to the public's attention. Let's look at the way they've apparently chosen to do it. Dolokhov came to you, Cassandra Wolfe, Reynolds' niece. Almost"—Nick's face was expressionless—"his surrogate daughter. In other words, about the least likely person in the world to accept the implications of the tape or to broadcast them if she did. That's always assuming, of course, that she understood them in the first place."

"Understood them?" Cass queried. "Why wouldn't I?"

"Well, you didn't till you talked to me. And I happen to be one of very few people familiar with the details of the Oracle case. One of only two or three, at least on the American side, who knew of Hal's link with Natasha."

"Two or three? Who were the others?"

"One was Sherman, my assistant in Brussels. I had him on loan from the local station. The corporal mentioned Natasha to him. I was forced to explain the situation."

"I thought you told the corporal to keep quiet."

"I did. But unfortunately, only after he spoke to Sherman."

"So presumably you told Sherman to keep quiet, too?"

"Of course. And he probably did, more or less." Nick paused. "I wouldn't have been surprised, however, to learn he'd confided in Quine."

"Quine?" She stared. "You mean Arthur Quine? The one who got the Militia off my back?"

121

"The same." Nick nodded. "Sherman worked for him in Brussels. Before I borrowed him, I mean. I don't know what he's doing here. Not running things, I hope. He never struck me as station chief material."

So Quine might have known about Natasha. Was this just, Cass wondered, another of the odd coincidences with which this situation was so fraught, or was it more sinister than that? It was hard to know what to make of it, she thought. It was hard to know what to make of anything.

"So in fact," she said, "the corporal told Sherman, who may have told Quine, who may have told any number of people."

"I doubt *that*." Nick gestured impatiently. "What's your point here, Cass?"

"Merely that your knowledge of Hal's alleged link with this woman may not be as exclusive as you think. So your point—that in order to grasp the full implications of the tape I would have needed to talk to you—loses, I would say, a lot of its force."

"In theory." He shrugged. "But my point is, you'd have to talk to someone. How could whoever dreamed up this smear possibly have known you'd be talking to me?"

"They told me to, remember? 'You could ask your father,' Dolokhov said. Better yet, 'you could ask your uncle.' What I'd heard on the tape, of course, more or less guaranteed that I would . . . and I did," she added. "I wish I hadn't."

"Amen to that. . . . So whoever was behind this *knew* I was coming to Moscow?"

"Possibly." She shrugged. "But not necessarily. The mail was still running, last time I looked. The telephone functions, occasionally. In any case," she went on, "I'm not sure I'd have had to talk to you. I'm not even sure I'd have had to know the full implications, or not, at any rate, about the quote/unquote possible link between Hal and this woman, Natasha. The tape suggests that the U.S. cabinet of 1990 included a KGB spy code-named Oracle. Once the existence of the tape became known, there were quite a few people besides you who could have made the connection with Hal—all those who took part in the Krasov debriefing, for starters, and anyone who read the debriefing report." She paused for a second, considering. "And that would have made it more convincing, don't you see? I don't *have* to know the

122

implications. All I have to know is what was on the tape. I make known the existence of the tape, let's say, not knowing beans about the possible identity of Oracle, and someone else makes the connection. I don't even realize I'm damaging my uncle."

She was smart, he thought, probably a lot smarter than he was. Her logical sense was at least the equal of his and was allied with a quickness of insight he lacked and a perfectly phenomenal memory. But here intelligence was blinkered by faith. Like some medieval schoolman puzzled by the motions of the planets, she would rather cling to an implausible theory, piling complication on needless complication, than dream of abandoning its central tenet. But he envied her that faith. It was easier than doubt and in some ways did her credit. It reflected better on her, he thought, than his demon of mistrust did on him.

"You make known the existence of the tape?" he queried. "And someone else makes the connection? But what tape is it, exactly, whose existence you're going to make known?"

"Why, Dolokhov's tape, of course . . ." Realizing what she was saying, she broke off. "Oh, you mean I don't *have* the tape."

"Precisely." He nodded. "You're going to 'make known' the existence of a taped conversation, allegedly in an archive not open to historians, which taped conversation you can't, alas, lay hands on but propose to quote, verbatim, from memory." Nick paused. "What learned publication, I wonder, would swallow a story like that?"

"I'm not dumb." She flushed. "I wouldn't try to publish without corroboration. But I wouldn't just drop the whole thing either. And they'd know that, too. They'd know I'd have to dig into it."

"You'd dig into it, then? Investigate the murder? . . . And at some point they'd arrange, these conspirators, to have their faked tape rediscovered?" Nick shrugged. "That's remotely conceivable, I guess. I can't say it strikes me as likely."

"I'm not sure it strikes *me* as likely," she conceded. "It's the best I can come up with at short notice. And it strikes me as a hell of lot more likely than that Hal was a spy for the Russians."

"Occam," Nick queried mildly. "What happened to Occam's Razor?"

"Occam? . . ." For a moment she looked blank. "Oh . . . you're

123

saying I should accept the tape as genuine because that's a simpler theory than the alternative?"

"A lot simpler." He nodded. "Your smear conspiracy theory suffers not only from the absence of the tape, it also presupposes an implausibly elaborate conspiracy." He paused. "Think about it, Cass—about what the conspirators would have to have known, what improbable alliances it would have to have involved. You'd have to have former or current KGB men, people who not only know about Oracle but also have access to the presidential archive—"

She interrupted. "Why access to the archive?"

"Because your faked tape would have to withstand all kinds of detailed scrutiny. Voiceprint analysis, for one. You can't just have actors reading from a script; that wouldn't fool anyone. You'd have to splice the faked conversation from actual recordings of Gorbachev and Kryuchkov. And you'd have to insert it into the tape of an actual Politburo meeting. And this means, since that's where those records are kept, that you'd have to have access to the archive."

"Okay," Cass conceded, "point taken. Go on."

"Well, it seems to me that if your smear is going to stick, it can't depend on the tape alone. It's going to need supporting evidence— namely some of the stuff I've just told you about the inquiry and Hal's involvement in it."

"No problem. They could get all that from Werner."

"Not all of it." He shook his head. "Werner didn't know about Natasha, remember?"

"That's true," Cass acknowledged. "But as I just pointed out, it's not clear they really need Natasha. I'll certainly grant she would help the smear stick, but I think it would do very well without her. . . . That's the thing about smears," she added. "Given the public's instinctive distrust of politicians, you don't need proof; suggestion is generally enough."

"If you say so." Nick shrugged. "But still we have to have Werner involved, and that's not all. The Russians and Werner need to link up somehow with the guys who want to trash Hal's chances of election and, since the Russians won't be doing this for fun, are willing to pay big money for it." Nick paused. "Now, you might say that this is no problem either. We can safely assume that among the other candidates are scumbags who'd be willing to join this little plot and other scumbags who'd be willing to finance it—"

"Correct," Cass cut in. "I might very well say that. And in view of Watergate and other recent history, I wouldn't have a problem believing it."

"No argument there." He smiled faintly. "But how exactly are our Russians to find them? Peddle the scheme on Capitol Hill? Take out an ad in *The Wall Street Journal?*" He shook his head. "You need a go-between, a broker, someone to put sellers and buyers together."

"That makes sense," she said. "But I still don't see the problem. Are you claiming there is no such person?"

"I suppose there could be," he conceded. "Just as there could be Russians with the inside scoop on Oracle and access to the presidential archive. And those guys could have gotten together with Werner and devised a smear campaign, though hardly one whose success depends on your willingness to believe and broadcast lies about your uncle. I guess what I'm trying to say here is this: Your theory assumes, one, an unlikely combination of unlikely circumstances, and two, some highly implausible psychology."

"I'll grant that," Cass said. "But couldn't there be other theories than the one you've so ably demolished?"

He thought about this.

"There's one I can think of," he offered. "Namely that the tape is not a fake."

She shook her head. "That's one I can't buy. Give me unlikely circumstance, implausible psychology. Give me anything rather than that."

"In other words, the hell with Occam's Razor?"

"Screw it." She nodded. "Instinct tells me Hal couldn't be a traitor. You were friends with him half your life. Don't you just know in your gut he couldn't?"

He shook his head. "Cass, believe me, it's not what I want to believe. But we can't let our heads be governed by our hearts."

"Can't we?" she snapped. "I don't find it difficult at all. But I wonder if your head has ever been governed by your heart. It certainly hasn't where your family is concerned."

Silence.

What galled him, he thought, what pissed him off, was less this

125

rehearsal of ancient griefs than her blindness to what he was feeling. Couldn't she see that what he had were not convictions but doubts, that her tape had raised ghosts he'd hoped had been laid to rest? Twelve years after the break with Hal, the ache of that loss was still with him. Did she think he *wanted* to believe his boyhood friend had betrayed him?

"You know what I wish?" he said bitterly. "I wish we'd never had this conversation. I wish to hell I'd never heard of your tape. Oracle either, for that matter."

"Well, you have," she snapped. "So what are you going to do?"

"What are *you* going to do?" he flung back at her. "You're all grown up. Grown up enough, it seems, to sit in judgment on me. This is your tape, your problem: Solve it. If you're so sure you're right about Hal, forget you ever talked to me, forget you ever listened to that tape."

*   *   *

BUT SHE KNEW forgetting wasn't an option. Doubt, like cancer, would spread unless rooted out. And doubt *had* been planted by what Nick had told her. Not a lot, but enough. She would have to dig to the root, to follow to the end, however bitter, this trail on which circumstance—or malice—had set her.

PART II

Moscow,
March–April 1996

Chapter Fifteen

ACCORDING TO THE LICENSING DIVISION'S computer, the address was in Tyoply Stan, a complex of identical fifteen-story shoeboxes at the nasty end of Leninsky Prospekt. In the planning stages, fifteen or twenty years back, some commissar had conferred on this complex the title "New Residential District." Accepted grudgingly by Muscovites at the time, this had been used, but with an overlay of irony, ever since. In fact, Sokolnikov recalled, the buildings had never looked new. Even under construction—it was their architect's most notable achievement—they'd managed to seem scruffy, years out of date. And strictly speaking, they'd never been new either, not entirely, since repairs to the exteriors had been necessary before the interiors were finished. Plain but not functional, sterile but not clean, they perfectly embodied, Sokolnikov thought, the Soviet bureaucracy's conception of the future.

A surprising habitat, though, for Comrade Dolokhov.

Or whatever his real name was. Sokolnikov, parking his Volga from the State Militia car pool in the asphalt wasteland adjacent to People's Apartment Cooperative Number 2, considered this issue far from settled. Dolokhov was the name the man had apparently used in his dealings with the American woman, but the Criminal Division's computer, on the other hand, had identified his fingerprints as belonging to a certain Grigoriev, Vladimir Alexeivich. And Vladimir Alexeivich— he'd been arrested once, in April 1993, charged with three counts of extortion, but not convicted or even brought to trial—was also listed as the registered owner of the white VW Rabbit found four days ago, abandoned and more or less gutted, in a side street near Komsomol Square. But in the eight days that had passed since the murder, no

129

missing-persons report had been filed under either of those names. So maybe the real name was neither Dolokhov nor Grigoriev.

Or maybe no one had missed him.

The foyer of People's Apartment Cooperative Number 2, which Sokolnikov now entered, boasted plywood furniture (unpainted), a table lamp (no bulb or shade), and a mural mosaic in brightly colored plastic from which about half the tiles were missing. The mosaic depicted a hero and heroine of Soviet agriculture, the latter nursing a gargantuan infant against a backdrop of cornfields and combines. A tactless image, it struck Sokolnikov, to have offered for the edification of Moscow's factory and office workers, whose experience of the shortages chronic in that era could have left them in no doubt whatever as to the achievements of Soviet agriculture. And maybe, he thought, it was this experience, not the achievements of Soviet construction, that explained the absence of so many tiles. But whatever the cause, their loss gave the mural a vanishing look, as though the heroes, knowing their day was done, were fading discreetly from the scene.

On the elevator door a handwritten notice was posted. Sokolnikov was unsurprised to learn that the elevator was not in service. A resumption, the notice assured him, could be expected at any moment.

The notice was dated—someone's idea of a joke—October 1917.

The apartment was on the thirteenth floor.

* * *

AT FIRST, in spite of protracted leaning on the doorbell, nobody answered Sokolnikov's summons. Then, just as he was trying to decide between his lock-picking skills and a well-directed boot, a voice, female and grumpy (or was it merely sleepy?), called out from somewhere inside.

"Chill out, for Christ's sake. I'm coming."

Then some seconds later, from just the far side of the door, "Who the hell are you, anyway?"

"State Militia. Open up."

She did, but only a crack, keeping the door chained, peering suspiciously around it.

"What do you want?"

"I want to ask you some questions." He could have shown his ID

130

but didn't. The uniform was ID enough. After twelve flights of stairs he was grumpy himself. "Will you open up, or do I kick down the door?"

She opened up.

The drive here, not to mention those endless stairs, had given Sokolnikov leisure to wonder who he might find in the apartment. Single occupancy was unusual in Moscow, especially in the poorer neighborhoods, and nothing about this Grigoriev, not even his preposterous overcoat or his white VW Rabbit, suggested he could afford the luxury of living alone. There'd be a roommate or perhaps a relative. Even, with a bit of luck, a wife.

What he hadn't expected was a nymphet.

But "nymphet" was the right word for her. Barefoot, barelegged—long, shapely legs, Sokolnikov noted—she couldn't have been more than fifteen, and if she was wearing anything under her T-shirt (souvenir, it proclaimed, from the Hard Rock Cafe in Houston), it certainly wasn't a bra. Half-formed breasts, the nipples prominent under the thin fabric of the T-shirt, forced themselves on his attention. Forced themselves with intent, he guessed, for there was something suggestive in the way she stood, something knowing and weary in the gaze that challenged his, a look far older than the features that wore it.

Behind her, in what he could see of the apartment, there was chaos.

He pushed past her into the living room. From there the rest of the place was visible. It looked as if a whirlwind had passed through. Bookcases and tables were overturned and smashed, LPs and papers strewn across the floor, the couch, its companion armchair, and a beanbag all gutted, their innards leaking from multiple slashes. In the bedroom, drawers and closets were ransacked, shirts and underwear littering the floor.

"What the hell happened here?" The unexpectedness, not to mention the mess, startled him out of his normal routine.

"Someone trashed it." Self-evident, her tone and shrug suggested. As indeed, he conceded to himself, it was.

"Someone . . . who?"

"How should I know? They didn't leave a card. . . . I came back, didn't I? Found it this way."

"Came back when? What day was this?"

131

She took a moment to consider.

"Maybe a week. Last Saturday, I think. Don't ask me dates. I'm not a diary."

He didn't need to consult his own. Saturday was the sixteenth, the day of the murder.

"What time?"

"Afternoon." Another pause for thought. "I don't have a watch, but it was light, I remember. I went out to buy food. When I came back, it was done."

"How long were you gone?"

"Dunno. Maybe an hour. Not much more."

She'd been gone for an hour, and when she'd returned it was still light. Sunset, these days, was about five. Most likely they'd done it not later than four. Less than six hours after the murder. But after, he thought, definitely after.

If she was telling the truth.

"It's been like this a *week?*" He stared. "It never occurred to you to clean up?"

If she registered reproach in his question, she ignored it.

"Not my mess, is it?"

She spoke as if this, too, were self-evident. And nothing she said, Sokolnikov thought later, spoke as eloquently for the child she essentially was than her genuine indifference to the chaos. She behaved as if it didn't exist, or as if it were somehow preordained, permanent, the upturned chairs and broken crockery simply features of an altered topography, something she was fated to live with.

"Whose mess would you say it was, then?"

"Volodya's, of course . . . it's his apartment."

"Volodya? Would that be Vladimir Dolokhov? Or Grigoriev?"

"He never told me his other name." She was suddenly wary, he noted, her tone neutral, manner guarded. "He was always plain Volodya to me."

"Is this him?"

The picture he handed her was from the morgue. A head and shoulders, full face, eyes closed, it made the subject look almost peaceful. But something rigid, masklike, in the features and the small blue hole in the middle of the forehead made it plain the peace was not of sleep. I should have prepared her, Sokolnikov thought, I shouldn't have sprung it on her like that.

She didn't seem very shaken, however.

"That's him." She handed the photograph back. "I see they finally got him."

" 'They'?" Sokolnikov queried. "Who's 'they'?"

"His enemies, of course." The response was prompt. "He was always talking about his enemies. Always going on about how people would like to kill him."

"He didn't happen to say which people?"

She shook her head. Emphatically. Perhaps, he thought, too emphatically.

"What about you?" He switched his attack. "Who are you, and what are you doing here?"

"I'm Olga." She tilted her head defiantly. "Olga Vorontsova. But people mostly call me Olyenka. . . . What I'm doing is answering a bunch of stupid questions. What I *was* doing," she added, "was sleeping. Until you woke me, that is."

Teenage bravado. Sokolnikov ignored it.

"You shared this place?"

"He lets me sleep here. In the daytime, when he's not using it. That is," she amended, "he used to."

"You sleep in the daytime? What the hell do you do at night?"

"Go out." Her look was suddenly opaque. "Party. . . . What I do is my business, I should think."

"Business" . . . an apt word, probably. No prizes, he thought, for guessing what business it was. He remembered now where he'd seen her type before. She was one of the kids who "worked on the railways."

"How old are you?"

"Eighteen." No hesitation.

"You have papers?"

"Papers?" Quick compression of the lips. Furtive, sideways movement of the eyes. "Lost them, haven't I? They were in my purse, along with fifty thousand rubles. Those bastards took them, the ones that trashed the apartment."

Not bad, he thought. Not bad as a spur-of-the-moment invention, but not even close to convincing.

"You told me you went out to buy food. You went out to buy it without your purse? What were you planning to use for money?"

A shrug. No other answer.

She could, of course, have been planning to shop, as the phrase went, "without money." For some of these kids it was a way of life, the only one open to them. The matter of her papers, in any case, could be cleared up later.

"What did you think had happened to him? Didn't it occur to you to wonder why, in more than a week, your Volodya didn't come home?"

"He wasn't my Volodya." Again the inevitable shrug. "I didn't think much about it. I reckoned maybe he'd gotten into a mess, pissed someone off, decided to take a vacation. He did that once before, you know. Took off for three weeks without saying a word. When he came back, he said he'd been in America. I figured he was probably lying, but maybe he wasn't. He brought me this T-shirt."

"You didn't think to call the Militia?"

She looked at him as if he'd lost his senses.

"He wouldn't have thanked me. He didn't like policemen. I don't much myself. No offense," she added, grinning.

The grin, animating her features, revealed what an attractive child she was. Sokolnikov, resuming his speculations as to what she might be wearing under the T-shirt, had to force his mind back to the business at hand.

"You weren't afraid they'd come back?"

" 'They'?"

"Whoever trashed the apartment."

"Why would they bother? Either they found it or they didn't."

" 'It'?"

"Whatever they were looking for."

"Whatever they were looking for"? Now, that made more sense. The criminal mind was irrational, of course, but the notion of taking revenge on a corpse might give even a lunatic pause. Searching, on the other hand, could explain their concealing the victim's ID.

"I thought you figured they were trashing the place. You thought he pissed someone off, you said. That was why they messed it around."

"Did I?"

In the pause that followed, her mask of indifference seemed to him to have slipped just a little, revealing, not anxiety perhaps, but calculation, a mind working harder than it ought to have been.

"Then I must have gotten it wrong, mustn't I?" She shrugged. Avoiding his gaze, she let her own wander around the apartment. "Trashing. Looking. What's the difference? Either way, they did a thorough job."

He let it go. He could always return to it later.

"What can you tell me about him, this Grigoriev?"

"Volodya? Don't know a thing." Instant resumption of the great stone face. "Hardly ever saw him, did I?"

"But according to you, you shared this apartment with him."

"Doesn't mean I have to know about him. I wasn't writing his biography, was I?"

"You must know something," Sokolnikov insisted. "What he did for a living, for instance."

"Don't know. Never asked. Most people," she added meaningfully, "don't like people asking them bunches of questions, especially questions that are none of their business."

Sokolnikov let that go, too. He didn't bother to point out that, since her former landlord had been murdered, this emphatically was the Militia's business. She wasn't telling the truth, of course, and equally clearly, she wasn't about to. Not that this meant very much, necessarily—she belonged to that majority of Russians for whom lying to the police came as naturally as breathing—but she'd fallen into what he recognized as the classic stonewaller's rhythm, intoning her responses in an obstinate singsong and phrasing them, where possible, as questions. Here, on her own ground, she was growing more relaxed by the minute. If he wanted anything out of her, he would have to get her onto his.

"Get some clothes on. I'm taking you in."

"Arresting me? What for?" If the outrage was simulated, the anxiety wasn't. "You can't. You don't have a warrant."

"Don't need one. I'm taking you in on suspicion."

"Suspicion of what?" Belligerent now. "What crime am I s'posed to have committed?"

"Delinquency . . . truancy . . . trespassing . . . breaking and entering." He shrugged. "Take your pick. While you're deciding," he added, "you can be getting your clothes on."

135

She didn't move.

"Breaking and entering? To take a nap? That's bullshit and you know it. So's trespassing. I've been living here for months, haven't I? I can show you my key."

"You say you've been living here. As for the key, how do I know you didn't steal it?"

She still didn't move, just stood there defiantly, head back and slightly to one side, eyes narrowed suspiciously, appraising. Then she smiled.

"Oh, you know." Broadening, the smile became conspiratorial, knowing. "And we both know what you want."

Before he could reply, she had taken off the T-shirt.

She was wearing nothing under it, and her body, child-woman's, was slender and perfect. Skin like ivory, breasts and hips half formed but rounded, nipples erect and delicate like rosebuds. Sokolnikov was jolted by a spasm of lust. He'd been offered bribes before, but nothing that had tempted him much. This seemed to hit directly in the prostate. . . . Well, at least—the thought helped him master himself—this settled the issue of the T-shirt.

"Get dressed," he said. "I'm not that kind of policeman."

"Aren't you?" She slid her hand between her legs, drew it up through the nest of pubic hair, middle finger parting the labia. "I didn't know there was another kind."

It was the stuff of fantasy made real. Sex pure and simple. Sex without tears. No complications, preliminaries, consequences. Absurdly easy, and it wouldn't change a thing. He could fuck her, *then* take her in. She wouldn't dare complain, and if she did, no one would believe her. In any case, no one would care. She was at his disposal, and the knowledge inflamed him. But then, by some odd lateral mind shift, Cassandra Wolfe invaded his thoughts. He imagined her watching him, despising. It was not, he assured himself, that he gave a bent kopeck for her good opinion; he just didn't care to earn her—anyone's—contempt. Whatever she and this little slut might think, there was more than one kind of policeman in Moscow.

"Get dressed." He said it roughly. Then, more gently, "Do your parents know where you are?"

She looked at him, her gaze a mixture of amusement and scorn.

"My parents? . . . Like they give a shit."

136

"I'm legally obliged to inform them," he said. "If you're underage, which I think you are."

"Best of luck finding them." She shrugged. "My mom died, and as for my dad . . . last I heard he was in Piatigorsk."

"Don't you have his address? A phone number, maybe?"

She shook her head vehemently.

"Screw him," she said. "Which I didn't, in case you're wondering."

"I wasn't." He shrugged. "Let's get going, shall we?"

She still didn't move.

"Think about this," she said. "I can go with you to headquarters or wherever, and you can ask me a bunch of dumbshit questions. But I can tell you now I won't know the answers. Then, after a day or two, you'll have to let me go. Or"—she paused—"you can save us both a bunch of time and trouble and skip right over to the last part—with or without the fuck," she added. "The offer's still open, but either way you won't hurt my feelings."

He shook his head. There was something appealing about her, and it wasn't simply her body; something tough, even healthy, in the practical way—no whining or self-pity—she'd attempted to deal with her current predicament. She would go a long way in life, he thought, if she made it through adolescence.

"The time and trouble I'm paid for," he told her. "What's so urgent in your young life that you can't take time out today to assist me in my inquiries?"

"What's so urgent? Use your head, Lieutenant."

When he didn't answer, she rolled her eyes.

"Let's say I've got a train to catch."

Chapter Sixteen

For cass the most uncomfortable result of her father's unwelcome revelations was the change it wrought in her relations with her uncle. To be more precise, since it was Josie she corresponded with these days, Hal being far too busy campaigning to do more than append an occasional brief message to his wife's communications, what had happened was that the change in her perceptions of Hal had placed a constraint on her relations with Josie. She hadn't wanted her perceptions of Hal to change—indeed, she had struggled not to let them— but the sad fact was that suspicion, once licensed to speak, was almost impossible to silence. When she thought about it, she didn't believe for a second that Hal was capable of betraying his country. But merely conceiving the possibility, the fact that she'd been *obliged* to think about it, robbed her bright image of him of a little of its luster. And since she couldn't, obviously, share with Hal's wife anything of what Nick had told her, she found herself, for the first time since her mother had died and just when she needed it most, without anyone to confide in. What made things worse was that Josie seemed to have sensed the constraint. This much was clear from her latest tape, which (her handwriting being no longer up to letters) had arrived by Federal Express this morning and which Cass, Tatyana having gone out early, played over on her boom box while eating a solitary breakfast.

> My Darling,
>
> Am I mistaken, or is your father's visit not going well? I ask because in your most recent letter you struck me as rather avoiding the subject. Or perhaps what I got was more the feeling that certain blanks had been left. You told me he'd arrived, of course, that you'd met him at

the airport and seen him "once or twice" since, that your roommate Tatyana seemed to be very much taken with him—what distinguished company *she* finds herself in—but apart from that, a conspicuous silence. Not a word, I observe, about *you* and him.

Have you two spoken at all? Really spoken, I mean. . . . If not, I think you need to, my love, and I'm afraid it will have to be at your initiative. While his claim of being sent there at his editor's insistence strikes me as a rather transparent fiction, I'm sure *he* believes his mere presence says everything that needs to be said. Men like Nick—I've found this to be true of surprisingly many professional writers—tend to be distrustful of words. They do, believe it or not, have feelings, but they seem to regard this fact (not to mention the feelings themselves) as self-evident and therefore in no need of discussion.

But you two do need to talk, you know, and for your sake as much as for his. It wouldn't be so bad if he'd always been an absentee parent, if you'd never been particularly close, but the fact is you used to *adore* each other. I remember very well how Patsy used to ruefully complain that though she was the nurturing parent—the one who got you up, dressed you, fed you, went to school plays, suffered through PTA meetings, remembered the stocking stuffers at Christmas, rallied around with Band-Aids and hugs whenever you hurt yourself—Nick was the one who got most of the love. She used to complain you were "Daddy's girl" first and foremost, that at times she felt like a privileged upper servant, graciously permitted to assist and spectate at the father-daughter love-in. And though you haven't cared to admit it, at least not since the divorce, it was very much a two-way street—he loved you as much as you loved him. What happened afterward, I think, especially when Patsy died and you more or less broke off relations, was not that he stopped loving you, but simply that he no longer showed it. You seemed to have turned away from him, and men like Nick (your uncle is another; at times they're as similar as peas in a pod) are too stiff with pride to acknowledge they've been hurt. They just nod and grunt and act as though nothing can touch them. So if things ever are to be mended between you, it will have to be you who breaks the ice. He can't, you see. He thinks it would be weakness.

Playing this over, I can hear myself lecturing you—saying, moreover, nothing you haven't heard before. I can almost picture you rolling your eyes, the way you used to as a teenager when Dolly gave you grief about the state of your room: "Josie, pul-eease," I hear you mutter, "turn the record over, give me a break." Well, I will in a moment, but first I want to say this: You're actually very like him, you know. You're as proud as he is and damn near as stubborn. And things can get left unsaid too long. You may not get many more chances, I mean, and *somebody* has to make the first move. People—and you're no exception, my dear, much as you might like to think so—need every bit of love they can get. I'd hate to see happen between you and your father what happened between him and Hal.

This was followed by a pause; then, in Josie's driest tones:

And with *that* endeth the lecture.

Feeling the need to reflect for a moment, Cass switched off the machine.

What happened between him and Hal? It was clear that Josie didn't *know* what had happened. Otherwise, of course, she'd never have suggested the parallel. That she *could* suggest it, in an effort, precisely, to promote a reconciliation with Nick, was almost more irony than Cass could bear. Josie, she thought grimly, wouldn't speak quite so kindly if she heard what Nick was saying these days about Hal. But what was one to reply to all this? Some platitude about wounds too deep to be healed? Some wise-ass feminist rebuttal of Josie's apparent assumption that peacemaker was properly the woman's role? The former, she thought, would be close to dishonest, the latter gratuitous and pert. . . . She wondered what would happen if she took the suggestion, if she said to Nick, "Look, let's sit down and talk out our problems." Probably nothing, she thought. Most likely he'd give her that look of his, as if she were threatening to be tiresome, and innocently ask her: "What problems?"

She switched the tape player back on.

Josie had taken a break, too, it seemed. No doubt she'd needed to. The voice that now issued from the machine, though still raspy and wavering occasionally, seemed stronger. Josie smoked like a chimney, of course, which didn't help matters any. Cass nagged her about it off and on, but not with much conviction. In Josie's case, as Josie herself pointed out, it didn't make a whole lot of sense to deny herself pleasure for the sake of her health.

The big news from here is more of the same: "The Reynolds Bandwagon rolls on." Since my last tape, as you probably know, Hal won the Wisconsin and Nebraska primaries. He hasn't lost a primary yet and, with more than two-thirds of them still to be held, he now has locked up about half the votes he needs for nomination. In a race with the president the polls have Hal leading, depending on who's doing the counting, by anywhere between twenty and thirty points, and according to the media, at least, the question isn't whether he'll win but by how large a margin. Things are starting to seem so one-sided that I'm feeling almost sorry for the president. I don't think even *he* believes he can win. The other day, at a press conference, some reporter with a doubtful sense of humor asked him what he expected to be doing after the election. The poor man put a brave face on things: He gave that lopsided country-boy grin of his and said he expected to be running the country. Everybody dutifully laughed, of course, but I think it was at him rather than with him.

I need hardly add that in spite of the foregoing, Hal is campaigning more or less nonstop. The convention's still two months and more away, the election more than six, and in that time, as he constantly points out, anything can happen. There's nothing more fickle than a voter, he says, so the worst thing he can possibly do is seem to take winning for granted. Actually, though he claims not to, I think he thoroughly enjoys the whole process. There's quite an element of the actor in my husband. The media have taken to calling him "Prince Hal," and I think that, like his Shakespearean namesake, he prides himself on having the "common touch"—going to barbecues and eating with his fingers, leaning on fence rails to debate the finer points of hogs, affecting to find in even the stupidest questions some serious underlying point. I'm not accusing him of insincerity; he never says what he doesn't believe, but he does rather play to his audience. They all do, of course, but he does it remarkably well. I sometimes suspect that he does it mostly for his own benefit, because he can and because it amuses him. I guess that's a sensible attitude to take—if you have to do it, you might as well try to enjoy it—but it strikes me as sad that he has to do it, especially since he's so clearly perfect for the job. I can hardly believe this traveling circus is precisely what the Founders had in mind.

Yours truly, of course, is for obvious reasons exempt. It's the only time in my life, I think, when I've been almost grateful for my affliction. I can usually muster enough energy to appear in the victory parades, but otherwise my duties are mostly shouldered by Dolly. She shoulders them, I may say, better than I ever could. If Hal, as the media keep insisting, is pretty much America's dream candidate, Dolly is America's dream candidate's dream mother. She seems to combine, someone recently said, the grace and charm of Rose Kennedy and the moral authority of Mother Teresa. We, who know her better, might consider this pitching it just a tad strong, but there's no denying her

141

appeal with the voters. She has an almost miraculous ability to make the tiredest of clichés seem profound. The other day she was on TV and the interviewer asked what made her proudest of her son, his political achievements or his Medal of Honor. She said it was not his achievements but his character; when the chips were down you could trust him to do what was right. The bit about character isn't inaccurate, of course, but, at least in these hypercynical times, it does tend to sound a bit corny. But when she says it you believe it, in part because you know she means every word. Hal declares she's his greatest asset, and following the lead of some journalist or other, has taken to calling her "the Dolly Factor," which he usually abbreviates to "the DF." "How's the DF doing this morning?" he asks her at breakfast, then proceeds to ply her with toast and cereal, insisting she needs to keep up her strength, at least for the duration of the campaign. Yesterday she threatened, if he didn't leave off, that she'd switch her endorsement to some other candidate. But hell will freeze over before that will happen. She's so proud of him she could burst.

Well, enough of *that*. . . . How are you doing, my darling? Is your research in those archives going well? I'm sure you're uncovering all sorts of fascinating secrets and that your dissertation will make your name. All the same, I wish you could come home. It gets lonely around here, with Hal gone so much, and I'd give my eyeteeth sometimes for a long, cozy chat with my favorite niece. Your letters are wonderful, of course, but no substitute for the real thing, and the Russian postal service is, to say the least, inconsistent. I think they must hold everything back until they have enough to fill a jumbo jet, for sometimes I get two or three letters in the same delivery, then nothing at all for weeks.

I'm afraid all this talking is tiring me out, so I'm going to have to bring this to a close. The trouble with recording machines is you have to know exactly what you want to say. I often don't know till I hear myself speak, and then it's usually not what I wanted to say, so I end up rewinding a lot and rerecording. You should try it sometime; it's not easy.

Anyhow, this will have to do for now. Hal sends his love, as does the Dolly Factor, and, of course, you know you have all of mine. And please, my love: Do talk to your father.

Chapter Seventeen

"Tatyana?" Nick stared. "You asked *Tatyana?*"

In the past ten days, in spite of Josie's urgings, Cass hadn't seen much of her father. This hadn't been altogether by choice; his time had been mostly taken up settling in to his assignment: getting a feel for the new democratic Russia, boning up on the political background, cultivating potential sources, "making his number," as he put it, "with the local movers and shakers." In this last endeavor, though her English was inferior to Cass's Russian, he had several times made use of a more than willing Tatyana. It was she he had asked to interpret, for instance, when he'd interviewed Zhirinovsky. Cass could have wished that, here at least, he had called on *her* to interpret, for the gentleman was in Nick's account "as crazy as a bedbug" and "the nastiest little vermin one has had the misfortune to encounter." Tatyana's version of the interview had been graphic and highly entertaining ("Your father is being *very* polite but looking all the time as if someone made a bad smell"), and the piece Nick later wrote was a small masterpiece of denigration, a portrait precisely and disdainfully drawn from the subject's own words and behavior. But if Cass was put out by her roommate's usurping a role she'd expected to be hers, she hadn't said so. Nor, since their original discussion, had she spoken with Nick about Dolokhov's tape. On this subject there seemed to be tacit agreement that, since positions were clearly staked out and nothing had happened to change them, discussion was pointless. In her case, silence had not meant inactivity; it was not her nature to wait for things to happen. But her effort to make things happen, it seemed, had earned her her father's disapproval.

"Why not Tatyana?" she demanded. "She's working on the official history, so she's perfectly placed to make inquiries. Granted, the subject's not exactly her period, but who would you suggest I ask?"

"Almost anyone *but* her." He sounded, it now struck Cass, not so much disapproving as worried. "She's known to be your roommate, isn't she? When she starts requesting documents she shouldn't need herself, you don't have to be a rocket scientist to figure out who she could be requesting them for." He frowned. "I don't think you understand what it is you've gotten into."

"Are you telling me you understand it?"

"I understand what seems to be escaping you. This Politburo tape your dead friend Dolokhov was trying to sell you—"

"*Alleged* Politburo tape," she cut him off. "At any rate, alleged discussion."

"It may not be alleged." Nick sounded weary. "Someone may have killed him to recover that tape. And you may just have let whoever killed him in on the fact that you're familiar with the contents." He paused. "Tell me, at least, that you didn't mention Oracle directly."

"I merely asked"—Cass was annoyed to find herself sounding defensive—"whether she could find out if the files for 1990 contained an assessment of the probable U.S. response to a Soviet invasion of the Baltic. I thought the answer might be revealing. If we learned, for instance, that there was no reporting, or none from sources considered authoritative, it would tend to indicate, wouldn't it, that Dolokhov's tape was a fake?"

"But of course." His voice was like chalk. "If it's not a fake, they're certainly going to *tell* us. They're willing to kill to plug this leak, but they'll happily release corroborating info to any stray historian who happens to inquire?"

Silence.

"What you're saying then"—she'd expected this but affected to think about it—"is that *if* the tape is real, the response to my inquiry is bound to be no?"

"Very acute." He nodded. "Go to the head of the class."

"So by that logic"—ignoring the sarcasm—"if the response isn't no, then the tape *must* be a fake?"

Silence.

He cocked his head, inspected her for a moment, amusement starting to glimmer in his eyes.

"This is a trap, isn't it? You set a trap, and I walked into it. You're about to tell me Tatyana came up with something."

"Very astute." She smiled sweetly. "Go to the head of the class. I'm not sure what to make of it exactly, but it sure as hell wasn't the absolute negative your logic would lead one to expect."

He rolled his eyes. "What was it, then?"

"An intelligence roundup from 1990. Subject: Probable U.S. responses to a Soviet invasion of the Baltic. Originally classified secret, it's culled from various unspecified sources and dated March fifth— one week prior, that is, to the Politburo meeting *allegedly* recorded on Dolokhov's tape." Cass paused. "So far, I'll grant you, nothing to build on. It's no doubt the kind of assessment the KGB was routinely called on to make. The conclusion, however, did rather grab my attention. It said—I quote verbatim—that in the event of an invasion, the United States *will yell murder but sit on their hands.*"

Silence.

"But that's the identical wording." Nick stared. "It's what Kryuchkov said on the tape."

She nodded, tried (but not very hard) to avoid looking smug.

"Did you see the document?"

"A photocopy." She shrugged. "It looked authentic, but then it would, wouldn't it? If the tape is authentic, on the other hand, then the people willing to kill Dolokhov to protect it would hardly be releasing corroborating documents to any stray historian who happened to ask."

"How did Tatyana get hold of this roundup?" He preferred to ignore, she noted, this use of his own arguments against him.

"She said she requested it in the normal manner."

"Which is?"

"You make a written subject request to the archivist. . . . Tatyana asked, in this instance, for all available material on, 'probable U.S. responses to a Russian invasion of the Baltic in 1990. They dug out what they had, ran it by the Declassification Committee, gave her what the committee told her they could."

"And this was everything they gave her? Nothing else?"

"Apparently." Cass nodded. "But it can't have been all they had. This was a roundup, remember, based on original sources, sources they apparently chose not to release." She paused. "If the bit about

145

the U.S. yelling murder, et cetera, had come from a source as valuable and sensitive as Oracle, they'd hardly have risked using it verbatim in the roundup, would they?"

Nick considered.

"You'd *think* not," he agreed, "but of course you'd be making assumptions. For one, that the Declassification Committee was paying proper attention. I gather it doesn't always. In the months after Yeltsin took over, I've heard, sensitive documents were released by the truckload. Stray cats were popping out of bags all over."

"Maybe then." Cass looked skeptical. "Not anymore. The *apparatchiks* are back in charge. Tatyana's always complaining to me that getting documents is like pulling teeth, especially from the First Chief Directorate. She says Colonel Schedrin works on the principle that anything historians want to see must, ipso facto, be something they shouldn't see."

"Schedrin?" Nick queried. "*Colonel* Schedrin?"

"That's right. Head of the FCD Declassification Committee."

"Given name Vladimir? . . . Patronymic Pavlovich?"

"I wouldn't know. Do I gather you're acquainted with a Vladimir Pavlovich?"

"By reputation." Nick nodded. "For most of the '80s, if memory serves, a Colonel Vladimir Pavlovich Schedrin was the KGB's resident in Bern."

"And?"

"Since the Bern resident controlled KGB operations for most of northern Europe, the man Oracle's case officer reported to would almost certainly have been him. . . . I don't know how common a name Schedrin is." Nick shrugged. "But it strikes me as unlikely that in 1984 there were two Colonel Schedrins in the First Chief Directorate."

"But wouldn't that make my case stronger?" Cass demanded. "If this is *that* Schedrin, he'd know about Oracle. And if Oracle were still active, he'd never have okayed the release of that roundup, would he?"

"Maybe not." Again Nick looked dubious. "But on the other hand, maybe. It's dangerous to argue on the basis of what you think others may be thinking. That kind of argument cuts both ways. As I pointed out, if Dolokhov's tape was genuine and the KGB killed him for it, they'd have to regard it as at least conceivable that before his death he confided the contents to you. On this assumption you could make the argument that, since their releasing the roundup suggests that the tape is a fake, and since *you* can be expected to make that deduction, what it actually suggests is the reverse."

Silence.

"Mickey Mouse." Cass rolled her eyes. "Humpty Dumpty thinking gone mad. If that's what passed for logic in the CIA, no wonder you screwed up so often. . . . The same set of facts supports contradictory conclusions?"

"The same *incomplete* set of facts," he corrected. "And isn't that almost always the problem, even in the groves of academe? You don't have enough facts to know what the ones you do have mean. Intelligence work, someone once said, is like diving for pearls in a sewer. It's next to impossible to know when you've got one, or even, usually, which way is up."

She considered this.

"If that's really the case, you wonder why anyone bothers. The billions devoted to gathering intelligence could better have been spent on cancer research."

"Not to mention"—he smiled—"the billions devoted to rewriting history."

She ignored this. What he'd argued made a certain sense. But so, by his logic, would almost any conclusion. It was clear the discussion was going nowhere. Perhaps it was time for another subject.

"You seemed bothered earlier by my asking Tatyana. Are you saying you don't trust her?"

He shook his head. "What I'm saying is that, if I don't have to, I'd rather not." He paused, then added: "On principle, you understand. No reflection on her."

She thought about this.

"Well, for someone you'd rather not trust, even on principle, you seem to be seeing her a lot."

His gaze was opaque. "Is that a question or a comment?"

"Maybe both." She shrugged. "I might have asked, since she's my close friend, what your intentions are toward her."

"And I might have said, had you done so"—he smiled—"that it was none of your goddamned business. Since you didn't, I will merely point out that the intentions here are not mine."

147

It was true, she thought. Tatyana had thrown herself at him from the start. Not that it made any difference. She hadn't noticed him trying to duck.

"You may have to screw her, in other words, just to be polite?"

"*Cass*"—he looked pained—"if I did, it wouldn't be to be polite . . . and screw wouldn't be the word I'd use."

He could use whatever word he liked, she thought. Screwing struck her as having precisely the right connotations.

"Would it bother you?" he pursued.

"Me?" she demanded. "Why would it bother me? Even if it did, why would you care? I can't see you arranging your sex life to suit my convenience. You never have before." She paused. "I'll confess to being a little apprehensive for Tatyana. I wouldn't want to see her hurt."

"Which she will be if she gets involved with me?"

"It's been known to happen. In my mother's case, to cite just one." She paused then, hearing herself and not liking it much. "I'm sorry, I don't mean to be a bitch. The subject seems to bring it out in me. Perhaps we should talk of something else."

"Some subject not off-limits? Can you think of one, offhand?"

"It's tough," she agreed. "All roads seem to lead to Rome."

"Then why not go where it seems one has to, in the end?"

Why go anywhere? . . . But she didn't say it. She'd been bitchy enough already.

"Look, Cass"—he hesitated, seemed to gather himself for a hurdle—"I wasn't sent here, I *asked* for this assignment. I asked because I wanted to see you. I wanted to patch things up between us. The last thing I had in mind was digging up the past, especially what happened in Brussels, but it seems I don't have a choice."

"All roads lead to *Brussels*, you mean?"

"Cass"—he sighed—"I'm trying to say something difficult for me. Do me a favor: Cut the wisecracks."

"I'm sorry. What were you trying to say?"

"I guess it's this: We'll get nowhere avoiding. Let's not have subjects off-limits. Whatever the issues between us are, let's face them. Otherwise we might as well not bother."

She could hardly believe what she was hearing. Could this be her father, that enclosed, private man? Could he really be issuing this plea for candor? It seemed he was. She was almost tempted—there was

148

something so appealingly simple about candor. If only, she thought, if only . . .

"We might as well not bother?" It was as if someone else were speaking, as if, till the words were out of her mouth, she didn't know what she was going to say. "I was under the impression you'd stopped bothering years ago."

He received this without flinching.

"I didn't do much to correct that impression, did I? . . . I was hoping"—he regarded her steadily—"you might let me do that now."

"But why?" she challenged. "Why now, after so many years? Belated stirrings of conscience?"

For a moment he looked at her without speaking, then he sighed.

"You know, Cass," he said wearily, "for a highly intelligent woman, sometimes you are amazingly dense."

Chapter Eighteen

"It's obvious," Tatyana said. "Simple: He was trying to tell you he loves you."

Simple? Cass doubted it. She regretted now what she'd said to Nick, blamed herself for not being more open. But things never were that simple, were they? You couldn't put wrongs right by talk.

"I don't believe it," she said. "And even if it's true, maybe I don't want to hear. Maybe I don't care anymore. Twelve years of absentee fatherhood can have that effect, you know."

"If you say so." Tatyana nodded, adding drily, "The twelve years, of course, were all his fault."

They *had* been his fault. Cass could still, without wanting to, recapture every detail of that day: the bone-white lilies; the grim, neo-Gothic interior of the chapel; the black dress and coat she had worn only once—they were still in mothballs in a trunk in Santa Barbara; the electric whine (which organ burble couldn't quite muffle) as the box slid away to its appointment with the fire. But the smell of the limousine was what always returned most vividly: that new-car scent (distinctive, expensive, a mixture of varnish and leather) that clung to the interior of the long, black Mercedes in which she and Nick had been driven from the chapel. Just the two of them, of course (as if they'd asked for the arrangement), just she and Nick in that congealing silence—a soundproof partition had cut them off from the driver—and for most of the journey they'd not even glanced at each other. "This is your fault," she had wanted to scream. "If you'd stayed, it wouldn't have happened." Maybe she should have, she thought. Maybe if they'd had it out, the wound, ransacked, cauterized by anger, might have had a chance to heal. But Nick wasn't a man you could have things out with. Despising "scenes," when he saw them coming, he withdrew. So instead, employing the polemics of subtext, she'd offered that silly, despairing gambit, laid herself open to his withering response.

"You're not being fair," she told Tatyana. "Granted, it was a stupid thing to say, but I was fourteen years old. Overwhelmed. My mother had just killed herself. He should have known I didn't mean it. . . ."

"Are you sure you didn't?" Tatyana's look was searching. "You were feeling anger. And guilt, you said. You wanted to punish him, I think. Yourself, too, of course."

Cass shrugged. "You may be right. But can you blame me?"

"Blaming is a great waste of time. That's what I've been trying to tell you." Tatyana paused. "But think for a moment how *he* must have felt—guilty, too, I'm sure. In the circumstances he could hardly not. And guilt embraces punishment as hurt embraces hurt. You offered him—perhaps you meant to—the completely appropriate penance."

There was probably truth here, Cass thought. But like most applications of pop psychology, it ignored as much as it explained. What tepid kind of love, for instance, would lay itself on the altar of guilt? . . . In any case, Tatyana was partial. What gave her the right to preach sermons?

"You seem to have it all figured out," she said. "And, in view of your brief acquaintance, to know him remarkably well."

Tatyana flushed.

"Ah, now you're being unkind and, forgive me for saying it, silly. Sometimes an outsider sees more clearly than a daughter with sand in her eyes." Encountering Cass's sardonic gaze, she met it with something like defiance. "I like him very much, your father. I would like to know him better."

"I've noticed," Cass said. "But I wouldn't be too eager. When you know him better, you may not like him so well."

"Cass"—Tatyana was startled—"how can you say such a thing?"

"I'm only trying to protect you," Cass said. "I've told you before. He breaks hearts. He'll charm you and take you to bed, but sooner or later he'll forget you."

"Is that so bad?" Tatyana looked at her sideways. "Worse things can happen to a woman my age than being charmed and taken to bed."

"Well"—Cass shrugged—"if you don't mind being used . . ."

151

"I happen not to see it that way." Tatyana's voice took on an edge. "I like to think it might be mutual. In any case"—she studied Cass intently—"is it me you're trying to protect?"

Cass pretended to consider. "I thought it was, but no doubt I'm wrong." Pausing, she added drily, "It's a thing I've noticed about amateur psychologists: They always know better than you what you're thinking."

Tatyana ignored this jab.

"Well, if it's me you're concerned for, thanks, but I'm willing to take my chances. Rather than dwell on what I could lose, I prefer to focus on what I could win." Tatyana paused. "Maybe you should focus on that. He's a fine man, your father. You won't find many better. And I may not know everything about him, but I know this"—she paused again—"he loves you."

Chapter Nineteen

IN THE RESTAURANT, Tatyana and Dima were still arguing. Tatyana and Dima were always arguing. They argued whenever they met. Dima liked to push people's buttons, and since Tatyana was passionate about practically everything, hers were very easy to push. The button this time had been the state of her apartment, in which she, Cass, Nick, and Dima had gathered for a predinner drink. More precisely, it had been the hobby responsible for the state of the apartment, the fact that except in Cass's bedroom and the bathroom, the place, which by Moscow standards was roomy (two decent-size bedrooms, dining room *cum* living room, bath and kitchen), resembled the nest of a scholarly pack rat, almost every available flat surface being occupied by piles of books or papers. The books were mostly journals and photograph albums, the papers mostly magazines and letters. There were also boxes, labeled by year since 1917 and stuffed with what the unenlightened might have taken for junk (restaurant menus, posters, proclamations, programs for the Bolshoi or the Kirov) but was actually the raw material of Tatyana's hobby. This—it struck Cass as more of an obsession—was to chronicle the fortunes of Tatyana's family (parents, grandparents, aunts, uncles, cousins) from earliest days of the Russian Revolution to its sudden end in 1991. What Tatyana hoped to achieve, as she'd several times tried to explain to Dima, was a kind of social history in miniature, a long-term study of the impact of the Soviet state on the fortunes of an average Russian family. Dima, predictably, had poured cold water on the notion. Since many of them had belonged to the *nomenklatura*, Tatyana's family, he'd observed, struck him as a long way from average. In any case, who cared about the average Russian family? Or the Soviet state, for that matter? The

Soviet state was as dead as a board and good riddance. The future was what mattered. Dima agreed with Henry Ford: History was bunk. Or to be more precise—here he'd paused, glancing sardonically around the apartment—junk.

The evening had gone downhill from there.

"But history"—this made the fourth or fifth time by Cass's count that Tatyana had made the assertion—"*starts* there, at the level of the family."

She shot Cass a defiant look, challenging disagreement. Cass didn't know if she disagreed or not, mostly because she didn't care. At the time it had seemed a good idea to accept Dima's dinner invitation. For one thing, she wanted to ask him about Dolokhov. For another, she'd thought the presence of others would keep the contact with her father formal, buffer the awkwardness that, after their previous encounter, both of them were likely to be feeling. Now she wasn't so sure. Maybe it would have been better to spend time alone with him. Maybe the presence of Tatyana and Dima was making her feel more awkward, because, as she knew, hostilities between her and Nick had merely been suspended, would resume when the others were out of the way. But whatever the reason, she felt on edge. She wished Dima and Tatyana would quit sniping at each other.

"Don't you think so, Cass?" Tatyana demanded. "Don't you agree it starts with the family?"

"I'm not at all sure what that means." Cass tried to give it her attention. "Does it mean, for instance, that if Stalin's mother had cuddled him more as a baby, if his father hadn't been such a drunk, then the gulag might never have happened?"

As she heard herself say it, saw the flicker of hurt in Tatyana's eyes, she knew it had come out wrong, not at all the way she had meant it. Worse, it had sounded as if she were siding with Dima. She knew Tatyana didn't like Dima, didn't much like it that *she* liked Dima, had accepted tonight's invitation, most probably, only because Nick would be present. She knew also that the current quarrel with Dima, though fought ostensibly on the narrow grounds of Tatyana's fixation on her family's history, was not just current and not just a quarrel but actually antipathy total and abiding. Tatyana's view of her country's history was moral. She believed Russia's past must be redeemed, the record set straight, people called to account. Dima, on the other hand, acted as if the past had never happened; as if, on that day in August 1991 when at last it was clear that the coup had failed and the Soviet state was dead and about to be buried, the past had vanished down some rabbit hole or other and Russia had been instantly reconstituted as a kind of scummy, used-car salesman's Eden into which he, Dima, had stepped apparently from nowhere, brandishing fistfuls of black market dollars and ready to set about wheeling and dealing. Which went a long way to explaining, of course, why Tatyana viewed him as "a little gangster, probably ex-KGB." And though she was stretching it too far, Cass thought, to some extent Tatyana had a point. On the subject of his origins, Dima was amusing but vague. "You could call me," he'd say, "stepchild of *perestroika*." He'd contrived to be equally amusing and vague in response to Nick's question about what he did: "I help the money get where it needs to go . . . most of it"—yelp of high-pitched laughter—"into my pocket." It made the joke better that in English, which in deference to Nick's halting Russian they were speaking this evening, he pronounced the word "pocket" as "p*a*cket."

"Easy to sneer." Tatyana sniffed. "If you make it too simple, anything sounds stupid. Why not something even more foolish: 'History starts with Adam and Eve'?" She wagged an admonitory finger at Cass and assumed a look of schoolmarmish severity, disguising hurt by converting it to theater. "Understand, please, before you mock."

"I'm sorry." Cass was contrite. "I didn't mean to. I'm feeling a little distracted tonight."

"Actually," Dima said, continuing to stir things up, "Adam and Eve would be close to the truth. Only one generation away at least. I think it begins with Cain and Abel."

"With some boy murdering another?" Tatyana looked pained. "Excuse me, Dmitri Petrovich, but what do you know, with your stocks and bonds, your futures contracts, your finder's fees and commissions, your champagne and caviar? What do you know about history?"

"Well, not where it starts, perhaps, but where it starts to get interesting." Dima grinned. "People raising kids, growing old, dying . . . show me the entertainment in that. Tolstoy said it best, I think: 'Happy families are all alike.' All alike and all boring. . . . It's when people start stealing each other's land, screwing each other's wives,

155

shooting each other in the head, that's when they capture our attention."

"In cheap novels maybe, not history." Tatyana sniffed. "Not Tolstoy either, as you'd know if you'd ever read him." Dismissing him, she turned back to Cass. "Actually, your example was not bad. A lot of what happens in the world, I believe, results from what happens between mothers and sons."

Or perhaps between fathers and daughters. Cass glanced at Nick, wondered if the thought had struck him. His eyes met hers, but they and his face were expressionless. Same old poker face, she thought; the same imperturbable, stoic mask with which he'd confronted her rebuff of yesterday, a suppression of feeling so seemingly effortless you wondered, in spite of Tatyana's assertions to the contrary, if it really was suppression.

"Mothers and sons, my God." Dima rolled his eyes. "You Russian historians are going backward. Now that Marx is out of date, you're falling back on Freud?"

"Don't be so quick to get rid of Marx," Tatyana retorted. "He still has useful things to teach us. For example, Dmitri Petrovich, I find he explains people like you perfectly." She turned to Nick. "Wouldn't you say so, Nick?"

Nick smiled. "I'm afraid I don't know enough to offer an opinion. Either about Marx or Mr. Kuznetsov."

Tatyana looked over at Cass. "Your father is a diplomat, I find. It is not a respectable profession." Turning back to Nick, she gave him a reproachful look. "Watch out, Mr. Nick. I may start to call you Nicholas, like your mother."

Time for a change of subject, Cass thought. Away from history and away from Nick. She turned to Dima.

"What can you tell me about your friend Vladimir Dolokhov?"

"Vladimir Dolokhov? My *friend?*" His face was a blank. "I have no friend of that name."

"Acquaintance, then. He was at your party. You must know the one I mean," Cass added disingenuously. "I'm sure I must have mentioned him to you before. He's the man I found shot at Novodevichy Convent."

She hadn't mentioned him. So Dima, of course, now demanded a detailed recitation of the facts. She was careful not to tell him any more than she'd told the police. It was not that she distrusted, especially. She certainly trusted him more than she trusted Arthur Quine. It simply seemed wiser, and safer, not to trust anyone she didn't have to.

Having heard her account, Dima persisted in disclaiming all knowledge.

"Never heard of him," he said. "So I can't have invited him to my party."

"Nevertheless, he was there."

"My dear Cassandra"—Dima threw up his hands—"consider where you are. This is Moscow, capital city of shortages. . . . There was free food, free music, free champagne. Half the people there were not invited."

"Could you find out who he was?"

He inspected her for a moment, quizzically. "I think it might not be a good idea."

"But could you, if I asked you to?"

He cocked his head to one side, considering. "The name was Dolokhov? Vladimir Dolokhov? A small man, you say? Dark hair, dark eyes, wore a fancy overcoat several sizes too large?"

She nodded.

"Then perhaps I could. I could make inquiries, at least. The thing is"—he paused—"are you sure you want me to?"

"Why wouldn't I?" She stared. "I mean, the man was murdered. He arranged to meet me to show me something, something he claimed would interest me as a historian, and when I showed up, someone had killed him. In the circumstances, wouldn't *you* be curious?"

"Extremely." He smiled. "But my curiosity would be tempered by caution. I might be thanking my guardian angel I hadn't shown up early for that meeting. And I think that in view of the fact that someone shot him, I might very well decide to forget all about him. I don't know who he is, or was, but I do know one thing." Dima paused. "He had some dangerous enemies."

"You mean because he was shot?"

"I mean because of *how* he was shot. I don't think this was a casual mugging. He was shot in the middle of the forehead, you said, by a small-caliber pistol, evidently silenced?"

"That was what I was told by the police."

"Sounds to me like professional work." Dima paused. "Mafia. Or worse."

"Worse?" It was Nick who inquired. "You mean the KGB?"

"Current or former." Dima nodded. "Which, given the timing, might seem to suggest that this man was murdered to prevent him from showing you whatever he'd planned to show you. Also to discourage you from pursuing the matter."

"And you think," Cass pursued, "that if *you* start making inquiries, he, or they, or whoever they are, will conclude that I haven't been discouraged?"

"It's conceivable." Dima nodded. "It's not a risk I would want you to take."

"Or a risk that you would want to take?"

"That, too"—he grinned—"though I have friends who have friends. . . . I doubt there would be much risk to me." He paused. "Do I get the impression that your interest in this Dolokhov is more than casual?"

"I don't know." She pretended to think. It was not an impression she wanted him to get, but where else was she to start finding out about Dolokhov? "Perhaps curiosity joined to the fact that I don't much like being threatened."

"Ah . . ." He smiled. "You don't like to be threatened. Very commendable, very American. But allow me to inform you, please, that this is not Connecticut. Here the Mafia do what they like; the Militia are powerless to prevent them." He paused. "Forgive me if I seem too blunt, but I think you believe that because you have money, because your family is powerful in America, the Mafia will hesitate to harm you. If so, I must tell you you're mistaken—"

"For once I agree," Tatyana cut in. "For once you should listen to Dmitri Petrovich. . . . When it comes to the Mafia and crime," she added darkly, "he knows what he is talking about."

Dima grinned. "Tatyana Nicolaieva is always so flattering."

"If I ask you, *will* you do it?" Ignoring Tatyana, Cass addressed herself to Dima.

"If you ask"—he shrugged—"I will do what I can. But unwillingly, you understand, because what you ask is foolish and dangerous."

"I'd be grateful." Cass smiled at him. "Because otherwise, you understand, I'll have to do it myself."

He turned to Nick. "Mr. Wolfe, I appeal to you. Have you no influence with your daughter?"

"None whatever." Nick shook his head. "She does what she wants. She has for years."

"In that case I will do as you ask." Dima turned back to Cass. "But only, you understand, because this way there's less danger for you. And very much I hope to learn," he added, "that this is Mafia business, not KGB. The Mafia are bad enough, but the KGB . . . those guys are murder."

* * *

"ENTERTAINING FELLOW."

The comment was Nick's. After dinner, for which he'd insisted on paying, Dima had excused himself on grounds of pressing business. The others had returned to Tatyana's apartment.

"And very solicitous of you, I notice."

The question hovering behind this comment had from time to time occurred to Cass herself. From their first meeting, just after her arrival, Dima had wined and dined her two or three times a month. Amusing and lavishly hospitable, he'd so far expected nothing in return but the pleasure of her company and perhaps the prestige among his circle of acquaintance (where trophy women were more or less the rule) of having in tow a blond American, fifteen years younger and six inches taller than he, and not obviously—she told herself quite obviously *not*—a hooker. Her own expectations were less clearly defined. He amused her, introduced her to circles that otherwise might have been closed, offered her, so to speak, a shark's-eye view of the waters he cruised, but her feelings for him otherwise were clouded by uncertainty as to who he really was. . . . He couldn't just be a predator—could he?—a bundle of reflexes linked to a relentless appetite. He was also articulate, detached, sardonic; a shark, at least, who had *chosen* to be one, selecting that role from the several available and ruefully amused by his performance in it. At any rate, she thought, he made a change from the graduate students and associate professors who normally fell to her lot.

"He's just a friend." She met her father's query with a shrug. "I thought you might find him entertaining. Your letter said you wanted to meet movers and shakers, not just the usual diplomats and officials.

Dima qualifies on both counts, I'd say. He's certainly not part of the cocktail party circuit. What exactly he does I've never understood, but since Yeltsin took over, Dima seems to have made a pile of money. I think he's one of those instinctive businessmen, someone who knows how to fish in troubled waters." She paused. "Tatyana doesn't approve of him much."

"Approve of him, never." Tatyana tossed her head. "To Cassandra he seems fun, but I think he is dangerous. He invites her to dinner, to Bolshoi, to parties. Always he is laughing, joking, spending money. But this money is money he steals. He makes it exploiting weakness in others. Now he is merely gangster, but before"—she paused—"before, he was Chekist, I think."

"KGB?" Cass laughed. "Tatyana, how can you possibly say so? Have you a scrap of evidence?"

"Evidence? No . . . but I live my whole life with those people. I have—how d'you say?—a feeling about him. You, my Cass, do not understand. You speak our language, but you do not have our history in your soul. When you live your whole life among these people"—Tatyana tapped her nose, then continued darkly—"you learn to recognize the smell."

Chapter Twenty

"So, Lieutenant . . ." General Rev leaned back in his chair. He seemed in a good mood, Sokolnikov thought; the appraising stare was sardonic but also genial. "What can I do for you?"

"The general will recall that he asked to be kept personally informed about the murder occurring last week at Novodevichy Convent."

"Ah, yes. That murder." That the show of recollection was a show was evidenced by the follow-up. "Do I gather that, at last, you've made progress in a *positive* way?"

Sokolnikov, tempted to respond to that "at last" by pointing out that for three days last week the Criminal Division's computer had been down, frustrating his attempts to match the victim's fingerprints, managed to resist the temptation. The general might think he was making excuses or, worse, reproaching him for the failure. Computers down were a fact of life, like understaffing or shortages of paper clips. Indeed, the propensity of computers—at any rate, Russian computers—to be down far more than they were up was so well known as hardly to be worthy of comment. It was best regarded as a property of the machines, one culturally induced, no doubt, an inherent and besetting moodiness. In this case, moreover, the computer's indisposition had probably been serendipitous. Had it not been down, he might not have chanced upon Olyenka.

Not that the little slut was helping very much.

"I believe we've made some progress, General. Two days ago, for the first time in almost a week"—he found himself unable to resist this sidelong "at last" of his own—"we were able to access the division's computer to search for a fingerprint match. . . . It seems the victim's

161

name was actually Grigoriev, not Dolokhov, as he told the American woman."

"He was in the computer? Had a criminal record?"

"Not exactly criminal, General. Nothing proven, that is. He was arrested, once, in November of 1989, charged with blackmail and extortion. The charges had to be dropped, however. The victims proved unwilling to testify."

"Unwilling . . . you mean intimidated." Not a question. Everyone familiar with police work here knew what "unwilling to testify" meant.

"It would seem so, General."

"Grigoriev was Mafia, then?"

"More a franchisee, I think. He put the scam together, I'd guess, but ran it under Mafia protection." Sokolnikov paused. "The Mafia wasn't his only connection. He also had links to the KGB."

"KGB links?" The general's eyebrows shot up. "What kind of links?"

"He worked for them," Sokolnikov said. "Used to, at any rate."

"The KGB." The general frowned thoughtfully. "Second Chief Directorate, I expect. Absconded with an armful of surveillance reports, used the contents for blackmail and extortion."

Superior in need of respectful correction. A formula existed for this situation. Sokolnikov employed it.

"That would have been my conclusion, General. It's certainly consistent with the record of extortion. But in fact he was employed by Yasenevo."

"A spook?" The general seemed surprised. Surprised and, as far as he was capable, impressed. "How were you able to establish *that?*"

"I asked them. Actually, I sent them a fax. I thought they might find it more persuasive." Sokolnikov allowed himself a grin; he was proud of the fax idea. "In due course I got this in reply."

Opening his briefcase, he extracted a paper, passed it across the desk. The general held it gingerly between forefinger and thumb, at arm's length, as if it might carry a contagious disease. Frowning and squinting, he read aloud the four terse sentences of text.

" 'Grigoriev, V. A. Employed FCD September 1974. Postings: European various. Resigned May 1985.' " He paused, inspecting Sokolnikov over the top of his glasses. "I don't call this wildly informative."

"Nor I, General. However"—Sokolnikov paused—"it seems to have told us more than it should."

He produced a second fax from his briefcase. Compared to the other, it was almost loquacious.

"This arrived about two hours later: 'Re your inquiry,' reference blah-blah, 'regret to inform you our previous reference in error. Subject Grigoriev, V. A., misidentified due to clerical confusion. Records list no such officer employed any time FCD.'"

Sokolnikov handed the fax across the desk. The general glanced at it, placed it on top of the other.

"Do I gather you place no reliance on this?"

Sokolnikov shook his head. "Since my inquiry included a photograph, 'clerical confusion' strikes me as unlikely. . . . Clearly whoever responded at first discovered that he shouldn't have and attempted, clumsily, to correct his error." He shrugged. "One wonders why he bothered. Covering his ass, I suppose."

"Lieutenant Sokolnikov"—the general's voice was stern—"I am going to tell you something I very much hope you will heed. In regard to the former First Chief Directorate, the word 'clearly' is one I would shrink from employing. Nothing those people do is clear. Nor, in my experience, are they apt to be clumsy."

"I see, General." Sokolnikov accepted the rebuke stone-faced. "You mean they may want to give the impression of not wanting their connection with Grigoriev known?"

"I mean"—the words were articulated coldly, dropped into the silence like pebbles down a well—"that I wouldn't care to speculate, one way or the other. I wouldn't advise you to either."

Protracted pause.

"Have you anything further to report, Lieutenant?"

Sokolnikov nodded. "The general may recall that when the murder was reported, the victim's wallet and personal papers were missing. My guess was that the killer had taken them in the hope of delaying identification of the victim. Developments suggest that my guess was correct."

"Developments? What developments?"

"Well, General, having matched the victim's fingerprints, we were able to obtain his address, an apartment building in Tyoply Stan. I

163

went there hoping to find someone who could tell us about him—a friend or family member, possibly a wife."

"A wife?" The general looked sceptical. "Men like that don't have wives. Not wives that they live with, at least."

Men like that . . . It occurred to Sokolnikov that the general had arrived rather quickly, and with virtually nothing to go on, at a very shrewd assessment of the victim's character. Men like that? Was there a type, familiar to the general? Was a former spook, dealer in stolen documents, prowler on the fringes of the Mafia, necessarily, by some rule of psychology, a man of irregular sexual morality? Or did the general, as he'd shown once before, know more about this case than he wished to admit? Sokolnikov, asking once again the question he'd asked himself the last time he'd spoken to the general, was just as much at a loss for an answer. For while his superior's original interest in this matter was explained by the U.S. ambassador's call to the ministry, what could account for his continuing interest?

"The general is extremely acute. The young person I found living in Grigoriev's apartment was quite obviously not his wife. She gave her name as Olga Vorontsova. Six months ago, as I learned when I checked, she was convicted of soliciting for immoral purposes at the St. Petersburg Station." Sokolnikov paused. "At the time she was not quite fourteen years old."

"A child prostitute?" The general frowned. "This Grigoriev was living with her?"

"He was, although," Sokolnikov qualified, "she claims not in the sense one would suppose. She said it was purely a business arrangement. He gave her daytime use of the apartment. In return, she paid a share of the rent. She hardly ever saw him, she said, because he was seldom around in the daytime. She, of course, was working nights."

"Working nights." The general rolled his eyes. "But how? Without anywhere to go, I mean. Where does she take her customers? Hotels?"

"They take the train," Sokolnikov explained. "In her case the overnight express to St. Petersburg. The man rents a sleeper and buys her a ticket. A similar arrangement brings her back."

"An instructive example of free enterprise in action." The general's voice was edged with distaste. "A fitting advertisement for the present regime. It makes one yearn for the days of order. However"—he paused, eyeing Sokolnikov severely, as if the problem were entirely his

164

fault—"we seem to have wandered from the point. I don't see how finding this slut in the victim's apartment confirms your theory about why his papers were stolen."

"Because the apartment had been wrecked," Sokolnikov explained. "And according to the girl, just hours after the murder. I believe what happened was actually a search. The theft of the victim's papers, delaying our ID of the body and hence our arrival at the apartment, gave the killer time to conduct it."

"Any evidence supporting this theory?"

"The timing, for one thing. Further support is given, I think, by statements made by the girl."

He gave the general an edited account of his encounter with Olyenka. The general thought for a while.

"Assuming I buy your theory," he said, "what do you think they were searching for?"

Sokolnikov hesitated.

"I'm not sure; perhaps the tape that the American, Miss Wolfe, claims Grigoriev offered to sell her."

"But wouldn't he have taken it to their meeting? If there really was a tape, and if it was why they were meeting."

"Certainly, General. But I was thinking of other copies. If, as you say, the American's story is true, I doubt he'd have sold her his only copy."

"If . . . if . . . if." The general made a gesture of impatience. "It seems to me, Lieutenant, that your so-called progress is mostly speculation, based loosely on the testimony of two female witnesses, both of whom are in your view unreliable." He paused. "This little prostitute, for instance. Did she give you any concrete reason for thinking the apartment had been searched?"

"Concrete? No." Sokolnikov shook his head. "She claims to believe it was wrecked for revenge. The suggestion that it might have been searched was, I think, a slip of the tongue. She certainly withdrew it as soon as she'd made it. I got the impression she was withholding something, knew a whole lot more than she admitted. I'd hoped a night in the cells might shake her, but she's cool as an icicle, that one, and as slippery. . . . I really can't hold her much longer," he added. "We can't charge her with trespass. Nobody's laid a complaint."

For some moments the general said nothing. His attention seemed to wander to the faxes on the desk. He picked one up, peered at it incuriously, put it down again. He leaned back in his chair and gazed at the ceiling. Finally he spoke:

"Lieutenant, I'm taking you off this case."

He inspected Sokolnikov for a reaction. Sokolnikov produced none. The general continued:

"This is not, I wish you to understand, because I disapprove of how you've handled it thus far, or because I doubt your ability or commitment. On the contrary, I wish to see them better employed." He paused, fixed Sokolnikov with his gaze. "I believe you will get nowhere with this case. Clearly our friends in Yasenevo are involved. And equally clearly"—he gestured at the faxes—"they intend you to get nowhere. I have few enough good men as it is. I can't have them wasting their time. However," he added with a smile, "when this interview is over, which is now, I will send for your personnel file and record in it my approval of the way you've conducted this inquiry."

"The general is very kind." Sokolnikov's relief and pleasure didn't quite make up for his disappointment. He could crack this case, he knew he could. Yasenevo or no Yasenevo, given time and just a little luck, he could crack it. "There is just one more thing, however . . ."

"Yes, Lieutenant?"

"The American woman, General, she telephoned me yesterday."

"She phoned you?" The general raised his eyebrows. "She wished to add to her testimony?"

Sokolnikov shook his head. "She called to ask how the case was progressing."

"So naturally you told her you weren't able to comment."

"Naturally, General."

"Perfectly proper. And yet"—the general's gaze wandered around the room—"and yet our colleagues in the Foreign Ministry would argue that, in this particular instance—in view, that is, of Miss Wolfe's family connections—the interests of the state might be better served by candor."

"The general is authorizing me to discuss the case?"

"I think it might be more accurate to say"—the general's expression was perfectly neutral—"that the general is instructing you to discuss it."

"Will the general be putting these instructions in writing?"

Pause while the general inspected his subordinate's features for impertinence. Finding none, he smiled faintly.

"No, Lieutenant, the general will not."

"Very good, General." Sokolnikov kept his face a blank. "Is there anything you wish me to withhold?"

"I don't believe so." The general thought for a moment. "I think you should tell her exactly what you've told me."

*　*　*

WHEN SOKOLNIKOV HAD LEFT, General Rev called for his file, then sat for a moment, thinking back on the interview. On the whole, it had gone very well. Sokolnikov was clearly dutiful and able, but equally clearly, he was not very devious. In attempting to obey his instructions to the letter he would, without meaning to, exceed them. His instructions, indeed, were so irregular he would hardly be able to obey without conveying, in the process, how very irregular he found them. Which, of course, was the object of the exercise.

They had asked for obfuscation. They had gotten it.

Chapter Twenty-One

CASS HADN'T VISITED Dima's office before. It was, she thought, looking around, instructive. Along with the usual status symbols—the spaciousness, Afghan rugs, massive desk in some blond wood or other, telephones in three different colors, desktop computer, fax machine, well-stocked bar, glass-top coffee table strewn with newspapers and magazines in four or five languages and surrounded by armchairs in squishy beige leather, receptionist whose extravagant nails proclaimed that whatever her duties might be (beyond making coffee and looking gorgeous) typing was not among them—along with all this standard equipment were features that struck you as distinctively Dima. The glass case of samurai swords on one wall, for instance, the photograph of Al Capone, enlarged and framed, on another; the editions of Mandelstam, Pasternak, and Akhmatova that rubbed shoulders, on his bookshelves, with Grisham, Chandler, John Le Carré. Since she seriously doubted that Dima found time for reading, let alone in the office, this library was mostly, like everything here, a series of carefully planted suggestions as to the character of its owner. Dima Kuznetsov, the room seemed to say, millionaire, warrior, poet. . . .

Gangster?

"My dear Cass . . ." Entering at a fast trot, he shed onto one of the armchairs his fur-lined overcoat and hat. "What a great pleasure to find you here, dropping in and brightening my day."

"You asked me, remember?" She made a show of consulting her watch. He was late by at least fifteen minutes. "You asked me to be here at eleven."

"Of course. And I apologize profoundly for not being here at that time. There was movement in the market for certificates of ownership.

It required some adjustment in my position. May I offer you coffee? A glass of champagne?"

"Neither, thank you." She paused. "There's a market in certificates of ownership? Is there anything you Russians don't speculate in?"

"I doubt it." He shrugged. "It's the most important lesson we learned from America. Speculation is the essence of capitalism. There's value and then there are expectations. And the expectations are frequently most extravagant precisely where the value is most doubtful, a tendency particularly marked in the case of certificates of ownership, where the value may be lacking altogether." He grinned. "Expectations are where the money is."

"So you buy these certificates, believing they're more or less worthless, because there are people who believe that they're not?"

"Precisely. That's what makes trading so convenient. You don't have to know business, or at any rate not much about it. All you have to understand are fear and greed."

"And you understand them?"

"Perfectly." The grin became broader. "Fear especially."

Fear and greed . . . Cass thought about this. Could he really believe in this pirate's philosophy? Or was he merely amusing himself, creating a fiction and pretending to live it? It was hard to tell sometimes, hard to know which part of him was real. The courtesy and charm, the reckless generosity? Or the predator's philosophy he claimed to espouse and took such pleasure in flaunting?

"Doesn't it bother you a little? The ship's going down and there you are, selling seats in imaginary lifeboats."

"Selling seats in imaginary lifeboats . . . I like that. I shall have to remember it." He laughed. "Perhaps I could also sell life insurance."

"But doesn't it bother you?" she insisted. "To be making money from people drowning?"

He shrugged. "If I didn't, someone would. A man has to follow his nature. Should the tiger apologize for eating meat?"

He paused.

"Speaking of tigers, I have news of our friend."

"Our friend?"

"Yours, actually. The man in the overcoat. Dolokhov, I think he was calling himself. Though I understand the name was really Grigoriev."

"Dolokhov? A tiger?" She considered it. "I shouldn't have thought so."

Dima shook his head. "A jackal, but a jackal who kept company with tigers. It was one of them, I think, who killed him."

"He was Mafia then?"

"Fringes only. Strictly small-time—black-marketeering, a touch of extortion." He paused. "I understand the child prostitution was a sideline."

"Child prostitution?" She was startled. "You mean he exploited children?"

"Exploited? I don't think so." Dima shrugged. "That kind of moralizing makes no sense to me. As you well know, they would sell themselves anyway. I imagine he was merely helping organize the market."

"Markets again." She caught his gaze and held it. "I should tell you, Dima, it's a word that since I came to Moscow I've gotten awfully tired of."

"Have you?" The grin was humorless this time, a sudden baring of large white teeth. "I apologize for boring you then. I, on the other hand, find its fascination endless. Perhaps the luxury of finding it boring is available only to those with inherited wealth."

She shrugged. "Perhaps. But let's not argue about it. I'm grateful to you for taking the trouble to find out about Dolokhov for me." She paused. "That's everything then? All you were able to find out?"

"Everything?" He looked pained, spread his hands in a pantomime of reproach. "My dear Cass, what did you expect? A family tree? An inventory of his business transactions? A life history?"

"I'm sorry," she said, "that came out wrong. I wasn't implying it isn't enough. It's only that when we spoke before, you seemed to find the way he was killed significant. You said it looked like a KGB hit."

"I did. And it does. But no one I talked to even hinted at a KGB connection." He paused. "It could be whoever shot him was KGB-trained or simply employing their methods."

From Dima's perspective, since she'd carefully told him nothing of the tape, this made a certain kind of sense; many members of the former Second Chief Directorate, especially those employed in what had been called "wet work," had ended up in organized crime. She, on the other hand, would be willing to bet that the KGB's involvement in all this went far beyond training or methods. Dolokhov had been killed for that tape, presumably by those he had stolen it from. And they wouldn't be Mafia, would they? But then again they might be, she thought, and precisely because of all those ex-secret policemen. Socialized crime had been privatized here; the KGB had gone into business. So the Mafia might well have laid hands on a tape from the presidential archive, then used it to devise a vicious forgery whose target was her uncle. But the question in that case was how had Dolokhov, that jackal who kept company with tigers, laid *his* hands on it? How, unless he had KGB connections—and very good KGB connections—had he known of its significance, its particular interest to her? So how come Dima, who conceivably had them himself, had drawn such a blank in that regard?

Or had he?

"It occurs to me to ask you"—she noticed he was studying her closely—"why so much interest in this alias Dolokhov?"

"I told you." She shrugged. "We had this conversation. . . . It's curiosity, pure and simple. You arrange to meet someone, you show up to find he's been murdered, it's only natural you want to know why."

"Ah, yes, I remember. And I remember suggesting at the time that in regard to the Mafia, curiosity might be unwise." He paused. "My inquiries incurred no risk to me, I think. But it will have been noticed that they were made. As will the fact that you and I are friends." He paused again. "You do know that I'm your friend, don't you?"

"I would hope so." She nodded. "Why do you ask?"

"Because I'm hoping that your interest in this matter will be satisfied with what I've been able to tell you."

She shook her head. "I'm afraid it won't. But what does that have to do with our friendship?"

"It has this to do with it." He sighed. "I have to tell you that, because I am your friend, I will take no more part in these inquiries."

Chapter Twenty-Two

CASS HAD LITTLE EXPERIENCE of police stations. Her only acquaintance with them, outside TV and the movies, was once in her undergrad days in Boston, when she'd bailed out a friend who'd gotten arrested for not responding to a traffic citation. What had struck her chiefly was the air of detachment, the sense that what happened there was mostly mechanical, cops and villains mutually dependent, playing their respective roles impersonally, without resentment or even much interest. She got the same feeling, more or less, from the midrise building just off Dzerzhinsky Street, into one of whose interview rooms she had just been ushered by Sokolnikov. The place smelled of stale cigarette smoke and boredom. The inhabitants looked as if their minds were elsewhere, and spoke, if at all, in a listless monotone. Most of them seemed to be doing paperwork. The sergeant, or whatever, who fielded her request to see Sokolnikov hadn't raised his head when she approached his desk. He'd been halfway through his routine catechism (Name? . . . Address? . . . Reason for visit?) before he'd deigned to look at her. When he had, admittedly, he'd brightened a little, complimented her on her Russian, practiced his English in the standard manner ("What do you do in afternoon tomorrow? You want I explain you Moscow?"), but even the effort at flirtation was half-hearted: His gambit conventional, her refusal expected, their exchanges reminding her of one of those tournament chess games where the players agree to a draw in advance. The building, too, contributed to the general lassitude. Drably functional, outside and in, the headquarters of the State Militia (Criminal Investigation Division) might almost have been designed as a rebuttal to the modernist philosophy in architecture. Though it could hardly be said to make anything as

172

positive as a statement, it nonetheless managed to convey quite clearly that, in Russia, less was less.

The message was underlined by Interview Room Number Four. It possessed no windows of any kind; lighting was provided by a single fluorescent strip. There was no wall covering. The floor was bare, unpatterned linoleum. The furniture consisted of a rectangular table, covered in the Russian equivalent of Formica, flanked on one side by a plain metal chair, angular and armless, and opposite by two others of similar design. (Each of these, however, had arms and a thin layer of padding on the seat.) Mostly because she knew it would not be expected—it was no doubt reserved for those whom the Militia referred to as "subjects"—Cass had taken the unpadded chair. It was hideously uncomfortable, no doubt by design, and she guessed that the "subject" whose arrival she awaited had spent many hours squirming in it already. This subject, she gathered, had so far been uncooperative, so determinedly that an exasperated Sokolnikov had described her as "an encyclopedia of ignorance." If she was to be persuaded to relent, it wouldn't, clearly, be by more of the same. Cass would need to appear sympathetic, unthreatening, not an ally of the Militia. In Interview Room Number Four this wasn't going to be easy.

It was hard to figure out, she thought, why the authorities were letting her do this, how in two days she'd been magically transformed from a suspect into something like a friend of the police. When she'd called on Thursday to inquire about what progress he had made, Sokolnikov's answer had been curt and bureaucratic: The investigation was progressing as expected. It was not the Militia's policy, moreover, to discuss ongoing investigations with members of the public. Yesterday, however, the attitude had suddenly changed. Sokolnikov had telephoned *her*. He had still not been especially friendly, but he had been amazingly forthcoming: The investigation was being discontinued. The file remained open, but due to lack of progess, resources now assigned to the case had been reallocated. If Miss Wolfe cared to call at headquarters tomorrow, Sokolnikov would be happy to share with her what little he'd discovered.

And what he'd discovered had not been that little. Not if one read between the lines. Not only was he able to corroborate most of what Dima had told her—Dolokhov's alias, the criminal charges, his probable links with the Mafia—but he'd also confirmed, if only obliquely, a connection she'd felt had to exist and that Dima's informants apparently had missed. Those fellows over in Yasenevo—Sokolnikov had prefaced this statement with a roll of his eyes and the sourest of smiles—were willing to swear on the lives of their mothers that Vladimir Dolokhov (alias Grigoriev) had *never* been employed by the First Chief Directorate. He had *not* had several European postings. He had *not*, emphatically, resigned in 1985.

"You can see," Sokolnikov had added sardonically, "how much progess we are to likely make. People falling over themselves to help us. . . . You don't know what he wanted to sell you. Yasenevo never heard of him. And as for that little slut of his . . . after living for months in his apartment, she doesn't know his last name."

* * *

THE "LITTLE SLUT" who in due course presented herself at the doorway of Interview Room Number Four confounded most of Cass's expectations. What was summoned to mind by "child prostitute" was mostly defined, she supposed, by the second word. She'd expected an overt, precocious sexuality, a child, in the expressive British phrase, "all tarted up" to look like a miniature woman, and probably wearing (since Russian notions of glamor still derived mostly from American fashions of the 1950s) a miniskirt, heels, and a beehive hairdo, with features obscured by a mask of rouge and mascara. She'd expected, too, an air of sullen rebellion, a mouth set firm in a discontented pout, eyes shifty, refusing to meet hers. What she got could hardly have been more different. Olga Vorontsova was going to be a beauty: elfin face, green eyes, dark hair, a body for which most women could exercise and starve themselves a lifetime and not have a prayer of achieving. She was also a schoolgirl who looked like a schoolgirl, her face quite innocent of makeup, her outfit (skirt and sweater, knee socks, sneakers) modest if not demure. She seemed, if anything, younger than reported and, given her circumstances, remarkably cheerful.

"Fantastic coat," she offered from the doorway. "Did you get it in America?"

"Thank you." Cass smiled. "No, I got it in Rome."

"But you are from America. You're the woman who wants to talk about Volodya?" She used, Cass noted, the polite plural form of the pronoun.

174

Cass nodded. "My name is Cassandra . . . Cassandra Wolfe."

"Cassandra . . . Cassandra." She rolled it around on her tongue. "I like this name; it's very pretty. But the other is hard to pronounce." She paused, subjecting Cass to continued and open appraisal. "I am Olyenka . . . Olyenka Vorontsova. But of course you know that. The officer"—she put the word in quotes—"will naturally have told you all about me."

Cass shrugged. "He told me something. Won't you come and sit down?"

"I'd rather not sit." She advanced, however, to prop herself against a corner of the table. "I've done too much sitting the past couple of days."

"Then you don't have to sit." Cass paused. "Actually, you don't have to talk. I don't have the right to question you. I couldn't make you answer if I did."

"Oh, I don't mind talking." The smile was winning, but the emphasis, Cass noted, on the "talking." "I haven't run across many Americans. American women, that is. At least you'll make a change from that officer . . . not that I'd call it talking," she added. "He kept asking the same stupid questions; I kept telling him I didn't know. Must have been like talking to an answer machine."

"Sounds more like talking to a no-answer machine." Cass gave her a conspirator's grin. "He did admit to finding you unhelpful. He wasn't too happy when he talked to me."

"He questioned *you?* . . . about Volodya?" Clearly Olyenka found this hard to credit. "What would you know about Volodya?"

"I was the one who found his body. They told you—didn't they?— that he'd been murdered."

"They told me. They even showed me a picture." Olyenka shrugged. "I guess he had it coming."

"Had it coming? What makes you say that?"

"Well he must have, mustn't he? . . . He was no plaster saint. Besides"—pause, slight narrowing of the eyes—"people don't get murdered for no reason."

It was hard to know what to make of this. Hard also to know how to proceed. Olyenka's manner had turned noticeably guarded. She clearly had no time for the police, and they'd held her now, barraged her with "stupid" questions, for more than forty-eight hours. But was her recalcitrance conditioned reflex, or did she have something to hide? Perhaps, Cass thought, it wasn't recalcitrance. Perhaps she was simply stating the obvious. In Olyenka's world people often got killed. Most of the time they had it coming. And Volodya *had* been no plaster saint. He'd been a pimp, an extortionist, possibly worse. So perhaps Olyenka, as her tone suggested, had merely been stating for her listener's benefit a fundamental rule of the war zone she lived in.

It couldn't be an easy place to live in, especially for someone just into adolescence. Cass was well aware that first impressions could be deceptive—in this case they almost had to be—but she found herself oddly drawn to Olyenka. No doubt this was partly because of her looks, but her personality also was appealing. She was tough, self-reliant, obviously intelligent, neither a pouter nor a whiner. Indeed, she seemed able to accept, and cheerfully, whatever life handed her. (How many fourteen-year-olds, Cass wondered—how many adults, for that matter—could handle with her evident insouciance forty-eight hours in a Russian lockup and Sokolnikov's persistent questioning?) It was troubling, depressing, to imagine what life might hand her in the future. Sokolnikov, when asked about it, had laid out the bleak probabilities succinctly: The jails were full, the cops overworked, the probation officers' caseloads enormous. There was no help available for girls like Olyenka, and in any case she didn't want it. When they let her go she'd be back on the streets in an hour. Sooner or later the Mafia would claim her. In five years, Sokolnikov predicted, she'd either be old or dead.

"Volodya had it coming, you say?" Cass pushed these unwelcome reflections from her mind. "What about the apartment?"

"What about it?"

She'd had switched into stonewall mode, Cass noted. It might be best to back off a little.

"Well, you can't really go back to it, can you? I expect the landlord will want to relet."

"I'll find somewhere else." Olyenka shrugged. "In the meantime, there's always the trains. He told you—didn't he?—about them."

Cass nodded.

"It's a way to make a living." The tone was factual, undefiant. "And no more dishonest than his."

176

Cass could find nothing to say to this that wouldn't be fatuous or impertinent or both. She said nothing.

"I'm not planning on doing it forever, you know. Only until something better shows up."

"What would you like to do?"

"Dunno." Olyenka looked vague. "Modeling, maybe. I think I'd make a good model."

"I think so, too." Cass nodded. "You're pretty and you have good taste."

"Good taste?" Quick, sardonic grin. "Because I liked your coat?"

Cass shook her head. "Because I like your outfit."

"Oh, these . . ." Olyenka looked down at herself disdainfully, shrugged. "These are my work clothes." She paused, interpreting Cass's silence. "They like us to look young, you see . . . young and innocent. Virginal." She rolled her eyes. "Sick, when you think about it."

Cass had nothing to say here either.

"What's your guess on why they trashed the apartment?"

"Look, Cassandra"—again the face had become a mask—"we need to get one thing straight: I'm happy to talk—it's better than sitting in a cell—but I've had it with Volodya as a subject. I don't know why his apartment was trashed, I don't know who his enemies were. I don't know anything about him. . . . I don't know, and what's more I don't want to."

"I know you don't know," Cass said. "I was asking if you could hazard a guess."

More silence. Olyenka regarded her coldly.

"You don't look dumb, but you're almost as bad as the Militia. I'll try to make this really simple: Someone killed Volodya and worked his apartment over. That someone is still out there, and I will be, too, when all of you get through with your questions. Now ask yourself what I stand to gain by "hazarding a guess," as you put it, then ask yourself what I stand to lose."

"I don't know what you think you stand to lose. This is just you talking to me. Who's to know what gets said?"

The response to this was withering.

"Oh, sure"—Olyenka rolled her eyes—"this is just between you and me, right? Like you won't run right out and tell that lieutenant. Like the cops don't have this whole place miked? Like three-quarters of the Militia aren't on the Mafia's payroll? . . . Get serious, Miss America, remember where you are. This is Moscow, not Washington, D.C."

Cass was tempted to reply that if Olyenka thought Moscow more lawless than D.C., then her notion of the latter was romantic. But the girl had a point. Especially about having nothing to gain. And that, Cass thought, was a notion that ought to be changed.

Reaching in her pocket for her notebook and a ballpoint, she wrote down her phone number. Tearing off the page, she handed it to Olyenka.

"Okay," she said. "You've made your position clear. I'd like to make mine clear, too. I'm not here fronting for the Militia. My interest in this is personal and private. Nothing you say will go any farther."

She stood up.

"Maybe you'll remember something later, when you've got the Militia off your back. If you do, you can call me at this number. Help me find out why Volodya's apartment was trashed, and you'll find me extremely grateful."

Olyenka said nothing. But she did, Cass noted, fold the page of the notebook carefully into four and tuck it into the top of her bra.

Suddenly Cass felt ashamed of herself.

"Look," she said, "call anyway, will you? Whether or not you remember anything."

"Call you." Olyenka's gaze was unblinking. "Why?"

"I don't know." Cass shrugged, feeling foolish. "I've enjoyed talking to you. Maybe I can help you somehow. Help you get started in modeling, perhaps. Find you something else to do."

Even to her ears it sounded lame: "Find you something else to do"? How was she going to do it exactly? What was there in Moscow for destitute, parentless teenage girls to do? What Olyenka needed was not some vague meretricious promise. She needed a different life, another childhood, a whole new country to grow up in.

* * *

"So," Sokolnikov said, "did you learn anything?"

"Not a thing." Cass shook her head. "She didn't trust me any more than you. I'm not at all sure she has anything to tell."

"Oh, she has something. She's just not willing to tell us what it is.

178

I'm not sure why," Sokolnikov added. "Maybe she's scared of something. Or maybe she's going on commercial principles: If you can sell it, don't give it away."

An exact intuition of Olyenka's sentiments, if indeed it was intuition. Olyenka, Cass thought, was no dummy.

"She thinks you guys were miking us. Were you?"

"We were not." Sokolnikov grinned. "Not that we wouldn't, but in fact we weren't. . . . As I told you, we're shelving this case. It appears the city has other uses for my time."

"And Olyenka? Will you just let her go?"

"What else can we do? . . . We could give her to Social Services, like last time. And they could assign her a probation officer, like last time, who she wouldn't report to, like last time. The streets are full of kids like her."

"Don't waste my sympathy, you mean?"

He shrugged. "Something like that."

"I don't think sympathy is ever wasted. Do you? She's not a problem, she's a person. The fact that others share her predicament doesn't make it less real or less painful."

He looked at her without speaking.

I didn't have the right to say that, she thought. He knows it much better than I. He sees it every day of his life, and here I am preaching at him.

"I'm sorry," she said. "I shouldn't have said that."

"It's okay." He shrugged. "Perhaps it needed saying. You can live so close you lose sight of it sometimes." He paused. "May I offer a suggestion?"

"Of course."

"It's one I've offered before. But then I was guessing, now I know." He fixed her with an earnest gaze. "I think you, too, should shelve this case. In fact, I think you should close it."

"Because of those people at Yasenevo?" Pointless to pretend she didn't understand.

He nodded. "Also those people at Lubyanka. They're still around, too, in case you didn't know. I don't want to see you, too, end up with a hole in the middle of your forehead."

First Dima, now this lieutenant—and both prompted by concern for her safety. Apparently. But mightn't one construe this apparent concern as actually a subtle form of threat? And if it was, it wasn't ineffective: "Also those people at Lubyanka." The prison was abolished now, of course, converted now into a kind of museum, but the name retained its power to chill. She had visited it once, just after her arrival in Moscow. In that infamous building just around the corner from here, she had stood and shivered in the courtyard where a chest-high frieze of pockmarks in the brickwork of one wall bore eloquent witness to the business conducted there. She remembered being struck at the time by the guide's tone of careful detachment, as if what he spoke of had been an aberration, something that happened centuries ago and in another Russia entirely. But most of them were still around, weren't they?—the gray-faced bureaucrats who'd signed the death warrants, the empty-eyed soldiers who'd carried them out. And wasn't it a fact, attested to by Tatyana, that in 1989, on the eve of the Communist collapse, the KGB's Second Chief Directorate had listed close to a million full-time employees? Bagmen, surveillance men, goons, gorillas, assassins, artists at the infliction of pain. But why, she wondered, when most of his countrymen seemed determined to forget, was this policemen reminding her of it?

"I appreciate your concern," she said, "though I admit it surprises me a little. The last time we met I got the impression that a bullet hole in the middle of the forehead was exactly what you thought I deserved."

"Did I give you that impression?" He smiled. "I must have been trying to scare you."

"I see." She affected enlightenment. "Not like now, you mean."

"Same intention, different motive. Then I was trying to get you to cooperate. Now . . ." He paused. "Now I would like to ask your opinion."

"About what?"

"Why would General Rev, my chief, who at first took so much interest in this case that he had me report to him directly, all of a sudden lose that interest? Why would he order me to shelve it? Why would he give me authorization—it was more than authorization, it was an instruction—to share the details of this case with you?" Sokolnikov paused. "What is your opinion about this?"

"I think it's fairly obvious." Cass shrugged. "I think someone scared him off, told him to try to scare me, too."

"I think you are right . . . Miss Wolfe." He paused, hesitated. "May I call you Cassandra?"

"If you want." She smiled. "My friends call me Cass."

"Then may I also ask you a favor?"

She smiled again. "You can always ask."

"I admire you," he said. "I would value being your friend. I think you are intelligent and courageous, but I think you are out of your depth. So the favor I want to ask you is: Please, Cass, *be* scared."

Chapter Twenty-Three

THE LOOP WAS FROM TATYANA'S APARTMENT near the university, up Komsomolsky Prospekt, left at Sadovoye Ring, another left on Smolenskaya, then back down the various embankments to rejoin Komsomolsky where it crossed the river. The distance, all told, was between six and seven miles. Cass ran it, or variants, three times a week, and except when the weather was particularly dismal, she'd done so since her arrival in Moscow. Her time was normally under an hour. So it didn't much surprise her that by the time they reached Lutsnezhkaya Embankment, she'd built up a lead of fifty yards. Actually, given the shape she was in and an age difference of twenty-five years, it surprised her the lead wasn't greater. Either Nick was fitter than she'd thought or else he was very determined.

Both, she suspected, but more the latter.

This hadn't been advertised as a race, but exercise by degrees had turned into competition. She wasn't quite sure who had started it, but no objections had been raised on either side. Halfway up Komsomolsky she'd noticed she had upped her normal pace and that Nick, instead of lagging, was actually pushing her a little. So, of course, she'd upped the pace again. On Savvinskaya Embankment he'd put in what was unmistakably a spurt. A few minutes later, she had countered. The second time he'd passed, he'd grunted, "Fie on this easy life," albeit through gritted teeth, to which, as she swept by a moment later, she'd responded with, "Last one home buys breakfast." Now it was openly a race, and she was going to win.

And not just win, leave him in the dust.

Not that there was any dust. The expected thaw had arrived and with it low clouds and thin drizzle. Only a lightening of the sky to the east indicated that somewhere the sun was up. At this hour the sodden streets were almost empty, such Muscovites as were about greeting the spectacle of her and Nick—a middle-aged man in furious pursuit of an amazon in green Lycra tights and shocking pink leg warmers—with responses that ranged from leers to looks of disapproval. These people were Americans, of course, tearing around the streets like this at the crack of dawn, half dressed. One heard a lot of loose talk these days about the blessings of democracy, the merits of the free enterprise system. If this was the sort of thing it led to, one wanted no part of it whatever.

When she reached the entrance to Tatyana's building her lead was close to a hundred yards, but she wasn't going to stop and wait here. "Home" was the door of Tatyana's third-floor apartment. She wouldn't put it past him to slip by, beat her up the stairs, claim the victory on a technicality. That would be typical, she thought. She wondered what made him so damned competitive.

History or biology? Or both?

Tatyana's building, which dated from 1917, aspired, in the public areas, to pre-Revolutionary standards of elegance. By U.S. standards the apartments were cramped and pokey—most had been drastically subdivided—but the lobby was spacious, tiled in marble, the marble staircase (with its handrail of wrought iron) rising to the second floor in a sweeping spiral. Above the second floor, opulence gave way to practicality: The stairs were concrete and uncarpeted, the hallways narrow and badly lit.

She didn't really need to keep running—Nick was still back in the street, half a block short of the entrance—but something, the exhilaration of victory or an urge to stretch the margin, made her sprint. She bounded up the staircase, taking the marble steps three steps a time, noticing only halfway up that at the top was a man coming down.

He was wearing a raincoat, she noted idly, both his hands thrust deep into the pockets. His skin was darkish, his features Asiatic. She didn't remember having seen him before. Probably he'd been visiting someone, though it was early in the day for that. Slackening her pace a bit, she moved to the right to let him pass.

She expected him to do the same, but instead he moved left, blocking her way. As he did so his right hand came out of his pocket.

It was holding something.

Instantly her reflexes took over. She wasn't aware of making decisions, only of having made them; only that in the heartbeat it took her to identify the something he was holding as a knife, she had stopped, spun around, and was galloping back down, taking the steps five or six at a time in a series of leg-breaking, heart-stopping leaps. Behind her, suddenly thunderous, terrifying, an accelerating clatter of footsteps.

She was already halfway across the lobby when Nick entered from the street.

It amazed her how fast he took things in. Before she could even call out a warning, he'd snatched up one of the lobby chairs and, brandishing it like a club, moved past her to confront her pursuer. As he did so, another man entered the lobby.

He also was holding a knife.

Alerted to this second menace, Nick halted. Motioning her to get behind him, he backed up to the wall that flanked the staircase, flailing the chair from side to side to keep their attackers at bay. The two men fanned out onto either flank, just out of reach of the chair. The second one was half a head shorter than the first but in other respects a carbon copy, even down to the raincoat. Not muggers, Cass thought, not amateurs at least. They moved like wolves, silent, unhurried, their faces expressionless and watchful, their knives—wicked commando models with serrated six-inch blades—held low and in front of them, ready to thrust upward or slash.

"Find out what the fuck they want," Nick whispered. "Say if it's money, we don't have any with us. Maybe we can work something out."

She passed this on. The men merely laughed.

"No money? . . . a pity." She was answered by the one on the right. "A bonus is always welcome. Especially dollars."

"They don't want money," she told Nick. "They want us."

"Figured they might." He sounded calm and even, astonishingly, cheerful. "Let's make them work for it, shall we?"

Great idea. The problem was execution. She hadn't, so far, had time for fear, but now, in this momentary lull, it gripped her. She wasn't paralyzed by it, not yet, but she knew if she let her mind dwell on those knives, if she gave her imagination rein, she would be.

She'd always had a horror of being cut.

"Here's what were going to do." Nick's whisper was urgent. "It's our

184

only chance, so don't argue. I'm going to yell and jump out of your way. When I do, make a dash for the door. Don't hesitate for a moment. Don't stop or look back. And keep on going when you hit the street."

She was going to argue, but he gave her no time.

"Go!"

As he yelled he feinted to the left, and almost in the same motion, as the man on that side jumped back, he whirled and went after the one on the right. The chair, catching this one moving forward, slammed him sideways into the wall. By that time Cass, accelerating like a spooked gazelle, was halfway across the lobby and yelling her lungs out for help.

At the entrance she found her way once more blocked.

By Dima.

Holding a gun.

Chapter Twenty-Four

"CHECHENS, BY THE LOOK," Dima said. "They come here from the Caucasus. Violence is a way of life to them. The Mafia hires them as hit men and thugs. There was no point arresting them, turning them into the Militia. The Mafia would just buy them out. Then I'd have a war on my hands." He paused. "I warned you something like this might happen."

They were back in Tatyana's apartment. It appeared that Dima, returning from some early-morning business, had been seized by the impulse to drop in and ask Cass to breakfast. His appearance on the scene, armed with a Makarov automatic, had prompted the Chechens to disorderly retreat. How he came to be armed was a matter he hadn't explained. Maybe, Cass thought, he always was. Or maybe the nature of his business this morning had required it. In any case, as even Tatyana conceded, his arrival had been providential.

"I know you warned me," Cass said. "It's incredible good luck you happened by. I'm just a stubborn American, I guess. Also relieved and very grateful."

She was grateful. Grateful to be alive, unhurt. Grateful to be sitting here safe, wading through the enormous breakfast Tatyana had insisted on providing and she to her considerable surprise was finding she had appetite for. Grateful, too, to discover in herself no tendency to dwell on what had happened. Later, perhaps, shock would set in; she might find herself reliving the encounter, having nightmares in which it ended differently, but for now her focus was entirely on the outcome. It might have ended badly, but it hadn't. No point worrying about what was past.

The future was another matter.

"Actually"—Dima shrugged—"maybe it was the Chechens who should be grateful. I'm not sure exactly who it was I rescued." He paused to flick a grin at Nick. "Your father is a dangerous man with a chair."

"For once Dmitri Petrovich is right." Modesty in Dima was rare; Tatyana was quick to endorse it. "The hero is Nick, I think."

She had a point. It was largely thanks to Nick, Cass knew, that the episode hadn't ended badly. His quick thinking had bought them the time to benefit from Dima's intervention. His quick thinking, or perhaps his instinctive aggression, which the Chechens had clearly not expected and from which, for those crucial few seconds, they'd backed off. And though Dima might joke about chairs, Nick would have been hurt or maybe even killed. He'd known it, of course, accepted it without hesitation, to buy her a chance at safety. And he'd done it as if the choice were automatic—for him, indeed, no choice at all. Cass was reminded of something Josie had once said, a remark she'd made about Nick and Hal. What Hal had was courage, Josie said; he was subject to fear but overcame it. What Nick had was a kind of freedom; he just didn't have a fearful bone in his body. It was easy to mistake this for machismo, Josie said, but it wasn't that, it was unself-conscious entirely. Nick did what he did because he was who he was. He didn't have to think about either.

Today Cass had reason to be grateful for that.

Grateful and almost proud.

"You were great," she told him. "You and Dima both."

"Adrenaline rush in my case." Nick grinned. "And perhaps just a touch of parental instinct."

"In my case it was entirely the Makarov." Laughing, Dima pushed back his plate. He stood up. "I regret this hero must say his farewells. There are markets everywhere requiring my attention." He kissed his fingers, with mock gravity, to Cass and turned with elaborate courtesy to his hostess. "Esteemed Tatyana Nicolaieva, the blintzes were delicious. They almost persuade me to reform my character, to give my filthy money to the poor and make you a proposal of marriage. If only"—sigh—"I could cure this fixation with the past, persuade you to set your eyes on the future."

The eyes in question flashed dangerously.

"Dmitri Petrovich, you honor me. It pains me all the more to have to tell you that the prospect of a future with *you* in it is unlikely to cure my fixation with the past."

"Thank you for your candor." He grinned and turned to Cass. "Maybe *you* would take pity on me."

"I don't know." She pursed her lips, looked dubious. "It's flattering, of course, to be your second choice, but if you want *me*, you'll have to give up markets. . . . Perhaps it wouldn't be too terribly painful. I wouldn't ask you to go cold turkey. You could ease into it, give up half a dozen at a time."

He shook his head. "The habit is far too strong. It seems I shall have to stay single. The loss, of course, will be entirely mine." He turned to Nick. "My friend, I leave these women in your hands. Try to persuade them, especially your daughter, not to get into any more trouble."

* * *

"THEY WERE WARNING us off," Cass said. "I'm sure they weren't trying to kill us. If you want to kill, shooting's easier than stabbing. They shot Dolokhov. Why not us?"

Nick thought before answering. Normally he would have tried to discourage her from dwelling on the morning's events. Dwelling encouraged imagination. And fueled by experience of the kind she'd just had, imagination was apt to turn morbid. But in her case this didn't seem to have happened. If anything, she hadn't been shaken enough.

"They didn't want to kill us *this time*," he said.

"The next time they may, you think?" She considered this briefly, shook her head. "That doesn't make much sense to me." She paused, continued somewhat defiantly. "I see their not having killed us as proof the tape is a fake. If it were real and I'd been them, *I* would have killed me right at the start, in Novodevichy along with Dolokhov. I mean, why take the chance? If dead men tell no tales, shouldn't the same thing hold true for women?"

"Gender discrimination unacceptable?" Nick smiled quizzically. "Even when the context is murder? . . . Face it, Cass, there's a difference here. Dolokhov was nobody, a petty crook who wouldn't be missed, a mere addition to the murder statistics. You and I are front-page news, or we are if we get our throats cut. . . . If I were in their shoes and the tape were real, I'd try really hard to stay out of the news. I'd give intimidation a go before resorting to murder."

"So in your view this morning doesn't prove a thing?"

"I think what it mostly proves"—he eyed her gravely—"is we're candidates for having our throats cut."

"You're saying we should give up? Quit when we're starting to make progress?"

"What progress? All I see is that we've managed to alert the opposition. Your tape may be real or it may not, but there's no doubt we're dealing with killers. I'd far rather let this thing go than have you murdered trying to figure it out."

"Then you *are* saying you think we should quit." She stared. "I wouldn't have thought it was your style."

Quit? . . . Nick thought about it. It wasn't a word he particularly liked, any more than he liked people warning him off. But how much progress were they likely to make? Not much, he thought. Not on their own. Not in this alien, lawless city where the criminals and cops went hand in glove and the *apparatchiks* had turned Mafiosi.

"Just sounding a note of caution," he said. "I think it needs to be sounded."

She shook her head.

"I don't think caution is a thing we can afford. The stakes are too high. If the tape *is* a fake, then someone's trying to ruin Hal's chances of election. Attempting to sabotage—assuming you don't care about Hal—our most important political process. If it isn't a fake"—she paused, fixing him intently—"if it isn't, I don't have to tell you what that means."

I don't, she thought, want to think about it.

"I know," he said. "I'm just trying to point out that the risks are high and the chances of success rather slim. Even the cops have given up here, and they've given up because they think they can't win. We're dealing with the Mafia or the KGB or both. They're ruthless and violent, and they have their eye on us." He paused. "I just want you to know what you're getting into. If you change your mind later, it's going to be too late."

Later, when things had gone terribly wrong, Cass would think back on this moment, like the moment at the entrance to the bell tower before she'd climbed up to find Dolokhov dead, as another of those crucial dividings of the way, those choices on which a whole future could rest. Maybe if she'd really believed where it could lead, maybe if her history had been different, if she hadn't been armored in that besetting illusion of youth and wealth—that somehow *she* was immune to disaster—then the choice might have seemed less automatic. As it was, there seemed no choice at all.

She said, "I think it's already too late. And the reasons you've given for changing my mind are precisely the reasons I can't. . . . The cops, as you say, have quit on this, and there's no one else we can turn to. If *we* don't figure this out, no one will. At least not till it's too late."

She paused. The look she gave him was imploring.

"It has to be us, Nick. Surely you see that? It has to be us, because there is only us."

Chapter Twenty-Five

IT HAS TO BE US, because there is only us.

It was easy to say, Cass thought later, as she lay in the bathtub soaking the tiredness out of her limbs. Easy to say and okay perhaps as a slogan for rallying the troops (though Nick hadn't greeted it with much enthusiasm), and it had the further merit that it happened to be true, but it didn't offer anything to build on. She could rally the troops until she was hoarse, but rallying wouldn't do any good if she didn't know which way to march them. And *that* was something of a problem at present, since every avenue she'd so far explored had led her into a cul-de-sac. . . . Take Tatyana's researches in the records of the First Chief Directorate; they'd turned up nothing that wasn't ambiguous. The same went for Dima's inquiries with his contacts in the Mafia; they'd told him nothing that helped at all, even assuming that what they'd told him was true. The police investigation into Dolokhov's murder had been shelved indefinitely, and Olyenka Vorontsova, who might know more than she was willing to reveal, had vanished into her twilight world—no doubt riding some midnight express—and would probably not be heard from again.

All they could do, Nick had argued, was wait. To do damage a libel had to be made public. If people were plotting to ruin Hal's chances of election, then sooner or later they would have to show their hand. When they did, *if* they did, he and Cass would know where to direct their attention. This made sense, of a kind, and it seemed to satisfy his patient temperament, but it didn't come close to satisfying hers. *When* they showed their hand—in her view the "if" was nonexistent—the damage would already be done. By then, indeed, it would be irreparable. In the court of public opinion these days, there was no such thing as presumed innocent. Mostly it was the other way around.

191

And, of course, there was an "if." Her heart might deny it, but her head couldn't, quite. If they didn't show their hand, if that damnable tape simply never resurfaced, she would never know the truth. Though the inference that the tape was genuine and her uncle a traitor could be resisted in various ways, it could never be refuted altogether. And because it could never be refuted, it would poison her relationship with Hal.

In fact, the poison was working already. Last week, when he'd won primaries in Kansas and Nebraska, they'd done a feature on the Moscow TV news. The commentary had focused, naturally, on what his election might mean to Russia, mostly in terms of economic aid. Watching the newscast, the film clips of Hal looking presidential (the echoes of John Kennedy no doubt deliberate), she'd found herself wondering, much against her will, what his election *would* mean to Russia. She'd found it next to impossible to banish visions of men breaking out the champagne—and not just in Washington, but in Moscow, too, in the inner sanctums at Yasenevo, in the offices of those who now controlled assets inherited from the former KGB.

Such visions were absurd, of course. Still, since the day Nick first told her about Oracle, her perceptions of Hal had undergone a change. She didn't know whether the cause was in him or in her, but the Hal she'd watched on the TV screen seemed unlike the man she had thought she knew. The physical grace was there still, and the intelligence, but the rest was almost unrecognizable. In place of the blunt common sense, the impatience with fools, the irreverence, was a kind of guarded, all-purpose gravitas. It was an act, of course. All politicians had to do it, especially in the Land of the Free, where hypocrisy was a fact of political life and the moral bullshit waist-deep and rising. It was easy to imagine the real Hal Reynolds, the man behind this marble facade, grinning sheepishly and holding his nose. But what bothered her—she remembered now that it had bothered Josie—was how well he did it. He did it superbly, and because he did, she found herself wondering what else he'd been faking.

Nick had wondered, too. She could see now how suspicion must have gathered in him. Earlier, with the shock of his revelations fresh, it had been natural to accuse him of bias, of malice stemming from broken friendship, but now that she was calmer, she knew it wasn't that. Nick had his faults, but pettiness had never been among them.

He hadn't *wanted* to wonder about Hal, any more than she did now; circumstance had forced it on him. And if he'd been too objective, too ready to wonder, had she, honestly, been ready enough?

It has to be us, because there is only us. But how? she wondered. Where were they to start?

In the bedroom the phone started ringing.

* * *

"MY PROFESSIONAL EXPERIENCE," Olyenka said, "has taught me an invaluable lesson: If you can charge for it, don't give it away. The price is one hundred dollars."

Her gaze veered off to inspect the restaurant's interior, a gaudy confection of gilt, plush, and marble. Presently she caught the eye of their waiter. Summoned by a toss of her head, he came hurrying over.

"I really *adore* this place," she informed him. "In Moscow it's my favorite restaurant. After McDonald's, of course. What I would like is another of these. And please"—she gave him a reproachful look—"tell them not to be so stingy with the chocolate sauce this time."

She must be working later, Cass thought, for her outfit was properly demure, suggestive of school or at a pinch, a convent: her blouse embroidered with pink and blue flowers, her blue serge skirt hemmed well below the knee, this maidenly ensemble accessoried by white ankle socks and black patent leather shoes of the type that in America were called Mary Janes. Slav Bazaar had been her choice of restaurant. For lunch, she'd suggested, though it was then after two. Her notion of lunch, it now appeared, was a Coke and three dishes of ice cream.

Her notion of business, however, was conventional.

"One hundred dollars," she repeated. "Cash. In advance."

This was a little rich for Cass's blood. After all, she thought, she was paying for the Coke and ice cream.

"How do I know it's worth that much?"

"That's the price." Olyenka shrugged. "Whether it's worth it is your decision. One hundred dollars for why the apartment was trashed." She paused. "Then we can talk about what else I know."

Sighing, Cass dug into her purse. Anticipating some such demand, she'd come prepared, but only just. A hundred and fifty was all she had in dollars. Since Olyenka, like the rest of Russia, had an absolute aversion to the ruble, further trading would have to be on credit. Cass counted out five twenty-dollar bills, passed them to Olyenka under the table.

"Okay. Why was it trashed?" She paused. "You might start by telling me how you know."

Olyenka looked up from her counting.

"I know because I was there."

"There." Cass stared. "You were inside the apartment *while it was being trashed?*"

"Not inside, outside. I went out to buy food, as I told that cop. When I came back I heard them inside. I heard voices and the sound of things being smashed; lucky for me I did," Olyenka added. "If I'd gone in and surprised them at it I wouldn't be here talking to you now. Come to think of it"—she paused—"a hundred dollars is dirt cheap. My life is worth more than that, don't you think?"

Cass did. But it wasn't a line of thought she considered it prudent to pursue. What conclusion Olyenka would draw from her assent was at this point only too apparent.

"What did you do when you heard them?"

"Hid, of course. There's a kind of closet at the top of the stairs where they keep the cleaning equipment—not that they ever use it," she added. "I don't think that passage had been swept in months."

"Then if you were hidden in the closet"—even in Moscow's inflated economy, a hundred dollars should purchase more than Olyenka's notions of good housekeeping, Cass thought—"how could you know why they trashed the apartment?"

"I heard them, didn't I? I left the door open a crack and I heard one talking as they left. I even caught a glimpse of him."

Cass waited for her to continue, but instead Olyenka became suddenly intent on her ice cream, thoroughly cleaning the dish with her finger, then licking the finger with a small pink tongue. This, Cass thought, was like trying to coax tricks from a cat.

"You heard him? What did he say?"

"He said"—Olyenka took a final lick—" 'If it isn't in the car, and it isn't in the apartment, then where the fuck is it?' Pardon my language," she added with a grin. "Only it isn't my language, it was his. . . . They were looking for something, it's obvious, looking and didn't find it."

"I managed to grasp that." Cass stifled a sigh. "Do you happen to know *what* they were looking for?"

"Oh, I think so—at least I can hazard an educated guess, as you put it." Olyenka paused, gave another of her smiles. "But not for any lousy hundred dollars."

At this point, perhaps fortunately, the arrival of the waiter with ice cream preempted Cass's response. You could say this for the Russians, she thought: The years of living in a socialist economy hadn't blunted their commercial instincts. This youthful heir of Marx and Lenin was obviously planning to nickel-and-dime her to death.

"I have," she told Olyenka when the waiter had left, "precisely fifty dollars in my purse. It's all you're going to get out of me."

Olyenka received this news with a sniff.

"Then you've had all you're going to get out of *me*."

"Then maybe I should turn you over to the lieutenant." Cass was starting to find this child tiresome. "He can hold you on a charge of withholding evidence."

"Oh, right." The reply was prompt and derisive. "He can hold me *if* he can find me. But I'm a woman of the streets, remember. No phone number, no fixed address. And he's not going to spend much time looking, because the last I heard of it, they'd shelved the case. Look . . . Cassandra," she added, wheedling, "there's really no reason to get upset. It was you who raised the subject of money. You promised if I helped you, I'd find you quote-unquote extremely grateful." She paused. In one of her lightning transitions from child to woman, she was suddenly as hard as brass. "Five hundred dollars is the price. It's a fortune to me, but nothing to you; you're loaded."

Five hundred dollars?

But she was right, Cass thought. Five hundred was nothing. She had *given* away ten times that sum without thinking twice about it. Why was she being so stingy here? Reluctance to contribute, or contribute any more, to the delinquency, seemingly incorrigible, of this minor? Or was she was afraid of being cheated? That would be stupid and, worse, petty. It wasn't as if she couldn't afford it. For someone who gave Dima grief for his unswerving devotion to the dollar, her own instincts, she thought, were getting alarmingly commercial.

"What will the five hundred buy me exactly?"

"Two things." Olyenka checked them off on her fingers. "One, I'll

195

tell you what those guys didn't find. Two, I'll show you where to find it." She smiled. "Do we have a deal?"

"You claim you heard them say they were looking for something." Cass wasn't ready to bite the bullet yet. "What makes you think you know what it was? You told the Militia you didn't know him that well."

"Of course I told them that." Olyenka looked pitying. "I wasn't going to tell them the truth, was I? If I had, I'd still be in jail answering their stupid questions. But I knew him, all right." Her look turned secretive, crafty. "I knew a lot more about him than I ever let him realize."

She paused for a spoonful of ice cream, continued.

"I know what they were looking for because he told me. There were people who'd kill to get their hands on it, he said. And then, not three weeks later, he gets killed. And then, that very afternoon, these guys turn his apartment upside down, looking for something they didn't find. I mean, it stands to reason they were looking for that—doesn't it?—the thing he told me about."

It probably did. The logic wasn't watertight, but it certainly made sense. Olyenka could have made all this up, of course, but somehow Cass tended to doubt it. It was worth five hundred to find out.

If she couldn't find out for free.

" 'That'?" she inquired. "What are we talking about, exactly?"

Olyenka's spoon, about to plunge into the ice cream, stopped in midflight.

" 'That,' " she said sweetly, "is exactly what we're *not* talking about. Unless I get five hundred dollars. If you keep trying to cheat me," she added, "the price is going to go up."

"Okay," Cass said. "I'll make you a deal. Tell me what it is and where to find it, and I promise to pay whatever it costs to get you started as a model."

Silence.

"You promise, do you?" Sardonic emphasis on the second word. "You promise to pay whatever it costs to get me started as a model. Tell me something, Miss America: What do you think would happen if I let clients pay me with promises? I'll tell you what would happen: I'd get fucked, is what would happen. So don't take this personally,

196

but no promises, please. My terms are five hundred dollars. Cash. In advance."

"I told you," Cass said. "I only have fifty on me. I'll have to get the rest from American Express."

"Where's that?"

"Hotel Mezhdunarodnaya . . . Krasnopresnenskaya Embankment."

"That's not so far." Olyenka consulted the clock on the far wall of the restaurant. "When do they close?"

"They don't. It's a cash dispenser, a machine."

"A machine." Olyenka looked dubious. "It'll just cough up five hundred dollars? Anytime you ask it?"

Cass smiled. "It will if I ask it nicely."

"That's fantastic . . . God bless America. Or maybe that should be God bless American Express." Olyenka stood up abruptly, bestowing on Cass a brilliant smile. "In that case, what are we waiting for?"

*　*　*

AS THEY ENTERED THE LOBBY, Cass spotted Dima. More precisely, she heard him before she saw him: a yelp of laughter, high-pitched, neighing, unmistakably his. He was in the middle of a group of men in suits. Evidently he'd been telling them a joke. They were business associates perhaps, though on the other hand, perhaps not. One of them—Cass recognized him only when he turned around—was Quine.

Quine from the U.S. embassy.

How on earth would Dima know *him*?

She was spotted before she could retreat. Dima's face lit up and, detaching himself from the group, he came trotting over, followed, a few steps behind, by Quine.

"Cass . . . what a pleasant surprise," Dima boomed. "Arthur and I were about to have a drink. Maybe you . . . and your young friend"—he treated Olyenka to a rapid scrutiny—"would join us."

Damn, Cass thought. Sudden ubiquity of Dima. Welcome earlier, now it definitely was not.

"Dima . . ." She did her best to seem pleased to see him, met, she suspected, with only moderate success. "Hello again, Mr. Quine."

"Arthur . . . please." He held out his hand. "I trust the Militia are behaving themselves?"

"Perfectly." She smiled. "Thank you again for your help."

She shot a glance at her companion. Obviously awkward, Olyenka was standing there woodenly, face expressionless, eyes down. Cass, feeling slightly awkward herself, hastened to perform the introductions.

"This is Olga Vorontsova, the daughter of a friend. We were just about to treat ourselves to ice cream. Olyenka, this is Dima Kuznetsov. And this is Mr. Quine"—she was damned if she'd call him Arthur—"who I gather is something important in the U.S. embassy."

"*Ochin' priyatna*," Olyenka murmured. Avoiding eye contact, she accompanied her greeting with the faintest suggestion of a curtsy. "It's a pleasure."

It sounded anything but.

"Olyenka . . ." Dima mused, his scrutiny affable but open. "Olyenka, the darling." He smiled approvingly at Olyenka, then turned to Quine. "I mean, of course, the Olyenka in Chekhov's story. I'm sure you remember the one."

Quine nodded, but without conviction. Whatever he'd studied at Yale, it had not been, Cass was willing to bet, Russian lit.

"And *are* you?" Dima restored his attention to Olyenka.

Olyenka looked blank. "Am I what?"

"A darling, of course." Dima's gaze was unwavering. "Are you a darling?"

Olyenka shrugged, continued to look awkward. "I think that's not for me to say."

"Dima, you're embarrassing her." It was time, Cass thought, to cut this encounter short. "As I said before, we're on our way to get ice cream. So if I may, I'll take a rain check on that drink. . . . Mr. Quine, a pleasure to meet you again."

She was turning away when Olyenka stopped her.

"Cassandra, I think you should go with your friends. We can do this another day."

Her tone, though still friendly, was decided. Her smile had no warmth at all.

"Nonsense, Olyenka. A promise is a promise. Dima and I can have drinks anytime. I'm sure Mr. Quine will excuse us."

"Of course." Quine smiled. "But maybe we should all have ice cream."

"Cassandra, I insist." This time Olyenka's tone verged on peremptory. "I prefer that you go with your friends. Another time would be more convenient."

She was right, Cass thought. It would be much more convenient. Dima might decide to latch on to Quine's suggestion, and when Dima latched on, he was hard to shake. Clearly this meeting was unwelcome to Olyenka, and it seemed that there was more to her reluctance than ordinary shyness. Perhaps she'd met Quine or Dima before, possibly in the line of business, and was terrified of being recognized. If so, Dima was the likelier candidate. He was always going to St. Petersburg on business, and his reference to Chekhov had certainly seemed pointed. Tasteless, too, though that shouldn't have bothered Olyenka. . . . On the other hand, why shouldn't it bother her? Would Olyenka's occupation necessarily destroy her capacity for feeling? And why, if being recognized would embarrass her, wouldn't Dima's sexist chat? But these speculations were beside the point. Since Olyenka quite clearly didn't want to be here, detaining her would be insensitive, unkind.

"Okay. We'll do it another time. But let's be *sure* we do. And not next month, you hear." Cass shot Olyenka a meaningful smile. "Soon."

Watching Olyenka say her good-byes—one could grant her this: when she wanted, the child had nice manners—Cass was assailed by a sudden infuriating sense of opportunity lost. She was certain she'd been on the verge of a breakthrough. Now, thanks to Dima and *bloody* Arthur Quine, she would have to wait. She would have to wait, and she was tired of waiting. She was tired of being circumstance's puppet, helpless to move unless someone jerked the strings. But though frustrating, it was going to be okay. Sooner or later Olyenka would be back.

For five hundred dollars, no question.

* * *

"YOUR FRIEND SEEMED CURIOUSLY ANXIOUS to be off," Dima said.

"You think so?" Cass shrugged. "I can't say I find it surprising. Your remarks about darlings were not in the best of taste. Girls her age are easily embarrassed, you know. If you'd said something like that to me, I think I might have decked you."

Moment of awkward silence. Perceptible drop in the social temperature. That, Cass thought, might have been more tactfully expressed. She hadn't meant it literally, of course, but in Russia that kind of violence was widely considered the prerogative of men. It didn't help, either, that she was six inches taller than he and probably could have decked him. Was it just her imagination, she wondered, or had that been anger in his eyes?

"Feminism"—he managed a lopsided smile—"it's threatening to take the fun out of sex. Attempted flirtation will soon be a capital crime. A compliment will need to be submitted for approval—in triplicate, verbatim, no less than two weeks in advance." He paused, adding casually, "Whose daughter is she, anyway?"

"A friend from the university. No one you'd know." Cass attempted to head off further questions. "Isn't your interest a little unseemly? She can't be more than fourteen years old."

He was unabashed.

"Unseemly? I don't think so. An interest in *les jeunes filles en fleur* is actually quite normal in men of my age. In normal men of my age, that is. The fact that the wine isn't ready for drinking doesn't mean one can't anticipate." He turned to Quine. "What do you think, Arthur?"

"I don't think I care to comment." Quine directed his smile at Cass. "I wouldn't want to risk getting decked."

It occurred to Cass then, with a rush of embarrassment, that if Dima had met Olyenka professionally, he'd know she was certainly not the daughter of anyone connected with the university; he would know that she, Cass, had lied to him. Not that he'd be in a position to point it out, though with him, since he seemed to lack all sense of shame, this might not be a deterrent. She was conscious of wanting, quite badly, not to be caught in a lie by him, especially this lie. She wasn't sure why, or that not wanting to be caught wasn't actually a wish that he not be able to catch her. She didn't want to think of him paying to have sex with Olyenka. Or with anybody. Which didn't mean, of course, that she wanted to have sex with him herself. She didn't know how she felt about that, but at least until the issue was settled, she wanted to be able to think well of him. He was amusing, intelligent, surrounded almost visibly by an aura of power that made him seem dangerous, therefore attractive, and perhaps for this reason she wanted to believe that somewhere beneath his disguises there existed a decent man. A man, at least, who would draw the line somewhere, preferably well this side of sexually exploiting children. But she didn't *know*, she thought, and thanks to her involvement in this Oracle affair she was beginning to wonder if, with people, one ever could. Most were mysteries, even to themselves, and in this business she seemed to be confronted with several, too many, cases in point—Hal, for instance. Her image of him, once sharply defined, was beginning to blur, its colors starting to swim. The same was true of her father. As for Dima—as for him, she didn't have a clue. All she had was a set of hopes, the chief one being that appearance *was* deceptive, that under the tiger's skin disguise there didn't lurk the beast itself. But among so much uncertainty, she thought, there was one thing she was sure of: It was time for a change of subject.

"How do you two come to know each other?" she asked. "I wouldn't have thought you moved in the same circles."

"We both know *you*." Dima seemed amused by the question. "That's a circle in common. We're satellites of the same planet"—he sighed theatrically—"condemned to orbit you, like dogs in space, until the attraction grows too strong and, entering your atmosphere, we plunge to a fiery extinction."

She made a face.

"That's an image I'd rather not examine too closely. Promise me you'll never write me poetry."

"I think I can safely promise you that." Dima grinned. "That's a market I have no ambition to enter."

"Thank God for that." She turned to Quine. "How does a respectable diplomat like you justify acquaintance with a shady character like Dima?"

Quine gave her the benefit of his boyish smile.

"Some people would say, you know, that 'respectable diplomat' was a contradiction—"

He was going to continue when Dima cut in.

"It's simple, really: Arthur's job requires him to cultivate the people in Moscow worth knowing. If he drew the line at shady characters, there'd be no one here left. No one worth knowing, that is."

201

He yelped with laughter, flicked a glance at Quine, perhaps to see how this had been received. Quine was laughing, too, she saw, but not quite as heartily as Dima.

"So your job is to cultivate the people worth knowing." Sensing that the subject wasn't comfortable for him, she decided, perversely, to pursue it. "Dima is worth knowing for all kinds of reasons, but mostly for his knowledge of markets. Which market has grabbed your interest, Mr. Quine? Foreign currency? Certificates of ownership? Military equipment, perhaps?"

"None of the above." Quine's smile looked as if it had been painted on his face. "Though in fact, to be quite honest, Dima and I do have a business side to our friendship: I happen, in a modest way, to be a collector of Russian art. Not antiques or icons. Twentieth-century stuff. There are still amazing bargains to be had, and since Dima gets around more than I, he has a kind of roving commission to make purchases on my behalf. Within my limited price range, of course. Within my *very* limited price range."

"How interesting . . . Russian twentieth-century art." Something, an insight gleaned from her own recent practice, perhaps, or his use of a phrase so frequently deceptive, suggested to Cass that Quine *wasn't* being quite honest. "Do you have any favorites?"

"Well"—Quine hesitated—"I do have a fondness for Mayakovsky. I have three or four of his. Etchings and lithographs, mostly."

* * *

THAT, CASS THOUGHT later, was an interesting statement. For one thing, Quine had not been frank about his price range. The last time she had looked herself, the going rate for a work by the painter in question had been about twenty thousand dollars. Moreover, to the best of her knowledge, Mayakovsk*aya*, a woman, had never done an etching in her life.

Dima and Quine—there were any number of reasons why they might know one another. And therefore, Cass thought, it was hard to see why Quine had improvised this unlikely cover story. It was clear, however, that he had improvised it, and that made you wonder what it was cover *for*, especially in view of the fact that when she'd met him at the embassy, Quine had shown interest in Dolokhov and his tape. When Hal had been in Brussels, moreover, Quine had been acting as chief of the CIA station, and Sherman, who'd been on loan from the station to help Nick with the Oracle investigation, had normally reported to Quine.

Sherman, of course, had known about Natasha.

Chapter Twenty-Six

"THESE," TATYANA SAID, "are the pictures of my wedding."

My wedding. . . . Why was it, Cass wondered, even in cultures as different as hers and Tatyana's, that when women spoke of this subject they almost always used the possessive pronoun *singular?* Was the reason perhaps that, though marriages were shared, weddings were seen as exclusively female occasions, at which men were merely regrettably necessary props? At her parents' wedding this suggestion had been captured, unforgettably, on film. In every picture of the happy couple her father was gazing fondly at her mother, while her mother was staring, in triumph, at the camera. In their case the impression conveyed was quite seriously misleading. The scales of affection had tipped well the other way. Indeed, it would not be inaccurate to say that if the wedding had been her mother's triumph, the marriage had been her father's revenge.

Tatyana's marriage apparently had not been like that (though the wedding pictures, as Cass noted with amusement, mostly showed *both* of them looking at the camera). Tatyana's husband, an infantry colonel, evidently had been devoted to her, and she'd clearly been devastated by his death in the Soviet invasion of Afghanistan. But flipping through the pages of black-and-white prints, while Tatyana, perched on the arm of her chair, brought this one or that to her attention, she found it impossible not to wonder why her friend had chosen this evening in particular to insist on her browsing through these albums. Was it simply whim, or was there perhaps a connection, even if only unconscious, between this excursion into the past and the fact that Tatyana had spent all last evening with Nick, coming home in the early hours and looking, this morning, conspicuously content?

204

Cass liked Tatyana, liked her a lot. If they stayed in touch—and she couldn't see why they wouldn't—Cass could see her becoming a life-long friend. Then why, she wondered, did she still so dislike the prospect (if indeed it was still only that) of Tatyana's having an affair with Nick? She didn't know, but whatever the reason, the fact was she disliked it considerably. It was hard not to feel that Tatyana, knowing how she felt, had deliberately thrown herself at Nick. (He, of course, had never been noted for resisting temptation.) Cass knew that her feelings were paranoid—her father's love life, and Tatyana's, were really none of her business—but this didn't make them any less real. At present she had little inclination to encourage Tatyana to wallow in nostalgia. She would have to try quite hard, in fact, not to be a bitch.

She had to admit, though, when she set aside her suspicions about Tatyana's motives for showing them, that these snapshots were fascinating. They shed light not only on an era that already, only a few years later, was starting to seem remote, but also on several aspects of Tatyana's former life. For instance, they raised interesting questions regarding her position in the Soviet system. Dima had accused her more than once of having belonged to the *nomenklatura*, an accusation she'd hotly denied. (She was "army," she said, which was different; the army had always been nonpolitical. This had drawn from him the withering rejoinder that if she, the wife of a colonel and the daughter of another, imagined that the army had been nonpolitical, she ought to leave history to others and instead write fairy tales for children.) But on the evidence of these photographs, Cass thought, Dima might be said to have a point. The ceremony itself had been nothing extraordinary—routine acknowledgment of legal obligations made, in the presence of apathetic witnesses, to some clearly uninterested official of the state—but the wedding reception had been something else. They had held it at a dacha outside Moscow, loaned for the occasion by the groom's commanding officer, and the guests—there were more than fifty—had eaten outside at elegant long tables (real flowers, linen tablecloths, silver, crystal) on which was spread the kind of feast most Russians of the time had encountered, if at all, only in literature, and subversive literature at that. But perhaps, Cass thought, browsing through page upon page of photographs in which the camera was invariably greeted by raised glasses, stuffed faces, bleary grins, perhaps in the army of the Brezhnev era binges like this

205

had been more or less standard. Maybe shashlik, beef Stroganoff, sturgeon, caviar, washed down with liters of Georgian champagne, had been aspects of the system's earnest endeavor to keep its army "nonpolitical." In any event the pictures made an interesting comment on the enterprise of which they formed a part. The stated purpose of Tatyana's hobby—hobby, *baloney*, it was close to an obsession—was to chronicle the impact on her family of a system she claimed to have detested. Yet these pictures and indeed certain facts about her life (the large apartment, the car, the attendance at special schools, the admission at a very tender age to the country's most prestigious university) suggested that this impact had been largely positive. Tatyana might deny till she was blue in the face having belonged to the *nomenklatura*, but she couldn't deny she'd been better off than most.

Cass couldn't deny it herself, of course. She was better off, materially, than almost anyone and in no position to cast stones at her friend. But the issue here was candor, not privilege. She wasn't casting stones, she was wondering. But this, the propensity to question people and things she'd normally have accepted without thinking, was precisely her problem these days. Wondering like this corroded what it touched, including (and especially) friendship. She mustn't let it touch things, she thought. Some things at least—her friendship with Tatyana, her belief in her uncle—must be kept very firmly off-limits. It was simply a question of exercising will.

Look at the pictures, she told herself crossly. Don't raise imaginary demons. Try, above all, not to act like a bitch.

Armed with this resolve, she flipped to the next page. Here she confronted what seemed to be family portraits: bride and groom (both still intent on the camera) surrounded by people of assorted ages—a group whose membership was constant throughout, though in different pictures their arrangement varied. Tatyana, in her bridal gown, was always the focus, but in every picture Cass found her eye drawn to a woman, roughly Tatyana's age, of insistent, remarkable beauty.

"This," Tatyana continued her commentary, "is my Uncle Nikita, the general. That is my Cousin Sergei, his son. And that"—she pointed to the woman Cass had noticed—"is my cousin the notorious Tasha."

Notorious . . . it was easy to see why. This cousin not only had the

206

kind of good looks men tended to find irresistible (huge eyes; an avid, discontented mouth; a figure both slender and voluptuous), she also exuded—neither time nor the camera had slowed it down a bit—a sexuality that came at you like a train. In the pictures, moreover, she was draped around some man—"clinging like ivy" was the phrase that sprang to mind—a man who seemed, when Cass looked at him more closely, oddly but decidedly familiar.

She had seen him somewhere. Recently.

But where?

The photograph was fifteen years old. The face that stared back at her seemed younger than it should have been, a rough-hewn, somehow unfinished version of the one she seemed to remember. A tune, it struck her, seeking final form, or a likeness emerging feature by feature from the marble. Not that such similes were particularly apt; this was hardly the face to inspire an artist. Not a Michelangelo at any rate, though a Titian might work, he of the shifty-eyed popes. It was with this thought that recollection came, recollection and a shiver of misgiving.

It was Dolokhov, of course, in his younger days.

Vladimir Dolokhov, alias Grigoriev.

Volodya.

* * *

"WHO'S THIS?" Cass struggled to keep her voice casual. "The man with your cousin. The one who looks like a used-car salesman, the kind you wouldn't want to buy from."

"Oh, him." Tatyana wrinkled her nose. "Some guy my cousin used to date. He claimed to be a diplomat, but *we* all thought he was a Chekist. . . . She always did have rotten taste in men."

"Tasha, you mean?"

"Natasha." Tatyana nodded. "The black sheep of the family. Actress, gold-digger, all-around hot pants. She believed she could sleep her way to stardom. Or if not stardom, money. She promised she'd get rich, or die in the attempt. And actually"—Tatyana paused—"she did."

"Did which? Die or get rich?"

"Not rich." Tatyana managed to look simultaneously indifferent and tragic. "In our family, nobody ever got rich. Maybe it was the

KGB, or maybe some guy she cheated. The cops called it suicide, but you know cops: Russian or Belgian, they never admit they don't know."

She paused for a moment, shaking her head. Whether in sorrow or censure wasn't clear.

"They were wrong, though," Tatyana continued. "I'd bet hard currency on that. Natasha would never have killed herself. At the time, for one thing, she had her hooks into some fat cat or other; she thought she was going to be rich. Anyway, she loved herself too much."

Belgian cops? Natasha? . . . Was it possible, Cass asked herself, that Tatyana's cousin had not only been Dolokhov's girlfriend, but also the Natasha with whom Nick suspected Hal of having an affair? The timing would fit: Tatyana had married in 1981, so her cousin could easily have been in Brussels in 1984. It also seemed, from the reference to Belgian cops, that she had died there, apparently by her own hand. Not only the timing, virtually everything fitted.

Perhaps, it struck Cass, a little too neatly.

Chapter Twenty-Seven

"I FEEL BAD ABOUT THIS," Cass said. "Sneaking around behind her back, poking through her possessions." She paused, then added with asperity, "You should feel worse."

"Worse?" Nick stared. "Why should I? She's your roommate. You've been friends with her longer than I."

"Of course I have. But your friendship with her is"—she pretended to consider—"not closer, exactly. More *intimate*, perhaps."

He inspected her quizzically, not quite smiling, his head cocked slightly to one side.

"Are we stating fact? Or flying a kite?"

"We're stating what we believe to be fact. Are we wrong?"

He thought about this for a moment.

"It seems to me," he offered presently, "a more pertinent question might be: Is it any of our business?"

"Oh, I see." She rolled her eyes. "The gentlemanly code. Refusal to bandy a woman's name. We can *do* whatever the hell we like as long as we don't talk about it."

He looked pained.

"That's horseshit, Cass, and you know it. I don't want to talk because I don't see the point. And it really *is* none of your business. The need to know," he added, "is a sensible principle, I think. Don't burden people with information they have no practical use for and may very well not want to know."

He was wrong, she thought, about its being none of her business, but right perhaps about her not wanting to know. (Though now she *did* know, since he'd more or less taken the Fifth.) What had started out as banter had, with puzzling speed, turned into confrontation.

209

She hadn't meant things to take this turn, but with him she always seemed to manage to take the wrong tone. But maybe here it wasn't just him; maybe guilt had played a part. What they were doing here wasn't, strictly speaking, an invasion of privacy. It wasn't as if they were reading Tatyana's mail. She was sure Tatyana wouldn't mind her showing these photographs to Nick. But what she would mind, with good reason, was its happening behind her back. By not telling her, Cass thought, by concealing their interest in her cousin, they were tacitly making an admission of distrust, conceding the possibility that Tatyana was mixed up in all this. If she knew, she'd be hurt. (At least if she *wasn't* mixed up in all this.) So Cass was feeling guilty. Nick should be feeling guilty, too, she thought, rationalizations notwithstanding.

He should because *she* was.

" 'Don't burden people with information they have no practical use for.' Does that include," she queried acidly, "people one happens to be sleeping with?"

He rolled his eyes. "You don't quit, do you?"

"I'm curious," she said. "Not about your love life as much as your habits of mind, the way you ex-CIA types reconcile these things with your conscience—*if* you have a conscience, that is."

"I don't reconcile them." His face was expressionless. "We're talking oil and water. Personal relationships and catching spies don't mix." He paused. "Think about this for a moment: If we tell Tatyana we're looking at her photographs, we'll inevitably have to tell her why. By not telling, we're not distrusting her, necessarily; we're merely declining to involve her in something she may very well not want to be involved in." He paused again. "Let's not agonize about this. Let's just look at the damn pictures."

"We're not distrusting her, *necessarily*"—quite some burden of ambiguity was balanced on the knife edge of that adverb. But here again he was right. They'd already made up their minds about this.

"Okay . . ." She shrugged. "I have to tell you I think you missed your vocation. You'd have made a wonderful Jesuit."

"Not really." He gave a lopsided grin. "I have the sophistical thinking mastered, but I'd flunk the morals requirement."

*   *   *

NO REACTION when he saw the photographs, she noted. For maybe half a minute he inspected them without speaking, eyes flicking from one to the other but revealing intentness, nothing more.

"Is it she?" she asked. "Is it your Natasha?"

She realized she'd almost said "Hal's Natasha" but had stopped herself in time. Ways of speaking implied ways of thinking. It was "your Natasha" unless proved otherwise.

"It's Natasha." He nodded.

"You're sure of that? You seemed to need time to decide."

"I'm sure," he said. "No doubt. It's little Miss Gorgeous, as I remember her in life. I knew her the moment I saw her."

"Then what was all the studying for? What doubt could there be?"

"About him," Nick said. "I know it's Natasha, but I think it's also him. I only saw photographs, so in his case I'm not so certain."

"Him? You mean Dolokhov?"

"Dolokhov." He nodded. "Grigoriev, if you prefer. . . . When he came to my attention he called himself Panev. He's the guy she was photographed with in Geneva. The Brits, you'll recall, copped them leaving a hotel. Which in view of the body language here"—he gestured to the photographs—"would seem to make a fair amount of sense. It was *afterward* they pegged him as KGB." He paused. "He was also involved with Werner in that so-called stamp sale transaction."

Dolokhov again. She was starting to hate him. He seemed to be everywhere in this. Whatever the hell was going on here, Dolokhov was at its rotten heart, the fountain and source of the spreading distrust that was threatening to take over her life. Her mind cast up a sudden, vivid image of the last time she'd seen him—the small blue hole in the middle of his forehead, the ambushed expression in his eyes. He'd gotten what he deserved, she thought. Whoever put that hole in his head had done the world a favor.

"I want to be sure I have this straight," she said. "If you're right about Panev being Dolokhov, then Tatyana's cousin, the notorious Natasha, was evidently having an affair with *him* the same time you think she was having one with Hal?"

"Evidently." Nick shrugged. "No doubt there are other reasons for renting a hotel room with a member of the opposite sex, though I can't think of any offhand. The affair with Hal is conjectural, of course, as I'm sure you were about to point out."

211

"I already did," she said drily. "The question in my mind is: Are you sure about Panev being Dolokhov?"

He shrugged. "Pretty much—as I said, I only saw him in a photograph. But that one, like these, was of him and Natasha together. My memory associates them, you see. When I saw these, something went click in my mind."

"Makes sense," she acknowledged. "What conclusions do you draw?"

He thought.

"I don't, really. Like everything else we've turned up so far, this supports contradictory theories. The most of obvious of which"—he stopped, corrected himself—"*one* of which is that Dolokhov was Hal's case officer and Natasha the cutout."

"You're saying this conjectural affair could actually have been a cover?"

"It's possible." He nodded. "A kind of first line of defense. If the contacts between them were discovered, sex would have seemed a natural explanation."

Natural to you, she thought, managing not to say it and awarding herself points for self-restraint.

"Of course," he went on, "there is a problem with that theory, a problem Hal himself pointed out. If Natasha *was* the cutout, why did she go to the embassy that evening, thereby guaranteeing my attention would be drawn to the possible link between her and Hal?" He paused, returned to studying pictures in the album. "If you think about it, these don't add very much. They confirm that Natasha had a KGB contact, but that was something we already knew. That the contact turns out to be Comrade Dolokhov doesn't get us any farther forward."

"I disagree." She said it flatly. "I think it helps a lot. And I think it works against your theory."

"It's not mine." He sighed. "It's just a theory. But anyway, make your case."

"Okay," she said. "We agree that either Werner was Oracle, in which case the link between Hal and Natasha was probably fabricated by the KGB in an effort to cast suspicion on Hal, or else Hal was Oracle and the stamp sale business was fabricated by the KGB in an effort to cast suspicion on Werner." She paused. "Are you with me so far?"

He nodded. "I agree that *taken by itself*, the first alternative seems the more likely. Unfortunately, we can't take it by itself. There's the awkward little matter of the tape."

"Agreed." She shrugged. "So let's think about that: Dolokhov, his tape, his involvement in all this, his motive for approaching me, the reason for his murder. Here again, it seems to me, there are two possibilities, directly opposed: One, the tape is genuine and Hal was Oracle, in which case Dolokhov was a KGB loose cannon, his motive probably blackmail, and his murder by his former masters intended to prevent him from leaking the tape and endangering their asset. Two, the tape was faked in a conspiracy to screw Hal's chances of election, in which case Dolokhov's approach to me was part of a strategy for leaking the tape, and his subsequent murder by his partners a treacherous ploy to persuade us the tape was genuine." She paused. "Still with me?"

"Lagging a bit here." He looked dubious. "I have to say that the tape-is-genuine scenario strikes me as more plausible than the other, which, of course, contradicts my earlier conclusion. I guess at the moment *neither* scenario makes sense." He shrugged. "And I don't see why this latest discovery works in favor of your position."

"Well then, listen up, and presently you will."

"I'm listening." He grinned sardonically. "Go ahead."

"For one thing, it strikes me that if Hal really was Oracle, he's poised to become the most important asset in the whole history of espionage, a president of the United States *who is actually working for the Russians*. And in that case the KGB's handling of Dolokhov, and me, has been unbelievably clumsy. Let's assume, for instance, that, finding out he'd stolen the tape, they killed him to recover it. You'd think they'd do it quietly and anonymously, but instead they did exactly the reverse: They left their signature all over the crime. They shot him in the head with a silenced twenty-two, which, as pretty well everyone in Moscow seems to know, was their favored method of assassination when they wanted people to know whodunit. Sokolnikov remarked on it right away, and so, when he heard, did Dima." She paused, fixing Nick with a prosecutor's stare. "Not exactly what we've come to expect—now is it?—from the fabled cunning of the KGB?"

213

"It's a point," he conceded. "I presume there's more."

"There is." She nodded. "It strikes me they screwed up again, and royally, when they gave Sokolnikov to understand that Dolokhov had belonged to the First Chief Directorate. They ought to have been desperate to keep that quiet, but instead they permitted Yasenevo to issue an utterly implausible denial, which Sokolnikov proceeded to communicate to me. It's as if they wanted to make sure I knew (a) that the KGB *was* involved and (b) that I wasn't meant to know it. That's another screwup," she added, "the dopey way they've dealt with me. If Hal Reynolds is really their asset, then Cass Wolfe ought to be dead. She ought to have been dead about five minutes after Dolokhov was."

"You've made that point before," Nick said. "I'm still not sure I buy it. Killing you would have caused a stink. Easier if they could scare you off."

"*I* don't buy *that*." She shook her head. "That would make sense from their point of view only if they knew I hadn't heard the tape. But they couldn't know, so why take the risk? They wouldn't have had to shoot me in the head. The murder rate here is pretty horrendous. They could easily have made me the victim of a mugging."

"They could." He nodded gravely. "In fact, you almost were."

"Those Chechens?" She looked sceptical. "Too little, too late to be really convincing. You said yourself it was pretty half-assed."

"Did I say that?" He smiled faintly. "That must have been *after* we were rescued. I remember finding it quite convincing at the time. Of course," he qualified, "I'll concede that if the object was to scare you off, it doesn't seem to have worked very well."

"No, it hasn't, has it? And it hasn't been repeated, either. So again I wonder if the object was to scare me off. Or was it perhaps exactly the reverse—to ensure my continuing interest?" She paused. "Because now, on top of everything else, we have this startling series of coincidences. Tatyana shows me her wedding album. She more or less *insists* on showing it. In it we find photographs of her Cousin Natasha, *your* Natasha, with her boyfriend, Comrade Dolokhov. . . . I mean, isn't it all beginning to strike you as just a trifle stage-managed?"

Nick thought about this, frowning.

"If it is, it would seem to implicate Tatyana."

"It would." Cass nodded. "And as you'll recall, she's been 'helpful'

214

before. It was she who came up with that intelligence roundup, the one predicting U.S. responses to a Soviet invasion of the Baltic, the one that echoed so exactly the phrasing used in Dolokhov's tape."

Silence.

"I have to envy," Nick offered drily, "your youthful flexibility of mind. Ten minutes ago you were fretting about seeming to distrust her. It doesn't seem to be bothering you now."

"I'm considering the evidence," Cass said. "And to use the words of a head no doubt wiser than mine, I'm not distrusting her, necessarily, I'm just declining to dismiss the possibility that she may in fact be involved in this." She paused. "Do you have a problem with that?"

"In my heart"—he nodded—"if not my head."

"You didn't in the case of Hal."

"I did." He caught her gaze and held it. "You've no idea what a problem."

"But you couldn't let your head be ruled by your heart?"

He nodded. "That's right. I couldn't."

"Well then," she said, "the same goes for me. It isn't easy, but I'm learning. Luckily," she added, "I've a wonderful teacher."

He let that go.

"You've made out a very good case," he said. "But in the end it doesn't persuade. You've highlighted the many problems with the Hal-is-Oracle theory, but you haven't offered a convincing alternative. Your conspiracy theory strikes me as implausibly elaborate. There are too many plotters involved, too many things have to fall into place, too many people have to act as predicted. I mean, fine machinery is all very well, but what sane person would design a conspiracy with more moving parts than a self-winding watch?"

"Fine." She shrugged. "Theory One is full of holes. Theory Two is way too complex. That seems to leave us sucking our thumbs. This is your territory here, not mine. What words of wisdom have you to offer?"

"Not many," he admitted. "Plots and plans were never my province. One thing I have observed: In the case of fine machinery, Murphy's Law applies with particular rigor—anything that can go wrong will. So plotters are advised to keep things very simple."

"Isn't that the point you've just been making? Theory Two is overly elaborate."

215

"Close," Nick nodded, "but not exactly. Plotters are advised to keep things very simple, but usually they don't keep them simple enough. We've been working on the assumption here that everything's going to according to plan. But things almost never go according to plan. Life's unpredictable. People screw up. The unforeseen is almost guaranteed to happen. . . . I suspect that whatever we're looking at here—and quite probably what I was looking at in Brussels—*didn't* go according to plan. Things went wrong, people got out of line, solutions were improvised on the run. That's why we're finding this so hard to figure out."

"That's wonderful." Cass rolled her eyes. "What you're saying is we have no chance. Life is so impossibly unruly we're *never* going to get this figured out."

"It's not that bad." He made a face. "I think it's a bit like studying history. We can't hope to learn the whole truth, if there even is such a thing, but we can arrive at a partial version. It's a question of gathering more facts. We don't *know* enough to make sense of this yet."

She considered this.

"I'm not sure I find that consoling. How are we to gather more facts?"

"If your theory's right," he replied, "we won't have to. If they're planning to screw Hal, they haven't done it yet. We can expect to hear from them again."

She didn't find this consoling either.

"In the meantime, I suppose, we just wait."

"Mostly." He nodded. "I don't suppose we'll have to wait long. In the meantime, there is one thing we can do. There's one person here who doesn't seem anxious to be helpful: your little buddy Olyenka. You promised her five hundred bucks, but she hasn't been back to you to claim it. You could find out what she was trying to sell, why she changed her mind so abruptly."

"I could"—Cass looked dubious—"if I could find her."

"That won't be hard." He shrugged. "I doubt she's gone out of business."

"Probably not," she agreed. "But something seems to have scared her off. Dima maybe. Or Quine. In any case, since she hasn't been back, she clearly doesn't want to be found." She paused. "She'll be looking out for me. You, on the other hand, she doesn't know from Adam."

"Me?" She was pleased to note he looked appalled. "But I don't know her either."

"Easy." Cass was enjoying this. "I'm sure Lieutenant Sokolnikov will oblige us with a mug shot."

"What about the language problem? My Russian isn't up to this."

"Hire an interpreter." She grinned. "I don't think I'd use Tatyana."

"But I can't do this," he protested. "You can't be expecting me to trek all over Moscow asking about the whereabouts of teenage hookers. For one thing, I have a job to do. For another, it wouldn't be decent. Not in a man of my age."

"Nor, one presumes, in a man of any age." Her smile was pure mischief. "Not to worry, old father of mine, I've thought of a way to solve both problems."

Chapter Twenty-Eight

"**I** DON'T KNOW, Dima. I just don't know how I feel."

This was only half honest, Cass thought. It was true that she didn't know how she felt, but as to whether she was going to bed with him she was really in no doubt at all. She supposed she should have seen this coming. He'd taken her out to the Millionaires' Club—one of his favorite haunts, though not hers; the millionaires eyed her as if she were for sale, and the number of bodyguards made her nervous—and he'd ordered a dinner extravagant even for him. The caviar had been washed down with Dom Perignon, and the Bordeaux he'd chosen for the *boeuf en croûte* had been of a vintage so rare and ancient you ordered it at your own risk (they'd had to open three bottles before they found a good one). When she'd asked whether this was a special occasion—had some market or other looked kindly on him?—he'd replied with an enigmatic smile that he hoped an investment in futures was shortly about to mature. So maybe she should have refused his invitation to come up to his apartment for a nightcap. But she'd accepted such invitations before without untoward consequences, and in spite of that remark about futures, she hadn't expected tonight to be different.

"You don't know how you feel about what?"

His voice, she was relieved to note, was relaxed and pleasant. She hadn't known how he would deal with a refusal. Probably he didn't get a lot of practice. But at least here he couldn't complain about having been led on.

"I don't know how I feel about *you.*"

"Ah . . ." He smiled faintly. "I think this is one of those cases where abstentions count *against* the motion. If you don't know

218

how you feel about me as a man, it has to mean you don't feel very much."

She shook her head. "I don't believe that's true, necessarily. The myth is it's always obvious; there's either chemistry or not. But aren't there times when there could be a reaction, but conditions aren't right, something is lacking, a catalyst?"

"Sure." He nodded, wry but still smiling. "The something lacking is called sexual attraction."

"It's not," she insisted. "There's a lot I find attractive about you. You're intelligent, amusing, generous, unexpected—"

"Et cetera, et cetera," he cut in, rolling his eyes. "No need to go on. When a woman starts listing your virtues, it always leads up to a 'but.'"

"I'll take your word for it. Women don't often list my virtues. . . . Do you want to know what the 'but' is in this case?"

"I've had the sugar-coating." He shrugged. "I might as well gag down the pill."

"You're being perverse now. You really are. I meant what I said, both parts of it. I like you, Dima, but I don't how much, because I don't know who you are."

"You mean morally?" He sounded amused. "You mean am I a gangster or not?"

"If you want to put it that bluntly, yes."

He appeared to consider. "It would help to know which answer you want. Some women find gangsters appealing."

"Well, I'm not one."

He grinned, then looked at her sidelong, eyes opaque. "In that case we have ourselves a problem."

"What do you mean?"

He continued to look at her with feline intentness. "If I told you I wasn't a gangster, would you believe me?"

She shook her head. "Not necessarily. Not just because you told me."

"That's the problem." He spread his hands. "You require a demonstration. But how, exactly, does one demonstrate that one is *not* a gangster?"

"It's hard," she said, "but it can be done. It's called establishing trust. It takes time."

She stood up.

"It may be that you feel I've had ample time already. If so, I'll be sorry, of course, but I'll also understand." She paused. "You have to admit you sometimes take pleasure in deliberately muddying the waters."

"Muddying the waters?" He stood up also, crossed over to the door. She expected him to open it for her, but instead he locked it, looking at her calmly as he did so and putting the key in his pocket. "You mean by doing something like this?"

He walked toward her, stopped a foot away.

"You may as well sit down," he said. "You're not going anywhere, not yet."

She sat.

"This doesn't muddy the waters, Dima." She tried to keep her voice calm. She could scream, she thought, but no one would hear her up here. No one except Dima's people, and there was no assistance to be hoped for from them. This wasn't happening, she thought, it couldn't be happening. "Actually, it makes them clear. Unless, of course it's a joke. . . . This *is* some kind of a joke, isn't it?"

This was her best chance. Give him an out. Let him think she thought it was a joke. For all she knew, it might be. His sense of humor was sometimes weird.

But it didn't feel like a joke.

"If I *were* a gangster, how would this scene continue?"

She didn't answer. Let him paint his own fantasy. She wasn't going to contribute.

"Are you *sure* you don't like gangsters?" His face was expressionless, but his voice contained a hint of lubricity. "Don't think I don't know what your girlfriend says: 'That little gangster, probably ex-KGB'. . . . But isn't that why you go out with me? The whiff of excitement, the thrill of danger, the turn-on? A princess walking a tame leopard on a leash?" He paused. "Did you think about what happens if the leopard gets bored?"

She said nothing.

"You Americans," he said. "You come over here with your money, your self-confidence, your patronizing attitudes. The winners being nice to the losers. You want a little taste of the Russian experience. Go

220

home and boast to your girlfriends in college how you used to go out with this cute Mafioso. As if I were some kind of clown in a circus. Well, I think what you need is more than a taste. I think you should have to swallow the whole thing."

"Dima," she said, "please stop this now. You're scaring me. Please stop."

For a second there was silence. He stood over her, motionless but sprung, as if he were held in precarious balance. Reaching down, he touched her collarbone with his forefinger, tracing its outline from shoulder to throat.

She didn't flinch or even move.

Suddenly he gave a lopsided smile.

"Cassandra"—his voice was heavy with reproach—"I don't believe it. I'm disappointed in you. If you're really scared, I'm actually *hurt*. I hoped you knew me better than that. Do you really think I would force myself on you?"

"That wasn't very funny, Dima." Relief brought anger, but she wasn't going to indulge it. At any rate, not very far. She wasn't sure yet that it had been a joke. He still had time to change his mind. Besides, there might be truth in what he'd said. Not about the excitement, maybe, but the rest. "If you had me fooled, you've yourself to blame. Sometimes you're too good an actor for comfort."

He smiled. "I am a good actor, aren't I?"

And with that it seemed to be over. He unlocked the door and got her coat. He walked her downstairs and into the street, where his driver was waiting in the white BMW. When he'd given her address to the driver and seen her into the car, opening the door for her with his usual courtesy, he gestured to her to roll down the window.

"I'm sorry about the charade," he said. "It was a joke. An impulse. I'm not sure why I did it. Maybe sometimes I resent a little the way you seem to think of me. Or maybe I hoped you wouldn't believe me. . . . You didn't believe me, did you?"

"Perhaps not," she said. "But I'm easily scared by things like that. Jokes like that one, you should know, work better for men than for women."

"Easily scared?" He shook his head. "It's one of the things I worry about with you. Especially in this city. There are very bad people in this city. . . . Sometimes I think you aren't scared easily enough."

He kissed the tips of his fingers, reached in, and touched them to her cheek.

"Don't worry. I will look after you."

Chapter Twenty-Nine

"SHE SAYS SHE DOESN'T KNOW any Olyenkas."

Another dead end. . . . Sometimes, or so it seemed to Nick, Cass's bright ideas were not quite as bright as she thought. This notion of combining the hunt for Olyenka with research for a background piece on child prostitution in Moscow had seemed at first to be almost brilliant. Though using this minor, though ugly, social problem as a metaphor for resurgent Russian capitalism had struck him as somewhat facile, it was just the sort of thing his editor loved. It also offered practical advantages: Little of the legwork would be wasted, and research that might otherwise have looked odd was provided with fairly respectable cover. This, at any rate, had been the theory. Practice, alas, had turned out rather different.

For one thing, even the interpreter's presence frequently failed to convince these girls that Nick's purpose in questioning them was as stated: his inquiries had met with sardonic smiles and comments that struck him as uncalled for. Moroever, when he did succeed in making his purpose clear, his reception tended to be hostile. Moscow's child prostitutes, by and large, didn't much *want* to talk to reporters. They didn't have any use for "talking," having done too much of it with cops and social workers. And since time was more or less synonymous with money, they expected, if they talked, to be paid for the service, and at rates that struck him as extortionate. He'd always had, in both his professions, a great dislike of buying information; what one paid for was always suspect. In this case he disliked it even more, since the money he was using was his own. It was all very well for Cass to call these interviews "research," but he couldn't see turning in claims for expenses. He was bound to end up explaining to his editor exactly how the money had been spent. He didn't care to even imagine the likely reaction to *that*. Worse, three days, five railway stations, and several hundred dollars into this thing, he now had enough material to write a *book* on child prostitution in Moscow, yet he hadn't so far managed to track down Olyenka.

He hadn't even come up with a decent lead.

"Ask her is she sure—she may have just moved her beat to this station."

That she *had* moved her beat was the only thing he was sure of. They'd been unanimous on that point, the girls at the St. Petersburg station.

The interpreter's flurry of Russian was met with a shrug and a shake of the head, followed by an answering flurry. This one must be about twelve, Nick thought. A sullen waif, with the listless gaze and affectless manner experience had taught him to expect from these interviews. And even to someone whose tastes ran this way, not, he'd have thought, appetizing.

"She says she's sure." The interpreter looked glum. "She says if this person wants to move her beat, she'd better think about somewhere else. The ones here are all taken."

"Ask her if she's ever seen this girl."

The photograph Sokolnikov had provided was the usual full-face head and shoulders shot, bad color, overexposed, the startled expression and unfocused stare resulting from a flash being used too close and pointed too directly at the subject's eyes. It was so obviously a mug shot, in fact, that he'd been using it only as a last resort. These girls, unsurprisingly, were all cop-shy. In spite of the interpreter and his own obvious foreignness, showing them a mug shot alerted their suspicions. Clearly this girl was no exception. As her eyes flicked over the photograph and back again to Nick, they seemed to lose what little expression they'd had.

She spoke briefly to the interpreter.

"She wants to know why you're looking for this person. Are you a relative? Her father? A cop?"

"Christ." Nick sighed. "Do I look like a cop? Tell her I'm a lawyer from America. Tell her I'm trying to find this girl because someone died and left her a fortune. Tell her that unless I find this Olyenka, ten million dollars will go to waste on a shelter for stray cats. Say there's a twenty-five-dollar reward for anyone who helps me."

Deadpan, the interpreter relayed this to the girl.

This time there was a reaction. The girl half smiled, a lazy, sceptical grin, her eyes flicking to a point behind Nick, then quickly back to him again. The ensuing volley of Russian was almost lively.

"She says she knows you're trying to hang noodles on her ears." The interpreter was grinning, too. "But if you mean it about the reward, she'll tell you right now where you can find her."

"Tell her I mean it." Once more Nick reached for his wallet.

She waited, he noticed, until the money was firmly in her grasp. Then, pocketing the bills and grinning, she pointed up the platform behind him.

He turned, following the direction of her finger.

Passengers from a train just arrived were surging up the platform. And among them, walking directly toward him, instantly recognizable from the mug shot, modest as a schoolgirl and dressed to suit, was Olyenka.

Chapter Thirty

"WHY DID YOU NEVER GET BACK to me?" Cass demanded. "There was money in it for you, remember?"

"Five hundred dollars . . ." Olyenka's look was withering. "You must think I'm really stupid."

"Stupid . . . why?"

Olenka said nothing. Her face was set in the mulish expression Cass remembered from previous encounters. There were two people here, she thought: the intelligent, humorous, outgoing child, whose idea of a treat was a bowl of ice cream; and this suspicious and resentful harpy, fourteen going on forty. Not that this was at all surprising. Suspicion would come naturally to someone like her; in the world she lived in it might be a condition of survival. There couldn't have been, in a childhood so tragically stunted, much encouragement to trust. And here her suspicions were not merely reflex; they'd also been aroused by that unfortunate encounter with Dima and Quine in the hotel. But which of them had scared her?

And why?

"Why stupid?" Cass repeated.

" 'Why stupid?' " Olyenka mimicked savagely. "Stupid for trusting you, for starters. Little Miss America, all sweetness and sympathy, so anxious to help me get my ass off the streets. What good is money when you're dead?"

Dead? . . . Cass thought she understood. Whoever it was had scared Olyenka; it wasn't hard to guess why. And in that case *she* must be suspect, too, if only by association. How was she to win the child's trust?

"Dead? You think someone's going to kill you? Is it him?" She

226

pointed to Nick. "Or me? Or is it maybe one those people we met when we went to collect your money?"

" 'Is it maybe one of those people'?" Olyenka's tone was savagely sarcastic. She turned to Nick and rolled her eyes. "Trying to pretend she doesn't know."

"I *don't* know," Cass said. "Just think for a second: I couldn't have known we'd run into those guys. I didn't even know we'd be *going* to get cash. That was your idea, remember?"

Olyenka wasn't buying. "I notice you know who we're talking about."

"Of course I know. It's obvious, isn't it? You were fine until we ran into my friends. Then you couldn't wait to leave."

"Friends . . ." Ironic emphasis. "Nice friends you have yourself there."

"That's right," Cass said. "I think so, at least. What do you know about them that's not?"

Silence.

"I think I can guess," Cass went on. "Those two men we met at the hotel, either or both, I'd imagine, were among the men who searched Volodya's apartment. You're scared that if they know you saw them, they might decide to kill you, too. And you're scared I'm going to tell them, aren't you?"

Silence.

"Okay." Cass shrugged. "Then there's something else I think you should consider: If I were going to tell them, don't you think I'd have done it already?"

No answer. But the shaft had hit its mark, Cass thought. There was indecision on Olyenka's face.

"Maybe you already have."

"That makes no sense." Cass pressed her advantage. "If that's the case, you should be dead. It wasn't that hard to find you, remember. We knew where to look." She paused. "Be honest, Olyenka, think about it. Do I really look like a killer? Does he?"

"That's stupid." The response was prompt. "If people *looked* like what they are, the killers would all be behind bars, and *I'd* have to find another job." Olyenka paused for a moment to think. "If I tell you, do we still have our deal?"

"Of course," Cass said. "Five hundred dollars. Two hundred to tell us what they were looking for, three hundred more if you show us where to find it. But first"—she didn't want to ask but knew she had to—"tell us who it was you saw that day at Volodya's apartment. Was it the older one, the American?"

One could hope, she thought; one could always hope.

"Not him." Olyenka shook her head. "The other one, the one you called Dima."

* * *

"ARE YOU OKAY?" Nick was looking concerned.

Cass didn't answer. Olyenka was gone now; they could talk without constraint. But for the moment she couldn't trust herself.

It was too much, she thought. It was just too much.

First Hal, then Tatyana, and now Dima—people she cared about, or could have cared about, one by one stained by doubt and suspicion. Olyenka's revelation, of course, had raised a lot more than suspicion. Dima had known of Dolokhov's death only hours after it had happened. How he had known was theoretically still an open question, but if the numbness at her heart were any guide, she thought, probably he had killed him. This didn't shock her—indeed, it was almost expected; she'd been preparing herself for it, or something like it, since that day at the hotel when she and Olyenka had run into him and Arthur Quine—but she was surprised to find how deeply it dismayed her. She'd no longer hoped, if she ever had, that her friendship with him might turn into something serious; the potential for that had been effectively destroyed by the creepy ending to their last evening together. Then why was she so upset? Perhaps, she thought, it was receiving such a brutal confirmation that her friendship, her trust, had once more been misplaced.

"Are you okay?" Nick repeated.

"I guess so. . . ." She hesitated, then shook her head. "This whole thing is getting me really paranoid. It's getting to where I don't trust anyone—and I'm getting so very *tired* of it." Quite suddenly she found herself fighting back tears. "I want people to be what they seem."

Nick studied her for a moment. "People—you mean Dima, don't you?"

"I mean all of them. Hal mostly." She paused. "I always knew the odds were Dima was a crook, but I thought there was just a chance he wasn't. Or else that he was a *nice* crook. It sounds stupid when you say it, but I guess it was what I wanted to think. He was funny and intelligent, and he seemed to like me. . . ." She broke off then, struggled to regain composure, but in spite of her efforts her eyes flooded with tears. "And here I go with that word again. He *seemed* to like me, but who knows what his real feelings were? Probably all he cared about was my connection with you and Hal."

At another time his look of dismay at her grief might have struck her as almost comical. He'd always had a horror of tears.

"You were . . . fond of him?"

"In love with him, you mean?" She shook her head. "I guess when it comes to men you like, that's an option you never close off, but I thought of him as a buddy mostly, someone I liked, someone I thought was my friend. That must be what's upsetting me here— discovering I was mistaken. Romances are a dime a dozen, aren't they? When it comes right down to it, romance is mostly glandular. But friendship is something else. If a friend betrays you, it hits you where you live. You feel—I don't know—diminished."

As she heard herself say it, saw Nick's face, it came to her that she'd spoken for them both. She'd spoken awkwardly, tactlessly even—that crack about romance being glandular was uncomfortably close to the bone—but she'd also explained to herself something about him she hadn't seen clearly before. It hadn't been envy, conscious or otherwise, that had made Nick able to suspect his friend; it had been love. Or rather, she thought, the self-absorbed aspect of it that made one always apprehensive of loss, fearful of the diminishment loss entailed, and (because people in their relations with each other were usually more or less paranoid) that much more willing, therefore, to entertain the prospect.

He was standing there, stone still, withdrawn, absent. She went over, touched him on the arm.

"I'm sorry," she said.

"Sorry?" He looked puzzled. "For what?"

"For lots of things. For what happened with you and Hal. For not understanding how you felt about it. For giving you grief about Tatyana. For being a bitch to you in general. . . ." She paused, mustered a watery smile. Knowing his dislike of "scenes," she attempted to lighten the mood a little. "That ought to be plenty to be going on with."

For a moment he said nothing. She thought he hadn't heard her. "Nick," she said. "Dad . . ."

"*You're* sorry." His look was disbelieving. "You think you owe *me* an apology?"

"It wasn't a question of owing. It was something I wanted to say."

"There's something I want to say, too." He looked awkward. "I've been wanting to say it since I got here. But all this other stuff came up. I never could find the right moment. I wanted to say"—he hesitated, offered her a rueful smile—"I want to say that as a parent I know I've given a spectacularly lousy performance."

"Not always." She smiled. "Sometimes, I'd have to agree."

"I regret that. I'll regret it all my life." He paused. "I know that doesn't help at all. It doesn't *change* what happened."

"I disagree. It doesn't change what happened, but it helps," she said. "It helps a lot."

Chapter Thirty-One

THIS TIME, THANK GOD, the footsteps on the staircase were *receding*.

If only people would stop moving about. They ought not to be at this time of day. With the Russian economy in its present disarray they ought all, Cass thought righteously, to be out at work. But instead they kept up this coming and going. . . . The carpet situation made things worse. The stairs weren't carpeted, but the corridors were, so until people were already on the stairs, you couldn't *hear* them coming and going, which didn't give you a lot of time to figure out where they were headed. This last was the third time in as many minutes she'd heard, suddenly and without any warning, footsteps only a flight below.

What the hell was taking so long?

She wished they hadn't made her keep lookout. It made sense, of course—Olyenka was needed inside, and she, Cass, being fluent in Russian, could always try chat to head off intruders—but it also made her nervous as hell. Actually, it wasn't just being the lookout; the whole thing made her nervous as hell. There were people who were suited by temperament to breaking into Moscow apartments and others who very clearly weren't. She fell into the latter group. It was all very well for Olyenka and Nick to assure her that the risk of being caught was slight; the risk *existed*, and it was all she could think of. Ever since they'd embarked on this endeavor, long before they'd even reached the apartment, her mouth had been dry, her palms sweaty, her heart rate about a hundred and fifty. And this at the mere *prospect* of being arrested, having to ask Quine to bail her out again, having to explain to some policeman—with *her* luck it was bound to be Sokolnikov—what she, her father, and a known child prostitute were

231

doing in Dolokhov's apartment. What worried her most, it seemed, was the embarrassment. She must be getting incurably bourgeois.

Not so Nick and his teenage accomplice. If Olyenka's sense of shame, the social *awkwardness* of being arrested, had been blunted by experience, Nick's didn't even seem to exist. By temperament, clearly, he was admirably suited to breaking into Moscow apartments. Or if not by temperament, by training.

Probably he'd had a lot of practice. The CIA had never been noted for respecting other people's rights, and he'd certainly known what to do. Some of it was common sense—picking a time when people were at work, ringing the doorbell to make sure no one was home, posting her at the head of the stairs, himself at the door to receive her signal and relay it to Olyenka inside—but common sense hadn't taught him to pick locks. He hadn't fumbled around at it either. When the keys in Olyenka's spare set ("I wasn't going to give that dumb Sokolnikov *all* my keys, now was I?") had turned out to work on the dead bolt only, and the new Yale-type lock had resisted the old credit card trick, it had taken him only a couple of minutes to fashion a pick from a length of stiff wire and persuade the new lock to yield to his probing.

Olyenka had found this impressive. Olyenka was finding this whole thing "fantastic." Particularly Nick. She seemed very taken with Nick.

Not that this wasn't par for the course.

A sudden clatter on the stairs startled Cass out of these sour reflections.

Footsteps.

Footsteps *descending*.

Should she warn Nick? The chances were it was someone headed for the ground-floor exit, but here "the chances were" didn't hack it. In the worst case, the *nightmare* case, it could be the new tenant of Dolokhov's apartment—given Moscow's housing shortage, it couldn't have stayed unoccupied this long—returning from a visit to a neighbor. If it was, they'd be caught red-handed. There wasn't a choice. She *had* to warn Nick.

She looked down the corridor.

He wasn't there.

He must have gone inside. Her mind flailed. What the hell should she do? The footsteps were halfway down the stairs. Not enough time to run in and give the alert. She could call out in English, hope that whoever was coming didn't speak it. But too many Russians did these days, and her tone—and the fact of her calling at all—might in any case give her away. Diversion, she thought. She had to create a diversion.

She started up the stairs.

The footsteps, she saw, belonged to a burly, belligerent-looking woman, somewhere in her midforties, with the rolling, backward-leaning gait of a sailor. She was dressed in the almost uniform of the urban Russian housewife: black, flat-heeled shoes; stockings of brown wool, darned in several places and drooping at the knee; a gray serge skirt; a blouse and cardigan; tiara of curlers under her headscarf. No coat, Cass noted with misgiving, which suggested a destination *inside* rather than out. One was dealing here with the familiar type who ruled her family with a rod of iron, took no crap from anyone, man or woman, and could be relied on *not* to mind her own business.

"*Izvinite, skazhite pozhalsta. . . .*" Cass planted herself squarely in the oncomer's path, smiling hard enough to crack her face and to her own ears practically yelling.

No answering smile. Stopping because there was no choice. Not at all pleased about it either. "Yes, young woman, what do you want?"

What *did* she want? A question, Cass thought, *any* question—she was looking, that's what she was doing. She was hovering inanely at the head of the stairs because she was looking for someone's apartment. But whose? She needed a name.

Any name.

Later she would blame herself for not coming up with anything better, but she didn't have a lot of time. The woman was already starting to push past, and under the pressure of that basilisk stare, her mind froze, emptied itself of all possibilities but one.

It wasn't the happiest of choices.

"Does a Vladimir Dolokhov live on this floor?"

Silence.

"He does *not*." Abruptly unfriendliness turned into hostility. "He used to live in three thirteen, but he doesn't any longer."

"Not any longer. . . . You mean he's moved? Can you tell me where he moved to?"

"Not anywhere *you* can find him, that's sure." The brief, thin-lipped, unpleasant smile reveled in its owner's superior knowledge. "He's dead. I heard someone shot him."

"Shot him?" Cass simulated horror. "Why?"

"How should I know? I can think of maybe half a dozen reasons. As I've no doubt"—nastily—"you can yourself. Girls," she added darkly. "Very *young* girls. Sluts, if you want to give it a name. Coming and going at all hours. And now if you'll excuse me, please, it isn't a subject I care to discuss with a stranger."

She made a sudden push to get past. Short of trying to restrain her physically, a move whose prospects of success seemed doubtful, Cass had no choice but to let her go.

But Nick must have heard them talking, she thought, and at least had the sense to shut the door.

It appeared he hadn't.

That the door was open was instantly noticed. With a cry of surprise and disapproval, the woman trundled toward it. Cass followed helplessly, heart sinking.

At the doorway, discretion reasserted itself. The woman paused for a moment to listen. From the bedroom there came a mutter of voices, and then, raised in triumph, Olyenka's:

"See, I was right. I *told* you I knew where it was. . . ."

Cass was never conscious of forming any plan or even a definite intention. It was rather, at this moment when her mind refused to function, as if instinct, body wisdom, took over. All she knew was that, when the woman turned back toward her, deciding perhaps that the better part of valor was retreat, she, Cass, gave her a violent shove, knocking her backward through the open door, then followed this up with a punch to the throat, knocking her victim onto the sofa and rendering her for the moment speechless. Then, caution reasserting itself, Cass turned and closed the front door.

It was then that, having heard the scuffle, Nick and Olyenka emerged from the bedroom. Olyenka was clutching a notebook computer. But Cass could spare little attention for it, not when she noticed what Nick was holding.

Nick was holding a gun.

* * *

"I FOUND IT in the cache," Nick explained. "Along with the notebook and the other goodies. Providential, wasn't it? When you and your friend made your sudden dramatic entrance, I thought it might come in handy—not that you seem to have needed any help," he added, shooting her a quizzical grin. "I thought you disapproved of violence."

"I do," Cass said. "If I'd stopped to think, I wouldn't have done it. And if you'd been where you were meant to be, I wouldn't have had to, would I?"

"Olyenka needed help." He shrugged. "She couldn't get the floorboard up. What was I supposed to do? Tell her to phone for the maintenance man? Relax, Cass. It's okay. All's well that ends well."

"I don't see that it's ended yet." His sangfroid struck her as almost offensive. "There's obviously someone living here now who could come back at any second. And then there's the minor problem of her." She indicated the woman, still gasping and retching on the sofa. "As soon as she gets her vocal cords back, she's going to start screaming bloody murder."

"Then we'd better gag her. Gag her and tie her up." He walked over to the woman and, squatting down, pressed the muzzle of the gun to her temple. Speechless still, she rolled her eyes in terror. "Use her headscarf to secure the gag, her stockings to tie her up with. Tell her not to make a sound meanwhile. Tell her if she gives you any crap, I'll give her a headache she'll never forget—and *mean* it," he added. "Mean it because I do."

Cass told her. The threat must have carried conviction because, though clearly outraged at the request, the woman silently removed her stockings, offering no resistance whatever when Cass and Olyenka gagged and tied her up, sat her down in an armchair.

"I think your father is fantastic," Olyenka whispered. "What is he in America? A gangster?"

"Close." Cass shrugged. Olyenka might be thrilled by all this, but Cass herself could hardly believe it was happening. Things like this *didn't* happen, she thought. They didn't happen to her, at least.

She turned to Nick.

"That seems to solve the immediate problem, but what about this one? This woman just happens to have seen us all and no doubt will be more than happy to give our descriptions to the State Militia."

He thought about this for a moment, then shook his head.

235

"I don't think so," he said. "Not when you tell her who she's dealing with here."

"Oh?" Cass said. "And who is she dealing with here?"

"Mafia." He had the grace to grin. "And not any half-assed, Russian imitation. *American* Mafia. The real McCoy. Tell her that, tell her when she's rescued to say she never saw us. Tell if she does, she'll be all right, we'll never bother her again. But if she tries helping the Militia, tell her"—suddenly his face went blank, the eyes dead, the features expressionless; he was bluffing, Cass knew, but even she was chilled—"tell her I'll come back and kill her."

Chapter Thirty-Two

"And now," Olyenka's eyes were shining, "we come to the happy moment."

They were back now in Tatyana's apartment. Tatyana herself was still out at work. What they'd found in Dolokhov's cache beneath the floorboards was laid out on the kitchen table. Except for the gun. That was in Nick's pocket.

"What happy moment is that?" Cass asked.

"The happy moment of settling up."

"Oh, that's right." Cass nodded, reached for her purse. "Two hundred for telling us what it was, three hundred for showing us where to find it."

She counted out ten fifty-dollar bills, offered them to Olyenka.

"Correct." Olyenka made no move to take them. "But you seem to have forgotten something. Specifically, my share of the loot."

"What loot?" Cass stared. "There wasn't any loot."

Olyenka met her stare composedly. "One notebook computer, including software, market value three thousand dollars. One twenty-two automatic—Makarov, isn't it?—on the black market, say, fifteen hundred. The key and the credit cards we'll forget," she added magnanimously. "Cards are always risky to use and, knowing him, they've probably been canceled. That's forty-five hundred total," she concluded, "making my share twenty-two hundred and fifty."

"*Twenty-two hundred and fifty?*" Outraged, Cass realized, an instant too late, that permitting herself to dispute the amount was tacitly conceding the main point. "But that's half. There were three of us in there, remember? Why would you get half?"

"Because you two are a team." Olyenka, stating the self-evident,

237

smiled brilliantly. "You're a team, and I'm a team. But if you want to get stingy about it, I'll stretch a point and settle for a third."

Cass tried to get the discussion back on track. "Olyenka, look: This wasn't like robbing a bank. We did it for information, not money."

"*You* did it for information, perhaps. But that's because you can afford it." Olyenka pointed to the notebook computer. "This is stuff I could have sold."

"You could have, *if* you'd been able to get to it. I seem to recall," Cass pointed out, "that we were of some assistance to you there."

"That's how come the split," Olyenka countered. "I'm being really generous. I'm giving you the information free. Volodya got *killed* for that. It could be worth millions and millions."

She made this assertion, however, with less than her normal conviction. Perhaps, Cass thought, it was hard for her to credit that mere information could be worth that kind of money. More likely, she couldn't imagine that kind of money coming her way.

"*You* say it wasn't like robbing a bank." She returned to the fray, her face taking on a hard, crafty expression. She held Cass's gaze for a moment, then her eyes wandered off toward the ceiling. "I wonder what the cops would say. Especially that Lieutenant Sokolnikov you told me gave you such a hard time about happening to find Volodya's body. I wonder what he'd say if he knew you'd ripped off the apartment." She paused. "You know what I mean."

"That's nonsense." Cass knew exactly what she meant. "You couldn't tell him. Not without getting arrested yourself."

"I think I could." Olyenka met this calmly. "And I'm used to being arrested. Besides, I'm a juvenile; I wouldn't go to jail. I doubt they'd treat you two as juveniles, however."

Extortion and now blackmail. Probably the threat was bluff, but with this child you never knew. Cass was torn between amusement and irritation, between whether to give her the money or slap her.

"Do I gather her ladyship has a problem?" Nick's Russian was not up to following these exchanges.

"The usual." Cass rolled her eyes. "She insists the computer and the gun are loot, demands that we give her her share. Originally she wanted half, but I've managed to beat her down to a third."

"Acquisitive child, isn't she?" Nick grinned. "How much are we talking about?"

"Fifteen hundred dollars."

"Sounds reasonable." Nick shrugged. "The computer's a top-of-the-line IBM. Even used, it's worth at least that."

"I'd say the value was hardly the point. Besides, do you have fifteen hundred? On you and in cash, I mean. She doesn't, you'll remember, take promises or checks."

He shook his head.

"Then we'll have to trek over to American Express. Otherwise we'll never get rid of her, and Tatyana's due home in half an hour." Cass sighed. "Sometimes I think I'd have liked Moscow better before they discovered the profit motive."

Nick thought for a moment.

"The Mezhdunarodnaya's one of Dima's hangouts, isn't it? I don't think we should risk being seen with her, for her sake as much as for ours. If she won't trust you, ask her if she'll trust me."

Cass did. Olyenka gave him an appraising look, thought very briefly, grinned, and shook her head.

Nick thought some more. He took off his wristwatch, handed it to Cass. "Give her this. It's a Patek Philippe; it's worth far more than fifteen hundred. Tell her to write down an address, somewhere she wants me to meet her. Tell her I'll meet her at midday tomorrow, buy it back from her for seventeen hundred—that's a two-hundred-dollar profit for waiting."

Cass explained. Olyenka, looking dubious, examined the watch minutely, holding it up to her ear several times to assure herself it was working. Finally she nodded and, strapping it onto her wrist, held her arm out to admire it. Then she asked Cass for paper and pencil, scribbled an address, and handed it to Nick.

"Tell him to be there when he says," she told Cass. "Otherwise I'll be forced to sell his watch."

Cass did.

"Tell her to be there herself." Nick smiled. "Otherwise I'll find her and beat her."

Cass did. The threat appeared to make little impression. Olyenka gave him a sidelong, seductive glance, pouting her lips and batting her eyelashes at him.

"Beat me?" She smiled. "Does he promise?"

239

Chapter Thirty-Three

Cass had never been much good with computers. Though she owned a Powerbook, which she used for her longer writing projects, she had never explored its capabilities, regarding it more with suspicion than affection, as if what it contained were magic—useful but essentially mysterious, and very apt to get out of hand. Dolokhov's IBM notebook baffled her, defeated her almost before she began. The keyboard was standard, the wretched thing seemed to run Windows, but once she got beyond the main menu, tried to pull up document files, it became mulishly obstructive, refusing every instruction she gave it and offering no explanation. Nick, whose computer expertise was only slightly greater than hers, was of the opinion that the problem was passwords. Probably he was right, Cass thought. In the light of Dolokhov's reported boast that the notebook stored secrets people "would kill for," it made sense that he'd protect his files. It made sense, but it didn't help. What good was knowing that, if you didn't know the passwords?

Moreover, it was still mere assumption that the notebook could shed any light on the vexed questions of Oracle's identity and the authenticity of Dolokhov's tape. Though intuitively this assumption had struck her as reasonable, it now occurred to her that it rested largely on evidence supplied by Olyenka. In view of that child's repeatedly demonstrated willingness to subordinate the claims of almost everything else—particularly truth—to her relentless pursuit of the dollar, this could, Cass thought, be a less than solid foundation.

"Has it occurred to you," she asked Nick that evening after he, too, had wrestled in vain with the notebook, "that maybe your teenage admirer has bamboozled us? Maybe those guys who searched

Dolokhov's apartment weren't after the computer at all. Maybe all the damned thing contains are stock market quotes or records of currency dealings. Maybe Olyenka invented that stuff she claimed he told her about it, and then, having conned us into helping her steal it, turned around and sold it to us."

Nick seemed entertained by the idea.

"If she did"—he grinned—"if she's capable of that much ingenuity and nerve, then I'd have to say she's welcome to our money." He paused to think, then shook his head. "I wouldn't put it past her, but I don't think she did."

"Why not?" Cass demanded. "The truth isn't in her."

"Possibly, but it isn't what she said that I'm relying on."

"What then?"

"What she did. Or rather what she didn't. We had to go find her, remember? She could have had your five hundred for the asking, but she didn't contact you. Instead, because she was scared of Dima, she ran like hell in the other direction." He paused, gestured at the computer. "I don't think we've bought a pig in a poke. I think there's something important in there, and it shouldn't be too hard to get to cough up. Any competent hacker should be able to help us. It's merely a question of finding someone we can trust."

A question of finding someone we can trust.

Merely.

"We'll have to take it to the States," she said. "There are people I know at Georgetown who could do it. But that'll take time. Weeks, I'd say, rather than days." She paused. "Could the credit cards help us at all?"

"They could." He nodded. "The American Express and Visa cards are both in the name of Grigoriev, like the passport. And according to the passport, he went to the United States earlier this year, entering at Houston, exiting via L.A. He probably charged his tickets and hotels, also meals, so the card-member statements—if we can get hold of them—should enable us at least to trace his movements. This may or may not shed light on our problem, but in any case, it's worth a try."

"*Can* we get hold of the card-member statements?"

He smiled. "All we need is an amenable attorney verifying records on behalf of the Grigoriev estate. You should be able to come up with one of those."

This, at least, should present no problem. One of the several fringe benefits of having inherited fifteen million dollars was that attorneys tended to be amenable.

"What about the key?" she asked. "It looks to me as if it belongs to some kind of safe deposit box."

The key had been in a waterproof wallet, along with the credit cards and passport. Maybe two and a half inches long, it was plain and flat, with no serrations for most the length of the tongue but three small rectangular teeth near the tip. The number 146 was stamped in the brass of an otherwise plain face. Cass had never rented a box, but her grandmother had, for her jewelry, and the key—Cass remembered it as very like this—had been prominent on her key ring. Carrie Wolfe had been fond of joking that this odd-shaped key was the key to her heart. When Cass discovered, as a teenager, what it was actually the key to, it had occurred to her that her grandmother may not have been altogether joking. Carrie had owned a great deal of jewelry and had loved it with a passion.

"It looks like that to me, too." Nick nodded. "But which bank, and where?" He shrugged. "Maybe the computer will tell us."

"Then we need to get started on it. Someone needs to take it back to the States, hire a hacker to unlock its secrets." Cass paused. "My nomination would be you."

"Me?" He looked dismayed. "You're joking, aren't you? I can't just up and fly home. I've work to do here, in case you'd forgotten. Some of us poor people do, you know."

"I do, too," she responded calmly. "Or doesn't researching a dissertation count?"

"Of course it does. Don't go all prickly on me. My point is that your schedule is more flexible than mine."

"Flexible?" she demanded. "Is it? You never told me you'd been demoted. Laid-Back Commentator File-When-You-Like is all of a sudden a reporter, meeting deadlines? Don't tell me you can't take a few days off."

"This could take more than a few days," he said. "You just got through saying so, remember? In any case, that's not the point."

"Then what is?"

"Listen, Cass"—he hesitated, looked uncomfortable—"I'm sure I don't have to remind you of this, but whatever's going on here,

242

Dima's involved and he's dangerous. At least one person's been murdered already—"

She cut him off. "What are you saying? You think Dima would kill me?"

He nodded. "I'm afraid I don't think there's any question. He knows you were inquiring into Dolokhov's death. It was shortly after he told you to drop it, you'll remember, that we nearly got cut up by those Chechens. In the light of what we've since learned about him, it's hard to see his arrival on the scene as pure chance. Nick paused. "Which suggests, perhaps, that he doesn't want to kill you, but he could decide he doesn't have a choice."

Which suggests, perhaps, that he doesn't want to kill you . . . Nick was right, she supposed. But still it was unreal; worse than unreal, it was ugly to be talking like this. Could anyone really dissimulate that well? Could a man you had thought your friend, with whom you had shared your thoughts, really just kill you out of hand? In jealousy or rage, that she could comprehend—the newspapers were full of *that*— but calmly, coldly, without feeling or even without malice? She knew it could happen, of course; psychology textbooks had a term for men like that—women, too, to be honest—and the term was sociopaths. But it was one thing to understand the theory, to know that there were people who saw others as abstractions; it was something else entirely to be the abstraction.

"Are you okay?" Nick was looking anxious.

"I am if you are." She attempted a smile. "A question here: Mightn't he equally kill you?"

He nodded. "He might . . . if he knows I'm involved."

"But he's bound to know; to guess, at least. I doubt he'd wait around for proof."

Nick shrugged, said nothing.

"What I think you mean," she pursued, "is you're a man. Able to take care of yourself."

"I didn't mean that. It might be true, but it wasn't what I meant."

"What *did* you mean?"

"I meant"—he hesitated—"I think my risk is less. He has to see you as the primary threat. If you go, he may think you've given up, that he doesn't need to bother with me."

"I see." She studied him. "I must have been mistaken. I thought

243

you meant that if anyone was going to get killed you'd much prefer it were you."

He looked innocent. "Why would I mean a thing like that?"

"I don't know." She pretended to think about it. "Perhaps that old lingering parental instinct."

"Forget it." He grinned. "It's not *that* lingering. I'm just being rational, figuring the odds."

"Head over heart, in other words?"

"You know me." He nodded, smiling.

"Well," she said, "be that as it may, I'm not going, and I'll tell you why: Dima's our key to this thing now. And I'm the one"—she was going to say "closest to him"—"the one best placed to watch him. He doesn't know we know he's involved, you see, so he might let something slip."

"Let something slip." Nick looked skeptical. "Like what?"

"How the hell can I tell you that? I won't know it till it happens, now will I?"

"You might not know then. That's what worries me," Nick said. "Dolokhov may not have known a thing till Dima, or someone, shot him in the head."

Chapter Thirty-Four

According to Nick's street map, Olyenka's address was some blocks off Mira Prospekt in the neighborhood north of the Riga station. After stopping off at his bank near the Arbat to withdraw money to redeem his watch, Nick went by metro to Scherbakovskaya, then made the remainder of the journey on foot. He had kicked himself frequently, since doing it, for entrusting the watch to Olyenka. An eighteen-carat Patek Philippe, gift of Cass's mother, it was probably worth, in Moscow's black market, many times more than he'd promised Olyenka. If she learned its true value before he redeemed it, he wouldn't see her, or it, again. He'd regret losing the watch quite considerably, of course, but her vanishing act even more. He needed to see Olyenka again.

There were questions he wanted to ask her.

Today, it seemed, spring was about to arrive. The snow was almost all gone from the streets, and the temperature was well above zero. As Nick walked south, down Mira Prospekt, the rays of a watery sun were doing their ineffectual best to penetrate the city's veil of smog. In spite of his anxieties regarding his watch, he found himself in an optimistic mood. Though Cass hadn't actually agreed last night to take herself and Dolokhov's computer to comparative safety in the United States, at least she'd agreed to consider the idea. A night's sleep and further reflection would persuade her, he hoped, of the wisdom of that course. Once she was no longer a hostage to fortune, he'd be able to turn his attentions elsewhere. Dima had had things too easy, too long. He needed to be made to worry a little.

The district Nick found himself passing through was an ancient part of the city, a part particularly fitting, Nick thought, to Olyenka's character and occupation. Not only was it conveniently close to her current place of business, it had previously, under the Soviet system, been about the only area of Moscow where commerce, most of it in stolen goods, had been free from the restrictions of socialist planning. Since Yeltsin had taken over, of course, the old Thieves' Market and the Rizhsky Market (no pun intended there, one presumed) had faced redundancy and virtual extinction, their functions usurped by that larger thieves' market whose boundaries had expanded to encompass, now, pretty much the whole of Russia. But if it was fitting that Olyenka should live here, in this hangout, historically, of thieves and receivers, it was also unfair to blame her. In most important respects, it struck Nick, she was merely a child of her time.

The address at which she'd appointed to meet him turned out to be an apartment building of the kind that in the nineteenth century had housed artisans, clerks, and small shopkeepers. Four floors, grimy brick exterior, tiny windows and not many of them, rickety metal fire escape running up one side. Inside there were no elevators, of course, none of the dubious social pretensions that so wasted space in Tatyana's building. No entrance hall here or sweeping marble staircase. Instead a dark and narrow passage, mailboxes ranged along one wall, that led to a steep and even narrower staircase. To judge from the number of mailboxes per floor, these apartments started small and dwindled as you got higher. On the fourth floor, where Olyenka lived, most must be one-room affairs, what the nineteenth century had bluntly called garrets. The passageway from which they led off ran the entire length of the building. It was lighted, very grudgingly, by grimy sash windows, one at each end, whose efforts were at times assisted, it appeared, by lightbulbs suspended from the ceiling and positioned on either side of the central staircase. But evidently power was supplied to them only at night, for although he found switches, when he tried them, nothing happened. He hadn't thought to bring matches or a flashlight, but by dint of starting at one of the windows (where the numbers on the adjacent doors were visible, though barely) and working his way from there, he was able to find the number Olyenka had given him.

He was in the act of reaching for the doorbell when he noticed, by feel, that the door was ajar. Or perhaps not ajar, not properly shut— not enough, at least, for the latch to have caught. At about the time he discovered this, his other hand encountered the doorbell. It appeared to be out of order.

So instead he knocked. Once, discreetly, then again, rather louder. No answer.

He was a little early. He'd left the metro at Scherbakovskaya at eleven-thirty by the station clock, and the walk couldn't have taken more than fifteen minutes. Maybe she'd gone out for a moment. Or maybe she was sleeping.

He knocked again, this time hard enough to make the door swing ajar. Nothing. He called out:

"Olyenka?"

Still no answer. And now, through the half-open door, he could see that the apartment—the room the door opened into, at least—was in virtual darkness, the only light a chink beneath the shades.

Almost without thinking—later it would occur to him that this could have caused embarrassment; he could have been in the wrong apartment, disturbing some late-rising Muscovite's slumbers—he pushed the door open and entered, as he did so, groping for the light switch.

Illumination proved he'd been wrong about the layout of these apartments. This one was a garret and very sparsely furnished—cheap deal table, wooden chairs, mattress on the floor (a blanket thrown over it) doing double duty as a bed and sofa—but there seemed to be more than one room. On his right was the usual kitchen area and, adjacent, a space enclosed by a plastic curtain—presumably the shower facility—but on the left a door, at present shut, proclaimed the existence of another room.

He went over, rapped on the door, called out loudly:

"Olyenka . . . are you there?"

No answer.

She'd stood him up, he decided. She'd discovered the value of his watch and decided to sell it on the black market. He was turning to leave when a further notion struck him: She worked all night, did most of her sleeping by day. And teenagers could sleep like the dead. (At Olyenka's age, he recalled, Cass could have slept through Judgment Day.) Silly to leave now, without checking, find out later that she'd been here all along.

He opened the door a crack and peered in.

Total darkness. Silence, heavy and oppressive. And permeating the darkness and silence, faint but persistent, unobtrusive but unmistakable, a smell.

Or perhaps a combination of smells. Smell, he knew, was the most vivid, most specific of the senses. Here his impression was of the familiar invaded by the also familiar to produce, in their combination, the strange. Something sweet, something salty and metallic, and mixed in with all this something charred.

Blood, he thought.

Blood and burning.

He groped for the light switch.

He had seen a number of dead people, several of whom had died violently. Some sense subliminally alerted by the smell had warned him of what he was about to see. Even so, he was not prepared. For a moment he stood there, stupid, frozen, eyes receiving pictures that the mind refused to process.

She was naked but for a pair of panties. A rag of some kind—perhaps more underwear—had been crammed in her mouth so her jaws were forced open in a stifled, silent scream. Her eyes were wide open, staring, terrified. Afterward, months afterward, when the afterimages of this returned like the visitations of an accusing ghost, what stayed with him, what haunted him, was not the throat slashed from ear to ear, nor the blood that soaked the blankets and mattress, nor the angry burn marks like hornet stings that spotted her breasts and belly, it was that look of horror in her eyes. A look of animal panic and terror but also of something piercingly human and baffled. Of a mind, an understanding, confronting what defied understanding, an intelligence failing to find words for the unspeakable.

But this didn't altogether defy understanding. The cruelty, perhaps, but not the motive. This looked like a sex crime, the product of unfathomable urges in a psyche that was wired up all wrong, and no doubt it was *meant* to look that way, but he knew instinctively that it was something else. Olyenka had been tortured not merely for pleasure (though clearly that had been a factor), but also to find out what she knew. What made it worse was the knowledge that *he* was at fault. She'd known this was dangerous, had wanted no part in it, but he'd tracked her down and bribed her, taken advantage of her ignorance and trust, ensnared her with her own cupidity and need. Then somehow he'd been careless, and she had paid this price.

I did this to her, he thought.

I helped, at least.

What to *do?* As the rush of horror receded, he retreated, deliberately, into the practical. He knew what he *should* do was call the police. But even as the thought occurred, he knew he wasn't going to. If he did, he'd be volunteering himself as a suspect. At the very least he'd be asked on to explain what the hell he was doing in a known child prostitute's apartment. And since policemen were professional cynics, nothing less than a detailed account of the truth would persuade them that his motive had been other than the obvious. Get *serious,* Nick, he told himself here; even the whole truth and nothing but the truth, attested to by St. Peter himself, would hardly succeed in persuading them of *that* . . . and he couldn't give a detailed account of the truth, not without revealing more than he could afford to about Oracle, Hal, and the Dolokhov tape. Not to mention, of course, his own previous involvment with Olyenka, an uncomfortably prominent feature of which was the recent commando raid on Dolokhov's apartment. He couldn't afford to call the police. He had to get the hell out of here.

At this point another thought occurred.

He wasn't going to call the police, but maybe someone already had. . . . As his mind, clearing, started to work, the full implications of the burn marks on Olyenka hit him like slaps in the face. Human capacity to endure pain was limited. If Olyenka had been tortured, there was no doubt she had talked. Whoever had murdered her—no prizes for guessing—would have learned that he, Nick, was to meet her here at noon. A well-timed, anonymous call to the police could land him in a shitload of trouble. And not just him—the further thought struck him with the force of revelation.

Cass.

If Olyenka had talked, Dima—it *had* to be Dima—would know who had Dolokhov's computer. But Cass, not realizing this, thinking she still had the advantage, wouldn't know the peril she was in.

He had to warn her.

He needed a phone. There was none here, not in the apartment and not that he had noticed in the building, but there had to be at Scherbakovskaya. And maybe there were others, even closer. He was

249

halfway to the door, already running, when a new problem hit him, pulled him up short:

His fingerprints were all over the apartment.

But where? he thought feverishly. Where exactly?

Calm down, he told himself. Remember what you touched. Retrace your movements in sequence, systematically: the door handle here, the two light switches, the doorbell, the doorjambs outside, *if* raw wood surfaces held prints. He thought they did, but he wasn't sure. Anything smooth would, surely. Better safe than sorry.

Going to work with his handkerchief methodically, forcing himself to be thorough, not to hurry, he backtracked through the apartment, wiping. He was desperate to know what time it was, but of course he'd given his watch to Olyenka. He didn't remember it on her wrist. Maybe she'd sold it or he just hadn't noticed. At this point he couldn't spare the time to look. It must be very close to twelve. If the cops had been called, they'd be here any minute.

But when he was finished, they'd still not arrived. As he let himself out of the apartment, giving a last wipe to the doorknob and the area around it, grateful there was no one about to witness this essentially furtive behavior, he felt himself relax a little.

That was one hurdle cleared. Now to find a phone.

When he reached the head of the stairs, however, he heard sounds coming from below.

Footsteps?

He stopped, held his breath, listened intently—sound carried amazingly here. With its staircases and corridors uncarpeted, the place was like an echo chamber. And now he was sure that he hadn't been wrong. It was not imagination, those were footsteps. Several sets, to judge from the clatter, maybe two flights below and ascending.

And now, to go with them, there were voices.

Men's voices.

Maybe it was not the police. Maybe it was just ordinary Russians. And even if it was the police, maybe he should walk on down, nodding politely as he passed, and maybe they would let him, wouldn't stop him. And maybe, he thought savagely, Santa Claus was Russian and Christmas had come early this year. It wasn't something you were willing to bet on. Not with Cass's life at stake.

There had to be another way out.

The fire escape . . . he remembered it was on the side of the building, presumably accessed from one of the corridor windows. With luck he might reach it undetected. Which side of the building was it on?

Orientation had never been his forte. Recalling the building as he'd seen it from outside, he tried to relate it to his present position. The fire escape—hadn't it?—had been on the right. The apartment was at the rear. The fire escape should therefore now be on his left, reachable (naturally) from the farther window.

The footsteps had reached the floor below.

The voices were clearly audible now. He could make out phrases, individual words.

Someone had just said the word *trup*.

Cadaver.

Not thinking consciously, reacting, he tore off his loafers—no shoe-laces to fumble with, thank God—and holding a shoe in either hand, made a panic-assisted dash for the window. The sash slid up easily, thank God without squeaking. As he clambered over the sill and dropped onto the fire escape, still in stocking feet, still clutching the loafers, the voices were reaching the head of the stairs. No chance of closing the window. He could only crouch and wait.

Pray that no one would notice the window.

As he waited he slipped the loafers back on. If he ended by making a dash for it, he preferred not to do it in stocking feet. He held his breath, listening, trying to ignore the pounding of his heart.

The footsteps seemed to coming his way.

But Oyenka's apartment was at the *other* end. Someone must have seen the open window. . . . In seconds he would have to choose: Run for it or get arrested. Probably he'd get arrested anyway. Running would only add to his troubles, underline, in the eyes of the police, his guilt in the murder of Olyenka. But he had to try, or Cass might be murdered, too. She might be already, but he had to try.

He had to try *now*.

Then a voice from corridor called out, "Pavel, you moron, can't you count? Thirty-six comes *after* thirty-five."

He froze. As the footsteps stopped, then retreated, he let out his breath in a noiseless sigh. In the corridor a muttered conference . . .

then silence . . . then a volley of knocking . . . then more silence . . . then a thump, and another . . . then a much louder thump and a crash. The splintering crash—it could hardly be anything else—of a door being kicked off its hinges.

He gave them ten seconds to get inside; then he took off down the fire escape, running.

* * *

NO PHONES AT ALL on the way to Scherbakovskaya. But there he found one not in use. Mercifully, he had the required fifteen kopecks in change and was able to remember Tatyana's number. He remembered also—it was something he usually forgot—that you had to dial 8 before the number.

Tatyana's phone was busy.

He tried to console himself, in the minutes he had to wait, with the thought that it might have been Cass on the line. At any rate, *someone* was on it. If it wasn't Cass, Tatyana was home and might know where Cass had gone. . . . He had the sensation, waiting, of being simultaneously in two separate dimensions of time. In one of them, it was like living in molasses; the seconds dawdled, stretched out forever; everything happened with excruciating slowness; it took a whole lifetime just to make a phone call. In the other, years streaked by like bullets: In a phone call's duration a lifetime could be over. A lifetime lost to him, he reflected miserably, a lifetime wasted in absences, silences, omissions.

If Dima harmed her, he would kill him.

When he tried again, he got through. His call was answered by Tatyana.

"Is Cass there?" Brusquely. No time for preliminaries.

"Nick? . . . No, she's not. She went shopping. I think in the Arbat."

"When did she leave?"

"About ten, maybe fifteen, minutes ago. She said she was going to browse the used bookstores."

"Do you know has she heard from Dima today?"

"Nick, you sound worried. Is something the matter?"

"Tatyana, *please:* Do you know if he called her?"

"Dmitri Petrovitch? Yes, he did. He called just now, as a matter of fact. He wanted to invite her to lunch. Why?"

"You didn't tell him where she was headed, did you?"

She sounded puzzled. "Shouldn't I have?"

Chapter Thirty-Five

SHOPPING IN ARBAT . . . Tatyana might just as well have said the East Village. Not that Arbat was anything like the East Village—in character it was actually more like St.-Germain-des-Prés—but for Muscovites, Nick knew, Arbat, *old* Arbat, encompassed a region whose boundaries tended to depend on who was giving the directions. Irregularly quadrilateral, it roughly extended, so far as he could gather, from Arbat Street to Prechistenka and was bounded, east and west, by the boulevards and Savodoye rings. In area, he guessed, it was rather more than a square kilometer; and at present, somewhere near the middle of that elastic interval Muscovites referred to as the "lunch hour," it was jammed with upward of a million people. Arbat Street itself, a thoroughfare restricted to pedestrians, was almost, on this springlike day, wall-to-wall humanity, an ocean of people through whose shifting currents his progress was halting and erratic. Cass could pass within feet of him here and he might never notice. Realistically, he thought despairingly, his chances of finding her were close to zero.

Used bookstores helped some, he supposed, or might if he knew where the used bookstores were. He'd run across several already, attempted to inquire, in his halting, phrase-book Russian, whether a young blond woman, a very *tall* blond woman—he'd wanted to say six feet but didn't know what that was in meters—had been in the store recently. He'd encountered varying degrees of incomprehension or uninterest. One store owner, who happened to speak English, did seem to remember a woman of that description, a woman who *might* have been an American, but he didn't think so—she was dressed like an American but her Russian was really too good—but she had left half an hour ago and he hadn't noticed in which direction. It occurred to Nick then that his inquiries were not worth the time it was taking him to make them. Unless he were right on her heels, it would do him no good at all to learn that, yes, she'd been in a given store and had left it headed east or west. He was acting without thinking, he realized, rushing around like a chicken with its head cut off. He'd always had contempt for people who did that—it seemed to him simply weak-willed—and now here he was doing it himself. On the other hand, he'd never felt this desperate before, never faced the prospect of a loss so insupportable. It mustn't happen. It *couldn't* happen. If she died, he thought, remembering Olyneka, he'd find it hard to live with himself.

Which was all nonsense, he told himself angrily. It could happen, would, if he didn't pull himself together. For a start he had to stop thinking like this. Or rather, *not* thinking like this. His resources here were limited—a pair of eyes, a pair of feet, a brain; he had to use them with optimum efficiency. Particularly the brain.

To this point he'd been working his way from Arbat Square down toward Smolenskaya, hoping, by walking in the middle of the street, to maximize his chances of spotting her. He now crossed over to the right and stationed himself in the doorway of one of the elegant, brightly painted eighteenth-century buildings that flanked the street on both sides. In this way, while he paused for thought he could scan the passersby.

It was clear to him now, thinking calmly about it, that if his chances of finding Cass here were slim, Dima's were not much greater. Dima, of course, knew the terrain better and had perfect command of the language. Moreover, he had transportation (which would do him no good on Arbat Street itself, but elsewhere would enable him to cover much more ground); also, quite possibly, he had help. But even with these advantages, the odds were still vastly against him. Almost certainly Cass would go home without either of them having found her. Which meant—Nick could have kicked himself for not having thought it through before—that instead of ignoring Tatyana's questions he ought to have told her to warn Cass against Dima. He ought to have warned her, too. She herself was not above suspicion, of course. His instinct was to trust her, but his instinct could be mistaken; sexual attraction, as he'd learned quite early in life, was no solid basis for trust. But in this instance it made sense to trust her; there was nothing to lose by it, everything to gain. If she was in this with Dima, he wouldn't be telling her anything she didn't know already; if she wasn't, a warning might save Cass's life.

Which meant, once more, that he had to find a phone.

No hope of it here this time of day. No hope of finding a pay phone, at least. But if he could get out of this scrum, into one of the less crowded side streets or alleys that led off Arbat Street, perhaps he could find a store with a phone and an owner who'd let him use it.

Setting off again toward Smolenskaya but keeping now to the right of the street, he plunged down the first turnoff he came to. At first glance nothing very promising here: a cafe two houses down on the right, but the overflow of customers spilling out into the street suggested he'd have problems even contacting the owner, much less getting use of the phone. Farther down on the left was a store that sold magazines and stationery. Strung across its glass front, apparently for the benefit of passersby, was a length of line from which sheets of newspaper were hung and attached with clothespins. This had potential. Anyone civic-minded enough to supply reading matter to the public, gratis, ought to be good for a local phone call.

Entering, he observed with relief that the store was almost empty; it contained only a couple of browsers. Behind the counter was a middle-aged woman, good-looking, severely but elegantly dressed, with a single streak of gray in her hair and an attractive smile.

"*Izvinite, mozhna sprasit*"—he fumbled for the words—"*mn'e nuzhna . . . tilifon.*"

"You need a phone?" Her tone was calm and pleasant, her English almost unaccented. "There are telephones for public use in Arbat, one hundred meters down on the right, and on the corner where Arbat joins—"

"I have an emergency," he cut her off. "The pay phones are all busy, lines of people waiting to use them. I was wondering, please, if you'd let me use yours . . . it's a local call," he added. "Of course, I would want to pay."

"You need the police? An ambulance? Perhaps I could make the call for you. Your Russian doesn't appear to be"—she smiled—"absolutely fluent."

He shook his head. "It's a personal emergency. Not medical but serious."

She inspected him briefly, then nodded.

"In that case, you are welcome to my phone. It's in the back on the right." She jerked her head toward the doorway behind her. "Remember, please, to dial zero eight before the district code. Payment will not be necessary."

*   *   *

HE WAS CERTAIN, the way his luck was running today, that Tatyana would be out, but she wasn't.

"Tatyana? This is Nick. Look—"

"Nick. My God . . . you are making me scared with these phone calls. Explain what is happening please."

"I don't have time. I'm sorry. Look, Tatyana. If Cass calls, tell her to go to my hotel, tell her to wait for me there in the bar or the lobby, somewhere with plenty of people around. Tell her not to move until I get there. If she returns to the apartment, tell her the same thing and go with her." He paused. "This could be a matter of life and death. Do you understand what I want you to do?"

"I understand, yes, but—"

"I can't explain now. Just trust me and do as I ask . . . and Tatyana, until she calls or comes back, don't let anyone in the apartment. And by anyone I mean *anyone*. Especially," he added, "not Dima."

*   *   *

As HE LEFT, thanking her, the store owner was still pleasant, still smiling. Her kindness, it struck him, posed a question for political philosophers to ponder: How a people individually so civilized and courteous could be, collectively, so incapable of governing itself, at least with any semblance of decency and justice.

"I hope your emergency has been averted?"

"I hope so." He nodded. "I'm extremely grateful."

"You're welcome." She paused, subjected him to another brief appraisal. "Come back sometime. Buy a book. In any case, enjoy the rest of your stay in Moscow."

Leaving the store, he hurried on down the alley, running as often as walking, heading in the direction of Ryleeva. He needed desperately to find a cab, and Ryleeva, unlike Arbat, was open to motor traffic. Once again—the thought had struck him while he was giving instructions to Tatyana—he hadn't been thinking well. He should have been viewing this from Dima's point of view. Dima was intelligent, eminently practical. *He* wouldn't be spinning his wheels trying to track Cass down during lunch hour in this teeming rabbit warren. Or if he tried it, he wouldn't count on succeeding. He might send henchmen to scour Arbat on the off-chance, but he himself would lie in wait where he knew she'd have to return in the end.

Tatyana's apartment.

* * *

LOGIC—NICK REMEMBERED having read this dictum—is the art of going wrong with confidence. Providence sometimes so orders events as to make their design inscrutable to reason. So far as he could see he'd made nothing but mistakes. He'd failed to confide in Tatyana when he should have. He'd come dashing over here, to Arbat, when a moment's sober reflection would have sent him back to the apartment. He'd tackled the crowds on foot, when he stood a much better chance cruising the district in a taxi. And then he'd decided to take a taxi home when anyone might have told him that during the lunch hour the metro was quicker. And yet . . .

And yet when he emerged from the network of alleys into the open expanse of Ryleeva, the very first person who caught his eye—his gaze, in fact, locked on to her as if directed by radar, as if no one else in that busy street *existed*—was Cass. She was passing on the far side of the street, maybe fifty yards away, and her face was turned away from him, but still there was no doubt whatever: mane of blond hair with the fur hat perched jauntily on top. Tailored coat with that faintly military cut. Striding out, as always, about twice as fast as anyone around her. Holding herself, as always, straight as a rifle. Very slim. Very tall. To his eyes very beautiful.

Alive.

But then, as he stood there, joy and relief flooding through him like a drug, he noticed, sidling up to the curb just ahead of her and stopping, a car.

A white BMW.

As he watched, she came up on it, noticed it, too. The door on the passenger's side opened and a man got out, no one Nick recognized, a nondescript man in a gray business suit. He beckoned, held the door open for her. She started toward him, stooping to look in the car.

"Cass!"

She was thirty yards off, the space intervening a hubbub of people and honking traffic, but his foghorn bellow cut through it all, turned every head on the street.

She stopped, hesitated, looked toward him.

"Cass . . . wait!"

As he yelled, he was sprinting toward her, dodging pedestrians and traffic, ignoring shouted protests and the outraged blasts of horns, hurdling, as he reached the far side of the street, the front wheel of a bicycle whose rider cursed him and fell off. He was conscious through it all of only a single imperative: Stop her getting into that car.

"Nick," she greeted him, "you must be utterly demented." He probably looked it, he thought. "That was a quite extraordinary performance. I hadn't realized you could move that fast." Then, noticing the look on his face, "Is anything the matter?"

Before he could answer, Dima had emerged from the driver's side. He came around the car, smiling, extending his hand.

"Mr. Wolfe, I was going to invite Cassandra to lunch. There's a restaurant, Praga, near here on Arbat. An eighteenth-century coaching inn. Czech food. Quite excellent. Permit me to include you in the invitation."

"Thank you, but I'm afraid we can't." Nick cast a meaningful look at Cass. "I've just received bad news from home. We need to get back to the apartment at once."

Silence.

Dima's smile didn't slip or falter, but behind it, Nick sensed, was a mind working overtime.

"In that case"—very smoothly—"it would be my pleasure to drive you."

Nick shook his head. "It's kind of you, but I need to talk to Cass alone." He paused. "I'm afraid this is *very* bad news."

Dima didn't answer immediately. He exchanged glances with his sidekick. Then his gaze surveyed the bustling street, rested a moment, or so it seemed to Nick, on the uniformed figure of a State Militiaman

259

at the corner some twenty yards distant. In the second or so required for this survey, he appeared to come to a decision.

"I'm sorry to hear of your very bad news." Had he merely imagined it, Nick wondered, or were those last three words in sardonic quotation marks? "In the circumstances, clearly, lunch will have to be postponed. But only postponed, you understand. I insist you accept— what's your charming American expression?—a rain check."

Chapter Thirty-Six

"**I** JUST DON'T BELIEVE IT," Cass said.

Nick had said nothing on the journey. When she'd asked, he'd just said, "Not now. Later." Normally she'd have found that unacceptable, but today there'd been something about him, something bleak in his look, something urgent in his manner, that had made her disinclined to argue. And the sense of urgency, her conviction that something disastrous had happened, was given force by the journey itself. They'd set out by metro from Borovickaya, heading, she thought, for Tatyana's apartment, but at Park Kultury they'd switched trains abruptly, exiting at the very last minute, Nick grabbing her hand, pulling her out of her seat, almost dragging her onto the platform. Thereupon they'd headed back north, changing again, in a last-minute dash that nearly got them caught in the doors, at Kievskaya. This was followed by their taking the next train *in the same direction*, getting off at the next stop, and heading back toward Borovickaya. When, at a point quite early in these proceedings, she'd asked if he thought they were being followed, he'd replied tersely: "Not by the time I'm through, we won't be." They'd emerged, finally (from the elegant arches of the station at Mayakovsky Square), still *north* of their point of departure and several miles from Tatyana's apartment or Nick's hotel on Teatralny Proyezd. It was only after he had checked them into a fleabag hotel on Tverskaya Street and searched the rooms very thoroughly for bugs that he'd told her what had happened.

"I don't believe it," she repeated. "I don't believe Dima *could* have done that."

She was conscious, hearing it, that her response was inappropriate, irrelevant. Compared to the horror of the act itself, the question of

261

who'd done it paled into insignificance. She knew this, but she couldn't help it. The question of who was a problem, something she could *think* about, therefore handle. Olyenka made other demands on her entirely. She wasn't ready, yet, to face them.

"Hard to believe *anyone* could have done it," Nick said. "But there isn't much doubt it was Dima, I'm afraid."

"Why not?" she demanded. "Granted the coincidence is somewhat disturbing, the fact that Olyenka was tortured and murdered just after she helped us find Dolokhov's computer, but why couldn't it have been some psychopath, some sadist? What kind of men, after all, pay to have sex with fourteen-year-olds? Perverts, every last one."

"It isn't just *that* coincidence," Nick said. "There's the fact that the door was left conveniently open, presumably to encourage me to go in. Also the fact that somebody called the Militia, and the fact that they arrived when they did. . . . I was lucky to be at the apartment early. Had I gotten there only a few minutes later, the Militia would have found me there." He paused. "Clearly they were meant to find me. Her killer knew I'd be there about twelve, knew because she told him so. And presumably"—he paused again—"her killer knows we've got the computer."

" 'Presumably'?" Cass shook her head. "What sense does it make to frame you for the murder? You said she seemed to have been dead for hours, also that you didn't find a weapon. Once those kinds of details were established, the Militia would know you couldn't have done it."

"Once those details were established, perhaps. But how long would it have taken to establish those details? Meanwhile," Nick said, "I'd be in custody, wouldn't I? Assisting the police with their inquiries. And meanwhile Dima gets a free run at you."

A free run—Cass knew what grisly suggestion was wrapped in *that* piece of delicate phrasing. But it was true—wasn't it? About the same time as Nick was discovering Olyenka, Dima had been looking for her. And was it really credible that Dima, with whom not wasting effort was almost a religion, had scoured Arbat for almost an hour *simply to take her to lunch?*

"I just don't believe it."

But even as she said this she knew it was true, that Nick was right; there was too much coincidence here. Dima, who'd offered to make love to her, had entered into some savage form of intimacy with Olyenka. Sadistic in the full, sexual meaning of the word, because he didn't have to strip her to hurt her—did he?—and because inflicting that kind of pain was always, in some twisted sense, erotic. And it hadn't just been to extort information. Olyenka would have talked right away. Offered the mere threat of what Dima had done, she'd have told him exactly what he wanted to know. Just, Cass thought, as she herself would have done, just as anyone would in that situation. But Olyenka had been covered with burns, Nick said. So the hurting had continued after she had talked. It didn't have to have been Dima in person, of course; it could have been some Mafioso, some hired degenerate exceeding his commission, but even then, how much difference did it make? Dima was still responsible, wasn't he?

I'm responsible, too, Cass thought. I involved her against her will, played on her insecurity and greed. It was my fault she came to Dima's attention, my fault she died in agony and terror.

She felt she was going to be sick.

"Are you all right?" Nick was looking at her anxiously.

"Of course I'm not." She almost shouted it. She felt the tears starting in her eyes, struggled with herself to hold them back. "How could I be? If you're right, if he"—she found she had to force herself to name him—"if Dima did this, he did it because of what I did. I'll never forgive myself for that."

"Sweetheart, look," Nick said. "I feel the same. But you mustn't start believing that. It's natural, I know, but you mustn't. . . . You didn't do it. You didn't will it. You had no way of knowing it would happen."

She shook her head, rejecting this comfort.

"Not this precisely, perhaps, but something . . . I knew it was dangerous, but I involved her. I shouldn't have. I didn't have the right. She was so fucking brave." Suddenly she could hold the tears no longer. "She was fourteen years old, for Christ's sake. She lived by her wits, dealt with whatever shit life dished out. And no one, ever, gave her a break. Not her customers, not Dolokhov, not the cops, not you and I—all of us wanted to use her for something. We stole her childhood, then we robbed her of her life. And for what? For a purpose she wouldn't have begun to understand, and even if she had, would have thought absolutely insane. For politics. *Fuck* politics."

Nick took her in his arms and held her, waited to speak until her sobs had subsided.

"If you're right," he said, "*I'm* in it, too. It wasn't just you, it was *us*. And I don't think you should dwell on it, not now, because now we have decisions to make."

"Decisions?" she asked dully. "About what?"

"About where we go from here."

She shrugged. "Who cares?"

"I care," Nick said. "And you will, when you get around to thinking about it. Dima must know we have that computer, and he's not going to rest till he gets it. Getting ourselves murdered, too, is not going to help Olyenka. Nothing we can do at this point is going to help Olyenka." He paused. "We need to get you out of here. Today. You and the computer both. I'm going to book you on the first flight out, put you on the plane myself. And between the time you leave and now, I'm not going to let you out of my sight. I'm not even going to let you out of this hotel room."

She thought about arguing, couldn't summon the will. She couldn't summon much fear, either. She tried to consider what all this must mean, how to interpret Olyenka's murder, but at least for the moment she found she didn't care. A numbness had descended on her. It was shock, she guessed, or more accurately shocks. Too many shocks, too close together. She wanted to be shot of all this—the tape, the murders, Dima, everything. She wanted to sleep for about three days, wake up, and find that the whole thing was a dream.

But it wasn't, and the proof of that—not that more proof was needed—came only a few minutes later. When Nick returned from making the travel arrangements, he looked grimmer than he had when he left.

"It seems we're both going home," he told her. "When I called the Metropol to get my messages, I learned there was a telegram from the office. I had them read it over the phone."

He paused. For a moment he was lost in thought.

"I don't know what to make of this. I sure as hell don't like it. But I think whatever's been going on here is about to come to a head." He paused. "It appears that in my absence I've been sued."

"Sued?" She could only gape. "For what?"

"Ten million dollars is the bit that caught my attention." He gave her a humorless smile. "The suit is for wrongful dismissal. The plaintiff is demanding reinstatement, back pay and benefits, and ten million dollars in malicious damages." Nick paused. "It's some consolation, I suppose, that I'm only one of four defendants. The others are the CIA and the State Department, and of course your uncle, Hal Reynolds."

"And the plaintiff?" Cass queried. "Is the plaintiff who I think it is?"

"Who else?" He nodded grimly. "The plaintiff is Marcus Werner."

PART III

Washington, D.C.–
Nashville–West Virginia,
May–June 1996

Chapter Thirty-Seven

"So," Hal Reynolds said, "my erstwhile good friend Nicholas Wolfe now believes I sold out my country?"

He and Cass were in his den at the Reynolds family home in Bethesda, a room Cass had always found remarkable for its lack of ostentation. Instead of the predictable vast shrine to an outsized political ego was a modest-sized working office, an untidy room full of books and papers that, apart from a portrait in oils above the fireplace of Hal's father, Senator Lucius Reynolds, offered almost no indication of the eminence of its owner. Of the many honors Hal had garnered in a long and distinguished public career, not one was on display. The sheaves of honorary degrees and scores of framed signed photographs of him with dignitaries domestic and foreign had, the last time Cass had looked, been gathering dust in boxes in the attic. The Congressional Medal of Honor and the two Purple Hearts were in a drawer of Hal's dressing table.

"I don't think Nick believes that," she said. "I think he doesn't know what to believe."

"He ought to know what *not* to believe. After twenty years of friendship"—Hal paused, took a moody swallow of his scotch—"I was never closer to anyone, not even Josie." Pausing again, he added sadly, "I might have expected more trust."

Cass said nothing, mostly because she couldn't disagree. For a while they sat silent, she looking over at him, he staring into the empty fireplace, slouched so deep in his armchair he was almost resting on his shoulder blades, his long legs, elegantly trousered and shod, stretched out straight into the hearth in front of him. Like Nick, Cass thought, he had kept the years at bay: his face unlined, almost no gray

269

in his hair, and his body, lean and graceful, that of a much younger man. They were so alike, he and Nick, both driven since boyhood by that ideal of excellence in mind and body that the Greeks had known as *arete*.

"And what do you think, Cass?" He turned his head to face her suddenly. "Do you think I sold out my country?"

"Of course I don't . . . I think someone's out to get you. Nick said, if this was a smear, they would have to show their hand. Now, with this lawsuit, they have. . . ."

She was tempted to go on, to elaborate, give reasons. But Hal didn't need evidence or logic, he needed faith. It was she—the knowledge almost made her ashamed—who seemed these days to need evidence and logic.

"Are you sure?" He might have been reading her thoughts. "Are you sure you've never once wondered?"

His gaze was reproachful. She met it and held it.

"That's not a fair question, Hal, and you know it. . . . We're all apt to imagine the worst, if only because it is the worst and because we can imagine it. If I said I hadn't wondered, I'd be lying, but I've never wondered seriously or long." She paused. "I know you didn't sell out your country. I know you wouldn't."

He smiled, a little wryly.

"Still the same old Cass, I see. Not an ounce of bullshit in you. Russia didn't change you a bit." He reached over and grasped her hand, gave it an affectionate squeeze. "I appreciate the confidence, sweetheart, the more so, perhaps, because of the honesty."

Russia hadn't changed her a bit? . . . Cass thought of Dima and Olyenka, of Tatyana and Nick, of the certainties that had deserted her, dissolving before her eyes. Russia *had* changed her; in a sense it had ended her childhood. She believed in Hal—that hadn't changed—but not with the instinctive trust of her youth; now, in part, it was because she needed to.

"Has Werner's lawsuit hurt you?" she asked. "Politically, I mean."

He shook his head. "Not yet. Not a lot. It's been reported, naturally, but the media have been fairly restrained. But they haven't gotten wind of this tape. Or the stuff about the Oblonski woman. When they do . . ." He smiled grimly.

"It'll be bad?"

"Worse than bad; disastrous." Hal paused. "Most politicians hold the public in contempt. I don't. Individually they're not nearly as dumb as they sometimes collectively look. But in the case of their elected representatives, bitter experience has taught them this: The presence of smoke implies fire. As people, privately, they may give me the benefit of the doubt; as voters who've been burned more times than they care to remember, they won't dare take the risk."

He spoke matter-of-factly, with a kind of stoic calm, and it wasn't, Cass knew, put on. If it happened, if it came to the worst and his burning ambition were denied him, he would simply shrug and get on with his life. She remembered what Josie had spoken on one of her tapes: "Granted he does many of the things we both dislike in politicians, but unlike most of the others, he's real. He stands up for what he believes in, he doesn't whine, and he's never mean. When I look at the rest of those creatures, I'm so proud of him I could burst." Cass was proud of him, too. If adversity defined a man, then Hal, she thought, stacked up with the best.

"It's garbage, Cass." Again he fixed her with his gaze. "I give you my word. It's all garbage. Not just the tape but the rest. . . . And it's not just me I'm concerned about, there's Josie."

"Josie won't believe it," Cass found herself adding, "any more than I do."

"I know she won't, but it'll hurt her all the same . . . and of course she'll wonder. Just as you did and for the same reasons." He paused. "I don't want her having to wonder, Cass. She doesn't deserve it."

And that was true. If Hal didn't deserve it—and he didn't—then Josie deserved it even less. Especially, Cass thought, she didn't deserve Natasha.

"Then we'll just have to kill the lawsuit, won't we?"

"Can we?" He looked dubious. "Have we anything to kill it with?"

"Sure we do. I told you, we have Dolokhov's computer. I'll get someone working on it right away. And I'll try to lay hands on his credit card records." Cass smiled, she hoped reassuringly. "Don't worry, Hal. Something has to give. Sooner or later it just has to."

He didn't look very reassured. "It had better be sooner rather than later. The timing could hardly be worse. There's five weeks to the

271

California primary—right about when the case should be coming to trial."

"Then we've got five weeks. That ought to be enough." She spoke with more assurance than she felt. How was she to do it? she wondered. How was she to do it in time?

"Let's hope." He didn't look particularly hopeful. "If not, I'll tell you this: If that tape and those lies get aired in court, my campaign, my whole political career, are over. . . ." He paused, smiled bleakly. "History."

Chapter Thirty-Eight

THE PRETRIAL HEARING for Werner's lawsuit had provisionally been set for June 9. The defense for the CIA and the State Department would be directed by their legal divisions, but though the services of these divisions were available to Nick and Reynolds, it was clear that the government's concern was chiefly with saving itself money, that preserving the good name of its former faithful servants was low on its list of priorities. So Nick and Reynolds were conducting a separate defense and, on advice from the Reynolds family lawyers, had chosen the Washington firm of Nathan, Orenstein, Willoughby, and Duvall to represent them. It was in the offices of this firm that on May 16 at 10:00 A.M. the two men met, for the first time in more than ten years, to learn in detail about the case against them and to help prepare their defense. Cass, who since her return from Moscow had acted as intermediary between them, was also present.

The offices of Nathan, Orenstein, Willoughby, and Duvall occupied floors nine and ten of a steel-and-glass box on M Street. Arriving at the reception desk at approximately five minutes of ten, Cass was shown into a conference room whose decor seemed to be doing its best to correct the modern, less-is-more, form-follows-function impression given by the building. Where not occupied by gilt-framed oil paintings of former senior partners of the firm, the walls were almost entirely lined with books, legal tomes in black and gilt bindings, that looked as if they'd been bought by the yard. Light was provided by a huge cut-crystal chandelier. The conference table and its twelve attendant chairs were imitation Sheraton but real mahogany. The present day was represented by telephones in various colors, a copy machine, and a pair of computer terminals, complete with screens and keyboards. The impression given, no doubt deliberately, was of ancient tradition married to modern efficiency, nineteenth-century legal values delivered with twentieth-century slickness.

This impression was confirmed by the contrast in the lawyers themselves. Ray Orenstein, the firm's senior litigation partner, had chosen to greet his new clients in his shirtsleeves. A burly, rumpled-looking man in his early fifties with bushy black eyebrows, iron gray hair, and eyes the color of glacier water, he surveyed the world over the tops of his half glasses with a gaze that struck Cass as shrewd and penetrating, deeply unimpressed by most of what gazed back, including, evidently, presidential candidates. He was, she thought, the kind of man who might in an earlier era have sat behind closed doors in smoke-filled back rooms, cutting the deals that determined the nation's future. Lisa Waters, at thirty-two one of the firm's youngest partners, seemed at first his complete antithesis. Lean as a greyhound, impeccable in a light fawn suit and cream silk blouse, not a strand of her ash blond hair out of place, she might have seemed colorless, even mousy, but for a certain quality of presence, an air of self-possession that made one notice her but without quite understanding why. Cass mentally labeled her the "Silver Wraith," but would find out later that the label, the connotation of fine, noiseless engineering, was only superficially apt; when she wanted to, Lisa could run over people with all the finesse of a tank. The third lawyer, an associate, Bill Unwin, seemed to merit less attention. In his middle twenties, elegantly tailored and shod, he was no doubt there to gain experience and to fetch and carry for the others. A litigation partner in training, Cass guessed, an Orenstein *in ovo*. When he hatched he'd be like his mentor, only smoother. An Orenstein in velvet.

Orenstein didn't waste time on small talk. As soon as the introductions had been made, orders for coffee taken, the group dispersed around the table, he got down to business.

"Okay," he growled, looking around him, "on the face of it what we have here is one sensationally nasty little lawsuit. The plaintiff, Marcus Werner, alleges he was wrongfully dismissed from his high-paying job with the State Department because you, sir"—he looked over his glasses at Reynolds—"in order to divert attention from your own wrongdoing, cast aspersions on his loyalty you knew to be unfounded, and because you, sir"—he looked over his glasses at Nick—"conducted the resulting inquiry, an inquiry that led to his dismissal, in a manner you knew to be biased and improper. He's seeking the following: from the State Department reinstatement and financial restitution, from you two ten million dollars in punitive damages." He paused, surveyed his clients genially. "Either of you have that kind of money?"

Nobody spoke.

Nick sure as hell didn't have it, Cass knew. Nor did Reynolds, not personally. Josie would stump up for him if he lost, of course, but it would leave even her feeling the pinch. The question struck Cass as an odd way to start: impertinent but perhaps deliberately so. Ray Orenstein was said to be brilliant, but it was quickly becoming clear from his manner—not to mention his shirtsleeves—that he didn't care much for celebrities. His clients might be an eminent journalist and a candidate for president of these United States, but here in this conference room they were just unfortunates in need of his services. To their credit, she thought, neither of them seemed to resent his tone, perhaps because they *were* in need of his services.

"Have it, perhaps, but don't want to part with it?" He seemed to construe silence as consent. "Which presumably is why you've hired me." He smiled, sharklike, showing teeth. "I'm expensive but not *that* expensive. . . . So let's begin at the beginning." He paused, nodded at the foot-high stack of documents on the table in front of him. "Is what the man says here true?"

"It is not." It was Hal who answered, very forthrightly. "My accusations were made in good faith. They were based on incidents I personally witnessed, incidents it was clearly my duty to report. As for his further allegation"—a look of disdain passed across the clean-cut features—"I prefer not to dignify *that* with an answer. I trust my record will speak for itself." He paused. "You described this suit as 'sensationally nasty.' It seems to me, Counselor, that you have both adverb and adjective right."

"You're suggesting it's politically motivated?" Orenstein exchanged glances with Lisa Waters. "I gather Ms. Wolfe has something to say about that. We'll get to her shortly, if we may. First I'd like to hear from Mr. Wolfe: What do *you* have to say to all this?"

Silence. All eyes on Nick. Especially Hal's, Cass noted. He and Nick hadn't spoken prior to today. Their encounter in this conference room

275

ten minutes ago had been, if not hostile, a lot more than merely reserved. They'd been civil, naturally—they were grown men, after all—but their way with each other had been noticeably short. No smile. No handshake. Just a nod, a muttered exchange of names, followed by a moment of awkward silence. Orenstein had picked up on this, of course—Cass had seen him frown and purse his lips—and it was only too obvious why. He might be steering the lifeboat, but they would be manning the oars; he needed them pulling in the same direction.

"Mr. Wolfe?" Orenstein prompted. "What's your position on this? The man is claiming he was railroaded. Was he?"

" 'Railroaded'?" Nick shook his head. "The Oracle inquiry was conducted in good faith. Every effort was made to be objective and impartial. The evidence against Werner was"—he paused, his tone, manner, the impersonal constructions, revealing a man choosing words with care—"was more than sufficient to justify our revoking his security clearance."

"More than sufficient to justify your revoking his clearance," Orenstein queried softly, "but *not* enough to support a prosecution?"

"I wouldn't know about that." Nick shrugged. "It wasn't my decision. It may not have been based on legal considerations entirely. In the CIA of my day we preferred not to wash our dirty linen in public. As well as the embarrassment of a prosecution, there were obvious security problems."

"But you personally believed he was guilty of spying for the Russians?"

"I did."

Past tense on both sides, Cass noted. And on both sides deliberate, she suspected. "Never ask more than you need to know," she remembered hearing a law professor advise a student. "Don't go wandering down blind alleys. You may not like what you find."

"Okay . . ." Orenstein seemed to relax a little. He sat back in his chair, put his hands comfortably behind his head. "That seems to cover the question of bias. What about 'improper'?"

"Depends what you mean by 'improper'," Nick said. "If you mean dishonest, the answer is no. If you mean unwise . . ." He paused and shrugged.

"It's not what I mean that matters here; it's what they mean." And what they mean is right here in the depositions." Orenstein pulled a document from the stack in front of him, flicked through the pages till he found what he wanted, began to read: " 'Evidence tending to exonerate the plaintiff and incriminate the defendant, Reynolds, was deliberately withheld from the plaintiff and the board of inquiry that revoked his security clearance. . . .' " He paused, shuffled through the stack of documents, extracted another, waved it at Nick. "Deposition of one Andrew Sherman, formerly employed by the CIA. Posted Brussels, 1983, as a member of the regular CIA establishment; temporarily detached, July 1984, and assigned to assist the defendant Wolfe in the Oracle investigation . . . blah, blah, blah." His eyes swept down the pages, scanning. "Ah, here we are: 'Wolfe told me to keep quiet about Natasha Oblonski. He said I shouldn't mention her to anyone, especially not to Werner. She wasn't relevant to the inquiry, he told me; he didn't want Werner flinging mud at Reynolds.' "

Orenstein put the deposition down, looked at Nick over the tops of his glasses.

"Mr. Andrew Sherman will repeat that statement in court under oath. It's the linchpin of the case against you. The rest of it—evidence of the polygraph expert who examined Werner, evidence of this alleged Politburo tape and the so-called expert who will vouch for its authenticity—is not much more than window dressing." He paused. "So the sixty-four-thousand, or perhaps I should say the *ten-million-dollar* question, is this: Is Mr. Sherman's statement true?"

"It's true as to fact." Nick met his gaze calmly. "I did tell him not to mention her to Werner, or for that matter anyone else. But it's also true that I believed her not to be relevant. And surely that's the issue here, isn't it? Whether or not I believed her to be relevant."

He was still using the past tense, Cass noted.

"What you believed is *part* of the issue." Orenstein nodded. "But only a lesser part and not at all easy to determine. What's more important is whether that belief was *reasonable*, based on the evidence then available to you. . . . The plaintiff, if I understand him correctly, and I do, is arguing both that it wasn't reasonable, and that you didn't really believe it was. He supports the first point with evidence, all of it known to you at the time, suggesting that Senator Reynolds was linked with this woman, Oblonski, who herself had links to the KGB. The second point he supports by arguing that had you believed

277

she wasn't relevant, you'd hardly have told Sherman to shut up about her. Which I must admit," he added sardonically, "does make a certain crude sense to me."

"Crude is right," Nick responded coolly. "You're making it sound much worse than it is."

"I sincerely hope I am." Orenstein didn't sound hopeful. He'd be deadly in court, Cass guessed, especially in cross-examination. There was a kind of power about him, a cool aggression guided by piercing intelligence, that most witnesses, herself included, would find devastating. "And I hope you can convince a jury of the fact. Because Werner's attorneys are going to be trying like hell to *make* it sound worse than it is." He paused. "Suppose you start by convincing me."

"Okay." Nick shrugged. "I'll grant there was circumstantial evidence linking Natasha to the KGB. What there *wasn't* was any significant evidence linking her to Senator Reynolds."

"Interesting, that word 'significant,'" Orenstein commented drily. "This woman comes to Senator Reynolds's office, way after normal business hours, asking to see him and only him. And when she's told she can't, she bursts into tears, has to be sent home in a cab. Later that night she kills herself." He paused. "If you didn't find all this 'significant,' why did you immediately try to suppress it?"

"At the time I didn't know who she was," Nick said. "I didn't know till later of her possible links to the KGB or that she had killed herself. What I did know was that Senator Reynolds said he had no recollection of ever having met her, and that I had no reason to disbelieve that statement."

"Not then, maybe." Orenstein shrugged. "But later, when you found out she had links to the KGB, you apparently repeated your instructions to Mr. Sherman. Hadn't it occurred to you to wonder why, if she didn't know Senator Reynolds from Adam, she'd come to his office asking for him?"

"Of course it had." Nick met this calmly. "One explanation that occurred to me was suggested precisely by what Werner appears to find so suspicious: her apparent links to the KGB. . . ." He paused. "Just assume for the sake of argument here what I believed to be true: that Werner was in fact the KGB agent Oracle. He knew he was under investigation because he'd already been confronted, so it was reasonable to assume he'd have told his KGB masters." Nick paused. "So they decided to muddy the waters. Knowing Werner's situation was desperate, knowing also that Reynolds was the source for much of the evidence against him, they sent Natasha to Reynolds's office with instructions to kick up a song and dance, hoping thereby to relieve the pressure on Werner, divert attention to Senator Reynolds instead."

Orenstein thought for a moment, eyes narrowed.

"You're suggesting that this is in fact what happened?"

Nick shook his head. "I'm suggesting it's what *could* have happened. There are problems with the theory, admittedly, but it's less implausible than the alternative. Had Natasha really been the senator's KGB contact, she'd never have risked drawing attention to herself, and him, by making a scene at his office."

Orenstein thought a little more.

"It strikes me," he said presently, "that the logic you use against Werner's suggestion applies with equal force to your own. . . . If I'm the KGB, hoping to deflect attention from Werner by creating the suggestion that this woman is Reynolds's KGB contact, then she has to be plausible in that role. I have to assume that you, the target of this so-called deception, are able to reason from A to B. So the logic that makes her implausible as Reynolds's KGB contact argues also against your buying the deception."

"Quite true," Nick said. "Which is why I admitted there were problems with that theory, too. The truth is, I think, that neither is correct. I don't suppose we'll ever really know why Natasha came to the senator's office that night, but my point was—and *is*—that however much evidence was subsequently found to link her with the KGB, it didn't make any sense at all to cast her in the role of KGB contact with Reynolds. And this, to get back to the point of this discussion, is why I didn't consider the Natasha incident relevant to the inquiry, and why I told Sherman to clam up about it."

Silence.

"That's not bad," Orenstein conceded. "If that was all a jury heard, they just might find it persuasive. But, alas, it won't be all they hear. The other side gets to cross-examine, and they'll do their very considerable best to present the business in a different and sinister light." He paused, turned to Lisa. "I think we should stage a dummy run, give Mr. Wolfe here a taste of exactly what he's going to be facing. Do you think you could work something up, be ready to run with it, let's say, next Tuesday?"

Lisa eyed Nick speculatively a moment, then turned back to Orenstein, nodded. "Tuesday would be fine."

"Tuesday okay with you, Mr. Wolfe?"

"Any day is fine with me." Nick shrugged. "Until this is over I'm at your disposal."

"Fine. Tuesday it is then." Orenstein paused. "Before we move on, a couple more questions: Did you make any effort to check into this Natasha?"

"At the time?" Nick shook his head. "At the time I—"

Abruptly, Orenstein cut him off. "Don't do that. Don't *ever* do that."

"Do what?" Nick looked blank.

"Don't ever qualify the question. It looks evasive and, worse, it assists the other side. If they can't figure out for themselves what questions to ask, don't help them." Orenstein paused, inspected Nick over the tops of his glasses. "Do you really want me, or for that matter anyone, to ask you whether you've tried to look into her *since?*"

Silence. Nick's face was a mask. So, Cass observed, was Hal's. This Orenstein was sharp as a tack and intuitive to boot; clearly he'd already figured out from slender evidence—the occasional hesitation, certain nuances of phrasing, the palpable chill between him and Reynolds—exactly where Nick stood in all this.

"*Did* you attempt to check her out?" Orenstein repeated.

Nick shook his head. "By the time I learned of her KGB links, she was dead. I'd already been given by the Belgian police what was known of her background. I had one inquiry going on already; I couldn't spare the resources for another."

"You never wondered why she killed herself?"

"I was curious, of course. But I doubted, for the reasons I've already given, that she or her death were relevant to my inquiry."

Orenstein seemed about to comment, but Hal beat him to it. He'd been silent up to now, and until the discussion focused on Natasha, impassive. In the course of the past few exchanges, however, he'd grown restive.

"If I might interrupt you for a moment, Counselor." Politics had trained him well, Cass thought; his voice was even, his manner apparently relaxed. "I'm not entirely clear as to the purpose of these questions. Or why you're considering this kind of defense."

Orenstein's eyes rested on him shrewdly.

"I'm endeavoring, Senator, to prepare a defense to the case I'm confronted with. What other kind did you have in mind?"

"I'll be frank with you," Hal said. "Refuting the charges point by point simply won't cut it for me. There isn't any merit in this case, not a shred of real evidence to support it, but I can't afford to have it go to trial. If it does, though I win in court, I still lose. I happen, you'll recall, to be running for political office. If this pack of lies gets aired in court, can't you just imagine the headlines? 'Reynolds Denies Link to Mystery Woman' . . . 'Did Presidential Hopeful Spy for the Russians?' " He paused. "This all happened twelve years ago. Werner has had all this time to sue, but, for reasons that aren't hard to guess, has chosen to do so only now. Isn't there some statute of limitations that applies?"

"Lisa . . ." Orenstein turned to his associate, Cass guessed to bring her into the discussion but also perhaps to allow her to strut her stuff. "Would you like to field this one?"

Lisa nodded.

"There is a statute," she said crisply. "It provides that in civil suits for wrongful dismissal you have to take action within two years of discovering you have grounds. It would therefore seem to disqualify Mr. Werner. There's a question, however, whether it applies in this case. For one thing, at least with respect to you and Mr. Wolfe, the plaintiff is claiming *criminal* wrongdoing, which isn't covered by the statute. For another, there's something called the Rule of Discovery. It provides that the two years permitted for filing start from the moment plaintiff discovers, or could reasonably be expected to discover, he has grounds. In this instance Werner will presumably claim that this was when he learned about Oblonski." Lisa paused. "These claims are open to dispute, and at the pretrial hearing we'll be making a motion for summary dismissal. But whether the statute applies in this case depends on questions of fact: whether there *was* criminal wrongdoing, and whether, more than two years before he filed, Werner *knew*, or should have known, that he had grounds for action." She paused. "Our guess, I'm afraid, is that the judge will rule these are matters for

281

a jury to decide. Which means, in effect, that the case will be tried *before* we get a ruling on our motion."

"In other words," Hal said evenly, addressing himself more to Orenstein than Lisa, "first Werner gets to use the court as a platform for publishing his libels, and only then does the jury get to say that he really shouldn't have been allowed to do so?"

"Something like that." Orenstein nodded gravely. "If you're telling me the law is sometimes an ass, then believe me, Senator, I know it. On the other hand, it's seldom an egregious ass. . . . The courts won't submit voluntarily to being used for publishing libels. Which would seem to bring us naturally to the question we earlier deferred." He paused, thought a little, continued. "Do you have any evidence at all—apart, that is, from Werner's twelve-year delay in filing this lawsuit and the inconvenience of his filing it now—to suggest that this *is* a politically motivated libel?"

"We do." Reynolds nodded.

"Cass"—he turned to his niece with a smile—"since this is mostly your story, I think you should get to tell it."

Cass had prepared herself for this. She gave Orenstein a brief account of her grounds for suspecting a conspiracy against Hal. Necessarily brief, she thought. Presenting it in summary made her awkwardly aware that her case was flimsy and that much of what she offered as evidence could be made to support quite different conclusions. When she'd finished, it was clear that Orenstein shared her misgivings.

"Not enough," he said flatly. "Actually, not even close. Everything is subject to interpretation. And one of those possible interpretations is strongly supportive of Werner."

"But doesn't it have the smell of a conspiracy?" Cass urged. "Doesn't it strike you, for instance, that if Werner's only motive here is to clear his name and get reinstated, he doesn't have to name Hal at all?" She paused. "As you said yourself earlier, this so-called Politburo tape is really just window dressing. Werner needs it to drag Hal into court, but otherwise he doesn't need it at all. And he doesn't need to drag Hal into court, doesn't need to suggest that he was Oracle. All he needs to do is show his inquiry was conducted unfairly. Natasha, surely, is enough for that."

Orenstein shook his head.

"In litigation, I'm afraid, enough is seldom as good as a feast. Lawyers tend to go in for overkill. And in this instance, I think, what you call 'dragging in' Senator Reynolds serves a legitimate forensic purpose. By suggesting a motive, it makes the alleged railroading of Werner more plausible." He paused, looked over his spectacles at Cass. "Young lady, personally I happen to agree with you that this thing smells like dead tuna. But that's based mostly on intuition, my estimate of your uncle's character, my feeling that winners of the Medal of Honor don't go around betraying their country. But my intuition won't get us very far. . . . What you're alleging is a criminal conspiracy involving Werner, God knows how many of his witnesses, maybe even his lawyers. Without some pretty solid support I can't go to court and start arguing that. I can't even hint at it. I'd get myself disbarred."

"So he has carte blanche to smear my uncle's character"—Cass felt very keenly the injustice of this—"but we can't even question his?"

Again Orenstein shook his head. "He doesn't have carte blanche; far from it. He has to produce evidence, just as we do." He turned to Reynolds, gave a piratical grin. "And if you think, Senator, that this tape of theirs will get itself admitted into evidence without a battle that will make the Tet Offensive look like a scuffle in a neighborhood bar, then you sadly underestimate the legal abilities of Orenstein and Waters." He paused. "We can fight this thing in court and we can win. But if you want to win without *going* to court, then you're going to have to get me a lot more to work with." He turned back to Cass. "I can give you all the help you need in terms of research, legwork, and what have you, but my people won't know what to look for, so you're going to have to direct the effort. You get me the ammunition, and I"—he made a pointing motion with his forefinger and thumb, accompanying this with a fair imitation of the sound of someone cocking a pistol—"will be happy to plug Werner and his cohorts right between their little piggy eyes."

Chapter Thirty-Nine

In the days following that first meeting with Orenstein, Cass kept herself almost furiously busy. Her motives were partly therapeutic—the more she did, the less she'd have time to brood about Olyenka—but mostly they were practical. In spite of the fact that press coverage had been fairly restrained, this case had dented Hal's support already. It must not come to trial, and it was up to her to see that it didn't. Whatever the legal outcome, a trial would be a PR disaster for Hal: *His* case would be tried in the court of public opinion, and in *that* court he couldn't win. Mud in large bucketsful would be flung at him, and a lot of it would stick. Not just his character, his adherence to the Republican "family values" that were such a central plank of his platform, but also his patriotism, his loyalty to his country—in short, every aspect of his fitness to be president—would be publicly called into question.

So the case must be smashed *before* it got to court. And not just for Hal's sake, either. Though materially Nick had less at stake, morally he had as much if not more. In his view (essentially male and limited but held, Cass knew, with utter conviction), what was at stake was quite simply his honor—whether he had acted as he should. On the witness stand this question would be subjected to withering scrutiny, to a detailed and hostile inspection of his motives. At this point it was unclear to Cass whether his motives could bear examination, whether, indeed, he himself still believed they could. To her it seemed that, far from suspecting too easily, he'd been a good deal too trusting of his friend. Relying too much on evidence from Hal, he'd made Werner the focus of his inquiry, given no weight to the counterallegations. He had held his nose, gagged, and swallowed his doubts about Natasha.

284

Cass herself still believed passionately—now that the suit had been filed, more than ever—that what Hal had told Nick was the truth. But she recognized that, viewed objectively, Nick's reliance on Hal's unsupported word, his failure to mention Natasha at the inquiry, was bound to seem like bias, if not worse, the more so because, as was clear from his manner these days, he no longer placed much reliance on Hal's word. For Nick, Cass thought, this lawsuit was a nightmare made real. On the witness stand he'd be forced either to prevaricate and lie, or else to air in public his unresolved doubts about Hal. Either course would be intolerable to him. If he chose the latter, he'd injure Hal; if the former, he'd forfeit his self-respect. Whichever he did—it was inconceivable to her that he would lie—he'd emerge with his reputation scarred. By the time the lawyers were all through with him, he'd be made to seem, in the eyes of the watching world, a fool or, worse yet, a knave.

But how was she to prove he was neither, that her uncle had not been a spy for the Russians? Her hopes were still pinned chiefly on Dolokhov's computer; its files, she was sure, would corroborate her suspicions. But the computer, entrusted to a hacker friend at Georgetown, had so far failed to give up its secrets. Eventually it would, he assured her; he would either crack the system of passwords or else go under that system, but since either course could trigger some self-destruct function, erasing the contents of the notebook's memory, he would have to tread lightly, and that would take time. But time was in short supply—the trial date was fewer than six weeks away—and whatever was in the computer's files might well take a lot of figuring out. She couldn't just wait on the files; she had to explore other options.

Reflection had revealed just three. One was the tape itself. Since her smear conspiracy theory required that the tape be a forgery, she needed to confirm at least that a forgery was technically feasible. By consulting a small firm in D.C., she'd learned that by a process known as voiceprint analysis, voices could be identified, like fingerprints. This implied that to have any hope of withstanding the technical scrutiny it could expect to meet, a forgery would have to have been spliced from words spoken (at some time or other) by Gorbachev and Kryuchkov. This is turn had prompted the question of whether such splicing could be done undetectably. According to the engineers at

Orion Recording and Duplicating, it could, even if the words were spliced one at a time. Armed with this knowledge, she had gone home and reexamined the critical passage on Dolokhov's tape. The vital word spoken, she'd concluded, was "Oracle"; this was the only vital word, and it occurred only once: When Kryuchkov referred to a "source with access at the very highest level," Gorbachev had asked: "You mean Oracle?" Kryuchkov had replied by imploring his esteemed friend not to specify sources, even in such a confidential gathering as the Politburo. . . . Assuming that Gorbachev had actually mentioned some currently active KGB source, not Oracle, and been admonished for the indiscretion, then the forgery could have been achieved by simply erasing the name mentioned by Gorbachev and substituting only the one word "Oracle." Even if this assumption stretched credulity too far—how many cabinet-level U.S. sources could the KGB have *had*, after all?—it was clear that, at worst, only the one query and reply—only twenty-one words in all—would have to have been interpolated. Clearly, forgery was perfectly feasible.

But proving it was feasible was different from proving it had happened. Though grateful for the technical information, Orenstein had questioned its practical value. It might help him argue the tape was a fake, but by itself it would not be enough, especially since Werner's attorneys proposed to submit direct evidence—the sworn testimony of one V. I. Schedrin—that the tape was a true and accurate record of the Politburo discussion. Schedrin, of course, had been a KGB officer; his evidence would be suspect, vulnerable to attack. But given its existence, Orenstein believed, the judge might very well admit the tape and allow the jury to decide authenticity. To be certain of getting it excluded, Orenstein said, he would need to produce evidence that it had in fact been forged.

So Cass had turned to another of her options.

If a forged tape implied a conspiracy, the converse was also true. By proving a conspiracy existed, she could get the whole damn case thrown out, this pernicious tape along with it. And the key to the conspiracy was Dolokhov. He had been involved in every stage. It was he, or so it appeared from the depositions, who'd supplied a copy of the tape to Werner; he who'd later offered it to her and been murdered before he could deliver. He was also, coincidentally, the KGB officer in the photographs with Werner—the "stamp sale" transaction—at which time, even more coincidentally, he'd been romantically involved with Natasha. In February of this year, moreover, just a few weeks before his death, he'd made an extended trip to the United States, traveling with a passport and credit cards identifying him as "Vladimir Grigoriev." Clearly the main purpose of that trip had been to contact Marcus Werner, provide him with ammunition for the lawsuit. But from "Grigoriev's" credit card records, copies of which Cass had obtained by the simple if risky expedient of forging his signature on letters to the issuing banks, it appeared that as well as visiting Werner, he'd made side trips to Houston and Nashville, Tennessee. Looked into carefully, as Nick had suggested, the expense records of those excursions might well provide clues as to what he had been up to. She'd been tempted to look into the matter herself, but realizing that she didn't have the time or the experience, she'd hired a private detective instead. Arnold Coleman had come highly recommended, for industry and unfailing discretion. Offered a retainer of five thousand dollars and a equally generous allowance for expenses, he had promised to get on it right away.

This left one last option: Tatyana.

Cass had been feeling bad about Tatyana. She had wanted to call her friend from the hotel, if only to let her know that she and Nick were leaving Moscow, but Nick had persuaded her not to take the risk. He didn't believe Tatyana could be part of this thing with Dima, but it wasn't a possibility he could totally discount. In any case, her phone might be bugged; Dima, quite clearly, had learned about Olyenka *somehow*. In the end they'd reached a compromise, phoning from the airport just minutes prior to their departure. They'd explained in somewhat guarded terms that a "family crisis" had summoned them home at short notice, and they had promised to return in due course. This last-minute leavetaking had struck Tatyana as offhand. On the phone she'd sounded hurt. And probably was, Cass thought, for there was no real evidence that she was in this with Dima, or was anything other, in fact, than the faithful and generoushearted friend she had always seemed to be. She was owed an apology, an explanation more truthful or, at least, more intelligible than she had so far received.

At the same time, she could be asked about Natasha.

This might be a mistake, but it seemed to Cass there was almost no choice. Even in the improbable case that Tatyana was part of whatever

Dima was up to, asking her about Natasha would elicit, at worst, just more misinformation—another shovelful of dirt, so to speak, stirred into waters already muddy enough. If she wasn't part of what Dima was up to, she might be able to shed light on the question. There was nothing to be lost by asking.

* * *

THERE WAS NOTHING to be lost by asking. . . . Afterward Cass would wonder how confidence could be so misplaced. Every new stage in this affair, it sometimes seemed, either knocked out some support essential to her theory or further eroded her trust in her judgment, especially her judgment of people. By the end of that forty-minute phone conversation she was almost convinced that Tatyana was her friend. If she wasn't, at least, she was simply the best actress Cass had ever encountered. She hadn't once sounded a wrong note, never seemed other than the woman Cass thought she knew. She'd displayed a startled and sympathetic interest in Cass's account of the Werner lawsuit ("Cass, my God, what a terrible thing for your family!"), but her chief concern had seemed to be for Nick: Was he bearing up well? Did Cass know when he would write? When was he likely to return to Moscow? Had he spoken of her at all? She had been so single-minded that Cass had persuaded her to talk about Natasha only by stressing how vital it might be for Nick. What she'd said had been very disturbing, for if what she said could be trusted at all, it meant that what Hal said couldn't be.

What made Tatyana's account persuasive, Cass thought, was that her recall of the details was vague. Twelve years had passed since that letter had arrived. Tatyana remembered it at all, it seemed, in part because it was the last Natasha wrote and in part because it had so shocked and dismayed her. Apparently Natasha had been up to her old tricks, sleeping her way to fame and fortune. And this time— hence the shock and dismay—her target had been a married man.

A prominent American diplomat in Brussels.

Tatyana still had the letter somewhere. Tatyana still had everything somewhere. If Cass thought it would be helpful at all, she would dig it out and send a copy. Cass had said thanks, she'd appreciate that; it might indeed be very helpful.

But to whom? she wondered.

Hal or Werner?

And here was another reason for believing Tatyana. The letter could be another forgery, but if it was and Tatyana was part of the plot, then how come it wasn't being used in the lawsuit? It hadn't been listed in the depositions, had it? Orenstein would surely have mentioned it, and she, Cass, would surely have remembered.

Maybe Nick was right. Perhaps Hal had lied about Natasha. A prominent American diplomat in Brussels, of course, could have been someone other than Hal. But if you were willing to swallow the coincidence of Natasha's having asked for him that night and being involved with some *other* prominent American diplomat, you might as well go all the way, believe in the Easter Bunny. . . . Really, Cass thought, there was no way around it: If Tatyana was telling the truth, then most probably Hal had lied about Natasha. And the misery this knowledge brought was sharpened for Cass by the question it naturally gave rise to.

If he'd lied then, when else had he lied?

Chapter Forty

THE DRESS REHEARSAL for Nick's cross-examination—he referred to it beforehand as his "ordeal by Waters"; afterward he avoided referring to it at all—was conducted in Orenstein's office a few days after Cass's phone call to Tatyana. It was conducted very like the real thing, with much of the formality that would attend it in court. This might strike Nick as theatrical, Orenstein said, but a courtroom, after all, was a kind of theater. He, Nick, would be giving a performance. It was important for him—for all of them—to know what kind of performance he would give. Lisa Waters conducted the cross. Her associate, Bill Pierce, stood in for the defense. Adjudicating was Orenstein himself. From some motive obscure to her but presumably masochistic, Cass was there as an observer. So, in spite of her efforts to dissuade him—he ought to be out campaigning, she said—was Hal Reynolds. He didn't have much heart for campaigning, he told her, when he wasn't sure whether, by the time this lawsuit got through, there'd be anything left worth campaigning for.

Lisa's colorless appearance and manner concealed the instincts of a shark. She began quietly enough—circling her victim, Cass thought later—by exploring Nick's background and qualifications for the job he had held with the CIA. Then she turned to his relationship with Reynolds.

"At the time of the Oracle inquiry, how long had you known Senator Reynolds?"

Nick did some mental arithmetic. "About twenty-eight years."

"You went to high school with him, I believe?"

"I did."

"Which high school?"

"Phillips Exeter Academy."

"That's a private school, isn't it? Rather exclusive?"

"It is private." Nick shrugged. "If you wanted to, you could call it exclusive."

"And you went on to college together?"

"Yes."

"Which college?"

"Yale."

"And after college you kept in touch? After you joined the CIA, that is?"

"Yes."

"Your wives were also sisters, weren't they? That would make you brothers-in-law?"

"Former brothers-in-law," Nick qualified. "My then wife and I were divorced in 1982."

"Then you've known Reynolds most of your life. You went to high school and college together, and for a time you were related by marriage?" Waters paused, treated Nick to a pale blue stare. "Would you describe yourselves as friends?"

"I've always had a very high regard for Senator Reynolds."

"No doubt." The stare didn't falter. "But that wasn't my question. Would you describe him as a friend?"

"No." Nick's face was impassive. Since this dress rehearsal had begun, Cass noted, he hadn't once glanced at Reynolds. He didn't now. "No, I wouldn't."

Cass looked over at her uncle. He was gazing out of the window, a study in indifference.

"*At the time the Oracle inquiry began*, would you have described him as a friend?"

"Yes."

"A close friend?"

"Yes."

"So you *were* friends, *are* no longer?"

"Correct."

"When did you stop being friends?"

"Sometime in 1984."

"At about the time of the Oracle inquiry?"

"Yes."

"That's interesting." Waters paused, regarded him with frank curiosity. "What happened?"

"Objection . . ." Bill Pierce addressed himself to Orenstein. "I don't see the relevance of this line of questioning."

Orenstein directed a look of inquiry at Waters. "Counselor?"

"Our contention is that the Oracle inquiry was conducted improperly," Waters said calmly. "We believe that evidence relevant to that inquiry, evidence tending to exonerate our client and incriminate his principal accuser, Henry Reynolds, was deliberately suppressed by the witness. Since the witness was in charge of the inquiry, the state of the relationship existing at that time between him and Henry Reynolds is clearly relevant to the plaintiff's case."

"But the state of the relationship has been clearly indicated," Pierce argued. "Do we need to invade the privacy of the witness by going into the whys and wherefores?"

"I believe we do." Waters nodded. "I believe this line of questioning will show that the ending of the friendship between the witness and Reynolds resulted from an incident that occurred during the Oracle inquiry, an incident vital to the plaintiff's case."

"If the incident ended the friendship," Pierce observed drily, "it can hardly provide evidence of bias on the witness's part."

"You get to do your arguing later, Counselor." Waters dismissed him, turned back to Orenstein. "I'd be happy to defer this line of questioning, move on to the incident in question."

"As you wish." Orenstein nodded, paused. "I'm calling a twenty-second time-out here." He turned to Pierce. "That wasn't a well-planned objection, Bill. One, you're displaying nervousness. Two, you'd almost certainly be overruled. Three, you've done Lisa's work for her, prepared the ground for her main attack." He turned back to Waters. "So go ahead, Lisa, let's see what you've got."

"Mr. Wolfe"—Lisa's pale blue stare returned to Nick—"in the course of the Oracle inquiry did you meet a woman named Natasha Oblonski?"

"Yes."

"Describe, please, the circumstances in which you met her."

Nick gave a succinct account of the meeting. So far he was doing well, Cass thought; making a good impression, not talking too much but answering the questions with every appearance of candor. He looked like a man at peace with himself and his conscience. There was rough water ahead, however, very rough water, and they were almost to it now.

"This Ms. Oblonski, what age would say she was roughly?"

"Then?" Nick thought for a moment. "Mid- to late twenties, I'd guess."

"Would you have described her as attractive?"

Pause. Bill Pierce, Cass noted, opening his mouth to object, caught Orenstein's look and thought better of it.

"Yes." Nick nodded.

"*Very* attractive?"

"Objection . . ." This time Pierce was not to be restrained.

"Sustained." Orenstein nodded. "The point's been established. Get on with it, Lisa."

"You've testified that she seemed distressed." Waters got on with it. "How distressed?"

"During the interview she was several times in tears."

"In tears?" Waters paused to emphasize the point. "Did you gather why?"

"No."

"Did you ask?"

"I asked if I could help in any way. She said no. She wanted to speak with Reynolds, no one else."

"And she claimed to be acquainted with him?"

"Yes."

"Did you believe her?"

"At the time I had no reason not to."

Pause. Waters seemed about to pursue this point but apparently decided against it.

"What did you do then?"

"I phoned Reynolds at home," Nick said. "The call was taken by a houseguest. She told me Senator Reynolds was in conference and asked if she could take a message. I told her Ms. Oblonski had called in at the office asking for Hal"—Nick hesitated, corrected himself— "for Senator Reynolds. I asked her to tell him so, find out what he wanted me to do."

"And what *did* he want you to do?"

"The message relayed to me"—Cass had the impression Nick was

293

choosing words carefully, "was that the senator had no recollection of having met Ms. Oblonski and couldn't, at that moment, spare the time to see her."

"You conveyed this to Ms. Oblonski?"

"Yes."

"How did she react?"

"She seemed distressed."

"Distressed . . . you mean she burst into tears?"

"Yes."

Pause.

"You didn't, yourself, speak to Reynolds that evening?"

"That's correct."

"Did you subsequently speak to him? About Ms. Oblonski, I mean."

"Yes."

"When was that?"

"About a week later."

"Did you ask him then to confirm that he had no recollection of having met Ms. Oblonski?"

"I asked him that." Nick nodded. "Among other things."

If he hoped to distract with this qualification, he didn't succeed. Waters, Cass noted, allowed the ensuing silence to drag on just long enough to be awkward. Then she dropped her question into it, like a pebble down a well.

"Why?"

"Several reasons." Nick's face was a mask. "The chief of which was that the subject happened to come up."

"It hadn't happened to come up *before*? . . . A week went by. You didn't speak of it? He didn't speak of it?" Waters paused. "You didn't find it strange that he didn't speak of it?"

"Not particularly." Nick shrugged. "I recall we were both very busy at the time. I think the opportunity just didn't present itself."

"So how *did* the subject happen to come up?"

Nick told her about Natasha's death, the inquiries made by the Belgian police inspector, Lem. If he was dismayed by the turn the questions were now taking, he didn't show it. He seemed unconcerned, almost bored. Waters, however, pressed toward her target.

294

"Did Inspector Lem share any information with you regarding Ms. Oblonski?"

"He did. He informed us she was originally a Russian national, who'd applied for, and been granted, Belgian citizenship. Also that at the time of her death she was pregnant."

"He told you, in other words, that Natasha Oblonski was a Soviet defector?"

"Yes," Nick said, "though 'defector' strikes me as overly sinister. In the CIA that term was normally reserved for refugees who were known to have worked for the Soviet regime."

Mistake, Cass thought. Don't argue, just answer. . . . Waters, however, chose to ignore the comment.

"Isn't it true," she pursued, "that Inspector Lem also told you that Natasha Oblonski had applied for work with NATO as a translator and had been turned down for security reasons?"

"Yes."

"Did that not strike you as sinister?"

"Objection." Bill Pierce was on his feet again. "Calls for a conclusion—"

"Of course it calls for a conclusion." Waters cut him off. "The witness was in the business of drawing conclusions." She turned in appeal to Orenstein. "The witness was in charge of a security inquiry in which my client was grievously injured. . . . The conclusions drawn in this inquiry by this witness—whether they were reasonable and made in good faith—are precisely what is at issue here."

"That's certainly the way I see it." Orenstein nodded. "The objection is overruled. The witness will answer the question." He paused, then added in a smiling aside to Pierce, "That wasn't such a bad one, though. At least you bought him some time to think."

He turned, with a less genial smile, to Nick.

"So now that you've had time to think, how *did* it strike you at the time, Mr. Wolfe?"

"It didn't surprise me much. The Cold War was at its height. All Western security services at that time cast a leery eye on *all* Soviet refugees. You could call it a conditioned reflex."

"A reflex," Waters queried, "that as a security officer you shared?"

"Of course."

"And was that why you found it necessary to ask Henry Reynolds to

295

confirm to you, in person, that he had no recollection of meeting Natasha Oblonski?"

For a moment Nick said nothing. Then he turned to Pierce and observed mildly, "This might not be a bad moment to lodge an objection. At least when I was in college, that would have been regarded as a rather nasty instance of Complex Question."

"He's right, Lisa," Orenstein said. "That wasn't one question but two, and one of them is prejudicial. He never said anything about 'finding it necessary to ask'; he merely said that he *did* ask. . . . Rephrase, please."

"*Was* that why you asked?" Waters looked unconcerned.

Nick nodded. "I asked because Senator Reynolds's message to me about Ms. Oblonski was, strictly speaking, hearsay. When I heard that Ms. Oblonski had been turned down for a job with NATO, it seemed a good idea to have him confirm, directly, the gist of his message to me."

"Why?"

"For the record. I wanted to be sure he'd been reported correctly."

"For the record?" Waters stared. "Did you in fact make a record of the conversation?"

"No," Nick said. "That was a manner of speaking. I meant that I wanted to assure myself that Reynolds had been reported correctly."

Cass expected Waters to make more of this point, but she seemed content to let it go.

"And he said he had been reported correctly?"

"He did."

Water paused. The pale blue stare seemed only curious, but the question, when it came, was like a knife thrust.

"Did you *believe* him?"

Pause. For the first time Nick appeared reluctant to answer. This is it, Cass thought. This is where she takes him apart.

"Did you believe him?" Waters repeated.

"I neither believed him nor disbelieved him." Now that he'd made up his mind what to say, Nick said it firmly and clearly. "I suspended judgment."

"In other words"—Waters was having none of this—"you believed it was possible that Reynolds might be lying?"

"One of them had to be lying," Nick said wearily. "I had to consider both possibilities."

Waters wasn't going to let this pass, either.

"To summarize your evidence so far, then: When your friend Senator Reynolds claimed not to know this young [beat], attractive [beat], *pregnant* Soviet defector who had come to his office asking to see him and burst into tears when he refused, you thought it was possible that he was lying?"

Pause. Nick glanced at Cass, then away quickly. His self-assurance had left him now. He was wearing a baited, stoic look, like a man being led to execution. She felt her heart go out to him. He was a decent man, a man who'd tried to the best of his ability to reconcile conflicting imperatives. His failure was coming back to haunt him.

"Yes," Nick said. "I did."

"What reason did you think he might have for lying?"

"I didn't know." Nick looked utterly wretched. "I didn't care to speculate."

"You didn't care to speculate?" Waters didn't attempt to hide her disbelief. "Are you asking the jury to believe that in fact you didn't speculate, that no reason whatever occurred to you?"

Nick's reply was barely audible. "No."

"You aren't asking them to believe that?"

Nick nodded.

"I didn't hear that," Orenstein said.

"I'm not asking them to believe that."

"In other words, you did speculate," Waters pursued. "*What* did you speculate might be the reason?"

"Objection." Pierce.

"Overruled." Orenstein.

"What did you speculate, Mr. Wolfe? What possibilities occurred to you?" Waters didn't wait for the reply. "Wasn't one possibility this: that your friend, Henry Reynolds, might be lying because he, a senior U.S. diplomat and a married man, was romantically involved with a Soviet defector?"

"Yes." Nick bit the bullet. "It was."

In the silence that followed this omission, Reynolds got up and walked toward the door. When he got there he turned. He caught Nick's gaze and held it.

"You," he said evenly, "are one sorry son of a bitch."

Then he nodded to the others and let himself out.

* * *

AFTER THAT it was shooting fish in a barrel. Waters went on to extract the admissions that Reynolds had asked specifically for him, Nick, to be entrusted with the inquiry and that the original basis for his suspicions of Werner had been incidents witnessed only by Reynolds. The subsequent admissions—that Natasha had been photographed with Dolokhov, that Dolokhov had been identified as a KGB officer, that Dolokhov was in fact the *same* KGB officer photographed with Werner in the "stamp sale" transaction—seemed by that time almost anticlimactic. At the end, when Waters reverted to the question of "the record," it was clear why she hadn't pursued it before.

"Mr. Wolfe, you testified earlier that, although you asked Reynolds 'for the record' to confirm that he wasn't acquainted with Natasha Oblonski, you didn't in fact include it in the record, even though you thought he might be lying. Is that correct?"

"Yes."

"Why did you not include it in the record?"

"I didn't believe it was relevant."

"You didn't believe it was relevant? *Even* though you thought it was possible Reynolds and Oblonski might be having an affair?"

"That's correct."

"And you didn't believe it was relevant when you learned that Oblonski was a Soviet defector who'd been refused a job at NATO for security reasons?"

"That's correct."

"And you *still* didn't believe it was relevant when you learned that Oblonski had been photographed coming out of a hotel with a man identified as a KGB officer?"

"That's correct."

"You didn't think it was worth including in the record." Waters paused, scepticism written all over her face. "But when Marcus Werner was photographed only two days later with the very same KGB officer, you thought *that* was worth including in the record?"

"In Werner's case it was part of a pattern." Nick endeavored to offer

298

some justification. "In Reynolds's case there was just the one incident."

"Just the one incident *that came to your attention. . . .*"

Nick attempted to reply, but Waters overrode him.

"Mr. Wolfe, do you know what the term 'honeytrap' means?"

"Yes."

"Will you explain it, please, for the benefit of the jury?"

"The term is used to refer to an agent who uses sex to entrap and blackmail an intelligence target."

"Ms. Oblonski was an attractive woman, a Soviet defector with continuing KGB contacts. You thought she might have been having an affair with Reynolds. Did it not occur to you that she might be a honeytrap?"

"It occurred to me. I didn't believe it was a serious possibility."

"You didn't believe it was a serious possibility?" Waters' face was a study in disbelief. "But if Ms. Oblonski was a honeytrap, didn't that in turn raise the possibility that Reynolds, and *not* Marcus Werner, was Oracle?" Before Nick could reply, Waters hurried on. "That possibility didn't strike you as serious? Not serious enough to include in the record?"

"You're confusing the issue," Nick said doggedly, "equivocating with different meanings of 'serious.' Had I thought there was any real chance that Oblonski had honeytrapped Reynolds, of course I would have seen that as serious. I didn't think there was any real chance."

"And that was why you omitted to mention Oblonski in the record? Because you didn't want to risk confusing *that* issue? Did you fail to mention her at Werner's security hearing because you thought the board might be confused by the incident? Or was it," Waters paused triumphantly, "because you knew they would *not* be confused, but in fact would understand it only too well?"

She waited a second. When Nick said nothing, she added:

"I have no further questions for this witness."

For at least ten seconds there was silence.

"I have a question for you." It was Nick who broke it.

"Yes?" Waters turned and looked at him inquiringly.

"Did you enjoy that as much as you seemed to?"

Then he, like Reynolds, turned and walked out of the room.

* * *

LATER, WHEN THEY'D ALL RECOVERED from their surprise, Lisa seemed upset by Nick's reaction.

"It wasn't personal," she said. "Compared to what the Werner team will dish out, it might even have been rather mild. Actually," she addressed herself to Cass, "I respect your father. I think he was honestly trying to be fair both to Werner and to Reynolds. I think he's an intelligent, decent man who conducted what he thought was a fair inquiry. But being fair and looking fair aren't always the same thing. Justice must be *seen* to be done." She paused. "Senator Reynolds put him in an impossible position. He really has himself to blame for this."

"Are things as bad as they look?" Cass asked her glumly.

"Perhaps not quite"—it was Orenstein who answered—"from the legal standpoint, at least. I get to do a redirect with your father, in which I would hope to present his position more sympathetically, make his failure to mention Oblonski appear less irrational and sinister than Lisa left it seeming." He paused. "From your uncle's standpoint, however, it's another matter entirely. By the time the Werner team gets through with your father I doubt there'll be a soul in that courtroom, or for that matter in the whole country, who *doesn't* believe Reynolds was having an affair with Natasha. What that will do to his chances of election, I'm not qualified to say. If we lose in court, I'd say they were nil. If we win, who knows?"

"If we lose?" Cass wailed. "But this lawsuit is utterly phony. It's a blatant attempt to tarnish my uncle and subvert the electoral process by using the courts to publish a libel."

"Is it?" Orenstein didn't look particularly convinced. "Well, whatever it is, I wouldn't call it blatant. So I think if you want to help your uncle, what you need to do between now and the trial is prove it."

Chapter Forty-One

Arnold Coleman, the private detective hired by Cass to look into Dolokhov's U.S. trip, had come highly recommended for industry and discretion. And as to industry, it seemed the report had not lied. Having promised to get back to her in a week, he was back in five days. In that time he had been, in turn, to Washington, D.C., Houston, Sacramento, and Nashville. In the process he'd spent quite a lot of Cass's money, but not, given the nature of his business, an inordinate amount, and he'd accounted meticulously for every penny. Almost every penny. Occasionally there were expenses reported as "gratuities" for which he was able to produce no receipts, but he'd warned her beforehand this might be the case. In investigations like this, he'd said, gratuities tended to run rather high; he hoped Cass would trust him in the matter. Since it seemed the money had been well spent, Cass did. Coleman had something to report.

"That first time, D.C. was a stopover," he told her. "Our boy got into Dulles late, stayed the night at a Howard Johnson's, flew out the next morning, early." He paused. "Odd that he went on to Houston, though. Nashville first would have saved him money. The way he did it, you have to backtrack."

Cass had noticed the same thing; also that instead of a round-trip ticket covering his entire U.S. journey, Dolokhov had purchased a series of one-ways. She didn't know how much extra this had cost him, but she guessed several hundred dollars. It was possible either that he hadn't cared about the money, or that he'd been ignorant of U.S. geography (and the pricing policies of U.S. airlines), but neither possibility struck her as likely. Russians were inveterate bargain hunters. For most of them money was hard to come by, and they took great pains not to waste a kopeck. Dolokhov, in her brief acquaintance with him, had seemed no exception to this rule. Had money been the only consideration, he'd certainly have shopped for the cheapest fare. His flying to Houston, then doubling back to Nashville, therefore, suggested that his business in the latter city was contingent on his business in the former. *How* it was contingent was another matter.

"Any idea what he *did* in Houston?"

"It seems that mostly he wasn't *in* Houston." Coleman made a show of consulting his notes. At least Cass thought it was a show. She'd have bet big bucks that Coleman, who wore horn-rimmed glasses and a gray business suit and looked like a cross between a C.P.A. and a minister, could recall from memory and recite chronologically every detail of what he'd discovered. The notes were for her benefit, probably, in case her memory was not quite as good. "He flew out of D.C. National Airport, at ten A.M., got into Houston three hours later. We're talking a Saturday here, remember. He checked himself into a downtown motel, made two calls to a long-distance number, Texas area code, and he hired a rental car. That night he ate dinner at the motel."

"The motel?" Cass queried. "Then he stayed in Houston. I thought you said he mostly wasn't there."

"The Saturday he was," Coleman said. "But Sunday, he seems to have gone on a road trip. He put just over two hundred miles on that rental—I know because he exceeded the mileage allowance—and he stopped for gas in a town called Huntsville, which is slightly more than sixty miles north of Houston and"—he paused—"in the same area code as the number he called from the motel."

To Cass, the inference here seemed elementary.

"So he called Saturday to set up an appointment Sunday with someone who lived in or around Huntsville. Were you able to find out who it was he called?"

Coleman shook his head. "Directory won't give out names or addresses. I called the number half a dozen times, got a message machine every time." Coleman shrugged. "I expect you're familiar with the kind. Doesn't tell you anything you don't already know: 'You have reached blah-blah-blah. If you want to leave a message, please do so after the beep.' I can keep trying," he added doubtfully, "but it's dollars to pennies it's not going to do any good. People who leave that

302

kind of message on their phone don't go around volunteering their name."

He was right: The message on Cass's machine was like that. And until she'd identified the caller, she never volunteered her name.

"Did he return the car that day?"

"Careful kind of guy." Coleman nodded. "Got it back at ten before five. Saved himself an extra day's rental. But here's what's odd: That night he ate dinner in a restaurant called Brennan's. Way the hell out of his normal price range. Check was *a hundred and eighteen bucks.*" To judge from his tone, Coleman found extravagance like this to border on moral outrage. "Must have been celebrating."

Celebrating. That could make sense, Cass thought. Maybe the careful Comrade Dolokhov had treated himself to dinner at Brennan's because his visit to Huntsville had paid off. And then it had been off to Nashville. Or rather *back* to Nashville.

Why?

"What did he do in Nashville?" she asked.

"Nashville . . ." Coleman screwed up his face, waggled his head back and forth, as though confronted with a dubious proposition. "I have to admit that Nashville is confusing. I mean, it looks like he was there to have a good time. He stayed three days, went to shows and restaurants, rented a car, but put no miles on it to speak of. But he also withdrew cash—a thousand dollars, in fact—from a downtown ATM. And he didn't spend it on the shows and meals, because *they* were charged on the Visa. So what *did* he spend it on?" Coleman hesitated. Before going on, he shot Cass a swift glance, appraising, slightly lubricious. "Women?"

Cass doubted it. Dolokhov had been, among other things, a pimp. He would think it beneath him to pay for sex, given that he'd been used to controlling the supply. It didn't make sense, either, that he'd spent three days just having a good time. Nor that he'd gone to Nashville for it, almost a thousand miles out of his way. He'd gone there for a reason, she thought; he'd stayed three days because he was waiting for something or someone.

"Phone calls?" she queried. "Long distance, I mean."

"Five." Coleman nodded. "Three to Sacramento, to a guy named Werner, and two international, to Moscow. I have the Moscow numbers, of course." He rooted through his briefcase, found the phone record, handed it to Cass.

So Dolokhov had called Werner . . . no surprise there. This merely confirmed what was already clear from the depositions. Someone had to have brought Werner the tape, supplied the ammunition for his lawsuit, and once she'd learned of Dolokhov's trip to Sacramento, it was clear that task had been his. But these two calls to Moscow?

Who had Dolokhov been calling in Moscow?

She inspected the numbers. Though the district code of the first belonged to one of the central Moscow exchanges, the number was otherwise unfamiliar. The second, however, was familiar. She'd called it herself dozens of times.

It was Dima Kuznetsov's office.

* * *

NOW PERHAPS she was getting somewhere. She had known, of course, that Dima was involved, just as she had known that Dolokhov was. Now, however, she could prove they were *linked*. When Coleman had departed, clutching a check for expenses and the balance of his fee, Cass sat down with a pencil and paper. In matters as complex as this, where much of the reasoning was provisional, she found it helped to write things down, to separate fact from inference and assumption. In that way errors in logic were less likely, easier to spot if you made them. At the top of the page she wrote "THE ORACLE CONSPIRACY" in capitals, adding beneath this a subtitle, 'State of play as of 4-15-96.' Then, in a kind of concession to objectivity, she put a query in brackets after the title.

Underneath she wrote:

1. (Fact) Dolokhov comes to the United States, traveling as Vladimir Grigoriev, arriving 2-3-96. He brings Werner a copy of the tape and supplies other "evidence" for lawsuit. (Sources: Grigoriev's credit card records, depositions.)

2. (Fact) Dolokhov makes extended phone call—cost, $82.76—to Dima Kuznetsov's number in Moscow. (Source: Motel billing records obtained—we won't ask how—by Arnold Coleman.)

3. (Inference) Dolokhov called Dima to report progress, which implies Dima was privy to the purpose of the trip. (Comment: This step

is a little dodgy, granted, but it seems reasonable to assume (a) that since he called Dima's number, he talked to Dima, and (b) that, given the length and cost of the call, they were not just shooting the breeze. What business *would* Dolokhov call Dima from the United States to discuss, if not the business that took him there? . . . I guess he could have called to discuss the long-term prospects for the ruble, but Dima's subsequent claims not to know him suggest their relationship was nefarious; I think the most likely reason for the call is the one given above.

    4. (Inference; implicit in 3 above) At least at the time of the phone call, Dima was in cahoots with Dolokhov. (Comment: But see 5 and 6 below.)

    5. (Fact) Dolokhov was murdered by a method suggesting to a knowledgeable observer (Lieutenant Sokolnikov) that the KGB was responsible.

    6. (Fact) Within hours of the murder Dima showed up at Dolokhov's apartment, with buddies, looking for something that "wasn't in his car." (Source: Olyenka.)

    7. (Inference) Dima had already searched Dolokhov's car, which after the murder was found abandoned way away from the site of the murder and several miles from Dolokhov's apartment.

    8. (Inference) Dima killed Dolokhov, or ordered it done, or at least knew that someone had done it. (Comment: How otherwise could he have known to search the car, also that Dolokhov wouldn't be in his apartment or return to it during the search?)

    9. (Inference) If Dima killed him the motive was *not* to prevent him leaking the tape to Werner. (Comment: This follows from 4 above.)

    10. (Inference) (?)

Here she paused. She wasn't too proud of these musings. They struck her as labored, prompted once again the unwelcome suspicion that when asked to do anything more than memorize facts, her mind was a blunt instrument, slow and unsubtle. She was also, now that it was set down before her in black and white, painfully conscious of how fuzzy it all was. The staircase of her logic was shaky, unfinished; vital steps were conjecture; the whole didn't take her where she wanted to go. Moreover, it suffered from a glaring weakness, one she suspected that Nick, inveterate and accomplished logician, would have spotted right away, but that had come to her only gradually. Underlying all her thinking, she now saw, was one crucial assumption, unstated and quite possibly unjustified. This assumption was that there was just *one* conspiracy here, only a single set of villains.

But this went way beyond the facts. As she knew very well from her own researches, the vast, unwieldy intelligence bureaucracy that Russia had been left by the Soviet Union was at present in a state of disarray. Following the upheavals of 1990, communications among its various branches had virtually come to a standstill. Ongoing secret operations had been stopped. Literally tons of documents later discovered to be vital and sensitive had been declassified, sometimes only to be *re*classified (when the cat was already out of the bag) months or even years later. Thousands of highly trained officers had been turned out overnight into the street to market as best they could their dubious skills and dangerous knowledge. Just because Comrades Dolokhov and Schedrin—Dima Kuznetsov, too, no doubt—had at one time been employed by the First Chief Directorate, one couldn't conclude that their current activities were approved or sanctioned by their former employer. Wasn't it entirely possible, in fact, to build an equally plausible theory on exactly the opposite assumption? Perhaps what Dolokhov had gotten hold of was a copy of a genuine Politburo tape. And then perhaps, because he was familiar with the background and understood its vast commercial potential, he'd conspired with Dima and others to exploit it. And perhaps, to take the scenario one stage farther, the current masters of Russian intelligence had somehow learned that the tape was missing, thereby endangering their agent Oracle. They'd have scrambled desperately—wouldn't they?—to recover the tape, and their efforts to do so might well have included killing their former agent Dolokhov.

Or to put the question in a more disturbing way: Even if Dolohkov, Dima, and others had conspired to use the Politburo tape against Hal, did that mean, necessarily, that it was a fake?

The answer—she conceded it reluctantly—was no.

There were arguments on the other side, of course, arguments other than those she had listed. If the tape was genuine and the Russian Secret Service had known of its loss, why had they stopped at killing Dolokhov? Why not her? she wondered. Why not Dima? And why had they been willing to confirm to Sokolnikov, and in such a transparently roundabout fashion, that Dolokhov had been a former employee? But even these arguments lost force, she realized, if you looked at the issue from a different perspective. What was it Nick told her made defectors so hard to assess? The fact that the other side *knew* they'd defected and could be relied on to obfuscate the issue with leaks. If the defector was real, they would try to suggest he was a plant, and vice versa. But then since they knew you'd expect them to try this, they might do the opposite of what you'd expect, and so on and so forth, ad nauseam, ad infinitum. In this case, once they'd known the tape was gone, they might well have acted simply at random, hoping to minimize the damage by confusing the hell out of anyone watching. If so, they'd succeeded. She remembered now the other thing Nick had remarked about problems like this:

Thinking about them made your head hurt.

Chapter Forty-Two

ON THE EVENING of May 24, approximately ten days before the preliminary hearing, Cass sat in her apartment contemplating gloomily a three-inch stack of eight-by-eleven paper. On it were printed, single-spaced, the entire contents of the document files from Dolokhov's laptop computer. She'd paid several hundred dollars for this stack of paper.

She hoped it would be worth it.

This job, she thought, could be worse than unsealing an archive. All the documents still to be classified and labeled. Untold quantities of information to be sorted, sifted, analyzed. No assurance that any would turn out to be of use. She didn't even know what she was looking for, only that something, some scrap from the great mass of electronic paperwork now piled before her, had struck Dima—or someone—as worth killing for.

But what?

Why?

When she got down to it, however, she discovered that the task was not as daunting as she'd thought. The documents didn't need to be labeled or classified; Dolokhov had done that himself. His life, though criminal, had at least been orderly, his piratical instincts controlled by the discipline of an accountant. The files were organized under half a dozen headings, each heading appending a list of the files it comprised, each file attaching a brief description of contents. Under "General Financial" there were files labeled "Trades, Currency (Dollar/Ruble)," "Trades, Ownership Certificates," "Bank Accounts," "Credit Cards," "Household Expense," "Car Expense," "Business Expense," and one, cryptically titled "Travelers," containing records of payments received. These were mostly in dollars but sometimes in rubles, and from sources identified in each case only by a single letter. Since the receipts were frequent, usually in the same amount, and the letter occurring most frequently was O, Cass guessed that those making the payments had done much of their traveling on trains; that in fact what the file recorded was Dolokhov's income from prostitution.

This reminder of Olyenda, leading her to thoughts of Dima, served only to strengthen Cass's resolve. Whatever it was and whether or not it succeeded, this plot had claimed at least one victim already. And though to claim that Olyenka had been innocent might seem to be wrenching the word out of shape, in a fundamental sense she had been innocent. Cass remembered Sokolnikov's chilling prediction about Olyenka's future. It had come true all too quickly. And just for that reason, because what had happened to Olyenka was precisely what Sokolnikov had *expected* would happen, the Militia would treat her murder as routine, just the death of another underage hooker at the hands of a pervert unknown. There'd be some kind of desultory inquiry, but the chances were it would be unsuccessful. Most likely Olyenka never would get justice now, not unless she, Cass, brought the killers to account. And she *would*, she vowed, she would if it killed her. Whatever else she might or might not accomplish, she was going to make damn sure she accomplished that.

There were twenty-nine files in the stack before her. In an effort to find a shortcut, she started with two that seemed to offer the most promise. The first was labeled "Bank Accounts." If there was a conspiracy, the Russians would be in it for money, so one way of proving it might be to follow the money trail. In view of the evident lack of faith between Dolokhov and his Russian partners, she doubted whether financial arrangements would have been entrusted to him entirely, but it was possible that his bank records might offer some clue as to where else to look.

They did, it turned out, offer *something* of the kind. In his own name, he'd had three accounts in Russia, none of them very suspicious or surprising: minimal balances, frequent transactions. Just about the pattern of activity you'd expect from a financially savvy Russian in a period of rampant inflation. He'd also, however, kept two U.S. accounts (balances in the low four figures, relatively infrequent transactions), both in the name of Grigoriev. He also had a numbered

309

Swiss account, to which he'd made deposits only. The balance here was close to three hundred thousand dollars, and the most recent deposit, dated February 28, was a wire transfer for one hundred thousand exactly. Also included under "Banks Grigoriev" was a single cryptic entry: "32785 RNBDC." Noticing that among the transactions recorded in the month of February for the Grigoriev account at Riggs National Bank in Washington, D.C., was a charge for "box rental," she concluded that "32785 RNBDC" was a safe-deposit box—the safe-deposit box, quite possibly, whose key they'd discovered in Dolokhov's apartment.

That key was now in her possession. In theory she could find out what Dolokhov had stashed there. In practice, however, she anticipated problems. She wasn't familiar with the procedure for obtaining entry to safe-deposit boxes, but probably she needed more than the number and the key. Probably she'd also need an ID. Maybe she'd have to sign something. Attempting to obtain unauthorized entry, moreover, was certainly a crime and not a crime she was prepared to commit, at least not without some assurance of a payoff.

She foresaw similar problems with the numbered Swiss account. Tracing deposits back to source was far more easily said than done. The Swiss were notoriously obsessive about the secrecy of their banking system. And even had they not been, even if she were somehow able to gain access to the records of that hundred-thousand-dollar deposit, they weren't going to tell her very much. People who made illicit payments were also obsessive about secrecy in banking. En route to Dolokhov's numbered account, that hundred thousand had no doubt traveled under various identities and made stopovers in such exotic places as Liechtenstein and the Cayman Islands. Tracing it back to the original source might not be utterly impossible, but clearly it would take a lot of time. That was what she didn't have.

Abandoning the bank records for the time being, she turned her attention to the file named: "Directory."

This, it seemed, was Dolokhov's little black book—a list, alphabetically organized, of telephone numbers, U.S. and Russian. With luck, when she matched it with the records Coleman had obtained, it would inform her who Dolokhov had called, other that Dima and Werner, on his trip to the United States. Unfortunately the owners of many of these numbers, and almost all the U.S. ones, turned out to be

310

listed only by initials. Dima Kuznetsov's number, for instance, was listed next to the letters D.K., while the *other* Moscow number Dolokhov had called from his hotel in Nashville was matched to the initials V.S. Cass consulted her watch: It was 11:00 P.M., 7:00 A.M. in Moscow. On impulse she dialed the V.S. number. Probably she wouldn't be able to get through—calling Moscow was always a pain— but there was just a chance she'd get lucky.

Much later she would have reason to wonder whether what she thought of as luck wasn't exactly the reverse, although, as honesty would force her to admit, stupidity had also played its part. For once the call went straight through. It was answered right away, almost before the first ring had sounded; almost, though the notion was clearly absurd, as if someone had been waiting for it.

"Schedrin." The voice was male, rather grumpy.

"I'm sorry"—the response, or its promptness, startled her into speech—"I seem to have gotten a wrong number."

"With whom were you wishing to speak?"

It occurred to her afterward that she shouldn't have made this call. Or rather that she should have planned it more carefully. She was seeking information, not handing it out; she should have hung up, not answered the question. And what she certainly shouldn't have done was answer it the way she did. Almost *any* name, she thought, even her own, would have served her better than the one that, in a moment of sheer brain cramp, she allowed to escape her.

"Grigoriev," she said. "Vladimir Grigoriev."

A silence, reflective, uncomfortably long, at the end of which the receiver was hung up.

She knew right away she'd been stupid but consoled herself with the thought that her blunder had not been that grave. Dima, after all, had known she had the computer. So all she'd given away, if anything, was the fact that she'd gained access to the files. Offsetting this was a certain gain. For though the nature of this game was still largely obscure, she'd identified yet another of the players: Comrade Schedrin, Vladimir Pavlovich, now scheduled to testify on behalf of Werner that the Dolokhov tape was a true and accurate copy of an original in the presidential archive.

Dolokhov. Kuznetsov. Schedrin . . . now at last, Cass thought, she was getting somewhere. In itself, perhaps, the link she'd established *proved* nothing; but these three, clearly, were the Russians involved, and now she could show them connected, via Dolokhov, to Werner. . . . There were gaps still left to fill in, of course. If the real purpose of Werner's lawsuit was to screw Hal's chances of election, the U.S. conspirators were still to be named. But the list of plausible suspects here should not be long nor hard to come by. You had only to ask yourself, she thought, who would benefit most from Hal's collapse. A glance at the latest polls would tell you that. The problem would be to find the links.

And then, of course, to prove them.

But finding was the immediate task. If they were anywhere, she thought, it was here in Dolokhov's phone directory. If she had to, she vowed, she would call *all* the U.S. numbers, find out whom each of them belonged to. But here again there were shortcuts available. This directory should include, for instance, the number Dolokhov had called from Houston, a number, she recalled, belonging to the same area code as Huntsville, the town in which he had gassed his rental the next day. . . . Retrieving that number from Coleman's notes, she quickly found a match in Dolokhov's little black book. Here it was listed next to the initials R.P. and followed, in parentheses, by a lower-case w. Below it was another number listed for R.P., this one in the Houston area code. This could belong to R.P.'s home, perhaps, and the (w) number to his work. But how many Houston residents, she asked herself, would commute to work in another town, more than sixty miles away? And if R.P. were this eccentric, how come Coleman had called the (w) number repeatedly and, according to his notes, during normal business hours, and each time only got an answering machine and a message omitting the name of the owner? . . . She cast her mind back over Coleman's account of his findings: Dolokhov had arrived in Houston on a Saturday. He'd driven through Huntsville the next day. Could the (w), conceivably, stand for "weekend"? Could this R.P., whoever he was, have a weekend house in the Huntsville area code? And had Dolokohov driven there to discuss with R.P. the business whose successful conclusion had encouraged him to treat himself that evening to a slap-up dinner at Brennan's?

She consulted her watch. It was now midnight, eleven o'clock in Houston. Was it too late to call R.P. at home?

She didn't think so.

Not if he were planning to injure her uncle.

There was no one home. A pause, after the call went through, was followed by the usual clicks. Answering machine, of course, and no doubt programmed with the same cagey message Coleman had encountered at the (w) number.

"You have reached 713-486-2200," the recorded voice, female and pleasant, informed her. "No one is here to take your call at present. If you'd like to leave a message, please do so after the beep. If it's Robbie you're trying to get hold of, good luck. Maybe you should call back after the election. If it can't wait, your best shot, which isn't very good, is to call 713-584-3130."

Call back after the *election?*

Had she, conceivably, just hit the jackpot?

No answering machine at the suggested number. This time her call was answered in person by a woman, brisk and businesslike.

"Democratic national campaign headquarters. . . . To whom may I direct your call?"

The temptation was to ask for Robbie, but Cass resisted. The chance that she might learn "Robbie's" surname was outweighed by others, less appealing. She could be asked *which* Robbie she wanted. She could be asked to identify herself. Worse yet, she could be put right through. These conspirators could start to get antsy if two of them got mysterious phone calls, one within hours of the other. Better to come at this from another angle entirely. It oughtn't to be hard to find out from other sources who, at Democratic national campaign headquarters, had the first name Robbie and a surname beginning with P.

"I'm sorry. I seem to have the wrong number."

It was then, as she was hanging up, that the implications of what she'd just heard really struck her: *Democratic* campaign headquarters? If if there *was* a plot to screw Hal's chances—and her latest discovery seemed to confirm it—then the ultimate beneficiary, surely, was the *Democratic* candidate, the incumbent.

The president of the United States.

* * *

IT TOOK HER NOT EVEN A PHONE CALL to discover the identity of Robbie P. It was printed out for her in black and white in column one of the inside front page of the next day's *New York Times*. There was even a photograph provided. The face staring back at her from the newspaper was one she now remembered having seen repeatedly since her return from Moscow, on TV and in newspapers and magazines. A player's face, she thought, not liking it much. A Beltway face, the impersonal smile presented for public consumption not quite hiding the self-satisfaction, the owner's not quite private elation at finding himself, a smart country boy from God knows where, at the center of the nation's attention.

Robbie Porcher, the blurb informed her, was the Democratic campaign manager.

But just in case, just in case by some odd mischance there were two Robbie P's employed in the campaign, Cass called up Directory Assistance for Huntsville. Could they give her the number for Robbie Porcher? . . . They were sorry—as usual, the singsong recorded response conveyed no sense of apology whatever—but that number was currently unlisted.

But her satisfaction at having the players identified, the plot in essence outlined, was qualified by knowing she could prove almost nothing. Though Dolokhov's phone list and the record of his travels established the links to her satisfaction, what would a jury make of it all? Would a jury, indeed, be permitted to *hear* it? On reflection she was sure they would not. It was easy, at any rate, to imagine how Werner's attorneys would react to attempts to get any of her findings admitted. . . . This "evidence" was hearsay—wasn't it?—and obtained illegally to boot. And who, apart from a woman closely related to two of the defendants and guilty (on her own admission) of stealing, was to say that this computer and these credit cards had actually belonged to Grigoriev, alias Dolokhov? And even if they had belonged to him, even if links between these alleged conspirators existed, even if it could be shown that these men had actually met and talked, did that tell the court what they had talked about? Did it prove that they were guilty of conspiracy?

She knew very well it proved nothing of the kind.

What would?

The tape, she thought. Everything rested on that. If she could prove the tape was a fake, the rest of her case would follow.

But how to set about proving it?

314

Back to the drawing board. . . . She cast her mind over her discussion with the engineers at Orion Recording and Duplicating. If the tape had been a fake, it had to have been done by splicing parts of a different conversation into an original Politburo tape. Undetectable splicing, though technically feasible, could be done only by professionals using sophisticated equipment. So Dolokhov hadn't done it himself, but had gotten someone else to do it for him. The only way, therefore, to prove that the tape had been spliced was to get whoever had done it to admit it, and to produce, in support of that admission, the originals used in the splicing. . . . This was fine in theory, she thought, but if Dolokhov had gotten the job done in Moscow, her chances of finding out who had done it were zilch. And if by some miracle she did find out, her chances of getting him to testify were worse.

She could think of several reasons, however, for Dolokhov *not* to get it done in Moscow, or anywhere else in Russia. Gorbachev's voice was well known there. So was the existence of the presidential archive. Almost any *Russian* hearing that tape would have known: (a) that it recorded a Politburo discussion, (b) that it was probably stolen, and (c) that splicing it was certainly illegal and beyond any question fraught with hazard. To someone who didn't speak Russian, however—for instance, an American recording engineer—the tape would be merely a jumble of sound, splicing it simply a technical problem, similar to working with music. . . .

Music.

It was then, by some sideways skip of thought, that she found herself remembering Dolokhov's U.S. itinerary. Everything in it made sense in terms of her conspiracy scenario *except* that backtrack he'd made to Nashville. Dolokhov had gone to Houston, met Porcher, secured his agreement to the deal. He should then have gone on to Sacramento—shouldn't he?—to acquaint Marcus Werner with the details of the plot and return to brief lawyers in Washington, D.C. Instead he had spent three apparently aimless days in Nashville.

Nashville. Home of country music.

It was now, riding a wave of inspiration, that Cass went back to Dolokhov's phone list. She was looking now for numbers with the Nashville area code. There was one, listed next to the initials R.S.M.

When she dialed the number, a receptionist answered. Rising Star

Music, it appeared, was an independent recording company. Their specialty was making demo tapes for aspiring country and western artists.

Dolokhov? An aspiring country and western artist?

Cass didn't think so.

Chapter Forty-Three

"WELL . . ." JUDGE ANDERSON sat back in her chair, smiled at the attorneys with evident satisfaction. "We seem to have our ducks pretty much in a row. The only issue still to be resolved is your motion"—she nodded to Orenstein—"regarding the admissibility of this tape recording. I propose we move to that issue now. When I've ruled, I think we can proceed to trial."

The pretrial conference on the Werner lawsuit had commenced at 9:30 A.M. in the chambers of Her Honor, Judge Laurel Anderson. Though only the lawyers were required to attend, and Reynolds—perhaps in a public display of unconcern—was off campaigning somewhere, Nick had elected to be present. It wasn't every day, he'd explained to Orenstein, that a man was faced with ruin and dishonor; he'd decided to live the experience.

By eleven-thirty he'd found himself fighting off sleep.

The trouble with the law, he discovered, was its nitpicking exactitude, its insistence, in all its documents and procedures, on dotting each i and crossing each t to the point, not merely of tedium, but of utter stupefaction. Thus far the conference had been devoted entirely to what Orenstein described as "housekeeping": verifying that the necessary papers—briefs, motions, depositions, interrogatories—had been filed with the court and exchanged between the parties in due time and proper form; that the parties were in agreement as to jurisdiction and the form of the trial; that the witnesses were all listed and available, et cetera, et cetera. All vitally necessary, Nick supposed, but hardly the stuff of drama.

And perhaps that was also the trouble, he thought. Perhaps this sense of anticlimax, of being caught up in some bureaucracy gone utterly bananas, could largely be blamed on false expectations, the fact that his only experience of lawsuits was derived from TV and the movies. These, since they preferred their audience awake (at least in the basic physical sense), demanded drama. Drama, in turn, demanded conflict, surprises. As normally portrayed on the silver screen, a trial was thus a process of unrelenting conflict and continual surprise: the unannounced last-minute witness, the unexpected devastating disclosure, the tearful confession from the witness stand. In life, it seemed, things happened differently. It seemed that in large part the function of this conference was precisely to *minimize* the conflict: to establish what the parties could *agree* on, and to limit, in advance and rather strictly, what was open to argument and on what grounds. Indeed, Nick thought, if the rules of engagement prevailing here could be reduced to a single guiding principle, it would probably be this: no surprises.

But now at last, or so it seemed from what had just been said, hostilities were going to be permitted.

Judge Anderson turned to Orenstein.

"I've read your brief and plaintiff's reply, both very clearly argued, I may say. Do you wish to offer oral argument?"

Orenstein nodded. "We do, if it please Your Honor."

At this the suggestion of a frown flitted across Judge Anderson's face. A slender, tense-looking woman in her mid- to late thirties, she'd been briefly touted as a candidate for attorney general in the last cabinet reshuffle, but had been passed over for some reason Nick couldn't now recall—smoking dope at Harvard, perhaps, or not paying taxes on her nanny. More important, she was a Democrat, which could be bad news for Hal and him. Alternatively she could be *pissed off* at having been passed over, which could be good news for Hal and him. . . .

And that, he reflected, was *really* the trouble with the law: Necessarily, it was administered by people, and people, no matter how intelligent and well educated, were mostly at the mercy of their prejudices, prejudices all the more insidious for being in most cases unconscious. Once you got caught up in the law, he thought, in spite of all the rules and safeguards, your fate could turn on whether the judge was a Democrat or whether a jury trusted your face.

"Okay . . ." Almost audibly Judge Anderson repressed a sigh, glanced at the clock on the wall. "Each side gets ten minutes. Hopefully we can be through in time for lunch." She paused, addressed herself to Orenstein again. "Let's see what we agree on here. As I understand it, Counselor, you're prepared to stipulate the identity of the parties and the accuracy of the translation?"

"We are, Your Honor."

"So once I've ruled, we'll be set for trial? You don't have any more motions up your sleeve?"

"Not up my sleeve." The implications of this figure of speech struck Nick as unfortunate and maybe ominous, but if Orenstein saw them that way, he didn't show it. "Depending on which way Your Honor rules, I may wish to make a motion to have the court cleared during presentation of the tape and evidence bearing on it. And, of course, I reserve my right to appeal Your Honor's ruling. But these are bridges we should cross only if we have to." He paused, smiled blandly. "My belief is that we won't."

"That"—Judge Anderson smiled blandly back—"is what remains to be seen. Please go ahead and make your argument, Counselor."

"The gist of it is set out in the brief," Orenstein said. "Our contention is that this tape is hearsay, and not just in one sense but two. It is hearsay, first, because the provenance is cloudy; we don't know whether this tape is a true and accurate record of the conversation it purports to reproduce nor yet whether the purported conversation took place on the date alleged. It is hearsay in another sense because, in the absence of direct testimony, we do not, *cannot*, know whether statements relied on by the plaintiff are truthful, or even whether what the speakers intended is what the plaintiff asserts they intended."

Orenstein paused.

"I'd like to elaborate briefly on each of these points. First, the issue of provenance. . . . As Your Honor knows, the tape in question claims to be a recording of a secret discussion held by the Soviet Politburo in March of 1990. If it is what it claims to be, it forms part of the so-called presidential archive and is the property of the Russian state; the archive has not been opened to the public or even to professional historians, and is in fact, under Russian law, still classified as top secret. The plaintiff claims to have obtained a copy of the tape from a Russian citizen, a Vladimir Grigoriev. Mr. Grigoriev—the name may well be an alias; in Russia he was also known as Dolokhov—is now unfortunately dead. We do not know how he came by his copy of the tape, but we do know that he must have come by it unlawfully. We also know that Mr. Grigoriev—or Dolokhov—was formerly employed by the KGB and that in 1984 there was contact in Geneva, Switzerland, between him and the plaintiff, Marcus Werner. This contact, indeed, was apparently part of the reason for the subsequent withdrawal of the plaintiff's security clearance—"

"Mr. Orenstein," the judge interrupted, "it's my understanding that the plaintiff has a witness, a Mr. Schedrin, who will testify in court that this tape is a true and accurate copy of an original in the presidential archive. If the tape is admitted into evidence, you will have—will you not?—the opportunity to impeach Mr. Schedrin's testimony in cross-examination. Are you suggesting now that his evidence should be tainted, discounted in advance, merely because this Mr. Dolokhov, or Grigoriev, or whoever, was formerly a member of the KGB?"

Orenstein smiled.

"Mr. Schedrin, who will testify as to the accuracy of the tape, was *also* formerly a member of the KGB. Which organization, may I remind Your Honor, was notorious for willingness to use any means . . . murder . . . blackmail . . . deception . . . *forgery* . . . to damage the vital interests of this nation. The KGB figures very prominently in this matter of the tape—indeed, in this whole lawsuit. Mr. Schedrin was a member. Mr. Dolokhov was a member. Mr. Kryuchkov, whose recorded statements the plaintiff wishes the court to rely on, was a member." Orenstein paused, continued calmly, "I'm confident that in cross-examination I'd be able to cast serious doubt on Mr. Schedrin's testimony, but I don't believe the interests of justice would be served by providing him and his former colleagues with a platform for broadcasting what I'm convinced is vicious innuendo."

Judge Anderson looked unpersuaded. But Orenstein had done a slick job, it seemed to Nick, in introducing the forgery notion without accusing anyone directly, at least not Werner or his attorneys.

"This brings me to my second point." Orenstein took a look at the clock, hurried on. "In the brief he submitted to the court, plaintiff's counsel argues that my second claim of hearsay is mistaken, since plaintiff relies not on the *truth* of statements allegedly made, but merely on the fact that they *were* made." He paused. "This argument is disingenuous. In point of fact the words relied on are not statements—they consist of a query answered by a request—but they are taken by the plaintiff to *imply* a statement, a statement whose truthfulness he very much relies on. This implied statement is, of course, that the KGB agent Oracle, whose suspected existence sparked the inquiry leading to plaintiff's dismissal, was still active five years later, *after* the plaintiff was dismissed. And the plaintiff relies on the truth of this statement to establish conclusions vital to his case: namely that the plaintiff couldn't have been Oracle, and further that this Oracle was actually the defendant, Henry Reynolds, who was thereby provided with a motive for attempting, falsely, to incriminate the plaintiff. . . . We contend that, even if the tape could be proved in every respect a true and accurate record, it would nevertheless constitute the very essence of hearsay, for not only would the jury be in no position to assess the *truth* of the statements made—or implied—but indeed the very *meaning* of the words relied on by the plaintiff would be, in the absence of direct testimony from the speakers, a matter for pure conjecture."

He paused. "Your Honor, we all know how it is with off-the-cuff conversations. People misspeak. Even at the time, they misunderstand one another. Who, apart from the speakers themselves, is to say now, seven years after the event, what the words relied on actually meant? Does the question 'You mean Oracle?' mean beyond any shadow of a doubt that a KGB agent of that code name was active when the question was asked, or did Mr. Gorbachev perhaps misspeak, mistaking either the agent or the code name? I submit that we don't know and we can't. . . . Similarly, does the response to that question— 'Respected Mikhail Sergeievich, I must once again implore you not to specify sources. Not even by their code names, and not even in these confidential surroundings'—necessarily, or even probably, imply an affirmative answer to Mr. Gorbachev's question? I would submit that it doesn't necessarily. It might or it might not, but if it *doesn't*, then it offers no support to the plaintiff's case."

Nick saw Judge Anderson glance at the clock. Orenstein must have seen it, too, for his words now came faster, his voice was more urgent.

"Your Honor, my client, Senator Henry Reynolds, has a most distinguished record of service to his country, not just as a soldier, but also

321

as a diplomat, a statesman, and a legislator. Is that record and indeed his whole character—his integrity, his honor, his *patriotism*—publicly to be called in question on the basis of evidence that is hearsay, deeply ambiguous, and vouched for only by some former hireling of a foreign intelligence service, whose methods are well known to include both libel and forgery and whose purpose was, and very well still may be, the destruction of the United States and everything it stands for?"

Silence.

"Very eloquent, Mr. Orenstein," Judge Anderson commented drily. She smiled. A touch wickedly, Nick thought. "So eloquent indeed that one is almost reluctant to deprive a jury of the pleasure of hearing it." She turned to Werner's counsel. "Your turn now, Mr. Raeburn. I'm sure you won't disappoint us either."

"I'll try not to, Your Honor"—Raeburn made a sketch of a bow— "though Your Honor has already stolen some of my thunder by stating with admirable brevity and concision my response to the first of Mr. Orenstein's points. The authenticity of this tape is attested by a witness, scheduled to appear before the court in person, whose competence and veracity Mr. Orenstein will have every opportunity to question. I submit that whether Mr. Schedrin's history is enough by itself to discredit his testimony is a matter for a jury to decide. Being formerly a member of the KGB, it seems to me, doesn't guarantee that a man is lying, any more, for instance, than being formerly a member of the U.S. Senate guarantees that he is telling the truth."

Here Raeburn paused and smiled pleasantly at Orenstein.

"With regard to Mr. Orenstein's second point, I submit that it is he who is disingenuous. I submit that the words relied on admit of one meaning, and one meaning only. And I note that in practice Mr. Orenstein, whatever confusion he claims is produced by those words, has no problem whatever deciding what they mean. The whole exchange could hardly be clearer: Mr. Kryuchkov claims that his information regarding U.S. intentions was obtained by a source 'with access at the very highest level'; Mr. Gorbachev inquires whether this source is the agent code-named Oracle; Mr. Kryuchkov replies, in effect, 'yes.' To Mr. Orenstein's further argument that our case relies on the truth of that 'yes,' we reply that it is not the 'yes' we rely on, but the fact that there *was* a conversation; the entire exchange makes no sense whatever if there was no KGB agent Oracle active at the

322

time. And that conclusion is not derived from hearsay but is, as I've already made clear, directly affirmed by a competent witness who will be present in court and available for questioning by Mr. Orenstein."

Here Raeburn paused and smiled blandly at Orenstein.

"Though I can't hope to match Mr. Orenstein in eloquence, I'd like to point out in conclusion that for twelve years now my client has been deprived of both his good name and his chosen career. *His* honor, *his* integrity, *his* patriotism have all been called publicly in question; he's been prevented from finding work commensurate with his talents and education. And all this as the direct result, first of accusations made by the defendant, Henry Reynolds, and second, of the way in which those accusations were investigated by Reynolds' codefendant and close friend, Nicholas Wolfe. The issue in this case is precisely whether my client was wrongfully deprived. I submit that this tape, which the defense is asking you to rule inadmissible, is not hearsay but legitimate evidence, vital to a just resolution of this issue."

Silence.

Good presentation, Nick thought. Stronger on the first point than Orenstein's, though possibly weaker on the second. Orenstein's features as he waited for the ruling were impassive. Hard to tell what he was thinking. Judge Anderson was also hard to read. She was gazing absently out of the window, lips pursed, frowning. Nick had formed the impression before the oral arguments that she was ready to rule on the motion without them. It seemed that now she wasn't so sure.

"I'm going to chew on this one over the weekend," Judge Anderson said finally. "I'll issue a ruling at nine-thirty Monday. Then we can get on with impaneling a jury."

*　*　*

"AM I GATHERING we could lose this one?" Nick and Orenstein had left together.

Orenstein stopped. "The case or the motion?"

"Both." Nick shrugged. "Am I wrong?"

"Hard to say." Orenstein thought for a moment. "With regard to the tape, I'm convinced it's hearsay and shouldn't be admitted. I believe the judge thinks so, too. I think she'll end up ruling in our favor, but she's human, so she worries a little. She worries about fairness, the big-guy-versus-little-guy aspect of this case. Because Werner claims to have been screwed last time around, she's anxious to give him no cause for complaint." Orenstein paused. "It's also possible that the tape bothers her a bit because actually the case bothers her a bit." Orenstein turned to face Nick directly. "I'll tell you the truth: It bothers *me* a bit. And what bothers me about it is you."

"Me?" Nick did his best to sound surprised. "Why?"

Orenstein tilted his head to one side, treated Nick to an appraising stare.

"Before I answer that," he said, "there's something I need to make absolutely clear: I am not about to give you advice on how to testify before a jury. My advice on that score has already been given: to tell the truth as you see it." He paused. "Nor do I expect or wish you to comment on what I'm going to say. In fact, I'd really much rather you didn't." He caught Nick's gaze and held it. "Do you understand what I'm saying?"

"Seems clear enough: What you're going to tell me isn't advice and you don't want to hear a reply."

"Correct." Orenstein's gaze didn't waver. "And actually, after our little dress rehearsal, it shouldn't come as any news. . . . Right now, Mr. Wolfe, you're not helping the cause. I don't imagine you actually believe that Senator Reynolds was a KGB spy or that Marcus Werner got shafted by your inquiry, but you're obviously uncomfortable about *something*, and it shows." He shrugged. "Maybe what you are is simply fair-minded, but it comes across as doubt. And juries pick up on that. They'll pick up on it, and they may misinterpret it. They may think you think that Werner was shafted, that maybe Senator Reynolds was up to something with this Natasha who had contacts with the KGB. And if they once start thinking things like that, then yes, Mr. Wolfe, we could certainly lose."

Chapter Forty-Four

"G<small>RIGORIEV</small> . . ." The receptionist repeated the name doubtfully, a syllable at a time, as if unconvinced that such names actually existed. "What kind of a name is that?"

"Russian," Cass said. "The man I'm inquiring about was a Russian."

"Grigoriev . . ." The receptionist, whose own name was Lettice, repeated the name thoughtfully. "In February, you say? . . . How would you spell Grigoriev, anyway?"

Cass told her.

"He could also have been calling himself Dolokhov," she added. "That's spelled with an o in the first syllable, even though it's pronounced like an a."

"Spelled with an o, pronounced like an a." The receptionist rolled her eyes. "That doesn't make much sense, now does it? Funny language, that Russian."

It was tempting to point out that in Lettice's own mother tongue the letter combination ou, to take just one obvious example, could be pronounced six different ways. Cass resisted the impulse, however. Since she couldn't compel answers to her questions, she needed the receptionist's goodwill. She supposed she could have asked Arnold to make this inquiry, but that would have meant explaining more than she cared to. Moreover, she had seen Dolokhov in person, which gave her the edge when description was called for. And probably it would be, she thought. She had with her the most recent available photograph, but it might be wise not to spring it on someone like Lettice.

Not right away.

"That's a lovely ring you're wearing," she remarked. "An engagement ring, isn't it? A diamond?"

"Fifteen hundred dollars." Lettice smiled. She cocked her head to one side, extended her arm, spread her fingers; displaying the object in question, Cass suspected, more for her own admiration than her visitor's. "Way too much to spend, I said, but Dave—that's my boyfriend—insisted. We're only doing this once, he said, so we're going to do it right. . . . Men." She rolled her eyes. "So sentimental when you get right down to it. And they say *we're* the impractical sex."

Cass nodded, smiling in what she hoped would be taken as rueful acknowledgment of shared experience.

"When's the big day?"

As a ploy to win Lettice's goodwill, she thought ruefully, this was amateurish if not utterly transparent. But Lettice didn't seem to share her opinion. With only minimal prompting from Cass, she rattled on for the next several minutes about in-laws (difficult), relatives (quarreling), gifts (inappropriate), caterers (recalcitrant), and the many other hassles involved in getting married. It took, in the end, a buzz from the switchboard to divert her from this theme and remind her that Cass was here on business.

"Sorry about that," she said when she'd routed the call. "I tend to get a bit carried away. . . . Well, now that you've learned more than you wanted to about little Lettice and her problems, maybe we could get back to yours. . . . You were asking about this Russian fella, Grigoriev or Dalokhov or whatever, whether we did business with him earlier this year?"

Cass nodded. She noted that the receptionist for Rising Star Music could not only remember both Russian names but also pronounce them more or less correctly. Lettice, obviously, was no dummy.

"D'you mind me asking *why* you want to know?" Lettice's manner, though still friendly, had become perceptibly guarded.

But Cass was prepared for the question. She handed over the business card she'd obtained from Coleman.

"I'm inquiring on behalf of a client," she explained. "A Russian client. It's a case of suspected fraud. We think this Grigoriev may have wanted a tape recording spliced and he could have asked Rising Star Music to splice it. No problems for you guys," she added quickly. "If you did it, you didn't do anything wrong. We'd just like to be able to prove the tape was spliced."

"You say you work for this inquiry agency?" Lettice hadn't seemed to find Cass's last statement reassuring. She fingered the business card Cass had given her, eyes flicking sceptically from Cass to it, then back. Almost visibly, pricing as she went, she took a quick inventory of Cass's outfit and accessories: designer jeans, silk shirt, suede boots, attaché case in Italian leather. "Seems to pay pretty well, your line of work."

"It pays okay." Cass nodded, shrugged. Inwardly she was kicking herself. She thought she'd dressed down for this interview. Clearly she hadn't dressed down enough.

Lettice inspected her a few seconds more, eyes narrowed.

"This Grigoriev, what was he like?"

"Small." Cass did her best to sketch a likeness. "Five-five or five-six. Plumpish. Dark hair. Very pale skin. His eyes were brown, kind of like a spaniel's, mournful. He spoke quite good English, but with a noticeable accent. When he walked, he sort of bounced. It was winter then," she added in an afterthought, "so he could have been wearing an overcoat. His was dark gray, fur collar and lining. It looked at least six sizes too large."

She paused here, scanned Lettice for signs of recognition. For a verbal picture, she thought, that hadn't been too bad. And the overcoat, if in fact he'd worn it, would surely tend to linger in memory. How many Russian customers, after all, could a two-bit firm like Rising Star Music have in an average year?

"I notice you said 'was.' " Lettice's face was expressionless. "He *was* like this. He look*ed* like that. . . . Am I gathering maybe that your Mr. Grigoriev is dead?"

Cass nodded, reached into her purse. She extracted the head-and-shoulders mug shot taken by the State Militia:

"He was murdered about a month ago in Moscow." She handed the photograph to Lettice. "This was taken afterward. It's not very pleasant to look at."

The warning didn't seem to daunt Lettice at all. She took the photograph, inspected it briefly, made a face, then handed it back. After thinking for a moment or two, she appeared to come to a decision.

"I remember him now." She nodded. "He didn't call himself Grigoriev then, or Dalokhov either, but I remember him, all right.

. . . And before we go any farther here, I think we should get Dave in the conversation."

Picking up the phone, she punched in a number.

"Remember that Russian came in a while back to talk to Les? Well, I've got someone here, a Miss Wolfe, asking questions about him."

Pause.

"She *says* she's from an inquiry agency."

Pause.

"No, I don't think the IRS." Lettice turned on Cass a look of cool scrutiny. "Some other government agency maybe."

*   *   *

DAVE FREEMAN was both the proprietor of Rising Star Music and— Lettice Scroggs's intended. About thirty, balding, a little overweight, he wore glasses and an anxious, harried look that, to judge from lines etched into his brow, was habitual. Cass also got the impression, however (perhaps because Lettice, abandoning callers to the care of an answering machine, had elected to be present for the interview), that his look today was a shade more anxious than usual. Rising Star Music, it seemed, had something to hide. Perhaps, Cass thought, Lettice's mention of the IRS had been more than casual.

"I'm not with the IRS. Nor any other branch of the government. I'm making inquiries on behalf of an attorney in a fraud case. Or to be more precise, what we suspect is a fraud case. We have absolutely no interest in the business or finances of Rising Star Music, but we may, depending on what you can tell me, wish to call you or one of your employees as a witness."

She paused, glancing from one to the other. Neither spoke. Dave, she noticed, rather than reassured, seemed more worried by what she'd said. She directed her appeal to Lettice.

"We know Grigoriev visited Nashville in February of this year, also that he stayed here three days. We found the number of your firm in his phone book. When I showed you his picture, you told me you remembered him. On the phone you mentioned that he'd talked to someone called Les. . . . As I've said before, I'm not for a moment suggesting that your firm did anything illegal or dishonest. I want to know whether you spliced a tape for him. Or if not, whether he asked you to."

She paused again. Again neither spoke.

"Oh, dear"—Cass sighed—"this is where it gets awkward. You clearly know something, and what you know may help us. If you won't answer here, in the privacy of your office, we can get a subpoena and ask you our questions in court. Are you sure you wouldn't rather save both of us the trouble?"

She didn't know how much of this was bluff, what Orenstein's powers of subpoena were, whether he'd be willing to use them. But even to her it sounded plausible. It must have sounded plausible to her listeners, too, for Dave directed a look of inquiry at Lettice, and Lettice, after a moment's hesitation, nodded.

"It's not that we don't want to help," Dave began. "But we've got a few problems of our own. I'm not even sure we know answers to your questions. Your Mr. Grigoriev was here in February and he did talk to Les about editing some tapes. It could have been a splicing job, I don't know. I'm not the engineer, you see, I handle the business side of things. All I know is he offered us cash—I think it was a thousand dollars—because he said the job was confidential and he needed it done in a hurry—"

"But could it have been a splicing job?" Cass cut in. "What I mean is: Had he asked Les to splice part of one tape into another so no one could tell it had been spliced, could Les have done it?"

"No problem." Freeman nodded. "We've got the equipment, and Les was an absolute artist. Les could have done it so not even God would have known." He paused for a moment, rolled his eyes. "The kind of musicians we deal with here, Les spent half his life splicing."

Past tense, Cass noted. Les *was* an artist, he *had* spent half his life splicing, but had moved on since, it appeared, to fresh fields and pastures new. She felt a twinge of irritation. More legwork for her, no doubt.

"And did he work on Grigoriev's tape?"

"Oh, yes," Freeman said. "I assume so, at least. If he hadn't, we wouldn't have gotten paid."

If he hadn't, we wouldn't have gotten paid? . . . If this was Dave's notion of 'handling the business side of things,' Cass thought, then maybe it was just as well he was marrying Lettice on Tuesday.

"I don't quite see the problem," she said. "You must have some record of what was done."

329

Silence. Freeman exchanged looks with Lettice.

"He told you, didn't he?" Lettice's tone contained a hint of exasperation; she might have been talking to a child. "Mr. Grigoriev paid *cash.*"

So that was it. An off-the-books transaction. Well, at least that explained Dave's worried look, why getting answers was like pulling teeth.

"So?" She shrugged. "Grigoriev paid cash. And maybe the cash never found its way into the books. I still don't see the problem, exactly. Presumably Les can remember what he did."

Another swift exchange of looks.

"I'm afraid that is the problem exactly." It was Lettice, finally, who answered. "Les can't remember. He's dead."

Chapter Forty-Five

As she parked her car on a side street near the bank, Cass tried to shake premonitions of disaster. Since she needed to go through with this, she couldn't afford to heed premonitions. They could make her look anxious or, worse, guilty; if they made her look either, she could end up getting caught. That she couldn't afford to heed them, on the other hand, was no doubt the reason they resisted her efforts to shake them. It seemed in the nature of premonitions, at least in the nature of *her* premonitions, that you only got them when they weren't going to do you any good.

Was it merely coincidence that her parents had christened her Cassandra?

Just how serious a crime, she wondered, was attempting to gain unauthorized entry to someone else's safe-deposit box? Probably pretty serious. "Attempting unauthorized entry" might be *her* description of her present intention, but the bank would call it "attempted robbery." She seemed to recall that robbing a bank, or attempting to, was a graver crime in the eyes of the law than robbing an individual. If so, this was absurd, *grotesque*, but it wouldn't surprise her at all. In a culture devoted to the worship of the dollar, robbing a bank was like plundering a church. Nor, she suspected, would it make any difference to the law that her motive was not gain, that actually she was trying to prevent a serious miscarriage of justice. The point—she could almost hear some district attorney making it—was that whatever use she planned to make of them, the contents of the box were not hers; her attempt to gain access was not only unlawful but also a threat to the integrity of the banking system and, by implication, to the whole social fabric.

It would also (which was of far more immediate concern than the state of the social fabric) deal a serious blow to Hal's chances of election.

Maybe even a mortal blow.

But Hal's chances were starting to look pretty shaky, weren't they? Though his lead in the polls was still substantial, the gap had started to narrow. "Don't know" had won legions of supporters these past weeks, and mostly at Hal's expense. What made this development even more ominous was that so far the press had been restrained. They'd picked up on the lawsuit from the start, of course, but as yet there'd been no feeding frenzy. If the case went to trial, all this would change. Then they would tear Hal apart. They would tear him apart regardless of the verdict, regardless of whether the tape was admitted. When Werner's attorneys got Nick on the stand and asked him about Natasha, the media would turn on Hal with that gleeful, vindictive relish they seemed to reserve for the mighty fallen.

So really she had no choice, did she? This was the only way forward. The others had all dead-ended, literally in the case of Rising Star Music. It was obvious what had happened there. It was as clear as if she'd watched him do it that Les Wooden had spliced the Politburo tape. But what good was her intuitive certainty of this if she couldn't prove it by producing Les in court? And the irony here was that what clinched it for her was precisely her inability to produce Les in court. Though there might be people able to see it as coincidence that, a bare week after working on the tape, Les had been killed in a hit-and-run accident in the normally tranquil suburb where he lived, she was not one of those people. Someone had made very sure that Les would never give evidence. But without him all she had to offer was a web of possibly suspicious circumstance; a web—she could almost hear Werner's attorney say it—that like all webs was mostly holes.

She needed to find the original Politburo tape.

It had to be somewhere—didn't it?—the original *unspliced* recording that Dolokhov had brought Les Wooden to work on and that Les, presumably, had returned to him later, along with the fabricated version. Dolokhov could have deep-sixed it, of course—that would have been the safest move—but somehow she couldn't see him doing so. It was way too valuable, and Dolokhov way too fond of money. He'd have stashed it somewhere for future use, somewhere secure, some-

where convenient, somewhere only he knew of. And where more secure and more convenient, she asked herself, than the safe-deposit
box he'd rented in Washington, D.C.? *Something* pretty vital must be
in that box; otherwise he'd hardly have hidden the key in his secret
cache along with the computer.

She had to get into that box. She had to try, at least. She couldn't
bear to think of her uncle politically ruined, her father disgraced,
publicly humiliated, because she had lacked the courage to act. If it
landed her in jail, so be it.

She wondered what it was like in jail.

Not, she reassured herself (entering the bank with what she hoped
was a businesslike air), that she really expected to end up there. Since
she'd taken the precaution, yesterday, of renting a box at another
branch, she was perfectly familiar with the bank's procedure. Two keys
were needed to open a box: one held by the renter, the other by the
bank. Once she'd produced an ID and signed a request for access, an
employee would go with her to the vault. He'd use his key to open one
lock, withdraw discreetly while she used hers on the other. Then,
when she'd completed her business, the whole sequence would happen in reverse and she could go on her way rejoicing. She'd be in
serious trouble, of course, if anyone realized she wasn't Dolokhov, but
she didn't see much risk of that. This branch of the bank was large
and exceptionally busy; Dolokhov couldn't have been in it more than
once or twice, most recently nearly three months ago. She doubted
anyone would remember him by name, much less know him by sight.
Since she knew the box number and had the key—it looked so much
like the key to the box she'd rented, it *had* to be the key—the only
obstacles she could foresee were producing ID and a convincing signature. And these were not serious obstacles unless the signature
Grigoriev had filed with the bank was not the same as on his Visa card,
or unless someone figured out that Grigoriev, V. A. (the name on the
account and presumably the box rental agreement, also the one ap-
pearing with *her* photograph on the forged driver's license that a contact of Coleman's, for a very stiff price, had somehow been able to
obtain for her) was a man.

This was rather too many "unlesses" for comfort, but they struck
her, individually, as reasonable risks. Most people had a signature and
stuck with it. Especially when using an alias, Dolokhov was unlikely to

be an exception. Americans, moreover, were mostly ignorant of Russian names. In the signature on Grigoriev's Visa, a signature she'd spent most of last evening practicing and could now dash off with some assurance, the first name appeared as Volodya. Though any Russian, and for that matter anyone else with a nodding acquaintance with Russian literature, would know Volodya was the familiar diminutive of Vladimir, a man's name, she hoped that to untutored ears, Volodya, since it ended in an a (like Maria or Natasha), could pass for the name of a woman.

If not, she was in a lot of trouble.

Starting, she thought, about now.

* * *

"I NEED TO GET into my safe-deposit box."

"Your name, please, and box number?"

"Grigoriev . . ." The first lie. As she spelled out the name, Cass had the queasy out-of-body feeling she sometimes got skiing, pushing off down a run she wasn't sure she could make. It was an odd combination of fear and detachment, a shiver that ended as a shrug. "The box number is one forty-six."

"I'll need to see some ID."

Cass handed over the driver's license.

The teller was a plump, comfortable-looking woman of about forty, who peered at Cass with friendly interest over the tops of her half glasses. She examined the fake license with evident care, eyes flicking from photograph to subject.

"Volodya . . ." She pronounced it more or less correctly, stress on the second syllable, y virtually elided. "That's an interesting name. Russian, isn't it?"

Cass's stomach gave a small, admonitory lurch. A chatterer. Damn. A "people person"—just what she didn't need.

She smiled, nodded. "My father was Russian."

"Volodya . . ." The teller repeated the name, but without, Cass noted, handing back the license. "My sister's boyfriend had a friend of that name: Volodya from St. Petersburg. What a flirt *he* was." She paused, shooting Cass a shrewd glance over the tops of her glasses. "Must be one of those unisex names, like Dana."

"In Russia it's normally a man's name. It's actually the diminutive form of Vladimir." Surrounding her deception with this packaging of truth, Cass hoped her smile looked better than it felt. What it felt was much closer to a snarl: a quick, tight baring of her teeth. "He'll never admit it, but I think my father was hoping for a boy."

And that part was true, she thought. She doubted any Russian, even in exile, would dream of naming his daughter "Volodya," but that last part was true.

"He should have been grateful for any child." The teller's smile turned wistful, faded. "Me and my husband couldn't have one. I think it was what doomed us." She seemed to recollect then where this conversation had started, for her manner became suddenly impersonal, businesslike, and her eyes strayed back to the license. "If you'll wait here, please, I'll be right back."

She turned and marched off, disappearing through a door in the rear. Cass felt panic rise in her throat. Like vomit.

Wait here.

Why?

She hadn't taken the license (which was reassuring), but on the other hand she hadn't given it back. Instead she had left it on her side of the counter, next to the computer terminal—but easily in reach. Cass fought off the urge to grab it and bolt. In two seconds she could be in the street, safe. But if she did, she'd forfeit forever her chance at the box, her last chance of helping Hal.

She never knew which way she would have decided. She might very well have bolted, she thought later (at a time when she very much wished she had). And had she, things might have been different. As it was, she was caught in a moment of perfect indecision, trapped between opposite but equal forces, when the matter was decided for her, flight removed from the list of options. The teller reappeared, accompanied by a man in a pinstripe suit.

She was going to have to bluff this out.

"Ms. Grigoriev?"

He was thirtyish and impeccably neat: shirt perfectly white, suit perfectly pressed, shave so close it was almost shiny. He could, she thought, have been a bank officer or alternatively a security guard. Impossible to tell from his manner, which was polite but impersonal.

"Yes?" Trying to sound indifferent but not, to her ears, succeeding very well.

"Would you sign this for me, please?"

He pushed a form across the counter to her, together with a pen. Cass recognized the form as the standard boxholder's request for access. If there was a Rubicon in all this, it was here. Once she signed there was no going back. If she signed, she was attempting robbery.

She signed.

He inspected the signature briefly, glancing at the card he had with him, then back again at her scrawl. His expression didn't change. If he'd seen anything suspicious, his eyes didn't show it. But then, of course, they wouldn't, she thought; the bank wouldn't want any unpleasantness in public. Banks were temples of propriety and order. Unpleasantness took place in private.

"Would you come with me, please."

Go with him *where?* . . . Again Cass fought off the urge to bolt. Go with him somewhere out of the public gaze? Somewhere she could be questioned quietly? Arrested without any fuss?"

She attempted a smile. "May I have my license back?"

"Of course."

The teller, handing it over, looked at her oddly, she thought. Turning to the man in the suit, Cass attempted another smile.

"Lead on, MacDuff. . . ."

He strode briskly to the end of the counter. Unlatching a gate, he held it open. She went through it with a sinking heart. Could she be leaving freedom behind her? She followed him down a corridor lined on one side with offices. At the far end stairs led down to somewhere—probably the unpleasantness room, she thought. The room where people like her were held, pending arrival of the cops.

At the top of the stairs he paused and turned, produced a ring of keys from his pocket. Then, for the first time, he smiled.

"You do have yours with you, don't you?"

She realized, with a rush of the purest relief she had ever felt in her life, that he was taking her to the vault.

* * *

SHE WAITED until she got back to the car to open the envelopes. She could have done it in the vault, but she couldn't bear to linger at the scene of her crime. Even here, in the relative safety of the car, her heart was beating about twice the normal rate and her breathing was rapid and shallow.

That was it for a life of crime. She wouldn't do anything like that again. Not for Hal. Not for anyone.

Two eight-by-eleven manila envelopes, no external markings, had comprised the entire contents of the box. One of them, which she put to one side, was flat and rather stiff: documents of some kind, photographs maybe. The second, bulkier at one end than the other, held something that rattled when shaken. Tape cassettes, or so she profoundly hoped. If not, her ordeal in the bank, those ten minutes of unrelieved terror, would all have been for nothing.

If not, furthermore, she was out of ideas. The trial would be held. Hal wouldn't be president. Her father would be publicly shamed, pilloried.

Closing her eyes and offering a prayer to whatever deity presided here, she tore the seal, upended the envelope, tipped the contents on the seat beside her.

She opened her eyes.

Cassettes, she saw. Two of them. Both of Japanese manufacture but otherwise without identifying markings.

Switching on the ignition, she placed one of the cassettes in the car's tape player, adjusted the volume, waited.

Silence. Then a hiss. Then a voice.

Speaking Russian.

"With the greatest possible respect, I must disagree with Mihail Sergeiivich. Failure to respond with military force to the repeated provocations of these so-called nationalists will be seen as a confession of weakness. It will only provoke more extreme, more outrageous demands. It will only . . ."

She listened to a few more predictions, all of them equally dire, then she hit the eject button. What she had here was a version of the Politburo tape—the Great Baltic Invasion Debate—though *which* version wouldn't be clear until she had heard the whole thing. . . . But, either way, she thought, there couldn't be any doubt. If this was the original, then the other would be the doctored version. These cassettes, accompanied by testimony from Dave Freeman of Rising Star Music, should be more than enough to explode Werner's lawsuit. They should blow it right out of the water.

She sat back, closing her eyes for a moment, allowing herself to savor the triumph.

Then she opened the other envelope.

In it were two photographs, identical eight-by-ten glossies, enclosed in a folded sheet of paper. The shot had evidently been taken in a restaurant, apparently without the subjects' knowledge. Hal Reynolds, a much younger Hal, was sitting across from a woman. She was a very beautiful woman, a woman decidedly not Josie. The instants it took Cass to remember where she'd seen her were the product, she thought later, of some inner prohibition; she didn't *want* to remember where she'd seen her. But she did remember. She'd seen her in Tatyana's wedding album.

The woman and Hal were holding hands.

On the folded sheet of paper was a pencil-scrawled sentence in Russian. The handwriting she didn't know but presumed it to be Dolokhov's. The sentence asked, perhaps rhetorically, a question.

Cass stared at it in utter dismay.

* * *

SHE MUST HAVE SAT there about a minute. Unaware, till she heard the click of the door latch, that she wasn't alone any longer. By then it was too late to do much about it. She could have screamed perhaps. Later she thought she *should* have screamed—at least it might have given them pause—but she wasn't a screamer, at least not by instinct, and everything happened too fast. She could only turn, in frozen amazement, as the rear door on her side swung open. An arm appeared around it, pointing a gun. At the same time the door on her right was opened. She turned just in time to see Dima Kuznetsov ease himself into the seat.

"If you yell or make any move," he said, "my friend will shoot you in the head."

She said nothing. Not because she was scared—she wasn't scared, she was outraged—but because she could find nothing to say.

"You'll be wondering why the unmannerly intrusion." Dima smiled. "Let's just say I found I couldn't live without you. Or maybe"—he reached over, removed the cassette from the deck—"what I really couldn't live without was this."

Chapter Forty-Six

SURFACING THROUGH DEPTHS of sleep toward the source of the sound that was drilling through his head, Nick grunted and rolled over, slapping reflexively at the snooze bar of his clock radio. Though failing to silence whatever had dragged him from his dreams, the action rendered him at least semiconscious and removed the alarm from the list of suspects. Identifying, an instant later, the telephone as a likely culprit, he fumbled for it on the bedside table, at the same time peering in peevish disbelief at the message conveyed by the clock radio. Six-twenty? Who in the hell had the brass balls to call at six-twenty on a Saturday morning? Cass, he thought, trying to shake his head clear. Presumably she'd come up with something. She'd *better* have come up with something, he told himself, lifting the receiver. She'd better have some damn good reason. If not, there were going to be words.

"Am I speaking to Nick Wolfe?"

Not Cass. A man's voice and familiar. Trace of an accent, probably Slav, hesitation on W suggesting Russian.

"Who's this?"

"I think you know who it is. We met several times in Moscow. I was quite offended, actually, that you left without saying good-bye."

Nick felt as if someone had doused him with water.

"Kuznetsov?"

No response.

"Kuznetsov . . . What the hell do you want?"

"I think it's more a question of what *you* want." The voice at the other end was silky, pleased with itself, now that he focused on it unmistakably Dima's. "If you want to see your daughter again, you'll listen very carefully to what I have to say. I want you to—"

"Are you telling me you've *kidnapped* her?"

"What I'm telling you is that I'm willing to trade her for the computer you stole from my colleague and former partner. I want you to get it from her apartment. I want you to do so as soon as I hang up. Cass has given orders for the porter to admit you. When you've got the computer, return to your apartment. Further instructions will be waiting for you there."

"How do I know you've got her?" His reflex was to stall. "If you've got her, put her on the line."

He did know, of course. He knew it in his gut. He recognized instinctively the presence of disaster, but somehow he had to extend the dialogue, keep Dima talking as long as possible, hope he would talk out of turn.

"Unfortunately, that won't be possible. I'm calling from a pay phone. I mention this in case you were thinking of trying to have the call traced." There was a pause. "I'm sure you remember your young friend Olyenka? . . . If you don't do exactly what I tell you, when I tell you, the same thing will happen to Cass."

Nick had a sickening vision of Olyenka as he'd seen her in that Moscow apartment, her blood soaking the sheets and mattress, her breasts covered with cigarette burns. For a moment he couldn't speak.

"Nick, are you there? . . . Do you understand me?"

"*You'd* better understand *me*, Kuznetsov. . . ." He had to struggle to keep his voice calm. "If you hurt my daughter, I will personally kill you. I will find you and kill you if it takes me the rest of my life."

"Threats, Nick?" Dima didn't sound impressed. "You're hardly in a position to make threats."

"This isn't a threat, it's a statement of fact. I will kill you."

"Then we seem to be at something of a standoff." Dima continued to sound perfectly relaxed. "If you don't do what I say, I will kill your daughter. If I do, you will try to kill me. . . . How much better for both of us—don't you think?—if you simply do as I say."

Better? Nick doubted it. The choices were clear: catastrophe or disaster. Best not let on you understood it, however. Best try to win room for maneuver, *time* for maneuver at least.

"I'm not even going to think about doing as you say unless you prove to me my daughter is alive. Get her somewhere there's a phone, call me, and put her on the line. Do that and I'll bring you the computer."

"And give you time to set up a trace? Dima sounded almost amused. "Nick, my friend, you don't understand your position. This is *not* a negotiation. There are my terms and they are final. The choice is yours, and in order to meet my deadline, you must make it now. And don't think of trying to involve the police. I've taken the appropriate precautions."

There was click followed by the dial tone.

Nick lay back for a moment, the receiver in hand. He felt as if someone had shot him. He'd been dumb, he thought, criminally stupid. Because Russia was no longer a threat, he'd behaved as if the same were true of Russians. He'd known Dima had tortured the truth from Olyenka, he'd known Dima knew that he knew, yet he'd let Cass run around investigating as if there weren't any danger, as if Dima were a snake whose poison was harmless outside Russia, as if being Russian somehow stopped him from getting on a plane. All the while Cass had been tracing Dolokhov's movements, Dima and his cohorts had clearly been tracing hers. Her father's stupidity could cost her very dearly. But it wouldn't, he resolved, not if he could help it.

If anyone paid here, it wouldn't be Cass.

Replacing the receiver, he got up and started to dress.

Chapter Forty-Seven

On the way to the apartment, he picked up a tail.

Actually, it was more like an escort. For one thing, their vehicle, a Mazda 626, was that noisy shade of scarlet the cops called "arrest me" red; for another, they made no effort at concealment. From the moment on the Beltway when he first spotted it in his rearview mirror to the time he reached Cass's apartment building in Georgetown, the Mazda was never more than ten lengths behind him and usually fewer than five. When he parked, it pulled up on the far side of the street, from which point the occupants, two men in leisure suits, observed him with undisguised attention. For a while he'd been tempted, from some urge to self-assertion, to pull some maneuver designed to shake them, but reflection had shown him this wouldn't be smart. They were watching to see that he was following instructions. He needed to let them see he was.

As meek as a lamb to the slaughter.

If there'd been any doubt whether Dima had Cass, the doorman quickly dispelled it. Miss Wolfe had called about ten last night. Not seeming at all like "her normal friendly self," she had sounded anxious, even upset, but had brushed off his efforts to find out why. She said that her father would be around in the morning and had asked to have him let into the apartment. . . . He'd be happy to do so, the doorman added, provided Mr. Wolfe could produce some ID. He felt awkward about asking this, he added, but Miss Wolfe's request was somewhat irregular. With so much crime in the papers these days, it was better to be safe than sorry.

Nick showed his driver's license, and the doorman, having summoned a replacement for himself, accompanied him up to the apartment.

*   *   *

THE COMPUTER was in the spare bedroom, which doubled as Cass's office. Next to it on her desk was the three-inch-high stack of eight-by-eleven paper on which the files had been printed out. Since Dima had said nothing about this—possibly he didn't know it existed—Nick didn't plan to volunteer it. Not that it would make much difference. What Dima wanted wasn't the computer.

Before he left, he took a look around the apartment. In the kitchen, not a cup was out of place: No breakfast dishes in the sink, no food left out, no messy saucepans on the stove. No clothes left around on the floor in the bedroom; the bed made; the closets shut; the jars and bottles on her dressing table all carefully arranged, all properly capped and stoppered. Even the living room looked hardly lived in, the windows spotless, the surfaces quite innocent of dust, the cushions on the armchair and sofa plumped, the carpet vacuumed, the magazines on the coffee table spread out in a careful fan. The place suggested an apartment hotel or perhaps an expensive furnished rental. The only traces of personality in it were the framed photographs on the mantelpiece and bookcases: one of Patsy, looking young and gorgeous; one of Josie before she'd gotten sick; one of Hal in his Marine Corps uniform; two of Dolly Reynolds, Hal's mother.

No picture of him anywhere, Nick noticed.

It struck him that there was something a bit bleak in all this. As a child Cass had not been noticeably tidy; indeed, she'd often been noticeably not. And she hadn't inherited from either parents any predisposition to neatness. Perhaps, he thought, the order she insisted on now was a reaction to the chaos of her adolescence. If so, it would hardly be surprising, but still the place filled him with a sense of something absent. There was little of her here or anywhere. If she died, she would leave almost nothing behind, as if her life had hardly been lived.

*   *   *

WHEN HE GOT HOME, a note was waiting in the mailbox, typed and unsigned, a set of terse imperatives:

"Come by car. Take Interstate 66 to 81. At 81 head south past Harrisonburg to Staunton. At Staunton take 250 heading west. Drive

9 miles to State Route 42. Make a left on 42. Drive 8 miles to the rest area on the left. Park. Get out of the car and lock it. Wait. Be there by 11:30 A.M. Do not attempt to organize rescue or surveillance. If you do, or if you are late, the trade will be considered canceled."

Ten-thirty. It was now a little after eight. Consulting a road map, he discovered the timing was well judged. For about 150 miles, 3½ hours gave him a reasonable margin for mishaps but not enough time to "organize rescue or surveillance." In any case, he couldn't take the risk. They had taken pains to show him they were watching. Possibly his phone was tapped as well. He couldn't risk taking a weapon, either. Dima was KGB-trained; if he made mistakes, they wouldn't be elementary. Maybe he wouldn't make any at all.

He would need to, Nick thought; he would surely need to.

Otherwise there wasn't a chance.

What Dima was planning here wasn't a trade. That had been clear from the start. He could have sent a sidekick to get the computer. He could even have done it himself. And unless there was something stashed in its memory whose significance Cass had so far overlooked, the computer was at this point more or less irrelevant. What was stored in its memory was what mattered, and that cat had been out of the bag for days. So the reason Dima was insisting that he, Nick, deliver the computer wasn't that he wanted the computer. It wasn't the message Dima wanted.

He wanted to shoot the messenger boy.

It wasn't a case of "Get me the computer, then you and your daughter can go free." What Dima had in mind here was more like a clean-sweep destruction of the evidence, deep-sixing the records of Dolokhov's travels and finances and eliminating at the same time the only people who knew enough to link him to the smear conspiracy and the murder of Olyenka. What this also seemed to entail, of course, was that Cass had been right all along—there *was* a conspiracy; the tape was a fake—but Nick noted this without much interest. Since the only people able to unmask the conspiracy seemed unlikely to live long enough, it no longer seemed important. From Dima's point of view, moreover, this wasn't just a case of eliminating evidence. It wouldn't hurt Werner's chances in the least if one of the defendants in his lawsuit went mysteriously AWOL on the eve of the trial.

But what if you *didn't* deliver the computer?

It wasn't an option. You could list it, Nick thought, but only to dismiss it. If you didn't go, Dima would kill Cass. He would kill her—and probably torture her first—whether there was anything to be gained by it or not, because that was the sort of man he was. So whether there was anything to be gained by it or not, you, Nick Wolfe, were going to give him what he wanted. Because not to would be to abandon Cass, leave her to die in pain and alone. It would tell her more clearly than words ever could that in this extremity of her need her father had refused to risk himself for her. You couldn't let her die believing that, and believing it, you wouldn't want to live. If she had to die, you would, too.

Except, Nick thought, that she was *not* going to die.

You were going to stop Dima if it killed you.

*   *   *

THE RED MAZDA fell in behind him a couple of blocks from his house, stayed with him all the way to the rest area. When he pulled in, however, it sped on by, perhaps to alert whoever was coming to meet him. It wouldn't be Dima in person, of course; he wouldn't be nearly as trusting as that. Though so far his instructions had been followed to the letter, he'd insist on screening for surveillance. Depending on how much help he'd brought, there'd be one, maybe several, cutouts.

The rest area was grade B or C. No soft-drink machines or bathroom facilities, just shade trees and a couple of picnic tables. Only one car in the parking spaces, and it pulled out as he pulled in. He parked next to one of the picnic tables, locked the car as instructed, propped himself against it, placing the computer on the hood beside him. Ostensibly the computer was what this was all about, so at least he should go through the motions of accepting their fiction. His Timex, replacement for the watch he'd pawned to Olyenka, told him the time was ten past eleven. If they were on time, twenty more minutes.

Without much interest, he inspected his surroundings. The rest area was next to a field. Beyond it were other fields—one had horses in it—and to the far side of them the ground was wooded and rising. In the distance, dim and blue, were mountains. It occurred to him that maybe he should pay all this more heed; since the screen of his awareness might very soon go blank, it behooved him to remark the final moments. The suggestion struck him as making no sense. Remark

345

them for what? When it was over, it was over. He'd never let *that* bother him much. And it didn't much bother him now. What bothered him—if he dwelled on it, he knew it would torment him—was the thought that he might never get to see Cass. Dima could have killed her already. Dima could kill *him* as soon as he gave himself up. Dima could . . .

Don't start imagining, he told himself sternly, don't start second-guessing. The latter had never done any good, and the former was simply distracting. Dima could do any number of things, and imagining wouldn't change one. There might not be much you *could* change now, possibly nothing, but you had to stay calm and alert in case there was. "Sufficient to the day is the evil thereof." It was the only piece of Scripture he'd ever been able to subscribe to. Things were bad enough already; no point imagining them worse.

He wished he'd been able to believe in a god. In tight corners it gave you someone to pray to. All he had was a kind of unfocused hoping. He wanted someone to pray to that Cass wouldn't have to die, especially not knowing how much he had loved her.

In the end, what life had come down to was that.

* * *

WHEN THEY CAME for him it was in a different car, a gray Toyota Forerunner with West Virginia plates. They cruised past the rest area once, rather slowly, presumably to check that he was alone. When they came back it was faster, sweeping into the parking lot and skidding to a halt beside his Saab. He thought they were the same men who had followed him in the Mazda. They were wearing the same beige leisure suits, and their coloring and the general physique accorded with his memory of the men in the Mazda. Both were heavyset, one six inches taller than the other, and both had dark skin and black hair. The smaller one was starting to go bald. They could have been Mediterranean or Arab or, he thought, conceivably Chechens. Since he couldn't see their eyes, he couldn't tell. But apart from impenetrable sunglasses, he noted, they'd taken no trouble to conceal their faces. In kidnappers this would have been serious negligence, but these, of course, were not kidnappers.

All the same, it was negligence.

346

Why take chances when you didn't have to?

He made it a point to memorize the Forerunner's license plate number. Probably it wouldn't do any good—most likely the plates had been changed or the vehicle was stolen—but he did it anyway because it was something he *could* do, a token but necessary act of resistance. Passivity was a state of mind. It was not a state he wanted to slip into. Besides, the plates might not have been changed. Negligence was also a state of mind, a rot that had a tendency to spread. It heartened him to note that the help were careless, also that there were fewer than he'd guessed.

They were careless but not grossly. They didn't pull guns or search him in the rest area, where some passing motorist might have spotted them and called the police. They didn't bother with tying him up, either, just took the computer and gestured him into the Toyota, the taller one getting in the back seat beside him. They didn't stop to search him—indeed, didn't speak—until they had driven some forty minutes, taking roads that led always upward, into the mountains, each one more deserted and narrower than the last. It was only when they were on unpaved track and deep in the West Virginia woods that they stopped and ordered him out of the car.

The smaller one did the talking. Though his English was passable, the accent could be cut with a knife.

Mafiosi, Nick thought, probably *rented* Mafiosi.

The taller one produced a gun. It crossed Nick's mind that they were going to kill him; he would die ignominiously, here in the woods, without ever seeing Cass. But before imagination could take hold of this idea, the taller one backed away, covering him with the gun, while the smaller one made him stand with his legs apart, hands resting on the roof of the car, then patted him down cop-style, feeling him all over, even around the crotch, in a way that was quite impersonal but still, because it emphasized how much he was in their power, maddeningly intrusive. The search had the single concrete result of costing Nick his Swiss Army knife, which he hadn't remembered was in his trouser pocket. The man felt it, reached in, extracted it, examined it briefly, and, smiling in a manner half pitying, half apologetic, shrugged and slipped it into his own trouser pocket.

Nick watched it go without regret. Since he hadn't known he had it, he wasn't going to miss it. And it wouldn't have done him any good. On the plus side, moreover, the theft had taught him something:

These were *small-time* rented Mafiosi.

* * *

THE CABIN STOOD at the edge of a clearing. It might have been used for hunting, Nick thought, or perhaps the owners had at one time run a still. It was of log construction, largish—two or three rooms, he guessed—with a brick chimney at one end and a rusty metal smoke-stack at the other. Neither appeared to be in use at present. Though the glass in the windows was intact, the place had an air of abandonment. There were two vehicles standing outside it in the parking area: a Jeep Cherokee and a Volvo station wagon.

When the Land Cruiser pulled up beside them and honked, Dima and another man came to the door.

The other man was Arthur Quine.

Not a good sign, Nick thought. It wasn't a good sign at all that Quine was willing to be seen by him. But then again, good signs weren't what he'd been expecting.

"My dear Nick," Dima greeted him expansively, as if he were the host at a party, "how sensible of you to comply with my requests."

Nick handed him the computer.

"I hope," he said, "it'll turn out to be worth all the trouble. My feeling is it won't." He paused. "And now, if you'll hand over Cass, she and I will be on our way."

Dima cocked his head to one side. "I'm afraid," he said, "that's not going to be possible."

"I see," Nick said. "Will I get to see her at least?"

"Oh, I think so." Dima eyed him curiously. "You weren't really expecting me to let you two go, were you?"

"Expecting you to keep your word?" Nick shrugged. "Dima, I have to confess the possibility never crossed my mind." He turned to Quine. "Can't say I expected to see you here. Not that I'm terribly surprised. What are you hoping for out of all this?"

Quine looked at him for a moment.

"Money," he said. "What else?"

Dima turned to the two Mafiosi.

348

"Put him in the woodshed with the girl. Tie him up and tie him tight. . . . You did think to search him, of course?"

They nodded.

"Fine." Dima smiled. "When you've done that, you can take off, I think." He turned to Quine. "You too, Arthur. I'm sure I can take care of things from here."

Quine stared. "Why the hell bother to tie him up? Take them into the woods and pop them. What's to be gained by delaying, except risk?"

"If you're worried about risk"—Dima shrugged—"take off. Speaking for myself, I'm not worried about it. In a few hours I'll be on a plane to Moscow. . . . In the meantime, I have a score to settle."

"Score . . . Christ." Quine looked disgusted. "This is business we're here for, not fun."

"A little of both, I think." Dima's voice had an edge. "Which is why you may not wish to wait around. These Wolfes, particularly the daughter, have caused me considerable pain and annoyance. It seems only just that I should repay."

Chapter Forty-Eight

For a couple of years in early adolescence Cass had had a recurring dream. The details and settings sometimes varied, but the action was always the same. She was called on to witness an execution. The method of execution was one of the details that varied; sometimes it was hanging, sometimes electrocution, more infrequently a firing squad. Mostly, however, perhaps because it offered some limited scope for resistance and therefore seemed the most cruel—she imagined the condemned clinging desperately to life, holding his breath until he was ready to burst, eyes popping, frantic with terror; it was the gas chamber. The location was almost always the same: a dimly lit cavernous room at whose center, elevated, stood a large drum-shaped metal cylinder surrounded by an observation platform. At intervals around the circumference were portholes, heavily glazed and reinforced around the perimeter with rivets. She'd be ordered to station herself at the porthole next to the door. Inside she could see the chair in which the execution would take place. Plain, high-backed, wooden, it had head- and armrests to which were attached leather straps. Similar straps were attached to the front legs. A spotlight was focused on the chair from above. It seemed to stand in an island of light in the midst of an ocean of darkness.

She could never tell how long she had to wait—dream time paid no regard to clocks—but the wait always seemed to last forever, attended by a mounting sense of panic. When the time at last came and the guards arrived, she would stand with her face pressed up against the porthole, hearing the footsteps approach from behind but not daring to look lest her eyes should meet the victim's. When she heard them open the door beside her, she would shut her eyes tight, determined

350

not to look. That was the moment she'd be seized from behind, pinioned, a gag clapped over her mouth, a sack pulled down over her head, and she'd know in her mind what she'd known in her heart all along: The death she'd been summoned to witness was her own.

It was always then, in that moment when numb disbelief turned into knowledge and her insides dissolved with the terror, that she'd wake and find herself safe in bed, gasping for breath and sweating, relief flooding into her mind like sunshine but never quite able to banish entirely the lurking, peripheral shadow. She'd always been left with the uneasy sense that what she'd been granted was only a reprieve, never an absolute pardon. In a year or two she'd stopped having the dream, but the imprint on her psyche had been lasting. Since then, whenever she'd read or even heard about executions, she'd been visited by that irrational dread, as if something out there were searching for her and had taken a sudden step closer.

* * *

SHE'D KNOWN from the start, or almost from the start, exactly where this was headed. Logic dictated that, even if he wanted to—and why should he?—Dima couldn't let her go. Though he had the tapes and the pictures now, he simply couldn't afford to. She knew about the smear and she knew about Olyenka. And Nick knew pretty much everything she knew. Dima's instinct for self-preservation was far too acute to tolerate the risk their knowledge represented. He would use her as bait to lure Nick here; then he would murder them both.

But though she had known all this from the start, she'd still somehow managed to hope. Maybe, once Nick brought him the computer, he'd feel safe. Maybe, once he'd destroyed all the evidence, he'd consider the witnesses harmless. There would only be her word and Nick's against him; and her word and Nick's, unsupported by fact, would never come close to convincing a jury. But Nick had brought him the computer and it hadn't changed a thing. Dima showed no sign of intending to let them go. Instead he'd tied them up, left them in this wood cellar, waiting.

Her nightmare had caught up with her at last. This time she wouldn't be waking up.

Not ever.

* * *

"HE'S GOING TO HAVE TO KILL US, isn't he?"

Nick didn't answer immediately, perhaps because no answer was required. She didn't know really why she'd bothered to ask. For the comfort of hearing his voice, she supposed, for the comfort of knowing he was there. He must know it as well as she, must have known it the moment he'd gotten Dima's phone call, just as she had known he would come. That was the only grace here, she thought, the small, steady flame bringing warmth and light in this onset of darkness and cold—that despite the troubled history between them, she had never for an instant doubted he would come. She had tried for his sake to *hope* that he wouldn't (she would like to think that, had she been permitted to talk to him, she'd have found the courage to urge him *not* to come), but the truth was that when Dima's men had bundled him into the cellar, she had felt a surge of love so intense it was all she could do to keep from bursting into tears. That she *hadn't* burst into tears, that she thought she could get through this thing now without screaming or begging or going mad with fear, was due to his presence. He would show her how to do this, she thought, because he knew how, because all his life he'd been obedient to at least one absolute imperative: courage.

"He's going to have to," she repeated.

"Let's wait and see." He might have been discussing the weather. In the gloom of the cellar she could just make out his features: calm, imperturbable, oddly reassuring. "No point *scaring* ourselves to death."

She was silent for a moment, then she said:

"But it's obvious he has to. It's always been obvious. *You* must have known it, too." She paused. "I can't find words to tell you what that means to me, Nick: You knew what would happen, yet you came."

"No words needed, Cass. You're my daughter. I love you." He paused, then added, "Let's not be giving up here. As long as there's life, there's hope."

"What hope?" She knew there was none. She didn't want to hope, she thought; at this point hope was the enemy. "What can we possibly do against Dima?"

"Do?" His voice was as level as ever. "If I get even half a chance, I'm going to fucking kill the little bastard."

Bravado, she thought, intended to keep up her spirits. Except that his tone was so matter-of-fact it was hard not to feel her spirits lift. And perhaps because the words were spoken so entirely without heat, it came to her that he absolutely meant them. What he was feeling here was anger—the knowledge struck her into something like amazement—not fear or desperation, anger.

* * *

DIMA CAME FOR THEM shortly afterward. He appeared to be alone. She heard footsteps, she thought just one set, descending the steps to the cellar, then the scrape and click of the lock. Then the door creaked open and he stood for a moment silhouetted in the doorway. As he approached her, she saw he was carrying a gun. Without speaking, he went over and stood behind her chair. She felt the muzzle parting her hair, the chill of it on the back of her neck. He was going to do it now, she thought; without preamble, Cheka-style, the quick bullet in the back of the head. For an instant her whole being rose up in revolt. It *couldn't* be now. It was far too soon. She still had her whole life to live. But she choked back the plea that rose in her throat. She wasn't going to give him the satisfaction.

But instead of shooting, he stepped back, propped himself against the table that ran along one wall.

"Not going to utter?" he asked. "You prefer to die in dignified silence. Very commendable, very American. But how long can you keep it up, I wonder?"

He took something out of his pocket. When he saw he had her attention, he placed it on the table beside him. A pack of cigarettes, she saw. A pack of Marlboros and a butane lighter.

Cigarettes?

But Dima didn't smoke.

"Remember that little slut Olyenka?" he asked.

Suddenly Cass understood.

He looked at her a long moment. "I see you do remember her. I expect you also remember that time in my apartment when I locked the door and you said you were afraid. I said there were terrible people

353

in Moscow. I said I didn't think you were afraid enough. . . . Have you learned to be afraid enough now?"

He was mad, she thought hopelessly. He was going to hurt her, but who knew why? For being a woman? For being an American? For being tall and rich and for refusing him? For not being scared enough? It was for all of these things, she thought, and yet it wasn't. In a sense it had nothing to do with her.

Out of the corner of her eye she saw Nick looking at her. Almost imperceptibly, he nodded.

She said, summoning all her will to keep her voice steady:

"I was afraid of you then, Dima. I'm afraid of you now."

"Very sensible." He smiled mockingly. "And sensible of your father to suggest it: 'Give the beast what he wants, placate him.' But in fact it wasn't necessary." He paused. "If I did what you thought I was going to do, we both know what would happen. And perhaps that's enough. No need to prove it, I think. I prefer to remember you the way you are."

Moving behind her, he untied her arms. Then, stepping back, he spoke again:

"I want *you* to untie your feet. When you're free, you can untie your father. Arms first, then feet. . . . Take care, both of you, to make no sudden movements. If you do I'll put a bullet in your head."

"Isn't that what you're going to do anyway?"

"Of course." His shrug was almost audible. "But I prefer not to have to do it here. I thought we might take a short walk in the woods. There's a sinkhole out there, maybe ten or fifteen meters deep. It's not the grave I would have chosen for myself, but it's going to save me a lot of digging."

It occurred to her to tell him to go to hell, that she was damned if she'd make this easier for him, facilitate her own burial arrangements. But if she did, he might change his mind about hurting her. Alternatively, he could just kill her now, while Nick was still tied and couldn't do anything. Not that there was anything he *could* do, she thought, but instinctively she grasped for a few extra moments of life. While there was life, Nick had said, there was hope.

There *was* no hope, but she hoped anyway.

It took her a while to get them both untied. The knots were tight, and her fingers were numb from the cold. From time to time she

354

would glance at Dima. He stood there watching her, some paces away, his pistol always pointed at her head. The pistol seemed rather small—she noted the fact but without much interest—a .22, perhaps. And that squat tube attached to the barrel must be a silencer. She remembered him telling her once, in Moscow—in another life, she thought—that a .22 was the classic assassin's weapon. It was small, he'd said, no stopping power whatever; but a professional, anyone who knew what he was doing, didn't need anything bigger. That must have been what he was, she thought, before the new Russia gave him new scope for his talents, an executioner for the KGB. He seemed to have no trouble meeting her eye, yet his gaze always seemed to look past her or through her. It wasn't hard to figure why. In his eyes she was already an object.

"I can understand you taking your time," he said. "But don't overdo it, please."

"My hands are numb," she told him. "If you want it done faster, do it yourself."

She looked up then from fiddling with the knots at Nick's ankles. Her gaze met Nick's. He was smiling at her, eyes shining. He mouthed something to her she couldn't quite make out. She thought it was: "I'm proud of you."

Then his ankles were untied, and she straightened up and stepped back. Nick didn't stand up immediately. Instead he sat there a moment, flexing his legs at the knees and rubbing his arms with his hands, restoring circulation.

"If we're all quite ready"—Dima sounded bored—"I will tell you how we are going to do this. You will go first." He gestured with the pistol to Nick. "Cass will follow. I will bring up the rear and direct you. If you make any sudden movement, Nick, Cass gets a bullet in the back of the head."

And if you *don't* make any sudden movement, Nick, Cass gets a bullet in the back of the head. But Cass wasn't, she suddenly resolved, about to go gentle into that goodnight. At some point on the trail she was going make a try, yell to Nick to make a run for it, hurl herself backward into Dima. Probably it wouldn't do any good, but at least she wouldn't have let herself be slaughtered unresisting, like some cow or sheep, some timid cut of meat.

Now Nick stood up. Moving slowly, she noted, and awkwardly; it seemed the cold had numbed him more than her. Dima backed up another pace, gestured Nick with the pistol toward the door. She needed to buy time, Cass thought, time for Nick to get the stiffness from his limbs. Otherwise her gesture would be futile.

"Before we do this"—she tried to keep her voice steady—"I've a couple of questions I'd like to ask you."

"A couple?" Dima considered. "We have time for a couple, I think."

"They're about Dolokhov. Why did you shoot him? It *was* you who shot him, wasn't it?"

He nodded. "It was all about money. Isn't everything about money in the end? . . . Dolokhov believed that because the idea was originally his, he should share double in the take. When the rest of us, naturally, disagreed, he decided to double-cross us, run a little scheme of his own. His plan was to blackmail your uncle, using the tape and the photographs you found in that safe-deposit box. He intended to use you, I think, as a conduit to your uncle. . . . Of course, when I discovered this, it was clear he would have to be stopped. I found out where he'd arranged to meet you. What happened then"—he paused—"you know."

She nodded. "You shot him. Then arranged him carefully on that parapet to scare whoever found him half to death. . . . And you knew it would be I who found him, didn't you? So why did you leave him like that? Simply a sick sense of humor?"

"Not at all." He looked surprised. "Actually, I was hoping to scare you off. I tried several times to scare you off," he added. "Several times with words and then by hiring those Chechens. But you just wouldn't let yourself be scared. And so now"—he shrugged—"here we all are."

He gestured them to the door with his gun.

"Actually, I regret this," he said. "I liked you both as people. It was Dolokhov's error involving you in this. Yours was letting yourselves be involved."

"And yours," Nick answered him calmly, "yours was coming in here with that stupid little gun."

For just an instant Dima was taken aback. And in that fraction of a second Nick launched himself at him with astonishing speed, hurling his body left, in front of Cass, shielding her from the inevitable bullet.

In Cass's stunned view of it, what happened then was like the moment just before a car wreck: Her senses were revved up to such a pitch that what took place in some fractions of a second seemed to unfold, unhurried, over minutes. It was clear from the start that there was no way Nick could make it. No way he could even have *thought* he could make it. And Dima was incredibly quick. He fired twice before Nick was on him. Cass didn't hear the bullets hit—one caught Nick in the stomach, she learned later, the other in the chest, piercing a lung—but they didn't do a thing to slow him down. Dima might just as well have tried to stop a grizzly with a slingshot. Nick's two hundred and thirty pounds slammed into him like a truck and he went down, Nick on top of him, the .22 flying out of his grasp, skidding across the dirt floor toward the doorway.

For an instant the shock of it held Cass frozen. Then she darted to retrieve the pistol. When she'd grabbed it and whirled around to point it at Dima—if he even breathed, she would kill him, she thought—she saw that Nick had no need of assistance. He had Dima by the hair and was pounding his head against the floor with a kind of systematic, destructive fury, as if determined to crack it like a coconut. Indeed, she thought later, but for the fact that the floor was dirt, therefore yielding, Nick might very well have done just that. And even then he might have done it had the .22-caliber slugs in his body not chosen, quite suddenly, to make their presence felt. A spasm seemed to shake him. He stopped, half turned to Cass, gave her a puzzled, unseeing look, then slumped forward on top of Dima.

*　　*　　*

The next two hours Cass would remember as being the longest of her life. Mostly, she thought later, what got her through them, kept her on task, was her single-minded urge to kill Dima. Had she not needed him to help her get Nick in the Jeep and to drive, she was sure she *would* have killed him. She'd have stuck his pistol in his face, looked him in the eye, and pulled the trigger. As it was, she kept willing him to offer her an excuse. While the Jeep bumped and lurched through the seemingly interminable miles of West Virginia forest, she sat behind the driver's seat, Nick's head cradled in her lap, the muzzle of the .22 resting on the back of the seat and pointed at the base of Dima's skull, and she watched with absolute unwavering attention for the sudden movement that would grant her her desire. And her craziness, for that must have been what it was, seemed to impress itself on Dima. He never did make that sudden movement. Instead he followed her instructions like a robot, drove her to the nearest town, parked outside a drugstore with a pay phone, stayed at the wheel, staring fixedly ahead, his back and neck still rigid with tension, as a passerby summoned the sheriff and an ambulance, and a crowd of whispering bystanders formed a circle around the Jeep. And he was absolutely right not to move, she thought, for even then, in front of all those people, she still might have killed him. Even when the patrol cars arrived, it was only after a deputy had put handcuffs on Dima that she could be persuaded to give up the gun.

Afterward, when she made her statement to the sheriff, which she found she could do calmly and lucidly, almost without emotion, she noticed he was looking at her oddly. His look was a little hard to interpret, seemed to hover somewhere between a frown and a smile.

"Did I do something wrong?" she asked him.

"No, ma'am." He shook his head emphatically. "If what you just told me checks out, and I'd venture to bet cash money it will, I'd say you did everything just about perfect." He paused then, flashed her a ferocious grin. "And I'd say this Russian must be thinking around about now that he sure as hellfire picked the wrong folks to kidnap."

Chapter Forty-Nine

THIS OUGHT TO HAVE FELT like coming home, but didn't.

In the iconography of Cass's memory, the drawing room of the Reynolds family home in Bethesda had always been an image both sanctified and constant. It was to this room—spacious, light-filled, elegant yet lived-in, the brocade of the couches and armchairs slightly faded, the huge Persian carpets showing traces of wear, books and magazines cluttering the tables, the spray of roses in their vase on her grandmother's Steinway spilling their petals on the gleaming black lid—that her thoughts retreated whenever she happened to be homesick. And she always, it seemed, imagined it in spring or in summer, always in the early evening, and peopled almost exactly as it was now: Josie in the armchair to the right of the fireplace, legs propped on an ottoman and covered with a traveling blanket, whatever she was reading resting in her lap; Dolly, Hal's mother, in the armchair opposite, holding her preprandial martini—she'd only ever permitted herself one—and sitting, in spite of her eightysome years, like an object lesson in perfect deportment; and, of course, Hal himself, standing between them, leaning casually against the mantel with a glass of something, usually Glenlivet, in his hand.

Tonight, however, it was champagne they were drinking.

Celebrating something? Cass wondered.

She had always *seemed* to imagine it this way . . . but perhaps, she thought, memory had tricked her. Perhaps the reason the tableau that now greeted her seemed so familiar (yet at the same time so wrong) was simply that she'd seen it a little too often of late. It, or some variation of it—always minus the alcohol, of course (no point forfeiting the teetotal vote)—had greeted her in half the magazines she'd

359

picked up recently. She'd even seen the TV version: When Hal had been interviewed by Barbara Walters, Josie and Dolly had been present there, too, arranged as now like some triptych in front of the fireplace. The two of them, Hal had said at one point, these two vital women in his life, spoke to what he stood for more forcefully than he ever could. It was then that Cass had turned off the TV.

What about Natasha? she'd wondered.

Hal was riding high again now. Higher than he had been before Werner's lawsuit was filed. "REYNOLDS VINDICATED," the eighteen-point headlines had screamed, "LAWSUIT WITHDRAWN," "RUSSIAN CONSPIRACY UNMASKED," and the polls had taken off like a stock market rally. She hadn't actually been present outside the courtroom when the news broke that Werner was withdrawing his suit—she had spent the day in Intensive Care watching Nick conduct the grim struggle for his life—but she'd gathered the scene had been pandemonium, the same kind of media fireworks display as had greeted last year's verdict in the trial of that football player. Not, she thought, that the hoopla was in any way surprising. For the story, which emerged in installments over days—you could hardly describe them as "leaks," Cass thought, they were more like releases from the Glen Canyon Dam—had been as sensational as the raciest tabloid could hope for. The centerpiece, of course, had been Dima's confession. The gist of it, obtained from the police and revealed by Orenstein at the conference in Judge Anderson's chambers (the same conference, ironically, at which the judge had been due to rule on the question of admitting the Dolokhov tape), had caused Werner's lawyers to withdraw from the case and Werner himself to abandon his suit in the face of the threat of a prosecution for libel. Though initially Dima had been reluctant to confess, he'd been brought to realize, in an interview attended by Cass, that a trial in the United States for kidnapping and attempted murder was actually the more attractive of his options. Once he'd started to sing, he had done so *molto con brio;* in its detail his confession had reminded Cass somewhat of the "Catalog aria" from *Don Giovanni.* A number of arrests had followed—Porcher and Quine were only the most notable—each extensively exploited by the media. Though the president himself was thought not to have known about the criminal activities of his campaign managers, the Senate was intending to appoint a select committee to investigate the extent of his involvement, if any. There were few in the country who didn't believe the scandal had doomed his chances of reelection, and those who didn't share this belief mostly felt his chances had been doomed already. . . . So Hal was riding high, all right. He had locked up all but thirty of the delegates he needed to win the first-round nomination at next month's Republican National Convention, and in the primaries yet to come the polls were predicting a win in Illinois and a landslide in California.

Cass wished she could feel happier about it.

She stood in the doorway awkwardly, the three of them—the people closest to her in life, her family—beaming at her, each of them genuinely overjoyed to see her. Now was not the time for this, she thought; some other time would have been better. But what other time? She had put this off long enough. Was any time good for what she had to say?

This morning, in the mail, she'd finally heard from Tatyana.

Hal approached, smiling, arms outstretched for a hug. Noting her expression, he stopped, his face clouding.

"Cass, what's wrong? Bad news about your father?"

Her father, she noted. Not her uncle's friend. Not Nick.

"Nick's hanging in there," she told him. "He hasn't completely won the battle yet, I think, but his chances are improving every day."

"He'll make it, don't worry." Hal's smile half returned. "One thing Nick Wolfe never was was a quitter."

He hadn't forgiven him, she thought. It was mostly thanks to Nick that Hal still had a campaign, but he hadn't forgiven him and he never would. And what he hadn't forgiven him for—the thought struck her now with the force of revelation—was doing him the injury of knowing who he was.

"You can say that again," his wife called out across the room. "In every respect except one Nick Wolfe has always been absolutely faithful."

Silence. Hal's smile took on a certain rigid quality. His gaze, avoiding Cass's, traveled downward to the legal-size beige manila folder she'd tucked under her arm upon entering.

"What's that you have there?" He seemed glad of the pretext for a change of subject.

361

"Documents." She shrugged. "Some photographs and a letter from 1984."

"I see." He considered for a moment. Possibly, she thought, about why she had brought them with her to this family gathering. "Some research project or other, I take it?"

"You could say that." She nodded. "It's my personal research project."

"You must tell us about it." He smiled. "But first, may I pour you a glass of champagne?"

"Please."

She watched him as he went to get it. There had always been something of Kennedy about him, an ease, a charm, an athlete's grace, yet he lacked the faint air of raffishness by which in her view—and perhaps it was colored by hindsight, the man having died before she was born—Kennedy's memory had always seemed tainted. Hal was more of the soldier, she thought; he had that aura of being born to command.

No wonder the voters seemed to love him.

"A toast to Cass." He handed her a glass and raised his own.

"A toast to me?" She was startled, disarmed. "What have I done to deserve this?"

"What *haven't* you done?" It was Josie who said it. "And the best thing you've done is to still be with us. I don't know what any of us would have done, my darling, if you hadn't."

"That was Nick," Cass said. "It's entirely due to him. He's the one you should be toasting."

"We will." Josie flicked a glance at her husband. "I will, at least."

"But there's something else," Hal ignored the comment. "In my case it's a personal thank you. You pretty much saved my campaign single-handedly." He raised his glass. "Thank you, Cass. I'll owe you forever."

"You don't owe me anything, Hal."

She paused. There never would be a right time for this, she thought. It might as well be now. "Except possibly an explanation."

He was suddenly still. "An explanation of what?"

She opened the folder, handed him the photographs. "To begin with, an explanation of these."

As he glanced at them briefly, one after the other, his expression

362

didn't change. When he looked at her, all she could see in his eyes was a look of innocent inquiry.

"Well, I recognize *him*." He handed them back with a smile. "But I can't say I remember her. . . . But obviously these were taken quite a while back. Where on earth did you get them?"

"I got them from Dolokhov's safe-deposit box. . . . You remember who he was, don't you? He was the guy who offered to sell me the tape. His other name was Vladimir Grigoriev. He took these in Geneva in 1984, at which time he was working for the KGB." She paused. *"Now* do you remember who she is?"

"No idea." His expression still didn't change. He was going to try to bluff it out, she thought, and so far he was doing it perfectly. He must be one hell of a poker player. "Since you evidently know, why don't you fill me in?"

"I will." She nodded. "Her name is, or was, Natasha Oblonski."

She didn't know what she expected exactly; whatever it was, she didn't get it.

"A-ha." Emphasis on the second syllable. But not much emphasis, she noticed. Not shock or dismay, more a grunt of acknowledgment. As if what she'd said had not been completely unexpected. "You're wondering, in that case, why I've been claiming not to know her."

"Among other things." She noticed that while Dolly was staring at her in open astonishment, Josie was not. Josie was staring at her, but not with astonishment. She knows, Cass thought. She knows something at least. "Things such as why you lied to Nick about her back in 1984. Such as whether you were planning to repeat that lie under oath. . . . How fortunate you didn't have to," she added. "Dolokhov and Werner must have been just praying that you would."

"I imagine." Very dry. "I'm surprised that I need to explain to you, however, that in the service of a greater truth sometimes one is forced to lie."

" 'In the service of a greater truth'?" She echoed the phrase dubiously. "What does that actually mean, Hal? I'm afraid it sounds like bullshit to me."

"Cass!" Her grandmother's stare had turned to disapproval. "Is that any way to talk to your uncle? Hal, exactly what is this all about?"

"It's okay, Mother." He didn't look at her, kept his eyes on Cass.

363

"Cass has raised a legitimate issue. I think she's entitled to an explanation. I just hope she can show a little understanding."

He paused for a moment to marshal his thoughts.

"You may not believe this," he began, "but when you showed me the photograph I really didn't recognize her. I remembered her when you told me her name, because, of course, I had had a brief acquaintance with her, back in Brussels in 1984, but if you hadn't told me I wouldn't have known her . . . because it really was just that," he went on, "not an affair, just a brief acquaintance. I met her once or twice at parties, and then in Geneva, when we happened to be staying at the same hotel, I took her out to dinner. That must have been where those photographs were taken."

He paused a moment, as if waiting for confirmation, but when Cass said nothing, he continued.

"That dinner was the last time we met. She spent the whole evening coming on to me like a bitch in heat. As you know, I've never been overly modest that way"—he gave his self-deprecating, boyish grin—"but it occurred to me to look this particular gift horse in the mouth. The Werner inquiry was getting under way and the whole situation smelled like a honeytrap to me. I said thanks but no thanks, and that was all there was to it. Or it was until she showed up at the office that night.

"What happened then was mostly bad luck, bad luck compounded by my own stupidity. It was bad luck your father happened to be there working late. Bad luck he let himself be wheedled into calling me at home. It was stupid that I didn't tell him the truth right then, and worse that I made that slip of the tongue when responding to his message via Patsy. And then, you see, I was stuck with my stupid lie. . . . Werner had just passed his polygraph test and was claiming that I had tried to frame him. It was obvious that if my contacts with Natasha were made public, those two or three innocent meetings would seem like a romantic involvement with a woman I suspected was a KGB agent, and if on top of this, I were known to have lied about it, it would have looked utterly damning. I decided to try to tough it out." He paused, looked ruefully at Cass. "It turns out to have been another bad decision."

He sounded and looked so convincing, Cass thought, she could almost have believed him. Probably she *would* have believed him, she thought, had she not known more of the details than he realized.

And then, of course, there was the letter.

"You know," she told him, "there's an irony here. Nick would have believed you if you'd told him. He might have thought you were having an affair with Natasha, but never that you were spying for the Russians. He trusted you more than you trusted him."

"Maybe so." He shrugged, unconvinced. "I notice, however, that when this whole business of the tape came up he didn't exactly fall over himself to come to my defense." He paused. "But that's all water under the bridge. It doesn't matter now what he might or might not have believed. The question is: Do *you* believe me?"

For a moment she was tempted to stop this here. What purpose would be served by going on? So what if she didn't arrive at the "truth"? Would the "truth" help anybody? Was it going to help Nick in his fight for his life? Was it going to help Dolly? Make Josie get better? . . . But she couldn't stop now, she knew. Too many people had been hurt by these lies. Too many people had died for them. They were owed the truth, those people. Whatever it was, they were owed it. She was owed it, too, she thought. She was owed it as much as anyone.

Almost sadly, she shook her head.

"I wish I could, Hal, I truly do. The trouble is, your bad luck wasn't confined to Brussels."

"What the hell is that supposed to mean?" His voice was starting to acquire an edge. "One can get a little tired, you know, of being called a liar."

"I'm sorry, but it's a title you seem to have earned. . . . And before you say any more, let me read you this." Cass extracted the letter from her folder. "It's a letter Natasha Oblonski wrote to her cousin Tatyana Rostova in April of 1984. Tatyana—this is where your bad luck comes in—happened to be my roommate in Moscow. It'd take too long to explain how this letter came into my possession, but there's no question it's the same Natasha. I saw a picture of her in Tatyana's wedding album. The letter's in Russian, of course, so I'll have to translate, but I don't think anything important will be lost. The meaning is right on the surface."

She darted a glance at Josie then. This was going to hurt her most.

But once again the look on her aunt's face defied expectation. Josie must be able to guess, at least anticipate, but she looked, Cass thought, neither pained nor apprehensive. Mostly she looked resigned.

" 'I've met a man. . . .' " Cass had read over the passage so often since the letter's arrival this morning that now she could translate it without having to think. " 'Of course, I hear you say, Tasha is always meeting men. But I want you to know, cousin, that this time it is going to be different. He's an American, a diplomat, very rich, very prominent; if I told you his name, you would certainly know it. I won't bore you with the details, but the bottom line, as they say in America, is this: I'm going to be married and I'm going to be rich. Or, if not married—he claims to have scruples about leaving his crippled wife— at least I'm going to be rich. Men should have to pay for their pleasures, don't you think?' "

Cass paused. No one spoke. She replaced the letter in the folder.

"That," she said drily, "was Natasha, the real Natasha. Not the heartbroken waif Nick imagined he saw in the office that night, who when Hal refused to see her went home and took her own life, but Natasha the brilliant actress, the hard-as-nails gold-digger, whom Tatyana had known from childhood as 'hot pants.' And Natasha saw in her 'very rich American' the chance she'd been waiting for all her life, and she planned, come what may, to seize it.

"She didn't kill herself," Cass went on. "Tatyana, who knew her as well as anyone, told me that directly. 'Natasha,' she said, 'would never have taken her own life, she loved herself too much.' . . . But if she didn't take it, someone else had to. And who had a better motive for that than the 'very rich American' she was gleefully helping to cheat on his wife, and also, quite clearly, planning to blackmail?"

The question hung there, terribly, in the silence.

"I see," Hal said quietly. There was something like appeal in his look. "Now I'm a murderer as well as a liar."

"Someone was." Cass ignored the appeal. "Someone killed Natasha Oblonski that night. And if it occurs to me now that the someone might have been you, then let me assure you I'm not the first to entertain that suspicion. . . . I got those photographs from Dolokhov, alias Grigoriev. He may or may not have been Werner's KGB case officer, but he certainly was Natasha's lover. Her *other* lover, I should say, for this was all going on at the time she was also screwing you. Dolokhov wrote a question on the back of one of those photographs, and the question he asked was this: 'Has it occurred to no one else that in all probability he killed her?' "

Cass paused again.

"When I started this I asked for explanations. Here's another thing I'd like you to explain: Nick told me he called you again that night, the night Natasha Oblonski died. About an hour, he said, after the first time he called. He was told by the maid that you'd gone out. . . . Did your very important meeting finish?" Cass's eyes never left Reynolds's face. "Or did you discover more pressing business elsewhere?"

Reynolds still didn't answer her, but a glance, she noticed, passed between him and his wife.

"Cass, I want you to drop this now." Josie's voice was quiet but decided. "For all our sakes I want you to drop it."

"Josie, how can I?" Cass's response was despairing. "All these years I've loved and looked up to Hal. I thought *he* was the prince I wanted my father to be. And now, when my father may not live, I'm finding I may have gotten everything backward. . . . What do you expect me to do? Shut up and forget the whole thing? Live the rest of my life not knowing?"

"You be better to . . . I know Nick would want you to."

Something in her tone gave Cass pause. It was urgent but not pleading. Or if there was a plea being made, it was not being made on Josie's account. It was almost—the suspicion struck Cass like a chill—as if Josie were making it for *her*.

But here, and before Cass could focus on the thought, Dolly entered the conversation.

Chapter Fifty

"WERE YOU HAVING AN AFFAIR with this woman?"

Dolly's eyes were fixed on her son. It was hard to tell what she was feeling, Cass thought, for in the midst of what must have struck her as an utterly appalling scene, unforgivable in any home, unthinkable in hers, the mask of her self-control had never been more firmly in place.

"*Were* you?"

Reluctantly Reynolds nodded.

"Did you get her pregnant?"

"She said so, yes."

"Was she blackmailing you?"

"Yes. Unless I paid her half a million, she threatened to go public with the story. She threatened to tell about us. Also—"

"Also what?"

"Nothing . . . she just threatened to tell about her and me. She knew it would wreck my political career. She said that must be worth half a million at least."

Dolly paused for a moment. She might have been carved out of stone. She reminded Cass of some Roman matron, prepared to lay any sacrifice required, even her family, on the altar of the republic. She had never flinched from anything in her life. She did not flinch now.

"She was blackmailing *you*, and then *someone* conveniently killed her? . . . Was it you?"

"It was not." Reynolds looked her right in the eye. "I'm mortified you think you need to ask."

"*You're* mortified." His mother's voice was like chalk. "I'm relieved I'm not alone. . . . Then if you didn't kill her, presumably you paid?"

He shook his head. "We didn't pay. We were going to, but before we could do it, she was dead."

Silence. Dolly seemed about to say something, but before she could speak, Cass did.

"We? . . . Who's 'we' exactly?"

Reynolds said nothing.

"How were you going to get the money?" Cass pursued. "You wouldn't have been able to raise it yourself, you didn't have it. Where was it going to come from?"

Another silence. Reynolds glanced at his wife.

"From Josie?" Cass's voice dripped scorn. "You're telling us 'we' was you and Josie? You went to your *wife* for the money to pay off your mistress?"

Reynolds still said nothing. He turned on Cass a look of pain, but it was pain mingled with something else. Pain, it struck her, and pity.

With sudden misgiving, she turned to Josie.

"Was it *you*, Josie? Did you give him the money?"

Josie shook her head. "God knows I would have if he'd asked me, but in point of fact no, I didn't." She paused. "I warned you to drop this, Cass. I begged you, but you wouldn't. Now I guess you'd better have the truth: The person Hal got the money from was your mother."

It was not, Cass thought later, a surprise. Not really. At some level of her consciousness, indeed, it seemed she had already understood it. She recalled now her father's evident unease when speaking of her mother and Hal. She recalled his account of the night Natasha had come to the mission. . . . It was Patsy, she thought, Patsy who had spoken of "some pretty young thing." That was her voice speaking, her phrase, not Hal's; that damaging slip of the tongue had been her mistake, not his, and afterward he had tried to cover for her. But earlier she had tried to cover for him. She had known about Natasha, had given Hal the money to pay her off. And not, it seemed, to spare Josie the hurt, for Josie, clearly, had not been spared. So why? Cass asked herself. *Why* had Patsy given him the money? And why, barely two weeks later, had Patsy killed herself?

What else had Patsy done for her sister's husband?

"So my mother raised half a million dollars to pay off your husband's girlfriend?" It seemed to Cass that her voice belonged to someone else, that her words obeyed a compulsion of their own. In the next moment she heard herself say, "I imagine you're going to tell me next that it was my mother who killed her."

Somewhere in the long, frozen pause that followed, barely perceptibly, Josie nodded.

* * *

IT SEEMED TO CASS that this was what real torture was like. What had happened with Dima in the cabin had been merely a pallid imitation, not even a dress rehearsal of horror, just a kind of cold reading, an improvised preliminary sketching out. And at least, she thought later, had the nightmare Dima planned been acted out, it would have been followed by oblivion. Here there was no such mercy. This would continue the rest of her life. If she lived to be a hundred, she knew she'd be able to repeat on her deathbed, word for word, the story that Josie now told her.

By the time Nick and Patsy were divorced, Josie said, her own illness had been far advanced. She'd known she couldn't satisfy her husband's sexual needs. She'd known also that her sister and he had always been attracted to each other. She'd encouraged them to start an affair. Hers was not a jealous nature. Sex had never been very important to her. The arrangement would benefit all three of them, allow her to keep close the two people whose love she most needed. With her sister assuming those wifely duties she couldn't, she'd thought her husband would be disinclined to stray.

"I thought I had it all figured out," she commented drily, not looking at Hal, "but it turned out I'd figured it wrong. For one thing, I reckoned without Natasha. Though I'd noticed the propensity of men in their forties to make idiots of themselves over women half their age, I guess I expected *my* husband would be different. Another person I misjudged was Patsy. I just never expected her to fall in love."

Besotted with Natasha from the first, Josie continued, Hal had found out too late her mercenary nature. By then she was pregnant and blackmailing him. Disillusioned, he'd attempted to break off the affair. And then, of course, Patsy had found out. Furious at first, she'd at length agreed to help. But though willing to give him the money, which she could easily afford, she'd advised him strongly against paying. Blackmailers, she'd counseled, tended to get greedy when their first demands were met; he'd be better advised to stall, plead the difficulty of raising half a million at short notice, while they looked for another, more dependable solution.

Natasha had responded by turning up the pressure. Her dramatic, apparently grief-stricken visit to the mission had implied a threat to go public if her demands were not promptly met. Patsy, receiving Nick's call and recognizing Natasha's message for what it really was, had improvised a response for Nick and, without telling Reynolds, had gone to Natasha's apartment with some of the money, hoping to persuade her to wait for the rest.

This, it turned out, had been a serious mistake. Natasha had divined at once the nature of Patsy's relationship with Reynolds, and understanding the added leverage she'd been handed, had simply laughed and upped her demands. She could see the headlines now, she'd told Patsy: "Diplomat's Harem Includes Sister-in-Law." A story like this, she'd figured, ought to be worth a million at least.

At this point Patsy had lost her temper. She'd rushed in a fury at Natasha who, falling backward, had hit her head hard against the edge of a table and collapsed, unconscious, on the floor. It was then, in Natasha's kitchen, with Patsy on the thin edge of panic and Natasha lying at her feet, that the other, more dependable solution she'd been seeking had suggested itself.

"Patsy confessed to me later," Josie said. "At first she thought Natasha was dead, but then she discovered she was breathing. If she'd come around quickly, everything would have been different, but five minutes later she still hadn't. By that time Patsy was half out of her mind with fear and guilt. She told me she thought that at the time she must have been literally crazy. Ten minutes later she was coming to her senses. She already knew she'd made a terrible mistake, but by then it was too late to correct it. Natasha was on the kitchen floor, gagged, tied up with Patsy's nylons, the windows shut and the gas turned on. Patsy could have untied her then, but she didn't have the courage. She told me she just couldn't face it, the probable charge of attempted murder, the imprisonment, the trial, the whole sordid story dragged out endlessly in court, the wreck it would make of all our lives, the scandal. Somehow it seemed easier to sit in the next room and wait for Natasha to die. . . ." Josie paused, turned a stricken look on Cass. "It seemed easier, but it wasn't."

Easier . . . in her mind Cass knew that what Josie had told her was true, but her heart refused to accept it.

"My God, you've been lucky in the women in your life!" She rounded in a fury on her uncle. "They get screwed by you, forgive you, pay for you, lie for you, die for you. And you? You just stand there and let them. Even now, I notice, you're letting your wife do the talking. What part did *you* play in all this? You never did tell us what you were doing out so late that night."

"You want to know what I was doing?" Reynolds said quietly. "Okay, I'll tell you. I'll tell you the whole thing. I knew nothing about this until after it had happened. Patsy never gave me Nick's message, and when he called me later that evening, I'd gone to the mission to put in a couple of hours' work. Before I left I was told that Patsy had gone out. The marine on duty at the mission mentioned that Natasha had been there, also that she'd spoken to Nick, who had left a message with Patsy. I knew exactly what Natasha was up to, so I fiddled around in the office for a while, then I drove to her apartment to see what I could do to head her off. As I arrived, someone was driving off. I couldn't see who it was, but the car was a gray Renault, the same color and make, though this only occurred to me later, as Patsy's." Reynolds paused. "Because it appeared that Natasha had just had a visitor, I rang the doorbell for what seemed like ages, but no one answered. Eventually I went home. When I got there I was told that Patsy was back. She'd come in a few minutes before me and gone straight up to bed. I wanted to find out what was going on, but when I went to her room the door was locked and she wouldn't answer my knock.

"In the morning I confronted Patsy. She looked like hell, as if she'd spent the whole night crying, but she said it was just a migraine headache. When I asked her about Natasha and Nick's message, she said she hadn't wanted to disturb me, so had made up a message from me to Nick to get him to send Natasha packing. We needed to take a firm line with her, she said; otherwise she'd take us for everything we had. When I asked her where she'd gone later, she said to find a late-night drugstore to get something for her migraine."

Again Reynolds paused. He looked from one to the other.

"I had no reason to disbelieve her. I noticed in the next few days that she seemed to be under a lot of stress, but when I asked, she said her headaches kept recurring. It was not till I heard Natasha was dead that it occurred to me to question Patsy's story."

"And all that time you didn't call Natasha?" Cass's tone was openly sceptical. "She'd already made one potentially devastating scene, but you simply sat and waited for another?"

"I was following Patsy's advice." Reynolds nodded. "It occurred to me that really she was right. Natasha had only the one card to play, and if she had to play it, it was worthless. I figured the only way to keep her greed in check was to let her know she could only push me so far. It seemed to me we were in a staring match; whoever blinked— called first—would be showing weakness. But after about a week or so, the police showed up at the office. I found out then why Natasha hadn't blinked.

"And of course," he went on, "I had it out with Patsy. There were too many things in her story that struck me now as not adding up. She held out on me for a while, but when I told her I'd seen her car outside the apartment, she broke down and told me what had happened."

He was silent for a moment. Lost in thought, he seemed to have retreated from the present to that moment in Brussels in 1984. Then, suddenly returning, he flung at Cass in anguish:

"What was I supposed to *do*? Tell me *that* as you stand there, judging. . . . Call the police and turn Patsy in? Ruin her life and mine and every life around me, yours included? Make everyone pay for my one lapse?"

He waited for an answer. Getting none, he continued:

"Well, maybe *you* would have found the strength, or whatever, to do that. I couldn't. I realized the suicide scenario was shaky, that if someone decided to lean on it at all, it would fold up; but that Belgian cop seemed to think it was all some spook business, not worth his time looking into. I thought there was a chance we could sit quietly and simply tough it out." He paused, fixed his gaze on Cass, added gently, "Your mother, unfortunately, just wasn't that tough."

"Not like *you*." Cass's heart was like ice. She knew, but she resisted anyway. "It doesn't seem to have bothered you at all. You just went blithely on your way, onward and upward. Patsy was expendable; so was my father. I'd guess that for you, everyone is expendable." She paused. "I can't help noticing, however, how very convenient all this

373

is. Patsy's dead. She can't defend herself. Let's blame everything on her."

"Cass, stop this. Please stop it now." Josie's voice was firm, but filled at the same time with tenderness and sadness. "Your mother was my sister. I loved her. I would never let her memory be slandered, not even to protect my husband. We aren't making this up. I can prove it. The police thought Patsy died without leaving a note. But she left one for me, hid it in the pages of a book she knew I was reading. In essence it was a confession, written, if worse came to worst, to clear Hal. I have it still, locked up somewhere safe. You can read it if you still don't believe me."

She waited for Cass to respond, perhaps to take her up on the offer. But there was no point, Cass thought. The letter would be where Josie said it was; it would say what she said it would say. The truth was out now. The graves had been opened and the ghosts let loose. She wondered if she could live with them.

"Along with telling, there was one thing Patsy asked me," Josie resumed. "That was to look after you . . . and that, of course, meant shielding you from this, and I did. I fully intended never to tell you. But the truth has a habit of finding its way to the light."

"So you kept quiet for *my* sake? . . . I'm touched." Cass was filled with bitterness and rage. She turned back to Hal in cold fury. "How fortunate, too, for the people of America. Their next president will not be a Russian spy. Just a perjurer, an adulterer, and an accessory to murder."

"He will be no such thing."

The words were very quietly spoken, but they cut through the silence like a whip. Somehow, in the stress of their confrontation, the other three had forgotten Dolly. She had risen from her seat and was standing now, head back, chin forward, eyes glittering, fixed upon her son.

"Your election would have been my proudest moment, but it isn't going to happen. Being president is not a job, it's a trust. What I've heard tonight convinces me that you, my son, are not worthy of it. . . . You are going to issue a statement tomorrow announcing your withdrawal from the race. You may offer whatever face-saving pretext you please." Dolly paused, added drily, "I believe it is usual in cases like this to refer to the needs of your family."

"And if I don't?" Reynolds challenged.

"If you don't"—his mother met this without blinking—"I shall have to issue a statement of my own. I shall say you no longer enjoy my support because, for reasons I am too ashamed to share, I have come to believe you are morally unfit for the office. If you think, in spite of that, you can still get elected, you are more than welcome to try."

Leaving behind her an astounded silence, she turned away and walked out of the room.

Epilogue

November 1996

A<small>T TWO MINUTES</small> after 9:00 P.M., Eastern Standard Time, the president went on television to concede the election. In a brief speech he congratulated his opponent, exhorted his followers not to lose faith in the party, and thanked his supporters, his campaign staff, and his family for their unstinting efforts on his behalf. Accepting all the responsibility for his defeat, he placed no blame on his former campaign manager (now awaiting trial, along with various members of *his* staff, for crimes including attempted electoral fraud). Indeed, he made no reference at all to the momentous events of early May—the arrests of Porcher and Quine, the appointment of a select congressional committee to investigate his own possible involvement in the attempted fraud, the subsequent, unexplained, and astonishing withdrawal of Hal Reynolds from the race—that had made this election among the most dramatic of the century. It was, it seemed to Cass, on the whole a rather graceful performance, and decidedly so from one for whom graceful performances hadn't exactly been the norm. Nick's verdict was more sardonic:

"He reminds me of that English king whose head was chopped off by his grateful subjects: 'Nothing in life became him like the leaving it.' "

Cass smiled and got up to take his tray.

"Would you like more soup?" she asked.

"Thank you, no." He regarded the tray with distaste. "What I'd *like* is a sixteen-ounce sirloin and three fingers of Talisker straight up."

She shook her head. "No steaks and no booze. Not for another month at least."

"Goddamn Dima." He made a face. "Now, this I really hold against him."

Cass gazed down at him with pure affection. The weeks in intensive care and months of convalescence had taken a great toll of his body. He had lost forty pounds since the day Dima shot him, much of which lost weight was muscle, and although the daily workouts in rehab were bringing him back—remarkably quickly, so his therapist assured her, for a man of his age and disinclination to follow doctor's orders—he still looked frail and shrunken. But he didn't look *old*, she thought; he didn't have that air of accepting defeat. What he looked like was a young man in hiding, forced to inhabit, but on a strictly temporary basis, an unfamiliar body.

Along with the affection, there was gratitude. He had saved her, she knew, in more ways than one. In fact, he had helped her, if that was possible, as much with his weakness as with his strength. Nursing him to health had given her a purpose at a time when, without it, she might have succumbed to despair. Indeed, there had been many days after Hal's and Josie's revelations in which but for him (not wanting, among other things, to render his sacrifice futile) she might have been tempted to follow her mother's example. That she hadn't was due also to the fact that she wasn't the suicidal type, but her father's love— and, when he was fit enough to talk, his common sense—had taken her through the temptation. He had made her see that, in her case at least, biology was not destiny; that, unless she let it, what her mother had done didn't have to blight her life. She'd decided, after a struggle, not to let it.

On the TV screen, to which her eyes now returned, attention had shifted to the campaign headquarters of the victor, a party hack whose mediocrity, Cass gathered—she hadn't had much time for politics of late—was almost universally acknowledged, even (in private) by his staunchest supporters. His speech was a farrago of mind-numbing platitudes, expressed with neither style nor verve, and uttered in a plodding monotone. After a minute or two of this, Nick reached for the remote and cut off the sound. What remained onscreen was a posturing dummy: a smiling mask, a well-cut suit, gestures devoid of meaning or substance.

"Okay with you?" Nick glanced at Cass. "I don't imagine it'll make much difference."

377

Cass made a face.

"Well, at least we've managed to elect a president whose past isn't actually criminal. Or at least," she amended, "so far as we know."

"Two cheers for that." Nick grunted. "To tell the truth, I think I'd rather have had Hal."

She had offered to take him to vote, but he'd declined. Being perfectly indifferent between the candidates, he'd explained, he didn't feel like making the effort. She had gone to vote herself, however; it always seemed irresponsible not to.

"To tell the truth, so would I." She paused. "To tell the whole truth, I voted for him."

"You voted for him?" Nick stared at her. "But he wasn't on the ballot."

"I know that." She looked at him sideways, grinned. "But that didn't stop me from writing him in, now, did it?"